THE
END-TIMES
ARMY
OF
GREENSVILLE

THE END-TIMES ARMY OF GREENSVILLE

How The Great Tribulation Became Their Doorway to Heaven

A Novel

by Phil T Porter

Xulon Press

Xulon Press
2301 Lucien Way #415
Maitland, FL 32751
407.339.4217
www.xulonpress.com

Unless otherwise indicated, Scripture quotations taken from the King James Version (KJV) – *public domain.*

Printed in the United States of America.

ISBN-13: 978-1-6628-0889-0

DEDICATION

To two real people I've known,
By the names of Don and Kathy.
Their lives inspired the creation of this book

Author's Opening Statement

This is a novel about end-times. Two points are important here. The story is about what it could be like living in the end-times, when such characters as the Antichrist and False Prophet, such events as the Abomination of Desolation and the Great Tribulation, and such other items as the Mark of the Beast and the Third Jerusalem Temple are all integral parts of the storyline.

The second point to keep in mind is that this is a novel. It was contrived in the mind and imagination of author – albeit after diligent study and meditation of the Scriptures, and after much time of prayer and consulting with the Author of those Scriptures, the Holy Spirit Himself.

And I ask you, Dear Reader, what mere human can possibly know with any certainty what will transpire during the end-times. Do you know? Neither do I. But in my mind, that's okay.

The story will be looking at interventions and strategies for survival among a hearty group of Believers from North Carolina; ideas that could apply in the face of any grand, life-challenging adversity. The problem is that the end-times, as portrayed in the Bible, is not *any* grand adversity. No, it is the grandest of them all! So very grand that the Lord said to His followers... *if it wasn't for the fact that the Great Tribulation will be cut short, no one could be saved: but for the elect's sake those days shall be shortened* (Matthew 24:22). So, get ready for an adventure and learn how it might apply to the end of times, that we are just beginning to witness in the world around us. Even though the book is not based on explicit facts about what will transpire during these end-times, it is what I hope you'll consider a sincere story of trust and faithfulness. (Plus, I think you'll come to love Doobie as much I did.)

Phil T Porter

CONTENTS

PROLOGUE

ONE DAY WHEN DON WAS 12 YEARS OLD, he was playing with some friends at a nearby creek. Suddenly he sensed that there was something seriously wrong at home. He ran home to see what was happening and discovered his mother lying on the kitchen floor. A small fire had started in the oven. His mother was trying to put it out when she slipped and fell backwards and broke her leg.

Young Don called the authorities for assistance and then proceeded to get his mother out of the house. Help arrived just in time to save the fire from getting out of hand. Of course, Don's mother was grateful. She commented, "Don, your sixth sense saved me from certain disaster. This is a gift from God. Treasure it and don't ever forget that He gave it to you."

Don was hailed as a hero in his community. He was reluctant, however, to think of himself as a hero. Over the years, Don did learn to appreciate his gift of *intuition*, as he called it. It paid a great dividend that day he saved his mother. And this heavenly gift would follow him the rest of his days, proving to be quite beneficial.

CHAPTER ONE –

The odyssey into unchartered waters begins

DON AND KATHY CRAWFORD WERE a typical middle-aged couple from the Midwest trying to make it through life the best they knew how. One day they embarked on a most challenging adventure, led by the Holy Spirit. This odyssey into unchartered waters was not something they desired, nor sought after. In fact, they had no idea what they were getting themselves into. Trusting in a God they were only casually acquainted with was the one thing that kept them afloat. Here's their story...

Don and Kathy would refer to themselves as nominal Christians. They would admit that the Lord wasn't the biggest part of their lives. On occasion, as the need arose, they would pray and ask for help with a teenage child or for the grace to make ends during a lean month. Typically, they enjoyed attending church mainly because of the many friendships they had formed there. But by and large they went to church only when their personal and family schedules allowed.

It didn't take Kathy long to discover that Don had an uncanny way of looking at the world. Over the years of raising two children, Kathy learned to trust in Don's premonitions. They were usually right.

One day, as the story unfolds, Don told Kathy of his latest glimpse into the future. He was sure that a move was in their near future - to where or when was still a mystery. For sure he had no clue about the marvelous plans God had in store for him and Kathy.

It was a bright Spring Monday morning when Don was about to leave the house for another week as an over-the-road trucker. He was aware of how his job was difficult for Kathy. That morning he particularly noticed her long face, so he tried to keep the conversation light and cheery.

"I'm telling you honey there is a move in our future. I can feel it in my bones! It's going to be happening soon! I haven't quite figured out where or when, but it'll be soon. Then I won't have to be gone for days at a time and you can quit that awful job at the factory."

"Oh, it's not that bad, Don; don't you give it another thought," replied Kathy in her usual gracious manner. She tried hard not to let on about her dislike for that factory work. But Don was especially aware of it today.

Finally, it was time for Don to be on the road. Another sweet but sad good-bye. Don assured Kathy that he would get after his *to-do-list* as soon as he returned. Repairing fences and shoring up a sagging hen house was low on his list of favorite things to do, but he knew it would be a blessing to Kathy.

Don mechanically made his way out East, across familiar roads and scenery ultimately to the little town of Greensville, North Carolina. He was delayed with his first unloading at the Chevrolet Dealership, on the edge of Main Street. So, to pass the time he went into a local sandwich shop. Before entering Don noticed a most difficult site: it was a family of five walking along on the opposite side of the street. They were obviously destitute, as evidenced by their shabby clothing and dirty faces, and a certain forlorn look about them. Don paused for a minute. It was difficult to imagine such a scene could be playing out in this great country.

Don entered the café and was greeted by a waitress, named Sybil. She led him to a booth nearby. As she began her usual spiel to highlight the main dish for the day, Don interrupted.

"Sybil, look at that across the street. That poor family: it looks like they are on their last dime. How sad."

"Yes, I know what you mean," she commented. "We're getting more and more of that these days. The economy has really taken a decided downturn; local factories are closing, and people are getting panicky about what the future will bring. It's so sad...So, what can I get ya today?"

Don ordered a ham and cheese, then continued to watch the drama across the street. Little did he know that the compassion that was welling up in his heart was a gift from God. And this empathy would form the basis for the ministry that God was calling and grooming Don to enter.

Suddenly, without giving it a second thought, Don took a bold step. He got up from the booth and went across the street to the family and offered them some money. At first, they declined, but after a little persuasion, they finally agreed to take the gift. The father and mother thanked Don profusely.

Other patrons at the café had noticed. As Don returned to his booth he was greeted by many wide smiles and positive comments. One patron was moved to pay for Don's lunch.

It was just a little act of kindness. Not a big deal to Don. But to God it was a big deal. It showed Him that the man He had picked to head up a ministry to the poor and the spiritually lost could hear and obey the Holy Spirit. Don was to be surrounded by other hand-picked helpers; they too would play a crucial role in this end-times ministry.

Two of those God was calling met Don by accident that evening, after he was able to finally unload at the Chevy Garage. One of those was Miss Verla, a starchy old maid who was the town librarian. She was walking along with a friend by the name of Doobie McKenna, a short, stocky young man who was intellectually challenged. Don quickly learned that this young man always presented a most pleasant and engaging smile. Everyone loved Doobie!

Don was walking down the sidewalk heading back to the café for another bite to eat and not watching where he was going, when he collided with Miss Verla. The collision knocked her off balance and she dropped a grocery sack she was carrying.

Doobie immediately came to her defense. "Hey, buddy. Watch where you're going!" He steadied Miss Verla. She was more concerned about her fallen grocery sack that was carrying eggs.

"Oh, dear. My eggs," she muttered. Don stooped down to help claim any unbroken eggs, so did Doobie. There they met face to face; Doobie glared. Don apologized. "I'm awfully sorry about this. Let me pay for your broken eggs." Don stood up and reached for his billfold.

Verla put a stop to that. "No. No. Don't worry about it. It was an accident. It was life bringing a little disappointment, that's all. Don't worry about it."

"Well, that's awful nice of you. Thank you...ah, Miss..."

Doobie stepped in. "This here is Miss Verla, the town Librarian."

Don pushed on. "And you, young man, you are...?"

"Doobie McKenna. I'm Miss Verla's friend, and her sometimes grocery store companion. But I wasn't doing a good job today, because the two of you collided – *Boom!* – and I didn't see it coming!"

"Yeah, I'm sorry. I was the one that caused the big *Boom*. Will you forgive me Miss Verla and Doobie?"

Doobie looked Verla's way and then nodded his head. "Yeah, we forgive you." Then he flashed one of his big smiles. And once again all was well in Don's world.

Don slept in his truck that night and headed out early in the morning. He had other travels and loads to deliver, from Florida to Georgia to Tennessee. The rest of that trip was uneventful. He couldn't wait until Friday morning came and he could head his rig home – to Kathy!

Meanwhile Kathy and her daughter, Jenny, were on the phone discussing the upcoming wedding. Kathy never let on about how much she was saddened at the prospects of having her younger daughter be the second and last to marry and leave home.

Jenny was painfully aware that her wedding was producing emotional hardship for her mother. Jenny tried to keep the conversation as light and as unfocused as possible about going to live in Colorado.

At one point, Jenny asked: "Mom, what are you and dad going to do after the wedding...Are you going to stay at home?"

Kathy replied: "Well, your father keeps insisting God is showing him that a move is in our future; just what that means I'm not sure, neither is he."

Jenny registered her disbelief. "Oh, one of Dad's premonitions...You can't put a lot of stock in them, can you?"

"Well, Jenny, he's right more often than not."

"Just when might this move take place?" Jenny quizzed further.

"Oh, it wouldn't surprise me if he starts getting really serious about it when your wedding is over and you and Jim leave for Colorado."

"How about your church? Won't it be hard to leave there, after all these years?"

"Not really. We've kinda grown away from the church since the Pastor left last year...Listen, Jenny, don't you worry about your father and me. We'll get along fine. Now, I've got some laundry to finish before he gets home. Love talking to you. Let's do it again real soon. Bye, honey."

"Bye Mom. I love you."

RIGHT ON SCHEDULE DON ARRIVED HOME late Friday night and was greeted by Kathy's warm smile. He promised to get after the *honey-do list* first thing in the morning, but before long Sunday morning came around and the *list* was still on the fridge without a single check mark. Kathy didn't mind. Truthfully, she would rather have his company than have the hen house repaired.

"Who's preaching today Kathy?" Don asked as he was getting ready for church.

"Oh, I think it's that man from Arkansas. He's been here before."

"Is that the one that talks on and on?"

"Yes, that's the one."

"I don't know, Kathy. Maybe we should skip church this morning."

"No, Don; we shouldn't," Kathy insisted. "Let's just go. Maybe he won't be so talkative."

"Okay, we'll go," answered Don. Kathy smiled.

As Don was finishing his preparations, he saw an old baseball cap and started reminiscing about his teenage years. He sat on the edge of the bed, as Kathy went downstairs and busied herself in the kitchen. Don fondly recalled his local church and Pastor Gibbons. This Pastor didn't need a microphone to get his message across. His messages were short and to the point. He was well respected by everyone in the Church. And he took a special interest in Don, keeping him on the straight and narrow, during some tumultuous teenage years.

It was as a young teenager that Don first got serious about the Lord because of the influence and urging of Pastor Gibbons. Don gave his heart and life to Jesus at a youth meeting when he was 13 years old. Soon after, however, Pastor Gibbons moved on to another assignment. They never stayed in touch. In the years since that time Don always compared other Pastors with Pastor Gibbons. So far, no one had compared favorably. Over the years, Don's interest in Church activities grew lukewarm – until he met Kathy, that is.

Kathy, by comparison, never had much Church background growing up. She had a brother who was thirteen years older. He was more like an uncle; they were never close. Her parents she would describe as hippies, not giving Kathy any encouragement to consider spiritual matters. They claimed to be *agnostics*. God wasn't mentioned in her household unless it was part of swearing.

So, while Don was learning about the Bible, Kathy was learning about Transcendental Meditation. It wasn't until she was a freshman in college and a friend talked her into attending a youth rally, that Kathy took any interest in the spiritual side of life. It was at the rally that she turned her life over to the Lord. After that, everyone she knew could see a big change. Kathy now had a Partner to depend on and a new peace in her soul. But God had a slightly different take on that arrangement, so He carved out a place in Kathy's heart for a handsome young Freshman, by the name of Don Crawford.

"Don, are you almost ready? It's time to go!" yelled Kathy from downstairs.

Don jumped off the bed to his feet and yelled back: "Yeah, I'll be right with you. Give me two minutes."

Off to church they went. As they both suspected, the Pastor talked on and on. And about really nothing...*nothing of importance*, was Don's assessment. Kathy had to agree.

Back home the two of them enjoyed a light lunch and a quiet moment together. Don had a yen to return to his reminiscing, what with all the talk about wedding floating in the air.

"Kathy, do you remember how we met at that Freshman Mixer?"

"You took one look at me across the dance floor and fell instantly in love. Right?"

"And I said to my friend, Sean, 'Someday real soon I'm going to marry that pretty young girl'..."

"...and before you knew it," Kathy added, "We were into the fastest romance on record!"

"Fast and furious, I'd say," Don added, smiling hard.

"And could the great Don Crawford wait for a normal wedding, with a minister, family and friends? Not on your life! He had to do it his way – elope!"

"That ladder I borrowed from your neighbor was a real doozy! Remember? A rickety old thing I never should have used. Thank goodness we picked a weekend when your parents weren't home, so you could walk out of the house instead of climbing down that junky ladder."

"And, after the Magistrate Wedding at the Courthouse, we wanted to see someone we knew to share the good news. My parents were on another one of their excursions, so they didn't know a wedding was even going on...and probably didn't care. So, where did we happen to go? To your parent's home."

"Yeah, I remember my mom wasn't too keen on the whole idea of elopement. And my Dad was a little cool himself."

"Can't blame them, however, seeing their favorite, and only, son was introducing me for the first time as their new daughter-in-law."

"But you quickly won them over, just like you did me...Wow! Just think! What a story book beginning. Somebody should make a movie out of our life."

"Really, Don? I think I could find six people to buy a ticket, and we'd be two of them, but after that who would be interested? Really?"

"I can think of Someone," said Don, as he looked upward.

"Well, yeah; I'll give you that...Say, Don, as much as I would like to sit around and chatter on like this, I have some work to do, before you take off again tomorrow bright and early."

"Okay, but I got one more part to add to this nostalgic scene, while it's still fresh in my mind. Remember that first night after the wedding when we went to my parent's house? My Mom took me aside and said: 'Don, I've been praying for you lately, a lot – and it looks like Kathy is the answer to my prayers...'"

"Oh, that was so sweet," said Kathy as tears began to well up. "I forgot that part. Then what?"

"Then I tried to change the topic; you know I don't like it when things get mushy...She asked about my plans and I told her I didn't want to go back to college. I wanted to get a job and get on with our life because I had a family to take care of now."

"How'd she take that?"

"Well, at first she thought I meant you could be, you know, in a *motherly way,* if you get my drift..."

"But you quickly cleared that up, right?"

"Right. I did. Quickly. Then, I told her I wanted to make something of my life. I wanted to make it big in real estate! 'In fact, Mom,' I went on bragging, 'Someday I'm going to have a city named after me, like *Crawfordville'.* And you passed by on the way to the living room and said, 'I like *Crawford City* a little better'.

"I turned to Mom and said: 'That's my Kathy. Ain't she something'?"

"Oh, that's so sweet! I forgot that you said that." Kathy gave Don a big hug and replied: "Well, here's what I say: there's no *honey-do list* for you. Let's take the day off!"

"Kathy Crawford, I like how you think! You are something!"

CHAPTER TWO –

Don chased after one dream and then another.

DON HEADED OUT AS USUAL WITH CARGO for Texas, Mississippi, and Georgia. As he raced across the interstate, he started recollecting again about his early years of marriage.

He and Kathy moved about quite often, as Don chased after one dream and then another. Finally, Don settled for a job at the local lumber yard and he and Kathy were focused on raising their family. Greg was the first, but he died when he was only three years old. That was a hard one to handle. The second one came along soon after. That was Sylvia, now an RN at a children's Hospital in Minneapolis. Then there was the miscarriage only a few weeks after conception. And lastly there was Jenny, who is now about to get married and move permanently to Colorado with her husband, Jim.

As the kids grew Don seemed to grow more dissatisfied with life. The lumber yard was a dead-end job, in his estimation; a long way from being the real estate mogul he dreamed of. He supplemented his income by painting houses in the evening and on weekends. Ultimately the lumber yard folded when a big box store came to town. Besides trying to paint houses on a full-time basis, Don also signed on as a school bus driver, a self-employed mechanic, tree trimmer, then electrician.

Don, looking back at those lean years, likened himself to a *jack of all trades and master of none.* Finally, thank goodness, Don's full-time over-the-road trucking job opened and he seized the opportunity. Don had to admit that the Lord had taken good care of his family, despite his sketchy work history.

This day, as Don was rolling down the road, he thanked the Lord freely for His continuing care. Then, he asked for the umpteenth time the now familiar question: "Lord what do You have in store for us now?"

Like usual, he never expected an answer but got one just the same. "Don, you are going to like what I have for you and Kathy in the months ahead. If I told it all to you now, you couldn't handle it. It will unfold in bits and pieces. But rest assured, it will be a great work and one that will satisfy every craving of your soul... So, stay faithful and stay ever so near."

"Oh, I will, Lord! Yes, I will! Thank You. Thank you."

Don was excited beyond belief, to hear the Lord's answer. "I gotta call Kathy this afternoon and tell her what He said!"

Don's run that week to the south and east seemed to breeze by. Everything went smoothly and right on schedule. Before long he was headed back home. And what awaited him there was the Jenny and Jim wedding and their departure to Colorado.

The wedding was scheduled for Saturday, June 16th. It was a lovely summer day. Blue skies and bright sun: absolutely picture perfect. That was on the outside. On the inside of Don and Kathy there was considerable dismay. After all Jenny was the last to be married. And, worse yet, she was planning to move so far away. I suppose for a trucker a jaunt to Colorado is no big deal, but to a parent anything more than a day's journey is a big deal.

Before you knew it, the reception was over and guests began leaving the Church Hall, including Sylvia and her family. Soon enough it was time for a quick stop at home, where there would be goodbyes to Jenny and Jim before they headed out to honeymoon in St. Louis.

Jenny's new husband seemed okay to Don; not outstanding, but okay. It was for sure that Jenny thought highly of him. There was something about him, however, that didn't sit right. In Don's estimation, Jim wasn't the type that you wanted to hang out with, man to man, you know. He seemed a bit naive and fragile to Don.

Back at the house, Jim was in a hurry to get on the road. He yelled at Jenny: "Hurry, Jenny. We have to be going!"

Don didn't like that. Kathy could see Don begin to drum his fingers as he sat at the dining room table. She went to him to soften some of emotional steam he was dealing with. "Hey, Don, how are you doing?" No response but a feigned smile.

Next came the "good-byes." Jenny was bubbling over with excitement and hugged her parents tightly. Jim too was excited; and Jim's excitement seemed a bit overboard in Don's assessment. A big hug was extended to Kathy as Jim said: "Thanks, Mom, for all you did for us today." Kathy beamed from ear to ear.

When it came time for Don's hug, Jim seemed to suddenly become a wet noodle. He said: "Thanks, ah, Daaa...Mr. Crawford. Hope to see you again soon." A two-second hug was the most either party wanted to give or receive.

"Oh, you will be seeing me again soon, Jim. You can count on it," Don replied.

"You two have fun in St. Louis," Kathy offered ("*But not too much fun,*" Don added under his breath, while sporting that same feigned smile for all to see).

Don and Kathy watched as the newlyweds got settled in their car. Once out of view the two turned back into the house. All the emotional upheaval of the day turned into a listless sigh of relief. Both sat - rather *slouched* - at the kitchen table without saying a word for a good five minutes.

Finally, Kathy commented that she noticed Jim was struggling with what to call Don. Don just smiled like the Cheshire Cat of old. In a strange way, only known of in the brotherhood of fathers of the bride, Don appreciated Jim referring to him as *Mr. Crawford*. He liked the respect that title conveyed...after all, Don thought, he was taking his Jenny all the way to Colorado!

HOW QUICKLY IT CAME: ANOTHER MONDAY morning to deal with. Don was ready to hit the road once again. His course this time took him back to Greensville, North Carolina. As Don entered the city, he noticed an overwhelming sadness come over him, that he couldn't explain. It was like he could sense the discouragement that was in the peoples' heart as they walked by.

He said to the Lord: "Lord, what is going on here in this community?" The Lord answered straightway: "Don, this is my place for you. I have a work for you to do here." He noticed how authoritative the voice sounded, how clear and to the point...

"You and Kathy will be anointed to address the needs of this community and to lead a group into the final hours of the last days...Don't try to figure how you might address these matters now, that would only be a waste of time. Again, I say, stay faithful and tuned into My Spirit that abides within you. More direction will be forthcoming; it will come in stages. When the time is ripe, you'll be fully equipped to do all that I've called you to do."

Don pulled over to the curb and paused to say, "Thank You, Lord. I'll do my best." The hard blare of a horn behind him let Don know that he should move on.

Don went about his business of unloading cargo at the Chevrolet Dealership, as usual, but with less than his usual upbeat, talkative manner. Others noticed: "Hey, Don, you down in the dumps?" "What's wrong, brother?" "Hey, do you feel alright, Don?"

Don tried to defuse the comments. "I'm alright, guys. Just had my daughter married last Saturday; I'm missing her already."

Then Don shifted the focus to the people on the street. "Hey, when I drove into town, I noticed the people seemed down in the dumps; and a lot of stores are closed or starting to close. What gives?"

The shop manager spoke up. "I suppose it's due to the economic downturn. Jobs are getting scarce. We had to let five of our own go last week. Bummer of a deal! Greensville needs a shot in the arm; something new to bring this town back to life! Got any ideas, Don?"

"Yeah, I've got an idea or two. I'll tell you about it sometime. See you guys later."

Don was looking forward to the end of this day. And he was to spend his evening at a little motel on the east end of town, called the Willow Creek Motel. He parked out in back and was checked in by a pleasant young man at the desk named Mark. When he finally got settled in Don searched for a place outside to be alone with his thoughts. He found a Bench out back away from public view. Perfect. But before long he wasn't alone. Who should come along but that young man he met by accident on his last trip to Greensville, Doobie McKenna!

"Hey, again, Mr. C," greeted Doobie with a big smile. "Is the room Okay? Anything I can get you?"

"Hi again; Doobie isn't it?" answered Don. "No, my room is fine. Don't need a thing." Don then recalled the details of his first meeting of Doobie.

"Say, Doobie, how is the Librarian, Miss Verla? Is she okay even though we collided on the sidewalk and she lost those eggs?"

"She's fine; just fine..." Doobie started to giggle, remembering the scene. And that started Don to giggle as well. Pretty soon, the two of them must have looked like two old friends reminiscing about a funny scene from their past – and that's pretty much what they were doing. An immediate bond of friendship developed between Don and Doobie.

Doobie had to move on. "Well, Mr. Don. Got to go, more work to be done. How long are you staying?"

"Just one night, Doobie, but I'm planning to be back in a couple of weeks."

"See ya then...Now don't go knocking down any ladies if you can help it, okay?" Doobie flashed a big smile as he turned back to the motel.

A few minutes later, Don caught glimpse of an older couple walking toward him. It looked like they on purpose were seeking him out. They were quite friendly and smiled as they sat on a nearby Bench. Before long they opened a conversation.

"Nice few days of weather we've been having," the gentleman said. Don replied: "Sure has been. It's great for a change."

"Hello, my name is Ben Tucker. This is my wife, Clair. We're new to Greensville, how about you?"

Don extended a handshake. "My name is Don Crawford. I'm a trucker who gets to Greensville about every two to three weeks, which started a month ago. So, you could consider me new to this city as well."

It was soon revealed that the Tuckers were also staying at the Willow Creek. Don asked: "What brings you folks to Greensville?"

Ben and Clair looked at each other, as if to wonder: *Should we tell the whole matter?* Ben seized the opportunity.

"Well, Don, we were both lead to curtail our retirement, pick up stakes, and move to this city. But for reasons unknown. We were assured in our hearts that God would give us more detail later."

"So, you felt led of the Lord to take this step, is that what you're saying?"

"Yes, that says it in a nutshell," answered Ben "It was kinda like what God did with Abraham. Are you familiar with that story?"

"Yes, I am. God told Abraham to move away from his country and family and He would lead him to a new place he never heard of."[1]

"Right you are, Don. That's pretty much like it was for Clair and me."

By now Don was becoming intrigued. "So, have there been any new instructions since your move?"

"None, so far. The Lord did tell us before we left home that we would meet up with another person, who would direct us into the next phase. We're still waiting."

"Folks, this sounds uncanny! But I too have been told by the Lord that Greensville will be my home someday soon. So, in a way, I'm in a holding pattern myself, awaiting further direction."

Clair spoke up for the first time. "So, I guess we can all conclude that it was no accident that we would meet up like this today and be staying at the same motel."

"I certainly agree with that, Clair," Don replied. "Say, have the two of you noticed anything out of the ordinary in Greensville?"

"Well, I wonder if the local economy is a bit depressed," said Ben

"And I wonder if the people aren't a little depressed also," added Clair.

"I was thinking the very same thing on both accounts," Don joined in.

"Say, where do the Tuckers hail from; not from around here, right?"

"Well, we hail from Upper State New York. I finished up a 40-year career as a counselor at a Community College. Clair had a home decorating business most of those years. No children. And you?"

"I'm an over-the-road trucker. My wife and I live about 600 miles due west of here. We have two adult children; our youngest got married this past Saturday. I just started coming to Greensville on a regular basis about a month ago, otherwise I'd have no reason to be here – except, of course, for the Lord's leading."

In a surprising way, Don felt an immediate kinship with the Tuckers. How their connection would play out in the weeks ahead no one had a clue. Don finally excused himself and went back to his room. He was planning to call Kathy and fill her in on the happenings of the day.

After his call, he looked around in the bed stand. There it was: a *Gideon's Bible.* He muttered to himself: *Thank God for the Gideons!* But he got out his own Bible from his backpack, instead, the one with a wealth of hand-written notes. He turned to a familiar passage that was overrun with notes: the 91st Psalm.

He wanted to read again about God's *Secret Place.* He paused and put down the Bible. He had a question for the Lord. "Say, Lord, where is this *Secret Place?*

The Lord answered: "It's very close."

"How will I know how to get there if it's a secret?"

"I'll show you. It's not a secret I want to keep from you; it's a secret kept just *for* you and others who seek after it."

Don was encouraged to go on. "Thank You. Now Lord, since I have your attention, there's another passage that's been bothering me for a long time. It's in Proverbs 10:22. I'll read it. No. You already know it. Oh, I'll read it anyway: *The blessing of the Lord, it maketh rich, and He adds no sorrow with it.*"

After a pause, the Lord asked: "Don, is there a question here?"

"Yes, in a way, I guess. I think I've been blessed, but I wouldn't exactly call myself rich...Are there some people more blessed than others and therefore richer? Where do I fit in?"

Don listened hard but didn't sense an answer. After a few long seconds he heard: "Don, I'll teach you more about this in the time ahead; just trust Me now...Soon enough, you'll find out what it's like to be truly blessed!"

Don said: "I do trust you, Lord. Thank You for taking such good care of me and my family. And thank You for Your blessings to come."

THE NEXT MORNING BRIGHT AND EARLY, DON was called by his dispatcher and told to wait 24 hours before delivering the next load. There had been some fracas about the union calling for a temporary walk off at two of his destinations.

Don went back to bed and tried to sleep again, but he was too keyed up. He was anxious to get on with the day; yet didn't have anything he wanted to do. He got dressed and wandered down to the check-in desk. There he found Doobie. Don asked if there was any breakfast available.

Doobie answered: "I know just the place for you. I was going there myself, so you can ride along with me, okay?"

Before long they were standing at the front door of the Riverside Café. Doobie explained that the Riverside is best known as Mama Blanchard's, the owner and day-to-day manager.

"Mama Blanchard has the best food in town. Her pancakes in the morning are out of this world! You gotta try 'em."

"Okay, Doobie," Don replied. "I'll do that. Lead the way."

When they walked into the crowded restaurant, they were surprised to see Clair and Ben already sitting in a small booth. They waved to Don and Doobie to join them, so they did. To Doobie's delight everyone was going to have Mama's pancakes.

Don got serious about his breakfast. After two bites he commented: "Doobie, you were right! These pancakes are delicious!" The Tuckers agreed they were out of this world.

As Don took his last bite of pancake, Mama Blanchard pulled up a chair and joined Doobie and his new friends. There were introductions all around the table. Mama took an instant shine to Don. Not one to hold back her thoughts, she went on in some detail about what she was sensing with her spiritual antennae.

"I tell you Don, Ben and Clair there is something stirring in my spirit. It's big too! I don't know exactly what it is, but something important is going on. Hey, Don, do you believe in the Holy Spirit, in His work in our daily lives?"

Don answered this way: "Yes, Mama Blanchard. I often have a sensing deep down in my spirit about things the Spirit is up to. My mother used to call my intuitions a gift from heaven..."

"Your mother was right, Don," Mama then turned to Ben and Clair. "And you folks...you believe in the Holy Spirit, too, I take it, or you wouldn't be hanging out with Doobie and Don, right?"

"Right you are, Mama Blanchard," replied Ben. "We're here at the leading of the Spirit and we're trusting Him to make His plans for us come to life in the weeks ahead."

There was a lull in the conversation, but Mama Blanchard didn't like any lulls, so she asked Don: "How did you happen to come here to Greensville? On business? Vacation?"

Don replied: "I'm a trucker from the Midwest and just started coming to Greensville about a month ago. Your town will be on my schedule about every two weeks...

"Two days ago, when I arrived, I had a great sadness come over me. I wonder if it was the Lord's compassion for the people that I was experiencing. You remember the Bible account of when Jesus looked over the multitudes...and they were like sheep having no shepherd."[2]

Suddenly the conversation was interrupted! A waitress came running to Mama. "Mama! Come quick! It's Barbara. She's fainted again!"

"Oh, dear. Oh, dear," Mama muttered as she and Doobie ran to the kitchen. There they found Barbara lying on the floor next to the refrigerator. She was wearing her same two jackets and a coat. She looked unconscious but had a pulse and fluttered her eyes as she lay there in a daze.

All the commotion caused quite a stir; all eyes of the patrons seemed focused on the kitchen door. The Tuckers felt led to join the scene in the kitchen and prayed softly off to the side. As they looked on two other kitchen workers stood off in the corner, crying.

The waitress who brought the first alarm to Mama Blanchard, tearfully recalled the fainting spell. "I told her Mama, didn't I, she shouldn't have been wearing all that clothing. She should go to a doctor and get checked out; how many times did I tell her that, huh?! But no, she was too stubborn!"

At this point Don joined the drama in the kitchen. Mama was on one knee patting Barbara's hand. Don proceeded to kneel on the other side of Barbara and take her hand in his as he prayed out loud: "Lord, You are our Healer. Please help this woman who has fainted; restore her and make her whole...Whatever may be going on in her body to cause this, I say to that malfunction: you be renewed and restored! Be healed from head to toe. I call this woman quickened by the power of the Holy Spirit. Thank You. Thank You. In the Name of Jesus, I pray. Amen."

Barbara slowly began to open her eyes. As she looked around, she became noticeably frightened when she noticed all the faces staring intently at her. Three of those faces she had never seen before. She pulled her hands away from Mama and Don and sat up, leaning against the refrigerator. She remained dazed. Ben asked Mama if he should call 911. Mama didn't think it was necessary. Within a few moments Barbara was standing.

Mama said, "Thank goodness child you're okay. And you're okay because this man thought enough of you to pray that God would heal you. And He did!"

Barbara darted out the back door and two other kitchen workers followed her. By this time, many onlookers had stood and gathered near the kitchen. Mama Blanchard went out to speak with them, to reassure them that Barbara was okay.

Mama then turned toward Don and said, loud enough for most to hear: "Thank you, Don, for being the man of the hour, with your prayer for her healing."

Don tried to deflect all the accolades extended by the people and return to his table. But to no avail; the patrons were intent on recognizing Don as a genuine hero.

The Lord spoke up in a hushed voice: *Don, the people need a hero at this time in their lives. Just smile and receive their praise. Be sure to keep your thoughts grounded on Me. This is part of the healing ministry that I've called you into. You did well.*

Don finally got the check from his waitress and began to get in line to pay, when Mama loudly insisted: "Don, you're not paying for breakfast today after all you have done for us, right folks?"

Most everyone in attendance was now fully aware of the scope of the good deed in the kitchen and Don's involvement. They began to applaud and pat him on the shoulder. Don himself just wanted to get back to the motel. He found Doobie in the crowd and motioned for him to follow out to the car.

On the ride back to Willow Creek, Doobie and Don didn't say a word. In the quiet of the ride, Don heard another bit of heavenly instruction. Deep down inside he heard this reassuring voice:

> *Don, it is My plan that you would be the glue to head up the people I have called into this ministry, to help them walk together and stay focused on Me.*

> Don thought, *But Lord, why me? Surely there's others better equipped than I am.*

> The Lord answered: *If you were already the perfect candidate, I couldn't use you, Don; I wouldn't want to. The way it is you'll have to lean on me all the time to get the assignment done. But that's the way I like it and that's the way you will like it also Don, believe Me.*

Don was encouraged by the Lord's comments. He said to Doobie, as he was getting out of the car: "Now there's a breakfast I won't soon forget, right?" Doobie replied with a wide, friendly smile.

As they walked to the front door of the motel, Doobie asked, "Why don't you go with me and Mama Blanchard to church tonight. I'll drive again."

Don said, "Great! I think that would be the best place to be tonight. Thanks."

"One more thing, Doobie: Why don't you start calling me Don. Okay?"

"Sure thing, Don. And you can call me Doobie."

"But I already do call you Doobie, you Dufus!" Don did a hip bump on Doobie that bumped him off his track.

Doobie returned the favor and bumped Don nearly off balance. There followed a brief light-hearted moment between two new friends. He didn't know how yet, but Don had a strong hunch that Doobie would play an important role in the Lord's coming assignment.

With his delay in deliveries, Don had some time on his hands that afternoon. He wanted to call Kathy and share with her some of the strange goings on, but she was still working. So, he would have to call later. The next best thing was to get out his Bible. He started reading the Gospel of John, and before he knew it, he was fast asleep on the bed.

Don awoke with a start and looked at the time. It was nearly 6:00 pm! No time for eating, so he went to the lobby and scarfed down a couple of doughnuts. Soon Doobie came by and off they went to the Church. They would meet up with Mama Blanchard there. The Tuckers also were invited to come along.

The scene at the little church was not too different from what Don was used to. There were about 25 people in attendance, and everyone seemed to know one another. It was a friendly atmosphere to be sure.

As the service began there were a few songs led by the Praise and Worship Team. Then the Pastor got everyone's attention by saying he thought there might be a special move of the Holy Spirit that night.

Before starting on his message, the Pastor started to move slowly down the main aisle and came to a stop where Don was sitting. The Pastor asked Don, "Would you please step out into the aisle? I believe the Lord has a word for you."

Don was extremely nervous, but you'd never know it. He complied with the request. The Pastor began to speak briefly in tongues and then in English: "I believe this is what the Lord has for you: *I have called you for a time such as this, in a place such as this. I will unveil more of My plans in the days and weeks ahead. You will find that Secret Place that you've been searching for. So, rejoice. Know that I am grooming you for a healing and teaching ministry and caring for the poor. The end is drawing near. Stay close to me for specific instructions.'"*

Doobie leaned over to Mama Blanchard and whispered: "Did you hear that? A healing ministry and it began today in your kitchen!"

The Pastor asked Don: "Does that Word speak to you? Is it a confirmation for something the Lord is already talking to you about?"

"I'd have to say *Yes* on both accounts," answered Don.

"Good! "It's good to know this Word tonight lines up with what the Lord has already been dealing with you about," the Pastor added. Then, he scanned out over the congregation to see if the Prophetic Gift might be touching anyone else. Assured that the Gift had completed its work he turned to the podium to deliver his prepared message.

At the close of the Pastor's message, he had an altar call, inviting people to come forward for prayer. One young woman came forward as did Doobie himself. Mama Blanchard leaned over to Don and said, "About once a month Doobie goes forward like this to rededicate his life to the Lord. No one really minds. His heart is so precious. He may be a bit slow in some areas, but his heart couldn't be bigger." Don looked on with a big grin on his face as Doobie came back to his seat.

As the service ended and the people were dismissed, the Pastor made a point to come over to where Don was sitting and introduce himself. "Good evening; I'm known as Pastor Daniel around here. And your name?"

"I'm Don Crawford, a trucker from the Midwest, just here in Greensville for my job. I've already met up with Mama Blanchard and Doobie. I'll be heading back home tomorrow."

"Well, Don, if your travels ever bring you back, I hope you'll pay us here at Cornerstone Church another visit."

"I'm sure I will, Pastor. Thank you."

As the Pastor noticed the Tuckers, he went over to them for a visit. In the meantime, Don was looking forward to heading back to Willow Creek, so he could talk with Kathy and tell her about his crazy day.

Kathy was quite excited about hearing all the news from Don. He rattled on and on, from the morning healing at Mama's restaurant to the evening prophetic word from the local Pastor.

Don commented: "Kathy, my head is swirling! I've got a lot going on in there; I don't know what to think about first. For sure I know I need to stay close to the Lord...

"Wow! Isn't all this something! I hope you're still glad you got hooked up with a guy like me. Boy, I wish you were here right now. I can't wait to get home, sit in my easy chair, and look at your lovely face. I should be home the day after tomorrow, in the afternoon...

"Oh, by the way Kathy I have a new song I want to share with you. I'm going to sing it all day long on my trip home. Do you want to hear it? Please say *yes*."

Kathy said: "Yes, yes. What is it?"

"Okay, Kathy, here goes, *I'm trucking down the interstate, slowly going home, soaking in the sun and pretty view. I'm trucking down the highway, going to see my Kathy. I can't wait to tell her I love you.*"

Kathy was touched. "Oh, that was beautiful, Don! I love it! I love it! Now get yourself home, you big Kahuna! I'll see you on Friday afternoon. I love you. Bye."

CHAPTER THREE –

Let's make sure we're following the Holy Spirit.

WHEN DON GOT HOME, HE MADE A BEELINE for Kathy and gave her the biggest hug ever. For a few moments Don and Kathy were 19-year-old college students, deeply in love.

Don's next destination was his favorite chair, looking forward to a relaxing evening. Kathy made other arrangements, however. She scheduled a time for her and Don to visit with the interim pastor that evening about all the recent goings on - just to get a different take on things and to make sure they were following the Holy Spirit.

When they sat down with the minister, Pastor Fred, Don got right to the point describing the prophecy from the Greensville Pastor on Wednesday night. Pastor Fred was quick to issue a strong voice of caution.

He said solemnly, "Don, I urge you to be leery about that bunch you have been dealing with. Don't put your trust there: He could just as well have been mistaken. And that tongues business smacks of the Twilight Zone in my view. I could tell you stories of how people had been led astray by ministers just like this one...Well, anything else?"

Without really waiting for a rebuttal by Don, Pastor Fred stood and called for a close to their meeting. "Well, thanks for coming in Don and Kathy. I hope to see you at Church this Sunday."

Don and Kathy walked out of the tiny office shaking their heads. Don couldn't wait to vent his frustration, which came after he got in the car. "Well, that was certainly a waste of time! He was no help at all! What are we supposed to do now?" Don smacked the steering wheel with both hands!

Kathy replied with a note of wisdom. "You know, Don, I never consulted with the Lord before making tonight's appointment. I'm sorry now that I didn't. He might have told us not to see Pastor Fred...

"Don, here's what I think we should do, at least for the rest of our weekend. Let's put this whole matter on a shelf and wait. If it's truly from God, He'll have to direct us again. If it's not from God, then it will pass."

That made perfect sense to Don. Under his breath and behind a smile, he muttered, *Thank You, Lord, for wise Kathy...and that she's a big part of my life.* "Good thinking, Kathy...But I honestly believe this is a God-thing."

"I agree, Don. That's what I think, too." Don reached over, grabbed Kathy's hand, and squeezed it lovingly.

The rest of the next day was involved with working on Kathy's to-do list. Sunday morning brought the same issue about whether to attend Church. This time Don thought he would beat Kathy to the punch. So, he announced: "Kathy, let's get ready for Church – and go despite Pastor Fred. We'll believe God wants to bless us and provide further direction about Greensville."

During Pastor Fred's sermon, Don inquired of the Lord. "Lord, Kathy and I haven't stopped believing that You are calling us to something special in Greensville. I'm still right about this, aren't I?" The Lord answered, "**Yes.**" It came deep down inside.

Don excitedly got Kathy's attention to pass on the Lord's affirmation. He flashed a big smile, shook his head up and down, pointed upwards with his thumb, and tried to mouth the letters *Y-e-s.*

Others sitting nearby may have wondered what was going on with Don and Kathy, but he didn't give that a thought. He was simply happy to hear from God.

Monday morning came once again. But it was different this time because Don wouldn't be gone for five days straight. No, this week he had local, day-long transporting to do. So, he would be home every evening. The good-byes were less stressful. Don thought he might focus on getting ready for the anticipated move during the week. Cleaning out the barn was number one; thinning out the basement was number two. After working at the factory, Kathy took the charge to thin out three bedrooms, no longer being used. The week went by ever so quickly.

Another Monday morning arrived. This time it signaled a return to Greensville. Kathy thought she'd never get used to the Monday morning good-byes. She never let on how much she hated it. Instead, today, she took some consolation in thinking that soon they would be starting a new life out East.

On his second day of travel, as Don approached Greensville, his spiritual receiver went into high alert. As he arrived at the west end of town, he experienced a depth of sadness in his heart, stronger than he had known before.

He quickly made his first stop and then headed to the Willow Creek Motel. He parked in the back as usual and then he spotted Doobie. What a happy vision that was. When he got out of the truck, he was greeted by Doobie in a most different way...a bit more starchy, aloof.

"Hello to you, Brother Don. Welcome once again." That was the first time Don had ever experienced that greeting. "I've got your same room ready for you. You'll be staying with us at least one night, right?"

"Yes, at least tonight. Thanks for taking good care of me, Doobie... Say, what's with the new name *Brother Don*?"

"Oh, I just thought it had a nice ring to it. Besides, after your healing of Barbara at Mama Blanchard's, I figure you ought to have a more important name than plain Don. Okay?"

"Well, first, it was the Lord that did the healing, not me. And second, I happen to like the name of *plain old Don*. It's me you know. So, let's just stick with Don."

"All right if you say so."

"Say, Doobie, how about dinner tonight at Mama Blanchard's?"

"Great idea! She'll be happy to see you again. I'll do the driving and maybe the Tuckers would want to go with us again. I'll check."

Suddenly Don had a call from his dispatcher. "Sorry, Doobie. I've got to take this call."

"No problem, Don." Doobie could tell by Don's expression that it was unexpected news.

"Well, Doobie, it looks like I'll be staying an extra day in your fair city once again. That was my dispatcher, who told me that my Wednesday drop off is embroiled in some labor-management dispute. So, I'll make their delivery the next day instead."

"Well, that's good. Now you'll be able to join us at Church tomorrow night. Mama Blanchard will be so happy!"

Don got settled into his favorite room for a two-night stay. He called and talked with Kathy to tell her the bad news about having the unexpected delay.

"But maybe I'll be able to make up the time with a change or two in my schedule," he wondered. "I'll talk to the dispatcher again. I sure want to get home at the regular time."

"Don, I know this must be hard on you...Maybe you can use some of your new spare time for prayer and getting the Lord's direction..."

(Don thought: 'Now, isn't that just like Kathy; here I give her some not-so-good news and she's thinking first about me!')

"Kathy, I love you. And I'm going to do just that: get more of the Lord's directions. I'll keep you posted. Bye for now."

There was a brisk easterly wind, keeping temperatures below normal, but Don decided he needed to get outside anyway, so off he went for a stroll toward town. A little roadside park came into view with an inviting picnic table near the entrance. And who should be sitting there but Ben Tucker. Ben spotted Don and waved at him to come over for a visit. Don obliged.

"Hello, again, Mr. Tucker. Good to see you," said Don walking over to the picnic table.

"Don't forget, it's Ben That's what all my friends call me; and I consider you a friend."

"Well, thank you...Ben. Thanks for thinking of me as a friend."

"Ben is short for Benjamin James. Same as my father. As I got to be a teenager, I wanted to change Benjamin James into something different, you know? I tried B. J. for a while, but that was too cumbersome, so I went from Benjamin to Ben."

"Yeah; I get it...So, you and Mrs. Tucker..."

"Clair! She would want you to call her Clair..."

"Okay. So, you and Clair have been in this fair city for a couple of weeks now, is that right?"

"Right, just getting the lay of the land, so to speak."

"I remember when I first met you two, you said there was a strong leading from the Lord to move here, but for reasons unknown. Is that getting any clearer?"

"The desire has grown stronger, but the specifics are still fuzzy."

Don paused to catch Ben's last point. "You know, Ben, that sounds a lot like my situation. I keep getting this yen to move here but the reasons to do so are not real clear. I know it – like I know a strong hunch – that it's from the Lord, but I sure wish He'd share more of that plan with me."

Ben could relate. "We're like two peas in a pod, huh Don...We just must be patient. I figure the direction will come in God's good timing... You know, maybe it's so big that we'd be scared out of our wits if we knew the whole picture at once."

"Yeah, that makes sense. Patience is not my strong point. I think I'll get into my search mode today by asking Him for more patience...Oh, by the way, where is Clair today. I hope she's alright."

"Yes, she's fine. Just back at the motel resting."

"Good. Well, Ben, I think I'll be moving on. Doobie is planning that I go with him to Momma Blanchard's later for supper. He was going to see if you two want to join us."

"We'd love to. Thanks."

Don headed out and turned to go back to the motel, probably a half-mile walk. He found a comfy spot on a Bench in the courtyard near his room on the far end of the building. There he got right into his business with God.

"So, Lord, I'm praying for two things: more patience and more direction. I know you have both to give me."

The Lord interrupted in His now familiar voice. It was not audible but a sensing deep inside: Don, I don't have more patience to give you. I've already given you all the patience you'll ever need. It's a fruit of the Holy Spirit, remember? Call on the Spirit that lives within you; He will gladly answer such a request...

Now as to the other area of direction for your life, Ben was right: If I let you in on the whole picture all at once, you couldn't deal with it. So, it will have to come to you piecemeal. But after all, that's all I'm asking of you – to trust Me day by day, one step at a time. You can do that, Don; I know you can.

"Yes, Lord, I can do that. I will do that! Anything else I should know at this point?"

The Lord spoke more directly "Only this for now: I'll be asking you to do things you've never done before. When you detect that in your spirit just know that a wave of My strength and provision is right at your heels. I'll help you in every way. You already know deep down that My promise is true: *I'll never leave you nor forsake you.*[3] Trust in that with all your heart and cast all your care onto Me. You'll see the victory!"

DON WAS CONTENT WITH WHAT THE LORD had given. He rested a long while on that Bench, basking in His Presence. A warm smile enveloped his whole face. "Thank You, Lord," he said softly. "Thank You."

His time of solitude was interrupted by Doobie poking his head out the front door and announcing it was time to go eat. "Hey, Brother Don, are you hungry?" he yelled. "Mama Blanchard has a table all set up, and Ben and Clair will be joining us!"

Don was hungry and eager to go to the diner. As he walked to the front door of the motel, Doobie sprang out the door to grab Don's arm. He pulled him in to the lobby. There behind the counter stood a tall, muscular young man, that Don knew as Mark. Nearby was a young lady tidying up the waiting area. Doobie introduced both.

"Don, Ben and Clair, this tall, handsome man is my younger brother, Mark." Doobie moved next to the counter, closer to Mark, to make his next point. "People say we look a lot alike! What do you think?" Doobie smiled from ear to ear. Tall, handsome Mark standing near short, dumpy Doobie was quite the contrast!

After a few chuckles, Don asked about the young lady. "Doobie, how about this young lady?"

"Oh, I almost forgot...Everyone, this is Suzy. She's worked here for many years, keeping this place clean and inviting."

"Will you be joining us for dinner, Suzy or Mark?" Don asked.

Both excused themselves; both had work to be finished at the motel. So off went the foursome to the diner. Ben drove. Mama Blanchard had her best table all set, even with a tablecloth.

"Welcome! Welcome!" was Mama's warm greeting. "Chicken and dumplings is our special tonight. I think Rusty, our cook, outdid himself this time."

"Chicken and dumplings sounds good to me," said Doobie. Don agreed. So did Ben and Clair.

"Four *Specials* coming right up!" barked Mama Blanchard as she walked back to the kitchen.

The only thing that outshined the great food that evening was the warm fellowship that followed, especially when Mama Blanchard joined the group. Everyone seemed to have their sights set on sharing what the Lord was doing in their hearts. And a sense of urgency and excitement filled the air.

A similar restless quality was detected at Church the following evening, in the Pastor's message and prayers. Both Don and Clair picked up on it. They glanced at one another with a knowing look several times.

Don decided right there that this would be the Church for him and Kathy. The Lord overheard and had a comment: "Don, this will indeed be your Church, at the beginning. But there is so much more to this than you know. Can you see yourself being a Shepherd for Me? Better get used to it; that's part of My plan. In the weeks and months before you, you'll get all the training and provision you'll need. Just stay close and trust Me! Okay?"

"Okay, Lord," whispered Don just loud enough for his friends to overhear. They turned to Don and smiled. His face turned red. He whispered again to the onlookers, "Sorry."

By the time Church let out, Don was yawning big time. This had been a long, long day. When Doobie arrived back at the motel, Don was more than ready to call it a night.

"See you all tomorrow; I'm beat," he announced. "Oh, by the way Doobie, does the motel serve anything in the way of breakfast?"

"Well, we're a little short in that area of service," he answered. "But we will have coffee, orange juice, and powdered donuts."

"Okay by me. Good night."

THE NEXT DAY DON HAD HIS MORNING available before taking off for his next delivery. He met up with Ben at the lobby, who suggested that the two of them have a quick tour around the city. Don agreed.

Their travel took them into an industrial area. There they saw an empty, boarded up, medium-sized factory. Ben drove around it several times, to see it from all angles. Don commented: "Hey Ben, you seem awfully interested in this empty place. What are you thinking?"

Ben stopped the car near the front entrance. His answer caught Don by surprise. "Shall we start it up again, rehire some locals for a new venture? Could we help revitalize the economy that way? That's how it seems to me. We could get Greensville cranked up again and this factory could be where we start."

"How could we have an impact on the local economy?" Don asked.

"What could we do? Well, how about a government contract? There are government-issued uniforms that are not being used because of some defect; usually something simple, like weak buttons, or incomplete hems. This is what my friend at the Pentagon tells me."

"So, how could that need fit into Greensville and this empty factory? I don't get it, Ben"

"Well, all we've got to do is get this factory up and running. Buy a few sewing machines, train some people, ship the defective uniforms here, fix the problem and send them back. In the process, the local out-of-work people get a good paycheck and start reviving. And the economy gets a big shot in the arm."

"Oh, is that all we've got to do! You make it sound easy and so doable, Ben"

"My contact at the Pentagon is a Major in the Quartermaster Corps. We served in the middle east conflict together many years back."

"You're serious about this? Really serious?" Don's skepticism was showing.

"Sure, why not...with the Lord's help all things are possible, right?"

Suddenly, Ben had an epiphany-moment! The Lord obviously turned on a lightbulb in Ben's spirit. Don witnessed it, sitting next to him in the car.

"That's it, Don! That's why I'm here! That's why God directed Clair and me here. Me with a close friend and contact at the Pentagon, me with an itch to organize people into a working crew and see them revitalize their own lives. Yes, this is it!"

Don was flabbergasted, but he had nothing to contribute. He was excited to see Ben's spirit grab hold of the Lord's unveiling.

Ben added, "This factory venture could be one way God's blessing could come on us and this community. God can use it that way – I believe he wants to...I'm going to call my buddy and see what he thinks. First, I've got to talk with Clair; she'll be so excited."

"Well, Ben, I hope this whole thing takes off. I could see it being a boon to Greensville. In the meantime, I need to be getting myself ready for the road."

On the ride back to the motel it was quiet in the car. Ben was busy thinking of ways to make the deserted factory become a reality. Don was considering his options. He was thankful that God had shined a light on Ben's role in coming to this place. But at the same time, he was uneasy, wondering *How do I fit into all this, Lord?*

The Lord spoke to his heart. *You and Kathy are right in the middle of My plan. More specifics are coming soon. In the meantime, you know what to do.*

"Yes, Lord, be anxious for nothing,[4] and always trust in You – with all my heart."[5]

"Did you say something, Don?" asked Ben

"No, more I was just thinking out loud, I guess." Since Don didn't go any further with that notion, Ben rightfully concluded that his friend had some things to work out with God. It got quiet again in the car.

Around the next Bend in the road the motel came into view. Don thought, *Lord, after I get back on the road, I want to be talking again with You. We have more to discuss and clarify.*

When they arrived, Don bid farewell to Ben, to Doobie and to Mark and headed for his room to gather his belongings. Within a few minutes he got into his cab and headed west, out of town.

He sat silently, but in no way peacefully, bouncing along on the interstate. Finally, he broke the silence. "Lord! Lord! I want to know what to expect; I want to know what You want me to do!" The Lord answered.

"Okay, Don, I can see you're not going to be satisfied until you know more specifics, so here they come, brace yourself: I want you and Kathy to move here to Greensville in two weeks."

"What? Two weeks? Are You sure? Of course, You're sure! Sorry, Lord."

"That's right, Don: two weeks! My plan calls for you and Kathy to live here on a permanent basis! This is your new home. Two weeks will allow you time to give notice to your employers, as well as your landlord. You'll have those two weeks of work, but it will be light. I realize you won't have much time to thin out your belongings, except on your two weekends home. That job will fall mainly on Kathy. I want you to give most of what you've accumulated away. You're not going to need much, just a few personal items, because I have a furnished place prepared for you here...Oh, and knowing you as I do, you're probably wondering about money..."

"Yes, Lord, You're right. That question has entered my mind a time or two...or three, in recent weeks."

"Well, give it no further thought. It's covered. In one regard, I have already taken care of that need at Calvary. Remember: *'I became poor that you might be made rich.'* [6] How specifically that will be manifested is still to be determined. I'm working on a couple of avenues. It depends a good deal on the cooperation of some people you don't know. But rest assured, either way you will be well taken care of. Keep trusting Me. And rebuke any unbelief or fear that tries to enter in."

"Okay, Lord, I'll keep trusting. I'll think of it as a *faith challenge*... I can't wait to call and tell Kathy!"

"And one final thing for now, Don: I want you to liquidate all your savings and retirement funds. Turn everything into cash. Sell that old pick-up to your cousin, Jake. He'll buy your farm equipment, too. Cash is what you'll need at the beginning of this venture. And soon enough that cash won't have any value or purpose anyway. I'm working with others who will be joining you to do the same thing with their assets.

"You'll begin to notice along the way that I am esteeming you in their hearts. They will more and more be looking to you as their shepherd. Don't object to that or dismiss their desire out of some false sense of humility. It's all part of the plan. In the days ahead I'll be talking more to you about *shepherding* this group. I know a thing or two about it, wouldn't you agree?"

"Yes, Lord! You know all about it. And I want to learn everything I can. Thank You! Thank You!

"I can't wait to make a call to Kathy," said Don to the rush of afternoon traffic passing him on the left. "She should be home from work by now..."

CHAPTER FOUR –

Devil, you take your hands off my wife! Now!

AS DON QUICKLY LEARNED, KATHY WAS less excited than he had hoped. She didn't like the two-week deadline for one thing. And she really didn't like that most of the business getting ready would be hers to shoulder. But the financial part of it all was the worst news.

"Don, are you sure the Lord told you to get rid of all our retirement and savings?"

"Not *get rid of* but turn it into cash, which will be most needed at the start."

"At the start, you say. At the start of what, Don? Where is all this leading us? And relocating? To begin living where? And doing what?"

Kathy was exasperated. Don had to admit he had dumped a lot on her all at once. Kathy took a few deep breaths to calm herself. She thought: *Don has been right there in the mix with God, getting His direction, basking in His Spirit, while I've been trying to keep everyday life going. I can tell that he's super excited.*

You must pull yourself together, girl! Lay aside those fears and catch some of his excitement. Be the helpmate Don needs you to be right now... Oh, Lord, help me!

Slowly she began in a calmer mood. "Don, you have laid a big portion on my plate...It's all happening so fast. I want to be able to keep up and do my part. But the devil's working hard to get me into all sorts of fears..."

In an instant, right there on Interstate 70, Don stood up in his spirit and took hold of his long-distance authority: "Devil, you take your hands off my wife! Now! In the Name of Jesus! You have no right or claim here! You take your fears and confusion and git! In the mighty Name of Jesus Christ!" Time stood still for the longest moment. Kathy finally spoke up.

"Thank you, Don. You always seem to know just what I need when I need it. Believe me I'll be talking to the Lord myself about making all this a reality, beginning tonight. I'll call the kids to bring them up to speed. And believe me you are going to have the longest *honey-do list* you've ever seen when you get home this weekend! And no chance of forgetting about it either. Bye for now. I love you."

"And I love you back. How about me giving you a long shoulder rub when I finish my to-do list?"

"Oh, so you've sunk to bribery now, is that it?" Kathy chuckled. "I don't care. I think I'll take you up on your offer. Bye."

"Bye. See you tomorrow."

Don smiled and then turned heavenward. "Thank You, Lord, for Kathy! She's such a blessing. You sure knew what You were doing when You put us together."

The Lord answered: "You're welcome, Don. If I were to look up *Helpmate* in the dictionary, I would find Kathy's picture there. And as we get further into these coming perilous times, you're going to appreciate her more and more."

Don smiled again, one of those silly-grin smiles. Then he let loose, bellowing out a "**Hallelujah**" that could have carried at least two football fields away! Passers-by may have wondered at Don's antics in his cab, but he didn't care.

Soon he began to see signs of his turnoff for the next destination. Right about then he had a call from Ben Tucker. It was unusual to get such a call, so Don wondered if he had something urgent to discuss.

Ben went on to explain: "Don, glad I caught up with you. I wanted you to know that the Lord has been talking with Clair and me about liquidating our retirement and investment accounts."

Don's ears perked up. "Tell me more Ben. This is sounding awful familiar."

Ben went on and on for a good five minutes. It was an encouraging confirmation to Don.

"I've concluded that we're going to need our cash right away," Ben explained. "Who knows, considering the unstable times we live in, but savings and cash as we know it could end up confiscated, or at least be found of little or no value."

"God has told me the same thing, Ben!"

In an unusually warm, father-to-son way, Ben confided: "Don we're on to something big for the Lord, you know that, right?"

"I couldn't agree more, Ben. It's more exciting and unnerving at the same time. But I'm sure glad we're together on this..."

"...and that God's the One in charge!" Ben added eagerly.

"Right you are Ben, God is definitely in charge. He'll see us through everything! And I just know you're going to like my Kathy when you meet her in a couple of weeks. We're moving to Greensville on a permanent basis, into the motel to start with. Praise the Lord! See you then. Say *Hi* to everyone back home. Tell Doobie to have my room ready. Bye for now."

Don was nearly beside himself with excitement. He thought about calling his mom and dad to let them in on the latest. But then he had a check in his gut: *They probably wouldn't understand. They'd just think that this was another one my wild schemes,* Don thought...

Don and his dad always seemed to have a strained relationship. Don felt like he never measured up. His dad was a successful accountant in his own business. He always thought of Don as following in his footsteps, but that was as far from Don's mind as anything could be. Don wanted his life to have excitement and purpose; he wanted his life to accomplish something important - for people's benefit!

True, Don had subjected his parents to some trying times over the years, as he floundered around trying to find his niche in life. He was never short on big dreams, but they usually fizzled to a zero. But now... things were different now, following God's plans. Don had plenty of excitement, and there was a promise that he would be directly involved in helping people accomplish something important, for themselves and for the Lord's Kingdom.

It tugged at Don's heart that he couldn't share all this with his parents. Still, he wanted to try. So, he called and talked with his mother. She listened politely but Don knew he was not getting through with the heart of it, like the Lord's calling to move out east and be part of a group of Believers. Don found it hard to put this into words his mother would understand; he could barely put it all into any words for himself to understand!

Don asked his mother to tell his dad about the phone call. She said she would do that. Don also promised to keep them in his prayers and to keep them informed about this new venture for the Lord. He ended the call on a somber note, in view of his mother's reaction; his eyes began to swell up with tears. Then, Don felt badly that he was relieved that the call was over.

"Oh, Lord, help me please...if there's any way I can get my parents to understand, please, please, let me know. I wish that could happen..."

Slowly, Don regained his composure. He had one more night on the road. And two more deliveries to make. By late afternoon Friday, Don headed into his own driveway. Kathy ran out and greeted him with open arms and the longest hug in the Guinness Book of Records! They talked and made plans well into the evening. [You know that the Lord was well pleased].

Don asked how the kids took to the news of uprooting and moving east. "Well," Kathy began, "they didn't quite know what to think...Sylvia and Mike said they wanted to help, but this was the busiest time of their year, work-wise and summer sports-wise for the grandsons. Probably can't count on them for much..."

"Who can we count on?" Kathy went on..."Jenny and Jim, the new-lyweds in Colorado! They want to come for the next two weekends all the way from Colorado to help us get ready. Go figure that!"

"Maybe Jenny is a little homesick for her mother. She didn't let on in any way that things were...ah, bad with Jim, did she?"

"No, nothing like that, Don, so put away your gun. She's still very much in love. Partly, they're just *foot loose and fancy free* for the next three weeks. They're both in-between jobs, you recall. And they said they don't have any firm commitments to take care of, so they're looking forward to coming home, and then traveling on with us to Greensville.

"I don't know if you realize this or not, Don, but Jim really looks up to you. You're the father he never had growing up."

"Really? Think so?" asked Don with his chest puffed out a bit and an approving smile pasted on his face.

"Yes, I really think so," Kathy replied. "Oh, by the way, I talked briefly with my mother. She didn't seem surprised about our move out east. She always considered you a bit of a vagabond..."

"She should talk," Don answered. "That's like calling the kettle black! How many far-out moves has she and your father done over the years... Twenty? Forty? Where is she off to now?"

"Somewhere off the beaten path in rural Peru...some place where tourists don't travel, that's for sure. She's not sure how long they'll be gone. I told her we'll keep her posted, but she thought they'd be somewhere where cell phones didn't work."

"And your brother?"

"He's off to Madagascar, for the University."

"He's a lot like your parents. I'm glad you're not. You're okay about being a home-body and looking after me!"

"Now there's a full-time job worth shouting about!"

"I know the pay's not great, but the benefits are outstanding!"

"Hey, let's go into the living room for our ice cream and cookies."

Both headed toward their favorite spot on the old couch. Kathy sighed as she ran her hand across the worn fabric. "I guess this old sofa won't be going with us will it? I'll miss this old thing. So many good memories. Every stain on it has a story to tell about this family."

Kathy switched gears and continued the planning session. "So, Don, let's get practical, where the rubber meets the road, as you truckers say. Just where are we going to live?"

"At the motel at first. For how long? I don't know. Nothing so far is on a long-term arrangement. A bunch of things are going on; it's a very fluid situation at the present. There's an empty factory building involved; could be a source of revenue for us. Ben is checking into that.

"More about that later. Once we get there, our first order of business is to get settled, get our bearings, and have you meet and get to know all the people I've been talking to you about..."

Don wanted to move away from the practical. Kathy had more questions than he had answers for. Don took her hand, looked her in the eyes and announced. "I hope you can realize, Kathy, how good it will be to have you at my side. And not 1000 miles away!" Kathy smiled back and gave up drilling Don with more questions.

The next two weeks flew by! Don completed his "to-do" lists with a gracious attitude that caused Kathy, Jenny, and Jim to marvel. The goal was reached of reducing their thirty-year collection of *stuff* to the barest of bones, so that it all could fit into a small U-Haul trailer. As the Lord predicted, Don's cousin, Jake, was quick to buy the pick-up and other pieces of farm equipment. Plus, he took care of getting rid of the furniture and other home belongings not going on the trip.

Kathy only had to work one of the two weeks, Thanks to a grateful boss, who bent the rules slightly. So, her second week could be devoted to last minute preparations. And Kathy appreciated having Jenny and Jim around for that second grueling week. Don, on the other hand, had to be on the road for both weeks, but at least he could be home every night. That was better than expected.

Jenny asked her mother one night if she and Dad had bid farewell to their Church and old Church friends. Kathy replied: "We tried, then quickly gave up. None of them understood nor seem interested. We heard several comments like: 'Oh, that sounds so risky in our declining economy. Are you sure God wants you to do that? Are you sure you know what you're doing? I hope it works out'...not the epitome of congeniality and encouragement wouldn't you agree.

"If it weren't for the fact that we needed that Church for your wedding, we probably would have discontinued there long ago. Your father is anxious to introduce us to a new, active, charismatic Church in Greensville, called the Cornerstone. He likes the Pastor and the people he's met there."

One afternoon in midweek of week two, Don called home to talk with Kathy. She was far away from her cellphone, so she asked Jim to answer for her. When Jim heard who was calling, he seemed to snap to attention: "Oh, Mr. Crawford, hello. Do you want Kathy? I'll get her…"

"Jim, I wish you'd start calling me Dad. Okay? Mr. Crawford is…it's too much. Make it Dad. Okay, Son?"

"Ah, sure, ah, Dad…Here's Kathy."

Jim tried to cuff the phone microphone as he handed it to Kathy, but Don could overhear his comment: "He wants me to call him Dad! Wow! We're beginning to really bond, don't you think?"

Kathy smiled as she began to talk softly. "Don, Jim is quite impressed that you encouraged him to start calling you Dad…So, what's up at your end?"

Don was resting in between jobs, he wanted to catch up on progress at home and to revel in the fact that he only had two days to go before he said goodbye to his boss and the semi that was often his home away from home. Otherwise, everything seemed to be going smoothly. "I can hardly wait, Kathy. Only two more days! I'll be counting the hours!"

Before hanging up, Don repeated the last line of his *Kathy Song*, delivered with a hint of Western Twang: "Oh, honnneey, I can't wait to tell ya, Ah luuuv you!"

"Oh, great, now you've gone *Country and Western* on me!" Kathy said with a big grin. "Don't we have enough changes to deal with these days…Just kidding, Don. I'll take your song as country-western or any way you want. Just hurry home. We all miss you. Bye."

CHAPTER FIVE –

We look forward to all You have in store for us

M OVING DAY FINALLY ARRIVED! THE U-HAUL was filled to the brim, even the back seat of the Jeep was cluttered with boxes and suitcases. Jim and Jenny were following in their own car. This would be a two-day trip with lots of driving. Half-way would be Memphis, Tennessee, for an overnight stop.

Before leaving, Don gathered all the travelers for a moment of prayer. "Lord, we believe You've brought us to this point and Your presence will continue with us as we travel on into Your plan. Thank You for taking such good care of us along the way. We commit our travels into Your care. We look forward to all You have in store for us. We trust You with all our hearts. You lead and we'll follow. Thank You. Thank You. In the Name of Jesus Christ. Amen!"

It was about 8:00 pm, two days later, when the travelers arrived at the Willow Creek Motel, weary after all the riding, but excited at the same time. They quickly checked into their room and then joined those who had gathered as a self-appointed *Welcoming Committee*. Doobie and Mama Blanchard had set up the meeting room with a banquet-style look, complete with a table of sandwiches and snacks.

All of Don's North Carolina family of friends were in attendance. Besides Doobie and Mama Blanchard, there were Miss Verla, the Tuckers, Ben and Clair, Barbara and Rusty from Mama's café, Doobie's brother, Mark, and the motel maid, Suzy. Don warmly greeted each one and introduced his Kathy and Jim and Jenny. Everyone agreed there were too many names to remember that evening.

Don noticed some new faces in the gathering. First, there was a well-dressed older man by the name of Henry Greyheck. He was cordial, but stiff and distant. He was an acquaintance of Doobie's brother, Mark. Then, there was a young mother, Mary Kay Johnson, with her three preschoolers, Gideon, Levi, and Natalie. She was a friend of Suzy, the motel maid. How these two new people were to fit in, Don had no clue. He convinced himself that God's hand was involved and that he would find out soon enough.

After everyone loaded a plate of snacks and settled in for some casual conversation, Don came to sit next to Doobie. "Thanks again, Doobie, for you and Mama Blanchard's work to pull all of this together. It looks so festive and inviting. Next time I want to throw a party, I'll put you in charge."

Just like Doobie to deflect any hint of praise. "Oh, it was all Mama Blanchard's doing. I just helped out a little."

"I bet you did more than help out a little," Don replied. "There's one thing I've noticed for sure..."

"What's that, Brother Don?"

"There seems to be an instant kinship among the people here. It was like everyone had known each other for years and still enjoyed being in one another's company."

"Yeah, I see what you mean," Doobie remarked. "I figure God had His part in getting us all together."

"Right you are, Doobie...Say, Doobie, I've been thinking...I'd like to do something...a bit peculiar. I'd like to change your name."

"Change my name? To what?"

"Einstein. Yeah, Einstein. *Einstein McKenna*. Now that has a real ring to it, don't you think?"

Doobie was silent, but his brain was going 100 miles an hour. "Say, Don, wasn't this Einstein guy a smart man, an inventor or something?"

"Yes, he was a very smart scientist and mathematician. But did you know, he never started talking until he was five. His family thought he was going to be a real slow learner. Boy were the parents surprised when he finally got with the program. Anyway, I'm going to call you Einstein."

Then Don knocked his fist on the top of Doobie's head to highlight his last point. "I believe there's more up there in your brain than people might think, including yourself. Okay, Einstein?"

"Okay by me. You call me Einstein McKenna and I'll call you Brother Don." Doobie answered as he flashed one of his contagious grins that melted Don's heart every time.

Don looked over at Kathy. She noticed and smiled, as she listened to Mama Blanchard rattle on about Don. To hear Mama talk, Don was just a tad shy from sainthood. Jenny and Jim were busy in their own talk with Mark and Mary Kay. Don used the occasion to introduce himself to Henry Greyheck, who was sitting all alone.

"Hello, Mr. Greyheck. Is that right? My name is Don Crawford. May I sit here?" Don extended a big handshake as he sat next to Henry.

"Of course," replied Henry. "Have a seat."

There were a few awkward moments. Don decided rather than try to chit-chat, he would just get right into the main question. "Say, Mr. Greyheck, I'm curious. How is it that you joined up with this rag-tag group?"

"Well, I'm an acquaintance of Mark McKenna. We've had some business dealings in the past. I've found Mark to be an innovative, thorough, and punctual young man. He got a lot of things done for me that I couldn't have done on my own. When I ran into a snag, I often came to Mark with it. He would say: 'Hey, no problem. I know some people. We'll make it happen' and he did. When he invited me here, I felt an overwhelming urge to come, but I'm not sure why. I understand from Mark that you're heading up this group..."

"...Oh, I'm not quite sure *heading up* is the right description," Don quickly added.

"Well, however you want to say it," Henry continued, "Your Group is focusing on a spiritual application to the economic woes facing this area, is that it?"

"That is a major thrust of what we want to work on, but there will be more than that in operation. What additional directions we might go is not totally clear yet. We're trusting in the Lord to provide that push. One thing we know is that the Lord is leading us by the hand. Most of us are certain that we're supposed to be here at this time and be a part of God's program, and that He will provide all that is needed to accomplish His purposes."

Another long silence, then Don continued. "Do my comments clarify any reasons why you might want to join up with us?"

"Well, not really. But I can tell you this: I will keep thinking about it. I'm a businessman, Don, faced everyday with important decisions to make. And over the years I've learned how to trust in my intuition to guide me, not my understanding. And I've been right most of the time. If that same inner urging that brought me here tonight rises again, I'll be in touch."

"That's good enough for me, Mr. Greyheck," answered Don.

"Henry. Call me Henry, Don."

"Alright, Henry. Happy to oblige. Nice to meet you."

Just as Don stood to join Kathy, a pronouncement came forth from Doobie.

"Folks, can I have your attention! Brother Don, I think the Lord has a lesson He wants you to teach us." Mama Blanchard echoed the thought: "I agree, Don. Tell us more about the end-times that we seem to be going into right now." Others encouraged the same.

Don stepped forward to reply. "Folks that sounds like a great idea. And on any other occasion I would welcome the chance. But not tonight, please. We're all bushed from our travels and would like nothing better than to catch eight hours of peaceful sleep at Willow Creek. Could we meet another evening soon? Tomorrow? No, that's midweek service at the church. How about in two nights? Whenever...Since we are now official *Greensville-ites*, our schedule is open. We'll do it very soon. Trust me!"

Ben stood to bid good night to others, when he had a sharp pain in his lower back. The pain nearly caused him to collapse. Onlookers were alarmed. Doobie and Mark rushed to his side to gently lower him into a card table chair. Don came immediately to the scene.

"Ben! Take it easy! Let me pray for you, alright?"

"Yes, Don, please do."

Don looked over at Clair; he was searching for some information. She recognized the unspoken question and promptly answered: "He's had this problem on and off for five years or more, but it's been getting worse over the past month. The doctors don't have any answers."

"Well, God has the answer! It's Jesus," Don insisted. By this time, all eyes were on Don and Ben. Don rested his hand on Ben's shoulder and looked out at the crowd.

"Folks, Jesus bore our sickness, disease and pain as our Substitute on the Cross, so we wouldn't have to have any of it. This pain has already been defeated; it's illegal and it has no right to inflict Ben's body. His body is a Temple of the Holy Spirit."

Turning to Ben, sitting awkwardly in the chair, Don went on. "Ben I'm going to place my hand on your lower back and pray, okay?"

"Yes, yes, Don!"

"Pain, I rebuke you in the Name of Jesus! You can't stay in this temple of the Holy Spirit. You go now! I call on the Holy Spirit that resides in this body to administer God's mighty healing work. Straighten out Ben's spine, Holy Spirit; correct any part that is not right...Ben, be healed and whole in the mighty Name of Jesus Christ!"

Don extended his hand, grabbed hold of Ben, and ushered him sternly to his feet (as Peter and John did for the lame man at the Temple in the Book of Acts).[7] "Now, Ben, I want you to say this out loud several times each day for the next week: 'I am healed, whole, restored and renewed!' Go on, you walk around the room and say it like you mean it: 'I am healed, whole, restored and renewed'!"

"I am healed, whole, restored and renewed...I am healed, whole, restored and renewed! Oh, my gosh, the pain is gone! I **am** healed! Praise the Lord!"

While no one was more excited about the results than Don, he didn't want to leave his friends with wrong thinking, so he jumped at the opportunity to teach. "Friends, we have witnessed a miracle, Ben receiving God's provision of health and wholeness. Like everything we receive from God, we receive healing by faith. We don't earn it or deserve it; we believe and receive. It's a question of the heart.

"Ben just exclaimed that he believed he received because he felt that the pain was gone. But that's just like the *Thomas-kind of faith* in the Bible. Remember him? He said he would believe Jesus had resurrected only after he could see Him and touch the nail prints in His hands.[8] In the days ahead we're going to have to rely on our faith to receive and walk in God's blessings. We don't receive based on what we can see or feel. We receive by faith – believing in what we can't yet see or feel.

"Friends, this business of faith is so important! And we'll be talking about it a lot...But look at the time. It's way past my bedtime. So, Kathy and I bid you all a good night. Thank you for coming tonight. We've never had such a welcome. I just know that Kathy and I are at the right place, at the right time. We'll plan on another time to get together real soon and let you know...Don't forget church tomorrow night."

There were a bunch of hands to shake at the beginning of the night. Now, at the close, it was all repeated. Don and Kathy were very tired but grateful as they made their way down the hall to their room. Jenny and Jim followed to their room next door.

As Don was beginning to wake up the next morning and he lay in bed in a half-conscious frame of mind, he began to hear from the Lord: "Don, Don, I want to talk with you. Are you listening, Don? You need to have a clearer picture of where I'll be leading you and your friends. You don't need the full story now, only a small portion."

"Yes, Lord. I'm ready to receive." Slowly Don got up and moved to a chair at the small kitchen table.

"Good," the Lord began. "Your new acquaintance, Henry Greyheck, is being groomed to help you financially in significant ways. He'll bring it up to you when the time is right; don't you push the matter, trust in Me. Also, you'll be receiving an anointing as a Teacher of My Word... And as a Shepherd of My sheep."

Don interrupted. "But Lord, You know how I sometimes stumble with my words..."

God interrupted, and sternly! **"Don, do you think I don't know what I'm doing? Do you think my Gift is insufficient? Inadequate?"**

"No, Lord! No! Never insufficient or inadequate!" Don quickly replied. "I'm sorry for questioning Your ways." The Lord brought the story of Moses to Don's mind, as He exclaimed: "As I was with Moses, so I will be with you. Remember how Moses was a stutterer at first and doubted that he could be used by Me.[9] But he grew into his anointing and soon became My trusted, capable voice to the Pharaoh and a great leader of the Jewish people. Remember?"

"Yes, Lord, I remember...I'll be quiet and let You unfold Your plan; and whatever you call on me to do, I will accept without question. With Your help I'll be like Moses: Your trusted and strong voice to the people you gather here."

"Good, now here's a couple of points about healing I want you to focus on with the others. First, healing has already been provided through the sacrifice of Jesus at Calvary. So, a Believer's job is to claim healing by faith and believe that you receive, much like you said last night. You're not asking Me to do something new, because the work has already been done. I paid the price by the stripes I bore."

"And, secondly, emphasize that sickness is not natural. Most everyone expects sickness and disease, especially as they advance in years, but that's not My best. Some see it as their ticket into Heaven, but that's not how I intended it to be, either. You don't have to be sick to die and go to Heaven. I'll help refine these points in your mind. Teach them to the people boldly!"

"Yes, Lord, I will. Thank You. One question I have: how does Doobie's Pastor fit into Your plan with us?"

"Can't tell you – can't because I don't know exactly. He's still wrestling with a couple of important issues that don't concern you. Once he gets through that then I'll be in a better position to do My work in his heart. I hope he'll choose to join forces with you; it all depends on what he decides."

"Lord, what I'm hearing from You is so new to me! You're saying that man can choose to override Your will and plan for them...?"

"But when I consider it, I can see how that's true. It's Your will that everyone be saved, but not everyone chooses to do things Your way."

"Yes, sadly, that's the case. My will is not always followed. My gift to man of a free will to choose his own destiny was My crowning glory, but I also regret all those who willingly turn their back on Me...If they only knew how much I long for them to draw near."

Don sensed a tinge of sadness in the Lord's voice. "I'll work hard to keep all these you have entrusted to me focused on You, Lord. I want You to be proud of me."

"Oh, I already am, Don...I already am."

Don was aglow with gratitude for the Lord's comment. Then he sensed that the encounter was over, for now. He turned and started to make some coffee. Before long Kathy was awake. She came to sit next to Don.

"Well, Mr. Crawford, what do you have planned for this beautiful September day?"

"Good morning, Mrs. Crawford. It was sure good to wake up next to you. Thanks for joining me in this venture." He sealed his thanks with a lingering kiss.

"Okay, but surely you had more in mind than just whisking me off to this exquisite, five-star motel," she replied smiling. Then Kathy got more serious.

"I'm not fully sure what I signed up for, Don, other than to be your awesome helpmate...Let me put it this way, Don: If I run into someone new at the grocery store and they learn that I'm a part of that *group* at the Willow Creek Motel and they ask, 'What is your group doing?' – how would I answer?"

"Right now? Not sure what you should say. You're in the same boat with a lot of others around here. They have a sense of wanting to be a part of what God is starting to do, but the specifics are still blurry. For one thing, it has to do with helping the locals deal with a definite economic downturn that set in here and across the Country, when businesses shut down right and left to deal with the virus scare. So, I see us providing food, shelter, and general assistance; maybe even opportunities for simple employment."

"But that's just a part of their lives needing attention, right?" Kathy asked.

"You're right. Their spiritual needs are even more glaring. I think I heard it said that only 13% of adults have any church connection around here. More Churches are closing than starting."

"Not unlike many communities around the country," Kathy added.

"Yeah, sad but true...Of course, the *kicker* for me in all this is that I believe that we are in the last of the last days. I believe the Bible teaches that we, even the Believers, are in for some hard times ahead, in the not-too-distant future...really hard times...so hard that we could turn our back on God."

Of course, Kathy was aware of the development of Don's desire to know about the end-times. It started out a few years ago as a biblical interest on his own, but quickly grew into a strong, consuming hunger, that he wanted to share with others. But she wasn't sure how it all tied in.

Lord, she said under her breath, *help me to know how all this fits together, so I can be the best helpmate ever for Don.*

She didn't expect an answer, but the Lord replied anyway: *I will be teaching you many things in the weeks ahead. You indeed have a big part in My plan for this venture. You are to Don what temper is to steel. Keep your eyes, ears, and heart open – and above all, trust in Me!*

Kathy stared off into space to savor every word that she heard from God.

Don noticed and tried to break into her reverie. "Earth to Captain Kathy...Earth to Captain Kathy...Are you there? Over."

"Oh, sorry Don. I wasn't out in space. I was trying to go over some direction that I just received myself from the Lord. He says I have an important part in His plan for Greensville..."

"Right you are, Kathy! What that's going to be I guess we'll both find out together."

"Say, I thought of another question. Couldn't God have done what He wants to do in Greensville back home in our own community? That way we wouldn't have had to move 1000 miles and turn our lives upside down. Our hometown needs some rejuvenation as much as Greensville. Why here?"

"Good question. I'm not sure. You'll have to ask God. He has called several of us to break loose from our former lives to relocate here. Maybe that way we are more likely to trust Him with every detail, rather than searching for comfort from our former lives. Remember how God called Abraham and Sarah to leave their homeland and family and go to a new place that He would be showing them? It's like we are a modern-day Abraham and Sarah. They trusted God and things turned out well; we need to do the same.

"Say, I think I'll run down to the lobby and pick up some juice and a couple of doughnuts. Okay? Be back shortly."

Mark was behind the desk and extended a warm greeting to Don. Don got his food to take back to the room but decided to talk with Mark first. Don was curious about learning more of Mark's connection to Henry Greyheck.

"Say, Mark. Got a minute?"

"Sure; what's on your mind?"

"I'm interested in knowing more about Mr. Greyheck. He told me that the two of you have had some business dealings together..."

"Yup, that's right. But it's not like I'm an Associate or an upper level anything for him. I'm more of a private contractor. He calls on me from time to time to help him find some out-of-the-ordinary items. I seem to have a knack for that; plus, I know some people that will help if needed."

"So, could you and I have a similar relationship? Like if I need something and have no clue where to find it, could I come to you for help?"

"Oh sure, Don. That would be great. I want your venture here to succeed as much as anyone, though I'm sure you've figured out by now that I'm not into this whole church or religion thing like Doobie is. He keeps inviting me, and he reminds me all the time that he's praying for me. But I figure a little prayer now and then can't hurt, right?"

"Right you are. We all need some heavenly help. This world can be a hard place to live, and I believe it's going to get much more challenging before very long...Well, I'd better get back to Kathy...Oh, oh, too late. Here she comes."

"Don, did you have to make those doughnuts yourself?" she asked tongue-in-cheek.

"Sorry, honey. I was just headed back to the room. Right, Mark? Right? Don't let me down now..."

"He's right, Kathy," Mark came to the rescue. "He was just leaving when you arrived."

"Okay. Why don't we sit here, Don, and have our doughnuts?"

As they were getting settled, in walked Ben. Don noticed his stride; he seemed to be maneuvering without discomfort. Don threw him a *test question*:

"Ben, how's the back this morning?"

"My back is healed, whole, restored and renewed, Thank you kindly!"

"Good answer, Ben. Regardless of how it feels physically, you just spoke the truth over it!"

Out of the blue, Ben bellowed: ***"My back is healed, whole, restored and renewed!"***

"Wow! Ben, great confession! Join us if you have time."

"Thanks, I will. Good morning to you two. What's on your agenda today?"

Kathy spoke up: "Not much. I want to get our room a little more organized. And there are still some things to bring in from the Jeep. Oh, another thing: I've heard you guys talk about this empty warehouse. Any chance we could see that soon?"

"Kathy, you took the words right out of my mouth," Don interjected. "That's just what I wanted to do today. In fact, I want to make an expedition out of it..."

Ben and Kathy looked puzzled. "What do you mean by *expedition*?" Ben asked.

"I mean let's invite some others to join us," Don answered. "Like Mark – 'Hey, Mark, could you give us some time today, and go to the vacant warehouse with us?' – 'Sure thing!' – And how about the realtor that must be handling the sale? – 'Hey, Mark, what realty firm is handling the warehouse?' – 'Eberhard Realty; Joseph Eberhard is the lead agent' – 'Thanks, Mark.'"

Then Don thought about Doobie. "'Hey, Mark, how about Doobie?' – 'He's down at Mama Blanchard's filling in,' — 'Okay, thanks.'"

"So, it would be Kathy and I, and you, Ben, and Mark, and the realtor, of course. That would make it an expedition. How about we go at 1:00? I'll drive."

"Okay," Kathy said with a smile, "But first you'll have to clear out the car, please...Let's see you make an expedition out of that, Mr. C!"

"Ouch! You got me that time, Mrs. C. I think I'll be an expedition of one!"

"One o'clock will work for me," answered Mark from behind the desk. "I'll have Suzy cover for me, and I'll call Mr. Eberhard. I'm sure he will want to be there personally. Besides, he'll bring the keys to get in."

"Great! I love it when a plan comes together!" Don roared. "That's a line from one of my old TV heroes...Remember, Kathy? What was his name?"

WHEN THE *EXPEDITION* ARRIVED AT THE warehouse, Mr. Eberhard was there to open the main entrance. Everyone was curious to have a look inside. It was simply a big, empty, dusty warehouse, that hadn't been occupied for the past 16 months. At one time it was a bustling manufacturing plant, making various auto and tractor parts, and employing several hundred workers. During its last year, it had dwindled down to mainly a storage spot for various trucking firms in the area, that needed more space for their own operations. Only about 30 or so employees were needed by then. Most of those trucking firms have since gone out of business or relocated.

The group spread out to take a closer, leisurely look. Don and Kathy walked together. In the natural, the place was dumpy, dirty, and depressing. But not for Don and Kathy. They were hearing in their spirits from the Lord.

"I want you to have this place, Don and Kathy. It's a big part of my plan."

"But how, Lord; how can we lease or buy such a huge building?"

"I've got that all worked out. You'll see soon enough."

After about an hour of milling around, the group convened at the main entrance for discussion and questions for Mr. Eberhard. He was the first to open a conversation.

"Well, folks, what do you think? A bit dismal, don't you agree? Back in its day this was a booming hub of prosperity for our community...I'm not sure what your intentions were about the warehouse, but if you can think of any way to lease part or all of it, I know the company owners would be more than happy to work with you."

No one had any comment. Mark seemed a bit glum: maybe *overwhelmed* is a better word. Ben seemed deep in thought. Don and Kathy were different; they were excited but tried to keep it in check. Just then there was a knock at the window of the front door! Everyone turned to look. It was Henry Greyheck of all people! The realtor quickly let him in. They knew one another.

"Henry! What are you doing here? Are you part of this group too?" asked Mr. Eberhard.

"Well, not exactly...well, sort of...I'm not sure. But one thing I know. This group is supposed to have this warehouse. And I'm going to make that happen!"

"Great, Henry. Let's talk for a few minutes...Excuse us folks." The two men went inside a nearby office, out of sight. Don took the opportunity to tell the others that the Lord had confirmed that they were to have the warehouse.

"Yeah, both Kathy and I heard from the Lord. He was clear about it. He wants us to be in this building! Hallelujah! And I suspect that good, ole Henry is going to come through for us...Wow! Folks, isn't this something!? Isn't this exciting?! We're watching God's plan unfold right before our very eyes!"

Henry and Joseph came out of the office. Joseph, the realtor, sported a large grin as he announced: "Folks, the building is yours! Thanks to Henry here. There are still a few details to be worked out, but that should be no problem. The owning corporation will do everything possible to make the transition go smoothly. Henry will be having some of his people assisting. I'm leaving you with two sets of keys."

Joseph handed them to Henry, who in turn gave a set to Don and kept the other set himself. Then Henry announced his leaving with a stern word.

"Folks, it is incumbent upon you not to leak my name with today's dealings, or even hint that I was somehow involved. This is for you, too, Joseph. If that should happen, I will disavow any connection and promptly withdraw my support. Is that perfectly clear?"

Everyone acknowledged their compliance. Henry looked each in the eye, and then turned and promptly left. The four-person expedition didn't know what to do: leave, stay? Joseph excused himself. Don and Kathy were beside themselves with excitement. Mark and Ben were flabbergasted at what just transpired.

Ben's mind started going on all cylinders, thinking of the potential benefits the warehouse could provide for Greensville. He finally spoke: "Don, everyone, just think of what we could do with this place, how we could help the people of Greensville."

For about ten minutes Ben held the attention of the others as he expounded on the advantages of the warehouse to the local community: work opportunities, shelter, food, and clothing distribution. None was more excited than Ben. Finally, Don announced he was ready to leave. On the ride back to the motel, Ben continued to articulate his glowing impression of the warehouse, while the others listened on.

As the group got out of the Jeep, Ben said to Don: "I'm going to call my friend at the Pentagon about some possible contracts we could do for the Military, now that we have full access to the warehouse. Boy, wait till Clair hears about this great news!" Off Ben scampered, with no sign of an ailing back, Don noted!

Kathy suggested that the two of them sit outside on the bench. As they got settled in, she couldn't help but notice that Don was deep in thought. "A penny for your thoughts," she said.

Don replied without much clarity. "Oh, I don't know...I'm certainly grateful to Henry for what he did for us today. Now, the question is: where do we go from here? The ball is in our court, so to speak. It was easier to brainstorm about what the Lord wanted us to do, when our main ministry resource – like a giant warehouse – was still a pipe dream, off in the future somewhere. But now that it's here, right now, it's time to turn those pipe dreams into reality. It's time to get on with the Lord's business...

"Lord, what do You want us to do?" Don said out loud, as he looked heavenward.

The Lord answered both he and Kathy in a still, soft voice: "Get organized. Look at all the talent you have around you. Tap into that; put them to work. Where do you think all that talent came from? Me, that's Who...Each of the members of this group has a specific work to do. Your job is to match up the talent with the work assignment...I'll help you get it done."

Abruptly, the Lord stopped giving directions. Both Don and Kathy were left hanging. Don finally said: "Kathy, I think it's time to get ourselves organized, rather than our room. I think the Lord wants us to turn our group into a well-ordered machine. Get the laptop out. We'll put our heads together and trust in the Lord's prompting to get us going."

"I'm with you. Let's go!" insisted Kathy, jumping up from the bench. The two of them worked diligently right through supper. Then, they noticed the time.

"Oh, my gosh, it's nearly time for church," Kathy said.

"We'll get something to eat afterwards," added Don, hurrying to locate his Bible and jacket.

When they arrived, the service had just started. Doobie was on the watch for his two friends and when he spotted them, he stood and waved to get their attention. Don and Kathy joined Doobie, Mama Blanchard, and the Tuckers.

Pastor Daniel spoke that evening on a topic near and dear to Don's heart: the end-times. The Pastor's message, like that of many others, focused in on the fact that time was short before the Lord's second appearance.

Don was at first encouraged at the message. Then, it seemed to take a sudden turn away from the truth as Don understood it. Pastor Daniel assured the congregation: "Folks, Jesus is coming very soon, but there are no worries for us as Believers. We'll be out of this mess of a world before anything bad happens, like the Tribulation. The next great event to look forward to is the Rapture of the Church, when Jesus will call us home to Glory, and that could happen at any time!

"My friends, if anyone tells you the Church will have to endure tribulation, they are not to be believed! They have their eschatology all wrong. After all, the Lord promised that we, His believing ones, would not have to suffer through the wrath of God. This is foretold in several

Scriptures. First Thessalonians, Chapter 1, Verse 10, is but one: *Jesus... (has) delivered us from the wrath to come.*"

Don had an overwhelming urge to stand up and announce: "No, you've got it wrong! The Church does have some serious hardships ahead, not at the Hand of God, but Satan, when he begins his reign of terror." Kathy noticed the mounting exasperation right off and gently grabbed his arm, as she whispered: "Don, don't let it bother you...and, **do not** challenge the Pastor! Not here!"

At Kathy's intervention, Don relaxed his fist, softened his scowl, and sat back in the pew. "Okay. Okay. I'll relax...Thanks, Kathy," Don said softly. He spent the remaining twenty minutes of the message, thinking about a variety of unrelated things. When the service was finished, Don and Kathy made a beeline for the door. They waited outside for Doobie and Mama Blanchard.

"Hey, Doobie. Over here." He and Mama Blanchard came right over. "Hey, Kathy and I are just going to grab a burger on the way home. We've gotten a new assignment from the Lord and we want to get right after it, beginning tonight. So, we'll see you tomorrow. Okay?"

"Sure thing," answered Doobie. "See you tomorrow, in the lobby for doughnuts."

DON AWOKE THE NEXT MORNING WITH a start, just as the sun was poking through the window. As he opened sleepy eyes, he knew that the Lord had something to tell him. He quickly got up to sit at the little kitchen table to wait. Before long, Don could sense the Lord's bidding. "Here I am, Lord. All ears and eager to learn what You have in mind."

"I told you, Don, I would be unfolding the plan in bits and pieces, not all at once, remember?"

"I do Lord. So, is this morning another piece to the puzzle?"

"Yes, Don. It has to do with the factory. I want you and the others to build a dozen efficiency apartments at the east end of the building.

You and Kathy will be moving there; others will follow suit. And several units will be available for the homeless, as their need arises."

"Wow, Lord! I had no idea that was in the plan. But it makes perfect sense. Any ideas on finding supplies and furnishings...and labor?"

"Yes, check with Mark. He'll be learning today of another motel in a neighboring city that is going out of business. Mark is your *go-fer* for the entire project. I like that young man. You haven't known him like I do, but he's beginning to warm up to Me because of all the prayers from his brother, Doobie, that bombard My Throne on a regular basis."

"Okay, Lord. I'll check with Mark later today."

"One more thing. I want you to gather all the people this weekend and give them an overview teaching on My end-times plan. Let's get that truth clearly out in the open, so you'll have a unifying, common ground on which to proceed."

"Yes, Lord. I'll make that happen...I love You, Lord. And Thanks for all You do for me and Kathy."

Just then Kathy awoke. "Ah, good morning, Don...any doughnuts and coffee?"

"No, not yet. I'll start the coffee and run down to the lobby for the doughnuts. Back before you know it. Then, I gotta tell you what I heard from the Lord just before you woke up."

Within a few minutes, the two enjoyed their breakfast at the table-for-two in their kitchen. Don began to share about his time with the Lord. Kathy took it all in stride. *Move to a new living unit to be built at the factory? Sure, why not? Why should that surprise me?* she thought.

By now Kathy was not astounded at anything Don told her about the Lord's direction. A few months ago, she would probably have been questioning Don's mental bearings or his understanding about God's instructions, but not any longer. Now she came to expect the unexpected. And no facet of this unfolding plan surprised her. She was learning to trust fully in the Lord. And she did so, sporting an upbeat attitude and broad smile.

After breakfast Kathy left to check in with Jenny and Jim, while Don went back to the lobby to talk with Mark.

Don caught him at his usual perch behind the lobby counter. "Hey, Mark, got a minute or two to talk?" asked Don.

"Sure, what's on your mind," Mark answered. "Let's sit at that table, near the doughnuts...

"It's about our newest acquisition, the empty warehouse, that God so graciously provided through Henry. I believe the Lord has directed us to put in a dozen or so living units, maybe more. I plan to move there so Kathy and I can be near the action, when that place starts being a blessing to the local community...Are you with me so far?"

"Yes, sir. I'm already thinking of some people I know that could help us out, most of whom are currently unemployed. A couple of them worked at that factory years ago."

"Good deal, Mark. I knew you'd have some contacts. Now these are good people, right?"

"Oh, yeah, good people...I only hang out with *good people*. After all, I'm hanging out with you, right?"

"Right, Mark. I didn't mean to imply that you'd lead me astray...I just want to do a good job for the Lord. So, if I seem a bit cautious, don't take it personal."

"No problem, Mr. D. I appreciate your scrutiny. I promise I won't intentionally lead you wrong."

"Thanks, Mark."

"By the way, who's going to pay for all this. These are good guys that I'm thinking could help out, but they will expect to be paid...as they go."

"Right you are. Not sure on that question. The Lord will provide for us, that I know. And we wouldn't be hiring anyone until we had that question answered...so, don't go to them yet with the news, okay?"

"Okay; sure thing...Say, I just thought of another angle on this plan. I learned that a motel in neighboring Titus, about twenty miles south of here, is going out of business and wanting to sell their appliances and furnishings, for pennies on the dollar. Now that could be a big help to us. I think I'll just pay them a visit this afternoon and check it out."

Don looked at Mark with a big, approving grin. "Great! Keep me posted."

Just as Don was turning to return to his room, who should enter the motel but Pastor Daniel. "Hi, Don. I was hoping I'd run into you. How've you been?"

"Fine, Pastor. What brings you out here? To see me, or maybe Doobie?"

"No, I wanted to talk with you. Is there someplace we could have a quiet visit?"

"How about right here is this empty lobby. Plenty of doughnuts and orange juice! Let's sit over here." Both took a seat at the table.

"Well, Don, this is a bit awkward to start with, but I've heard from both Doobie and Mama Blanchard that you are a serious student of eschatology."

"We're talking about end-times?"

"Yes. Oh, sorry for the big churchy word, *Eschatology.* That's a word Preachers get out every now and then when they want to impress. I'm not trying to impress you, Don. In fact, I'm a bit nervous actually."

"Nervous? No need to be nervous around me."

A long, awkward moment followed, then Don spoke: "Well, back to the topic: Eschatology. Yes, I would consider myself a serious student of what the Bible teaches about the end-times, which I think is fast coming upon our world."

"Don, you were at Church last night and heard my teaching about the end."

"Yes, I did."

"What did you think?... As you maybe could tell, I'm not a serious student of end-times. I'm mainly passing along to the folks what I learned myself in Seminary...I'd like to hear what you think. Do we agree on anything about the topic?"

"Well, Pastor, in a word: *No.* Well, not much anyway. My under-standing of the Bible's teaching on end-times is that we the church will have to go though some extremely difficult times, when the Antichrist begins his reign of terror on the earth, after he declares himself God. I believe the Lord called this time the 'Great Tribulation.'[10]

"It's true the Bible teaches us that we will not have to endure God's wrath; that His horror is reserved for the wicked who have turned their hearts away from Him. But before that wrath happens, you know, the trumpet and bowl judgments, the Antichrist will unleash his own terror and destruction, to overcome God's faithful ones awaiting the return of Jesus. This is where the Mark of the Beast comes in.[11] There will be such pressure to turn against God and to take the Mark...I believe it will be pressure like the world has never known.

"Your teaching, Pastor, is like most current views in the Church. You believe that the Church will be raptured before any bad things unfold. But I'm saying that the Church will have to undergo some very, very harsh times at the hand of the Antichrist before Jesus returns to rapture us home. And that going home will happen just prior to the final judgments of God.

"One of the important points about all this for me is being ready for the worst, while staying faithful to God. We will all need to be ready for that reality, to band together, encourage one another during this great testing...And I'm almost 100% sure this will happen in my lifetime."

Pastor Daniel sat there silent.

"Well, I could go on and on," Don interjected.

"Yes, I wish you would...Listen, Don, is there any chance you could present this teaching at next week's Wednesday night service?"

Don gave a sober reply. "It's not something to be grasped at in one session – in fact, it could be too overwhelming for the people. Rather than that how about this idea: let's think of it as an 8-week seminar. We'll make it happen at another time than Church as usual, say, Friday evenings? And we could meet at the Church; we might even think about inviting other churches to join us. As you promote the idea at Church, encourage the people to make the 8-week commitment...We could start a week from this Friday. What do you think, Pastor Daniel?"

Pastor Daniel was deep in thought, thoughts of regret. "Just think of all the years I've assumed, and taught others, that we wouldn't have to go through any hardship. We would be raptured out of here before the tribulation unfolded. In fact, the next great event on my end-times calendar was the Rapture itself – nothing had to precede it, and it could happen at any moment!"

"Pastor, I think I know what you mean. It was kinda the same for me, when I came face to face with this new teaching – that put the faithful Church smack dab in the middle of Satan's tribulation through the Antichrist...This can't be true, I thought over and over. These people are wrong! But, when I finally stopped fighting it and got serious about studying the Bible myself, my blind eyes were opened. Now the Scriptures about end time events fall into alignment and make perfect sense...That's what I want for you, too."

"Well, I say, let's get this seminar started ASAP. I'll promote it this Sunday and next Wednesday. I'll get a committee formed to help make it happen. We'll invite other Churches. And we'll see you and your friends at the Friday opener. Don, this has truly been a helpful meeting. Thank you so very much."

"You're very welcome. Have a good day," Don answered.

CHAPTER SIX –

A buzz around town about purchase of the factory

THERE WAS QUITE A BUZZ AROUND TOWN about the purchase of the old factory, and consistently Don's name was connected. Several businesses wanted to know more. Suddenly Don was the main sought-after guest speaker to address the service clubs in the area. He was also invited to present his plans to the Chamber of Commerce, to the City Council meeting, and to the Mayor's City Betterment Advisory Council.

Soon, after all the community hubbub began, Mr. Greyheck came for a surprise visit with Don, and found him sitting on a bench just outside the motel's front door. He wanted again to make it clear that he did not want his name mentioned at all, or even hinted at, as Don was making the benevolence and ministry plans known to the public.

"Don, I want it clearly known as you go about your speech-making: you are to keep my name out of this! I don't want anyone to identify me as part of your project, or...or, I'll get hounded by every bleeding heart in the State!"

Don agreed. "I've already given that promise, Henry, but I'll say it again today. I won't in any way mention your name. I'll avoid the question as much as I can, but if anyone insists on knowing, I'll just talk about a kindly person that God raised up to be *Our Benefactor*. Would that be okay?"

"Oh, I guess so. And if they pressure you to give more specifics, just tell them you're not at liberty to disclose anything else."

Don went on. "Sure thing. And, of course, I want God to get all the credit for the complete project, so He'll get a lot of mention by me."

"I don't care about any of that. Just keep my name out!"

Henry got in the last word on the matter. He abruptly left, and then within ten seconds, he came back for another word with Don, like he was a different person.

"Don, I'm sorry...I didn't mean to leave in a huff like that. As soon as I got to my car, I suddenly had this tremendous urge to give you and your companions the money you'll be needing for the next step in your plan. Now, what's that all about?"

"Well, Henry, we are planning on putting in some efficiency studio apartments in the east section of the warehouse. Several of us want to begin living there, and we'll have some rooms available for those in need. Mark is checking into a construction crew and into ways we could buy some furnishings and appliances from a neighboring motel about to go out of business...

"Mark asked me, 'Where are you going to get the money to finance this apartment project?' I told him, 'I don't know, but I'm trusting God to provide.' And now today...here you show up wondering how you can bless us even more than you have already. It must be God's Hand in all of this.

"Maybe you're not aware of it, Henry, but you're being used by God in a most tremendous way. And considering God's principle of *Sowing and Reaping*, He must be getting you in position to receive a mighty great harvest in return."

Henry stood silent for the longest time, without expression, apparently deep in thought. Without so much as a smile, he turned to Don and said: "Tell Mark to keep record of all costs and expenses, and I'll take care of it...all of it!" Again, he promptly turned toward his car to leave, without further comment.

Then, before reaching his car, Henry returned. "Don, also tell Mark not to scrimp in any of his negotiations. We want to have the best of everything, including labor and materials. That seems to be the best way to do business, don't you agree?"

"Ah...well, Henry. Yes, I guess that is the best way. This I know for sure; it would be God's way to go for the best. After all, He gave us His absolute best, His Son, Jesus."

Henry looked on expressionless. "Yes. Well, good-bye for now." Off he went for his third departure.

Don watched him drive off down the winding road toward town. Then he went in to give Mark the exciting news about God meeting the need through Henry Greyheck. Mark was elated and said he would get right on talking with possible carpenters and visiting the neighboring motel.

"And get this part, Mark: Henry said as you take care of expenditures, don't scrimp along the way, but have the best in manpower and materials! That's what Henry said, bless his heart."

"That sounds just like Mr. Greyheck," Mark commented with a smile.

The next one to share the good news with was Kathy. And that good news was not only about Henry's generosity but also of Pastor Daniel's desire to start an End-Times seminar at Church. *She'll just flip over all this!* Don thought as he sped down the hallway. *Lord, You are too much! Thank You! Thank You!*

Don paused before going in his room...*In fact, Lord, we've got to get the whole crew together to talk about these latest developments,* Don continued to ponder. *There's planning to do and assignments to make. I'll get Doobie to help me set up the meeting. It's time we get this Show of the Road, right Lord?*

"And the teaching, Don. Don't forget the teaching on end-times," the Lord added.

"Oh, yes Lord, the teaching. I won't forget. That's coming up real soon."

THE MEETING ROOM AT THE MOTEL was packed. Nearly everyone was in attendance. The quaint motel meeting room at the motel was decidedly cramped, but no one seemed to mind. Doobie had done a masterful work to get all the participants together, and with only a two-day notice. Mama Blanchard closed her restaurant for the evening, so her staff could come, including Barbara and Rusty. Clair and Ben were there, as was Miss Verla, the Librarian. Mark came with his co-worker, Suzy. He invited Mr. Greyheck, but he declined. Surprisingly, Pastor Daniel from Doobie's church accepted the invitation, along with his wife, Marybeth.

There was great elation among the people; you could feel the excitement in the air. But there was a somber note as well. This would be a night to bid farewell to Jim and Jenny, who would be starting their return trip to Colorado the next morning. Doobie had enlisted their help with the drinks and snacks. When it was all laid out on the 4 x 8 table it looked to be enough food to feed a small army.

Don made that very observation during his opening remarks, saying that he felt like he was part of a *small army* for the Lord about to embark on a campaign to defend God's Kingdom and even expand it, as the days of the end were fast approaching. Don's intent for tonight's meeting was mainly to get to know one another better, so he invited all in attendance to do two things:

"First, let's go around and give your name." Everyone did so easily.

"Second, I want you to be free to ask questions and to make comments; don't overlook to share any leading that you think might be from the Lord...

"I don't mean to put anyone on the spot," Don explained, "but I think it's important that we be open to share like this. Even if you have something that might seem strange, don't judge it, and say nothing. It might be something the Lord is trying to get us to look at and you're the best person He could find to make His wishes known...Anyone like to start?"

After considerable squirming in their chairs, one brave soul spoke up. It was Jenny. "It's going to be so sad to leave all of you tomorrow," she said. "Jim and I have really enjoyed our time with you at Greensville. We know God is behind your plans and efforts, and we wish you all of His best...Anything to add, Jim?"

"Nope. You pretty much said it all."

Ben was next. He was itching to share. "Well, folks, first I'll join Jenny in saying that Clair and I have really enjoyed getting to know you. We have known for some time that God had a special work here in Greensville. It has been exciting to see that plan unfold before our eyes... and to recognize that much, much more is yet to come. And, Pastor Daniel and Marybeth, we're so glad that you are here and interested in this move of God...Well, I don't want to hog the limelight, so I'll turn it over to anyone else."

Don jumped in. "Ben, I know you had some talks with God about money issues. Anything you want to share along that line?"

"Sure, Don, love to." Ben seemed to enjoy *the limelight,* but he was generally gracious about it. "Folks, I believe the Lord is directing – at least me and Clair, maybe others too – to turn our savings and 501(c) k's into cash on hand. So, we'll have that resource for the uncertainty of the days ahead. I believe God is helping me to see that investments and savings as we know them are not going to be of much use or value. So, consider what I'm saying. Now whether you follow suit is up to you and the Lord. But I urge you to seek Him about the matter...I could say more, Don, but I want to hear from the rest of the group, too."

"Who else would like to share?" Don asked.

Mama Blanchard had her turn. "I'm just grateful to be a small part of this ministry...I've been wondering – maybe with God's help – how my owning the restaurant might come into play. I know a lot of food vendors and distributors and they have contacts far and wide. Perhaps that will be a factor in the food distribution focus for Greensville and the area. We'll see."

"Keep after it, Mama Blanchard, I mean keep asking the Lord about all this," Don encouraged.

"Oh, I will for sure, Don."

Barbara, sitting next to Mama Blanchard, tugged at her arm, and whispered in her ear.

Mama Blanchard said to Barbara: "Sure thing, child, you can say that right here."

Barbara cleared her throat. She obviously was shy about speaking up, but she ventured forth anyway: "I just want to say Thank you to Don for praying for me several weeks ago. I have not fainted any more since then. So, I'm happy to be a part of this group; and I'll help out in any way I can."

"Well, thank you, Barbara," replied Don. "I appreciate your willingness to help. I'm glad you're a part of this group, too."

Now it was time for Mama Blanchard to lean over to Barbara and do the whispering. Then Mama spoke up: "And please notice that Barbara is wearing only a light jacket tonight. Since being prayed for she has stopped being bundled up with several layers of coats in any kind of weather." Barbara smiled from ear to ear.

Mark cleared his throat and shared. "Just one thing I can think of to say. I've changed my opinion about the lot of you. You are not a bunch of crackpots, as I originally thought – well, maybe there still is one crackpot in the room and that's Doobie of course, but he's always been a bit weird."

Doobie was taken by surprise. He didn't know if he should laugh or retaliate. He finally laughed. Several others joined in with him.

As the laughter subsided, Don brought the focus to another area most did not know about. "I've been talking with Mark about his finding a crew of workers to do some renovations at the factory; by that I mean adding a dozen or so apartment units along the inside eastern wall. I believe I've heard from the Lord about this. Kathy and I would plan to move in one of the units, to be closer to the action, you might say...And if you're wondering how this will be financed, the Lord has taken care of it, once again, as only He can do...And we're so thankful!"

Kathy took the floor. "Folks, there is still much to be worked out here, but we're confident that the Lord will reveal the next steps to take as we continue to seek His direction. I see us all becoming a well-greased, working machine for the Lord – each bringing some special talents and dedication to bear. He's the One Who brought us all together at this time and in this place. He has a special purpose for us to fulfill that will be a blessing to many, many people as we deal with the challenges ahead."

Don beamed broadly. "Isn't Kathy great? She has a way with words; that's one of her many talents," he said. "She can make sense out of the most confusing situations. If you ever need some muddled mess cleared up, just ask: 'Kathy, what does this mean?' And she'll get right to the heart of the matter. Thanks, honey!"

Don continued. "There are several others we haven't heard from. Any other comments from anyone?" as he looked in the direction of Rusty, Suzy, Doobie, Verla and Pastor Daniel.

Pastor Daniel said: "Well, folks, I and my wife are new faces here. I only have a small grasp of what directions your ministry will be going. But I have no doubt that the Lord is behind it all. I hope that we at Cornerstone Church can play a part in it. I'm certain that some of our regulars would like to get personally involved in your work. I'll be talking it up in the weeks ahead. In the meantime, I look forward to hearing Don's teaching on end-times, which will be starting a week from today at the Church. Don has graciously agreed to this becoming an eight-week seminar. You're all invited to attend. In fact, I hope that you all will be coming. Thanks again, Don."

"Sure. Happy to do it," he replied. Don was okay that a few didn't speak up, considering this was the first time many had been to such a gathering. But there was the exception of Doobie. Don knew that Doobie was not shy, so his reluctance now was a bit baffling. So, Don pushed the envelope, you might say: "How about you, Doobie? Anything on your mind you'd like to share with us?"

No reply. Don pushed again. "Come on, Doobie, I know there's something going on in that outstanding brain of yours. Want to share?"

Doobie gave out with a big sigh. "Well, Don, there is one thing...I think we should give all the credit to God for providing the money needed for the factory and now for the apartments. You've been talking, and Kathy, too, about how we have gifts for this ministry. And I figure that our gifts come from God, and one of those is the financial part.

"I Thank God for the gifts that all of you here bring to the table – and as soon as I figure what mine is, I'll thank Him for that, too. But in the meantime, I want to make sure that we thank God for the money, not the ones who give it...That's all I wanted to say."

After a few seconds of silence, the small group broke into a round of applause! "Right on, Doobie!" and "Good point, Doobie!" and "You are so right!" and other such comments could be heard.

Don joined in. "You are right, Doobie. I stand corrected...Pastor Daniel, you can see why I like having Doobie around. He keeps me on the straight and narrow...Thanks, Einstein McKenna! That brain of yours is working on all cylinders!"

Doobie smiled one of his great smiles. Mark came over to him and offered a high-five! *Whap!*

Don was wrapping up the meeting. He turned to Kathy: "Is there anything else to bring out tonight? Did we miss anything?"

Kathy replied. "This has been a great time. And we all seem to be on the same wavelength...at least with regards to wanting to do what the Lord is calling us to do. But there's an important question I raise. Are we all on the same wavelength with regards to our personal relationship with Jesus...Don?"

Don took over. "Folks, Kathy raises a most important point. Let's ask ourselves this: Is Jesus my Lord? Have I received His gift of Salvation? If I were to die tonight, do I know for certain that I would go right to Heaven? If you can answer 'yes' to these questions, then you are what the Bible describes as a Born-Again Child of God...But if you can't say 'yes' then tonight is your night to make things right with Jesus.

"Friends let's close our eyes. If you couldn't truthfully say 'yes' to the questions I posed, please raise your hand. I want to pray with you to make things right between you and the Lord...Anyone? I see that hand. I see that hand. Anyone else? There's a hand, I see it.

"You that raised your hands are about to embark on a most exciting adventure with the Lord, to a life of peace and blessing to last forever. Let's all of us here repeat this prayer together and mean it with all your heart: 'Jesus, come into my heart...I confess You as my Lord and Savior... Thank You for Your gift of Salvation...Thank You that Heaven is now my home for all eternity...I am now a Born-Again Child of God...I just traded my sin and iniquity for the Righteousness of God...Thank You! Thank You! In the Name of Jesus. Amen!'

"We cheered for Doobie. Let's cheer for these new ones in the Kingdom of God." Applause abounded.

"Now, folks, join me in digging into some of this great food that Doobie and Mama Blanchard provided. Amen?" Don looked over at Kathy with a broad smile and gave her a *thumbs up*. Kathy returned the gesture.

Everyone seemed to be blessed and encouraged by the meeting that night. And they looked forward to other such gatherings. This would have been the perfect evening for Don and Kathy to celebrate, but unfortunately their hearts were a bit heavy anticipating the departure of Jenny and Jim.

In accordance with their wishes Jim and Jenny wanted to have an early departure time, to avoid any contact with other group members. So, Don and Kathy were the only two to be up at the crack of dawn to see them off. And what a beautiful morning it was. The sun was warm, the sky was deep blue.

After their van was loaded there was a moment of silence; all eyes turned to Don to pray. But Don turn the tables, when he said: "Jim, why don't you pray this time and we'll all agree with you."

Jim took an instant shine to the request. He prayed this way: "Oh, Lord, Thank You for this glorious time we've had in Greensville. May Your Hand continue to be upon Mom and Dad and the rest. We look forward to continuing good reports of this outreach. And now, Thank You for Your protection on our trip to Colorado...We declare, *No evil shall befall us!* In the Name of Jesus. Amen."

There were final hugs all around. In the process, Don whispered to Jim: "You know, son, I'm getting to like you more and more all the time." Jim was flabbergasted; all he could muster was a faint "Wow" as he slid into the driver's seat.

Don and Kathy watched as the car drove off, down the dusty road. Then Kathy asked Don: "What did you say to Jim at the last?"

"I just told him that I was getting to like him more and more." Kathy squeezed Don's hand ever so tightly, as she got her last glimpse of the car.

Well, that's finished. Now, what's on tap for this day? Don wondered. *I know... orange juice and doughnuts!* "Kathy? I think..."

"I know what you're thinking. You're thinking about something round and soft and sweet, right? And it's not me. Something with a sprinkle of powdered sugar and cinnamon on top, it must be a what-chamacallit...a doughnut! Right?"

"You know me like a book, Kathy Crawford! Let's go get one, or two!"

CHAPTER SEVEN –

God works through Doobie in a most unique way.

LATER THAT SAME MORNING, DON AND KATHY meet up with Mark and Ben for some discussion about where to go from here. Don opened with a brief prayer and then made this proposal:

"People I think that the four of us should consider ourselves as a planning or steering committee for our new ministry, as it steps into this formative stage of operation." Everyone agreed.

"I was hoping that Doobie would be joining us. You know, over the past few months I've grown to appreciate that God works through Doobie in a most unique way. That young man seems to have a no nonsense and bonified connection to God's heart...Where is he, Mark?"

"He's working at the restaurant, busing tables again," Mark answered. "He fills in like that every now and then when Mama Blanchard needs extra help. But I'm sure he'd be happy to be a part of this Committee... he likes to be in the middle of everything going on, you know."

Don continued. "So today, Mark, why don't you start and bring us up to date on the construction of the apartments at the factory."

"Sure; be happy to. I've located a great carpenter and general contractor, by the name of David Levine. I've worked with him before. He does great work. And he knows he could get up a crew of five or six other qualified workers, who are likely out of work with our recent slump in the economy. David's going to work with a friend at an architectural firm in town – someone who owes him a big favor, he says - to get some sketches of possible apartment designs...Could I get a key from you, Don, for the building, so David and his friend could see the layout first-hand? I'd be with them all the while."

"Sure; no problem. Remember Henry Greyheck's request that his name be kept out of public scrutiny, which would include your contractor and his architect friend."

"Oh, yes, Don, I remember...But Henry's got to know that sooner or later the public is going to learn of his generous hand in all this."

"My sentiment exactly – but for the time being let's be sure to do everything we can to honor his request...What did you find out about that neighboring motel that was going out of business and selling everything?"

"Well, I checked them out. They have a lot of stuff we could sure use, like appliances, furniture; fixtures, you name it. And the price is good – about half of what it would cost wholesale, I figure."

"And you recall Henry Greyheck's admonition to us, not to scrimp or settle for seconds," Kathy added.

"I do remember. I'll be extra cautious when I go about picking items for us to use. I'll get a crew together myself to begin loading up what we need from the motel. We'll probably get after that beginning next Monday and bring it to the factory."

Ben was listening to Mark's report with great interest. "Wow! That's exciting news, Mark. So glad you know so many people that we need to get our venture off the ground...Well, I think I have some exciting news too. I've been in touch with my friend who's a *higher-up* in the Quartermaster Corps at the Pentagon. We've talked about the possibility of getting a government contract to do some repair or replacement work for the military on some of their uniforms."

"What do you mean, Ben? What could we do for the U.S. military?" asked Don.

"My friend tells me there are storage units filled with uniforms needing repair, like redoing shoddy button work, fixing faulty zippers. Or the military has gobs of equipment in need of some minor tweaking – not serious repair requiring experienced hands, but simple repair work, to make the items perform to their full potential. It's the kind of low-end work that most big companies wouldn't even think of bidding on. But it might just be up our alley, to get our local unemployed back into the workforce."

"Now that sounds really exciting, Ben," offered Kathy. "I used to spend some time at a sewing machine; I could teach our ladies from the community what I know. It would bring in some income for them and give them a sense of purpose. And I know God would want us working, so we can be a blessing to others."

"You know, gang, I think we are headed in the right direction," Don remarked. "God is giving the direction and the resources. He has found us a man who liberally supports us. We've got two *movers-and-shakers* here in Mark and Ben who know how to get things done. As exciting as this brainstorming is, I know the actual application of these ideas is off into the future."

Kathy jumped in: "And I just know that if I were to ask Mark, 'Where are you going to get a crew to help you move that furniture and stuff' – he'd say: 'Don't worry; I know some people.'"

Everyone busted out in laughter; then Don broke into a volley of praise: "Praise to You, Lord! Thank You, Thank You for taking such good care of us! Thank You for witty inventions. Thank You for sending Mark just the right people along the way...Wow, I'm hungry. Any dough-nuts left, Mark?"

"Yup! All you can eat. The distributor just came by earlier this morning."

"Before we break, are there any other points or issues we should be discussing?" Don asked. No one had anything new. Of course, by this point everyone's mind was dancing with images of doughnuts.

"In closing, folks, let's plan to meet like this every day and about this time, as our schedules allow."

Everyone got up from the table, with doughnut in hand. Don looked on with a big smile as he saw Mark put his arm around Ben and say: "Mr. Tucker, I know people that could provide some manpower for your projects; maybe even a few sewing machines."

"Oh, that's great, Mark," Ben replied. "And by the way, call me Ben"

"Will do, Ben"

THREE MONTHS LATER..."Kathy, you're going to love this!" shouted Don from the bedroom. "It's your daughter, Jenny! She wants to talk with you." Kathy came running. Don handed her the phone with a wacky grin on his face.

"What! What's going on?" Kathy whispered to Don.

"Take the phone; you'll find out soon enough."

"Hello, Jenny. What's up? Is this your average I-just-want-to-see-how-you're-doing call, or is it something special?"

"It's something extra special. You better sit down, Mom," came the reply.

Kathy looked puzzled, even a bit alarmed with this special phone call. She sat on the side of the bed. "Okay, I'm sitting. Now what's going on?"

"Well, there are two big news items to share...let's see, what should I tell Mom first? Hmmm..."

"Jenny! You're just like your father! Just get on with it!" Kathy replied in a muffled command.

"Okay, Mom, enough kidding around. Two things: Jim and I want to move back to Greensville and...and, we're going to have a baby!"

Stone silence. Kathy's mouth fell open. But no sounds. Vocal cords *Out of Order*.

"Mom, Mom, did you hear me: We want to move back with you and Dad; and you're going to be a grandmother again...What do you think...? Hello, are you there?"

"Yes, I'm here, honey. I heard you. Are you sure about all this?"

"Yes, Mom, we're sure. Jim wants to move back as much as I do. And I think he's even more excited about the baby than I am!"

"Wow! Honey, I'm speechless...Of course, this is great news! We would love to have you and Jim back with us...And the baby, oh Jenny, that is so special. Is it a boy or a girl?"

"Too early to tell, is the word we get. It doesn't really matter to us. Does it matter to you?"

"No, no, not in the least. The Lord will provide a healthy baby; that's all that matters."

"That's the way Jim and I feel."

"So, when will you guys be moving to Greensville?"

"Well, we have some loose ends to tie up here...probably should take us about three weeks we figure, maybe a little more."

"Oh, this is the best news ever...Well, it's the best news out of many great things that are happening around here. We've had one miracle after another! If I had another hour or so, I could give you a bit more detail... and I'll do just that when you and Jim arrive!

"Listen, Jenny, you and Jim just get here as soon as you can. Hopefully, we'll have a cute, little furnished apartment waiting for you to move into at the factory, but you might have to start out in the Motel. It depends. Anyway, honey, I'll let you go for now. Thanks for the great news, on both accounts. Bye."

"Bye, Mom; give Dad a big hug for me."

Kathy set the phone on the nightstand and looked up at Don, with a smile that could stop a freight train.

"Did you know about this before today?"

"No, I just found out about it right before you."

Kathy got up and went over to Don to deliver a hug. It was a hug to be remembered.

"Thanks, Kathy."

"Jenny told me to give you a big hug."

"Well, you need to listen to that girl..."

Later that day, Don gathered in the break room with Mark, Ben, and Doobie. Kathy elected to skip the meeting. She excused herself with: "Too much to think about with Jenny and Jim coming back."

After opening prayer, Don shared the good news about Jim and Jenny by first asking Mark: "Mark, do you think you could get that crew of yours to build another apartment, in about three weeks' time? Jenny and Jim are wanting to come back to Greensville. And they have some other great news: they're going to have a baby!"

"Wow!" "That's great!" "I'm so happy for you!" came the replies.

Mark said, "I think we can make that happen. I'll get right on it after our meeting."

"Great!" Don answered..."What should we be talking about today?"

Ben was the first to reply. "You guys know that I've been taking some pictures of late. I've designated myself as the *Historian* for this ministry. It seems important to me to keep a running account of what we're doing, with narrative and photos..."

"And I for one am mighty glad you took this on, Ben," added Don.

"Thanks, Don. Well, I was hoping today to get us all thinking about the ministry's challenges and accomplishments since we started. Was that about six months ago, by now? More? Hard to believe."

Don was the first to recollect. "I remember our first meeting, Ben, at the Willow Creek. You and Clair had moved here lock, stock, and barrel on some wild idea that God told you to pack up and go. I was kinda in the same boat; I felt the Lord's bidding to be in Greensville, but *why?* I had no idea...

"Then we met up with this character, called Doobie...talk about a country bumkin, and now I call him Einstein McKenna! He led us to Mama Blanchard, to the Cornerstone Church, to Mark and Suzy..."

Doobie continued with the tale. "...We started talking about rejuvenating Greensville's economy, about a healing ministry, helping the homeless, about our banding together to face some harsh upcoming end-times possibilities..."

Ben went on. "But we needed a place of operation to accomplish all we felt the Lord was leading us to do. That's when the vacant factory came into view. And the Lord sent us a Mr. Henry Greyheck as our beloved financier to give us nearly a blank check for ministry operations and growth."

Mark chimed in. "What an unexpected wonder that was. After years of knowing Henry as a stoic, grumpy man of means, he has changed into a...a stoic, grumpy man of mega-means. No, I was just kidding a little. Henry is softer and more congenial than he ever used to be. Why, I've seen him smile several times over the past few weeks. I know he appreciates what we do here, but he doesn't let on much."

Don continued the discussion. "So, just what is it that we've been able to do?" He pulled out a hand-written list filling most of two pages. "I've got some notes I've been working on. We have constructed twelve units of efficiency apartments here at the factory. Six of those are being used by the community on a revolving basis, to meet emergency housing needs. Four of these are in use right now. Six are being used by us. One more is going to be constructed, right Mark? And the motel itself is occasionally used for housing and meals on an emergency, back up basis, like the time about two weeks ago we had that family of eight literally camp at the front door – the factory was full, but the motel had two vacant rooms we could use, Thank God."

Doobie raised his hand, itching to get into the discussion.

Don chided him: "Einstein, you don't have to raise your hand; just jump in there..."

"I like it that we are getting to be known around town as a place where people can come to get their needs met, without cost and without forms to fill out. Police, emergency workers and others are relying on us more and more. And here's what I like, too: we shouldn't forget about all the great group discussions we have had. Everyone seems to like the get-togethers and potluck dinners. It's like we're one big happy family. This is like the big family I never really had. Mark was my only family – until now that is."

Mark used the moment to praise his older brother." I think Doobie should be congratulated for his success with the garden out back. It is proficient, well used, and delicious. I never knew it was in him to do such a thing. That's the way to go, Big Bro! High five!" (Smack).

Ben took up the charge. "I think a valuable accomplishment for us was completing the eight-week class on the coming end-times. Thanks, Don. It was very enlightening and well received. And another benefit was seeing this ministry grow closer to the Cornerstone folks, many of whom are directly involved out here now, when we do community outreaches and the like."

"And, thanks Don, for your day-to-day leadership and encouragement to us to stay faithful to God during these times," offered Kathy, who quietly snuck into the break room almost unnoticed.

"Thanks, Kathy. Thanks to all of you. Without your involvement, none of this would have been possible," said Don. "Right, Grandma Kathy?"

"Kathy, I bet you're busting out with happy thoughts about your Jenny and Jim coming back to us," Ben said.

"Oh my, yes," Kathy replied. "Couldn't be happier!"

Getting back on track, Don asked Ben: "How is your Pentagon Project coming along?"

"Slower than molasses! That's how it is! You talk about government red tape! I'm surprised anything gets done in Washington. We've got six beautiful used but efficient sewing machines – Thanks to Mark – just sitting in the corner, gathering dust! Thank goodness, Mama Blanchard has stepped in to help Kathy train us on the machines. But more than that, she has opened several doors for our folks to do some home cleaning in the community, and Clair's real excited to help. That might be the next direction to take for our people to find some gainful work and earn a little income: through a home cleaning and small repair kind of outreach. Clair and I will be talking with Mama Blanchard about how to move more in that direction...

"We all agree that work, no matter the kind, is important to help people regain self-esteem. I wish you all could see their faces beam when they come into the office and give Clair 20% of what they earned during the week, to offset their room and board...A lot of times they comment: 'You wait, Miss Clair; next week it will be even more.'"

The discussion paused for a long moment. Beaming faces were evident across the table.

"I've seen it time and again," Don interjected. "To have local citizens and strangers come to the factory with any number of individual and family needs, and then watch them begin to recoup their sense of well-being, when those needs are addressed, will never cease to amaze me. And we owe it all to You, Jesus! Thank You! Thank You!

"Folks don't get me started. We need to wrap up this planning meeting." Don went back to his hand-written list. "First, I wanted to share a few ideas for the immediate future...Let me throw these out for us to be thinking about and I'll talk more about them later at our Potluck and Teaching meeting tonight. Things like: I think we need an official name for this ministry; maybe even design some ministry tee shirts. Maybe Jenny could help us with that when she returns. I think we need to look at how to involve more of our guests in the day-to-day operations – like Doobie, you could use some help in the garden, right? And I know Clair could use some help in the office. Mark you could probably appreciate some help at the motel from time to time. Hey, how about if we make cleaning the office, factory, and grounds one of our ongoing cleaning and maintenance accounts. Maybe we could write up some job descriptions, post them, and invite people to apply – just like in the real world..."

Mark intervened. "Don, I'm in need of a janitor at the motel and of a part-time front desk worker, and I've heard that Mama Blanchard could use a dishwasher at her place. Let's include those openings in the job search."

"Great idea, Mark. Let's do that. And maybe there are other uses for the factory – other job possibilities that we haven't even thought of yet... Hmmm. Well, I could go on, but I gotta stop there. We can pick it up later. See you tonight. Have a good rest of your day."

THAT NIGHT'S MEETING WAS WELL attended, which surprised no one. Everybody seemed to enjoy getting together for scheduled or impromptu gatherings for food, fellowship, and teaching. For the first such meeting, several months ago, there must have been fourteen or so who came. Tonight, the number was thirty! Adding Jenny and Jim would bring that to thirty-two; and others were on the waiting list to move in.

Once again, the serving table was laden with great dishes, Thanks to Doobie and Mama Blanchard. Don was sitting with Kathy, Mark, and Doobie, enjoying some awesome potato salad, when David Miller poked his head into the room and motioned for Don.

Don went out into the hall to talk with him. "What's up, David?"

"I'm not quite sure. I was on my first evening patrol as usual, but this time I sensed something bad going on, but I couldn't find anything out of the ordinary."

David was a trusted friend of the ministry; he and his family were one of the first to arrive at the factory, homeless, out of work, out of money, and with three little ones to look after. He was eager to work and volunteered to do any job that came up. So that included cleaning toilets, painting walls, mowing the lawn. But then there was an area that David seemed to gravitate toward, given his background as a *Green Beret,* and that was security. So, for the past three months David became the self-proclaimed security team for the ministry, and he took his job quite seriously. He typically set out on his patrol when others were ending their day. Tonight, was something unusual for David to encounter. He had run-ins with others peeking into windows and the like, or snooping around, and he quickly scared them away. But tonight was different.

"So, tell me David. What are you sensing? Someone or something outside?"

"Not sure, boss. I just got a creepy feeling when I went near the front entrance. I went outside to look around but found nothing. Maybe it's my imagination...maybe it's the pepperoni pizza from lunch."

"And maybe it's the Lord prompting you, David. We've talked about this: becoming sensitive to the Lord's voice. That Holy Spirit that lives in you might be telling you to be on your toes tonight. How about if I get Mark and we go to the entrance with you to check this out."

"Sounds good to me. I'll wait here."

Within minutes Mark and Don came to David, each carrying a flashlight. Without saying a word, the three of them proceeded to the entrance of the factory. As they drew near, David had that same gnawing feeling spring up in his gut. Mark began walking more slowly and cautiously. Don did likewise. Flashlights were scanning the surroundings. Nothing seemed out of order.

Suddenly Don called for silence: "Sssssh. Something up ahead," He whispered.

Then they all heard it – the moaning. It was coming from the storage room at the end of the corridor. Slowly they tiptoed in that direction without a word. David moved to the front, readied his pistol, got his hand on the door handle, and flung it open.

There lay an older man, in obvious anguish. He was clutching his left upper arm, frightened beyond belief. The stench of urine could not be denied. He was lying in a pile of rags. Don got down on both knees. He asked: "Are you hurt? What happened? ...Don't be afraid. We want to help you."

David yelled, "Boss, I'm going to get my wife; she's an LPN, remember? I'll see if Miss Kathy could look after the kids." He darted down the dark hallway.

Don continued talking to the gentleman, but he gave no reply. His eyes were fastened on Don and he twitched whenever Don moved in the slightest. Mark stood at the doorway with both flashlights aimed at the man inside.

Soon David returned with his wife, Dianne. She brought what medical supplies she had. She quickly stooped down, as Don gave way. She had a soothing voice as she asked about pain and symptoms; still the man gave no reply. Dianne asked Don and Mark to turn away their flashlights and to back into the hallway. With that change the man seemed to relax a bit. He allowed Dianne to look at the wound on his left arm. She used some scissors to open his blood-stained shirt. The wound looked like a bullet grazing to Dianne. She asked particulars about what happened, but the man only said: "I can't tell you. Don't make me tell you."

Dianne dropped the subject and went on to dress the wound with some antibiotic cream and bandages. She said: "You know, we really should get you to the E.R. for some x-rays and stitches."

"No. No. No. I can't do that." He started to get up but fell back into the pile of rags.

Dianne stood up and went out into the hall to talk with Don and Mark. "He refuses to go to the hospital. It looks like his arm was grazed with a bullet. It's a fairly deep wound, and he's likely lost a lot of blood. He would heal faster and better with some further medical attention... What should we do?"

Don had a friend on the police force that immediately came to mind, a Sergeant Becker. The Policemen appreciated the work of the ministry and arranged for there to be two or so courtesy patrols around the factory every day, just to keep an eye on things. Don called the headquarters and spoke with the Sergeant.

"Sergeant Becker, we have a situation out here. We found a wounded man hiding out in our building, who was possibly grazed by a bullet. Anything going on that you know of that this man might be a part of?"

"Nothing much happened yesterday or today; been quiet," the Sergeant went on. "Oh wait, there was a shooting over on Mullen Ave early this morning, but that's an open and shut case. We know the assailant and he's confessed to the shooting; it's from a family feud that's gone on for years. The victim is at the hospital resting comfortably. Neighbors saw everything and we have their statements. As I recall, there was a possible witness standing in the doorway as all this took place on the victim's front porch, but he got away in all the confusion."

"I think we might have the witness with us now," Don responded.

"Ask him his name. If it's Nelson, that's the witness."

Don cuffed his phone, looked in on the man and asked, "Sir, what is your name?" No response.

"Is it Nelson?"

"How did you know?" came the wary reply.

"Oh, it's a long story, Mr. Nelson. Don't panic, but the police want to ask you a few questions about a shooting that went on earlier this morning. It's just a few questions."

"Don! Don!" the Sergeant spoke over the cellphone Don was clutching. "I'll come right out and talk with him."

Then Doobie came walking down the hall to see why Don and Mark were not returning to the dinner. "Where have you guys been?" he asked Don.

"Oh sorry, Doobie. We've been detained by someone in trouble who broke into the Factory. The Police are on the way to investigate...Why don't you go back to the others and tell them we're all safe and we'll only be a few more minutes."

"Okay, I guess...Do you want me to come back and stick around with you and Mark?"

"No, go back to the others and wait...tell them a joke or two. We'll join you soon,"

Within minutes Sergeant Becker was at the front door. David let him in. The officer recognized the victim and greeted him by name: Jerry Nelson. They talked in the closet for a few minutes, as the others hung out in the hallway. Then the Sergeant spoke privately with Don. "I got his statement; he was the other witness looking on from the front door of their house (he lives with his son, J. R.). He's not in any trouble with us; he'll likely have to appear before the Judge when charges are brought. He says he doesn't want to stay here, but this would be a good and safe place for him tonight. I understand, he's afraid of reprisal from the assailant's family. We're keeping an officer with the son tonight in the hospital as a precaution. We could post an officer here at the Factory for the night; if that would help."

"Yes, Sergeant, that would be great. We'd all feel better," Don quickly answered.

"Any chance the two of them could stay here later for an extended period as they both recover?" asked Sergeant Becker.

"Sure. We could do that. What do you think, Dianne? We could look after this man for a while, couldn't we?"

"Yes, I think that would work," she answered.

Don looked at his watch in amazement: "Wow, we've been gone close to forty-five minutes! Hey, folks, I should get back to the meeting. They're probably wondering about us..."

Don extended his hand. "Thanks, Sergeant, for coming out here on such short notice."

"No problem, Don. You folks out here do some good work for Greensville and make our job easier. It's the least I could do."

"And thanks for the courtesy checks you do for us. We appreciate your concern; that makes our job easier."

As the Officer left, Don turned to David and Dianne before leaving the scene. "David, Dianne, can you take it from here?"

David was first to speak: "Boss, I'll take care of our guest tonight. First job is to get him cleaned up and then into some different clothes. I'll get him some food from the potluck table. Then, I'll put him into the spare, single unit and curl up in the comfy chair there right beside him. We'll go from there in the morning."

Dianne said: "I'll check on him later this evening; probably need to change his dressing by then. First, though, I should retrieve my three kids from Miss Kathy, before they drive her nuts!"

"One more thing," added Don gazing toward the storage closet, "Maybe our guest - Jerry Nelson, right? - would like the use of that office chair over in the corner with four wheels on it. I'm sure it must be hard to navigate by foot after all he's been through...If there are any questions or concerns, you guys know where to find me...Now, I wonder if my sumptuous potato salad is right there where I left it."

Don headed back down the hallway with Mark alongside. David and Dianne situated Jerry on the rolling chair and off they went for an overdue shower and change of clothes. "Here we go, Jerry; Hang on to Dianne's arm," encouraged David. Jerry looked forlorn and hung on dearly; David was having a great time!

The way things turned out seemed, in David's mind, to be a good outcome to an otherwise stressful evening. One thing that continued to bother him was the question of how this Jerry character got inside the factory in the first place. *Did I leave a door unlocked? Or did someone else?* he wondered. *Did he get in by breaking a window? Somehow, some way, I'll get the answers to those questions as we spend some time together...I know, when Dianne comes by to change the bandages, I'll take a quick look outside to see if there are any broken windows or other clues.*

When Don and Mark arrived back at the meeting, the meal was finished, and people were chatting with one another. Their attention got focused when Don stood to speak. He gave a quick rundown on what just transpired and reassured the folks that things at the factory were safe.

"David is on the scene for us, and we all know how thorough he is!" People nodded in agreement.

Don went on. "Well friends, let me save this great potato salad for later and we'll get on with the rest of our evening, even though we're running a little late. If any of you think you should leave, feel free to do so." No one budged. So, Don started a teaching about end-times.

"Many of you attended some of the teaching sessions that were held at Cornerstone Church, so tonight may be a repeat of sorts. But can a person learn too much about the Bible? And about end-times? Really? Do you think Paul the Apostle is up in Heaven now lounging on a thick cloud, eating grapes, thinking about nothing he'd rather do? No, he's either attending a lecture or leading one. He probably figures we have all of eternity to learn about God and His ways, because there's so much to understand.

"As you've heard me say many times, I believe this current generation is going to see the return of Jesus. That means me! That means you! Aren't you glad? We're going to meet up with Jesus in the clouds, as He calls His Church home, sporting our new glorified, eternal bodies and forever live with Him.[12] Most everyone who knows anything about the

Bible agrees that that will be the result. It's the *how-do-we-get-to-that-point* understanding that separates us.

"In most circles the popular, more common view is known as the *Pre-Tribulational Rapture* position. That says that the next great event on the end-times calendar is the Rapture of the Church itself. Nothing else needs to precede it; so, there are no signs to be on the lookout for. And, in this view, the Church will not have to endure any great hardship or tribulation as it awaits the Rapture. A comforting thought, wouldn't you agree?

"But my viewpoint, my understanding of Bible teaching in this area, is 180 degrees different. My perspective is understood as the *Pre-Wrath Rapture* position. I agree with the first group that we are not to experience God's wrath, namely His trumpet and bowl judgments, scheduled to come upon the unbelieving earth. The Bible is explicit about this. But...and there is a big *but*...I believe the Bible also teaches that we, the waiting Church, will have to endure great hardship, not from God, but from Satan when he unleashes the full fury of the Antichrist upon the earth. This character will direct his terror at Christians and Jews. This is what Jesus referred to as the *Great Tribulation*,[13] when He taught His disciples about end-times just before the Last Supper. The Lord was talking about a tribulation so awesome that many Jesus-loving Churchgoers would give up their faith, turn on one another, and publicly scorn the promise of Heaven.[14]

"Can you image yourself doing such a thing? '*No way would I do that*,' you say, '*Not me!*' Well, before you get all bent out of shape, do you remember the Apostle Peter? He vowed his allegiance to the Lord at the Last Supper. Jesus told Peter that he would deny Him three times that night before the cock crowed. Peter couldn't envision such a thing. He protested and said: '*Though I would die with You, yet will I not deny You.*'[15] Peter had no idea what he was in for, but when it was all said and done, he put personal safety over his commitment to the Lord...like the Bible tells us many others are going to do.

"Many Christians will find themselves faced with the same dreaded option. I imagine each of us will have that choice as the end draws near. How are we going to react? Will we bend like dear Peter as the pressure turns intense?"

Don couldn't help but notice that his friends seemed to be struck speechless with the sheer reality of that possibility. No one moved or spoke. Even Dianne's kids sat at attention. Don wanted to end the session on a brighter note.

"Awesome to think about, right? But I believe God doesn't want us scared about the coming tribulation. He wants us prepared for it: *Not Scared but Prepared*...Hey, that sounds like a good title for a book about end-times, doesn't it?

"Or maybe it should be our slogan! ***Not Scared but Prepared.*** Let's make that become the focus of this community in our remaining time. Let's get ourselves so trusting in the Lord that we will not be shaken off course. Amen? Amen!"

Several *Amen's* were heard around the room. Don was happy. To him the *Amen's* signaled the desire in the hearts of the people to win in this coming battle.

Don went on. "I just had another thought about our dear friend, Peter. It's easy to criticize him for his apparent weakness when he chose personal safety over his allegiance to Jesus. But let's remember that Peter at that point of denying Jesus did not have the Holy Spirit in his heart like all of us here do. That Holy Spirit comfort, strength and wisdom wouldn't be coming to live in him until later at the feast of Pentecost..."

"Folks, we for sure will be learning more about this topic in the days and weeks ahead... Okay? For now, change of topic. Let's close with this final announcement. We're going to have a contest. It's a *Name-the-Ministry-Contest*. I want you all to put on your creative hats and think of a name, and present it as a full-color, 8 ½ x 11 poster. We're looking for persons who are not only creative, but adept at design and computer skills. Members of the Planning Committee will be the final judges. Submit your entry within a week. Turn it in to Clair in the office."

"And what does the winner get?" piped in Doobie.

"I was waiting for you to ask, Doobie. The winner will get a fifty-dollar gift card to their favorite eating establishment...Namely, Mama Blanchard's fine restaurant, because we all know she has the best in town, hands down!

"And...and, whoever wins has to take me with them!"

Pause. "No, I was just kidding about that last part! Well, folks, have a good rest of your night. Thanks for coming. Good night. See you tomorrow."

THE FACTORY ENJOYED A PERIOD OF CALM and growth in the weeks that followed. The name **The Factory** was chosen as the winner for the contest. Dianne submitted that entry. The judges liked the simplicity of that choice and it seemed to reflect how the public had come to know the ministry: it was a big factory that did a lot of good things. Period.

Don and Kathy were thrilled when Jenny and Jim arrived home. Their new, two-bedroom unit was ready and waiting for them. Kathy took on the job of picking paint colors and carpet and adorning it with neat fixtures and decorations...things that she knew would please Jenny.

After a week of readjustment, Don talked with Jenny and Jim in the break room about their role at the Factory, with a box of doughnuts and hot coffee available. "How do you two see yourselves fitting in here? What jobs or responsibilities would you want? I have some ideas myself along this line, but I want to hear what you think."

Jenny spoke up first. "Well, dad, I was wondering if I might plug in to public relations, social/media outreach, or something along this line. Maybe organizing and publicizing a community outreach of some sort, for example, or a newsletter. I could develop our own webpage and get us started on Facebook, too."

"Bingo!" replied Don. "That's what I was thinking too. I've been dreaming about a community outreach event, like an Open House, where we would highlight our ministry services; and let the public look us over. You could fit in there as organizer and coordinator of such an event. What do you think?"

"Yeah. I like the idea, dad. And after the Open House? Then what? I was kinda wondering about helping with childcare and teaching for the little ones. Aren't there about six or so pre-school kids here now?"

"I think that's right. Oh, that would be great, Jenny. Suzy would love to have your help. And how about you, Jim?"

"Well, I'm not real sure, Dad..."

"Oh, say that again, Jim..."

"I'm not real sure? Oh, I'm not real sure, **Dad**! Is that what you mean?"

"That's it. Music to my ears! Go on."

Jim smiled broadly. "My background is in human resources, but how would that fit in?"

"Not sure right now," answered Don. "But until we carve that out, I'd like you to start meeting with our Planning Committee. There are five of us that meet, mostly impromptu, but at least three times a week lately; some weeks every day. You see, Jim, I have you in my mind as being my associate, my right-hand man. I need someone with your skills who could take over in my place if I were gone...Reaction?"

"Ah...that sounds most interesting. Yeah, sure, I could fit in there. There's a lot I don't know about this place, you understand."

"That's why I want you to start tomorrow shadowing me. We'll start with a Planning Meeting at nine. Then, we'll make the circuit, meet the people, see what some of their issues are. Are you gamed?"

"I am. Tomorrow at nine." And, with a smile Jim added, "Thanks, Dad."

CHAPTER EIGHT –

Are you sitting down? I have some disturbing news.

MAYOR TOM REILY LED A GROUP OF LOCAL Dignitaries to the Open House. Sergeant Becker came with several of his friends on the Force. Fire Chief, Mac Johnson appeared, as did Director of the County Social Services, Betty McPherson. Pastor Daniel and his wife were in attendance, along with six other church Pastors. And when you add in members of the Greensville community, that must have equaled 160 guests. Several of the Factory faithful agreed to lead small groups on tours of the facility. Doobie was the gracious host at the refreshment table. He invited people to fill out a comment card at the same time. Most of the comments were positive and appreciative.

One highlight of the open house was the personal testimonies given by those who had been personally touched in some way by The Factory. A particularly moving account was given by D. J. Nelson. He talked about how The Factory took he and his dad, Jerry, in to recuperate from gunshot wounds. The ongoing family feud turned violent a month after the shooting, including the Nelson home being burned to the ground by the other family. D. J. and his dad had few options to consider. So, the offer to stay on and live at The Factory was a great blessing. D. J., once a Master Plumber, helped with construction and plumbing needs; his father has plugged in with the vegetable garden and general janitorial help.

D. J. closed his testimonial with this thought: "We were without a home, income, clothing, or any job. I don't know what we would have done if The Factory hadn't stepped in to help. May the Lord continue to bless this great humanitarian work."

As the open house wound down and the clean-up crew went into action, Don spotted Jenny and went over to talk with her. "Well, Jenny, I'd consider the open house a big success. Thanks again for all you did to get this off the ground."

"Thanks, Dad. I'm exhausted and excited at the same time. I'm about ready to count the attendance. There must have been at least 150 here. Do you want to see the comment cards yet this evening, or can it wait until tomorrow?"

"Tomorrow would be soon enough for me. I think I'll find Kathy and call it a night. See you later."

The next morning arrived too soon for Don. He was awakened by a most disturbing phone call. It was from Mayor Riley. Usually in an upbeat mood and one of The Factory's most vocal supporters, this morning he sounded grumpy and he was the bearer of hard news.

"Don, are you sitting down? You better. I've got some disturbing news to share," the Mayor began.

Don sat at the kitchen table and braced himself for the worst. "I'm ready Mr. Mayor. What have you got to share?"

"Don, it has to do with some repercussions from the open house. Some people took strong issue with The Factory's lax attitude about meeting certain health, fire, food, and State safety guidelines. You know as well as I that I've not really pushed you to comply; I wanted to focus mostly on the good work you and your people were doing.

"The negative comments came from persons who accused me of showing favoritism, in violation of certain laws and standards. And they promised - no they threatened - that if there wasn't some immediate sign of you attending to the deficits, then they would start a petition to get me to step down as Mayor and have The Factory close its doors."

"Oh, man! That is terrible, Mr. Mayor. I'm so sorry to have put you in such a predicament. I'll get right after it. We'll set up a task force out here to map out plans to work on compliance issues..."

"I hate to be real downer, Don, but I have the sinking feeling that no matter how hard you tried and how visible your changes were, it would not be enough to satisfy some people. It's almost like there are those who want your hide; and want you out of business!"

"Sounds like you've had some past dealings with this crowd. Right?"

"You're right Don. I've put out a few fires on your behalf for some months now. But with their attendance at the open-house they have bolstered their desire to have The Factory roll over and fade away."

"Man, oh man, what a mess. The way I see it, it's the work of the devil coming against us. So, in a strange way, I take consolation in the community persecution. To me it means we are doing something right and good for the Kingdom of God! The Bible tells us to count it all joy when we fall into temptations, or tests and trials...[16]

"But that doesn't help you much out your predicament with your critics. Can you think of anything we could do, Mr. Mayor? Mr. Mayor?"

"Oh, sorry, Don. No, I can't."

"Well, at the least, I would like the opportunity to sit down and talk with those raising the stink. Do you think that could be arranged, Mr. Mayor?"

"Yes, it probably could be arranged. That might be the best way to get this started. Maybe a week from today, say at 9:00 am."

"By the way, could you tell me who is raising all the ruckus?"

"Three are spearheading the drive: The head of Social Services, Betty McPherson; the Fire Chief, Mac Johnson; and a relatively new Church Pastor, Robert Skilling. And I understand there might be a snitch who's part of your Factory personnel. I'm not sure of the name. I didn't push the matter; I didn't want to know."

"One more thing, Mr. Mayor, would you join me in a quick prayer? God didn't bring us this far to fail...

"Dear Lord, we're not real sure what to do here. But, like King Jehoshaphat of old our eyes are on You. We ask for and expect You will provide Your wisdom of how to deal with the persecution. I know I have Your heart when I proclaim that The Factory will not shut down until its work is done. So, I say to the kingdom of darkness: No weapon from you against us can prosper. We will have the victory! May your

Blessing, Lord, fall heavy on our good friend, Mayor Riley. In the Name of Jesus. Amen."

"Good-bye, Don. If anything comes up about this before next week, I'll let you know. Bye."

"Bye, Mr. Mayor."

Don put the cellphone down and immediately noticed that Kathy was sitting on the edge of the bed looking at him. Don asked: "Did you hear?"

"I heard enough. We're in some trouble, huh?"

"It appears that way; but let's call it a *challenge* instead of *trouble*... And let's call it an *opportunity-for-God-to-shine* instead of *terrible*, like I first said to the Mayor...And here's another important question: Do we have any doughnuts in the room?"

Kathy stood up and hurled two pillows at Don. "I take it that means No?" Don asked as he stood and threw the two pillows back.

The Planning Committee met that morning for a scheduled session. All were present to hear Don recount his crucial call from the Mayor. People were stunned. At first, they had nothing to say. Talk about extremes: yesterday everyone was riding high over the success of the open house; and now after hearing the Mayor's report, those same faces were shocked and saddened. Then one voice took center stage. It was Jim's.

"They can't do this to us! What are their names; I'll give them the full internet search. We'll find some dirt from their past that we can use to silence their allegations!"

"No, Jim, that's not the way we do things around here. So, just *cool your jets*!"

"Okay. Sorry, Dad."

"What are some other options we have? Put on your thinking caps, guys."

Ben said: "Don, short of a miracle by God Himself, I don't see that we have any recourse to deal with this problem."

"People, like I told Kathy this morning, let's not call it a *problem*, let's refer to it as a temporary *challenge*. Scripture tells us: *Whatever we call it is what it is to us.*"[17]

"Well, whatever we call it: problem or challenge," Mark asserted, "it seems likely to have the same result – to shut The Factory down...and none of us want that!"

"Gentlemen, as we speak, Kathy and Jenny are forming a prayer group, to intercede in this whole matter," Don shared. "We could all agree that we need God's wisdom, and His power, right?"

Doobie looked across the table at the other members, then he spoke slowly. "Men, we are in a pickle. And it's not God's fault. We ourselves turned away from trying to comply with the regulations, thinking we were somehow above such everyday matters, since God put all this into motion. I think that's a case of pride.

"Now we have the consequences to deal with. And here's where the Lord can help: He can turn around even the most stubborn and unfriendly heart. He can '*Make a way where there seems to be no way,*' as the Bible tells us.[18] We need Him in on this."

The men at the table were flabbergasted at Doobie's insight and clarity; they looked on with amazement.

"What? What are you looking at? What'd I do?" Doobie asked.

Don answered for them all. "It's nothing bad Doobie; it's all good! You were speaking for the Holy Spirit what we needed to hear. The ladies are praying for God's wisdom and here it comes through the mouth of our dear friend, Doobie. You are something else, you know that Einstein?"

"Time for another high-five, big bro," Mark exclaimed, as he reached across the table. Smack!

Don went on. "Men, I learned that the Mayor has been running interference for us for many months, holding at bay those that would like to see us go under. But that favor is wearing thin and about to come to an end. As Ben said earlier, short of a miracle we seem to have no choice but to make a herculean effort to comply."

"What does *her-cue-leon* mean," asked Doobie.

Ben answered. "It means enormous, superhuman."

Doobie thought a moment and then replied: "Instead of *super-human* let's make it *supernatural.* Like I said before, let's get God involved. Only He can take us above the natural"

Jim added: "Let's humble ourselves and ask for His help...That's where I need to start."

Mark added this: "Let's believe He can and wants to turn it all around."

"You're all right," Don asserted. "We've got a work here to do and God's not finished with us yet. And let's not forget that there are other actors in this drama, from the Kingdom of Darkness. They are either directly interfering or using those arrayed against us as pawns in the battle.

"Okay, men, the question on the table is this: Where do we start?"

There followed a time of spirited, practical planning. Two trends were identified: Don would be facing his accusers in a week at the Mayor's office, so he needs to be armed with as much information as possible with which to give a meaningful argument for clemency - because of needing time to comply. Secondly, Don would call the City Office of Inspections, to arrange a meeting at The Factory to get that person's take on how much work needs to be done. In the meantime, the planning group would be meeting daily. And each would commit to keeping the whole matter lifted in prayer. And they all echoed a resounding: AMEN!

AS SCHEDULED, DON HAD A MEETING with the opponents of The Factory that Mayor Riley identified. It was held in the Mayor's meeting room in City Hall. All were present and accounted for. These included: the head of the County Social Services, Betty McPherson; the Fire Chief, Mac Johnson; and, a relatively new Church Pastor, Robert Skilling.

And there was a *surprise participant* not expected by Mayor Riley. The surprise guest arrived about five minutes past the hour. It was the

Lieutenant Governor, Carroll Leonard. It was obvious from the start that he was the brains behind the movement, or (as Don thought) the Kingpin behind the conspiracy to squash The Factory. It was not so much that Mr. Leonard set out to control the proceedings, because he had little to say. But the other three conspirators seem to defer to him and seek his "go-ahead" before participating.

The accusers did not add much about their concerns, to what Don already knew from talking with the Mayor and with the County Inspector. And there was really no rebuttal, or argument, Don could offer. The Factory was indeed out of compliance with the building, health, and operational standards. Don conceded that much but tried valiantly to convince the others that The Factory was prepared to take all the steps necessary to get into compliance.

So, while the company of accusers went out of their way to cast The Factory in a dark light, part of their thunder was stolen by Don's soft response to the concerns. The Mayor was all set to mediate a fracas, but it never happened. Don knew that sections of the various codes allow for a set amount of time for the one in non-compliance to have to become compliant. And he banked on that provision to stand in his defense. There was no arguing about that. The deficiencies had been identified by those at the meeting, but those same ones had to acknowledge that The Factory had an agreed-upon latitude of time within which to address the infractions. Don insisted that his people would take on that task immediately.

After nearly 45 minutes, the accusers seemed to simply sputter to a stop. To have the last word, so to speak, they demanded that Don show evidence to their "Committee" of his meeting the standards, over and above the normal course for reporting when compliance objectives are met. They spent the next 15 minutes discussing how that might be done. Don was content to allow them as much leeway as they wanted, even if their demands seemed unreasonable. Don was happy that the results of the meeting gave him a "green light" to proceed. There would be no shutdown of The Factory!

"Hallelujah," Don said under his breath. On the outside he maintained his gracious and grateful demeanor; inside he wanted to stand up and dance around the table, or maybe on top of it!

He considered what the actual role of the Lieutenant Governor was to be in all of this; it was unclear, since he was not an active participant. After the meeting officially ended, the Mayor excused himself. Then Don left, while the Lieutenant Governor stayed behind with the other three.

There was a little nagging voice that asked: "I wonder what those four are going to cook up now to impede the work of The Factory?" But a stronger *Voice* prevailed: "Thanks for being so open and gracious, Don. Your easygoing manner compelled them to do the same...What you sowed is what you reaped. Now, let's get busy with all the work ahead of you."

"Yes, Lord. We're going to do just that!

"By the way, Lord, I could tell that You were there in the meeting. I sensed Your presence and Your peace. Thank You. Thank You."

By that afternoon, it was "all-hands-on-deck" to deal with compliance and inspection requirements. As Don walked by a group of workers, he yelled out: "Somebody come up with a song that we can sing – like the Seven Dwarfs did for Cinderella. Remember: '*Whistle while you work...*'"?

Doobie took the assignment as a personal challenge. As he mopped the meeting room floor, he strained and strained to think of a song. Soon he presented it to the Lord as a prayer request: 'Lord, help me to come up with a song we could all get behind to make this work go easier.'" No ideas came forth, so Doobie prayed in other tongues. Then it came, sung to the tune of: *Mary had a little lamb.*

Who's gonna take The Factory down? Nobody can, Nobody can!
With God we are victory-bound, through His mighty hand.
Who's gonna stop the work we do? Nobody can, Nobody can!
God will see we make it through. Like when we first began!

"Brother Don! I got it! I got a song," yelled Doobie from the meeting room.

"Doobie, where are you?" asked Don. "I don't see you."

"I'm right here...in the meeting room! Oh, I left out that part, sorry."

"I'll be right there...Oh, there you are. Ok, let's hear it."

Doobie proceeded to joyfully sing his new song. "What do you think, Don?"

"What do I think? I love it, Doobie. It's great! You can teach it to everyone. It will be our rallying cry and our great confession...Thanks, Einstein. You did it! Again!"

Don had the notion to add a section in The Factory that would house a score of beds, like in a dormitory setting arrangement. D. J. was busy with his crew of plumbers, adding new restrooms. Mark worked with David Levine and his troupe of carpenters, as they provided some finishing touches to apartments and addressed the electric code deficiencies.

Part of David's crew included one Derek Johns, who, unbeknownst to David was the fink who reported directly to the "Committee of Adversaries," through his Church Pastor, Robert Skilling. In this way he kept the Committee informed about progress and problems at The Factory. Don often wondered how the Committee seemed to be one jump ahead of him. Before Don reported on steps taken at The Factory, the Committee was already aware.

Don decided to talk with Mark about his concerns that an informant was on the loose at The Factory. They decided to put the matter before the Lord in prayer. A prayer circle of Don, Kathy and Mark arose. All three had a list of everyone involved with The Factory in some capacity, whether directly receiving assistance or engaged as an outside worker. They prayed over the list, asking God to show them the informant. In less than four days the prayer circle came up with the same name: Derek Johns.

Next came the plot to fed Mr. Johns some false information and see how it got back to the Committee. What would that be? What faulty info would work?

Mark had an idea: "Let's arrange to have Mr. Johns overhear us talking; we'll talk about how we're going to sidestep the building code section on garbage disposal size and food freezer capacity in the kitchen area – and when the inspector comes, we'll find a way to divert his attention away from the kitchen."

"Yeah, that might just do the trick," Kathy added. "But you, Don, would come to the Committee meeting armed with an official inspector verification that those two areas *did meet* the standards."

"Right! And Mr. John's reputation in the eyes of the Committee would fall out of sight," Don said gleefully. "The Committee would sit there with egg on its collective face, and The Factory might just get some reprieve from the Committee's relentless scrutiny and disfavor. Now wouldn't that be a blessing...Let's make it happen."

Kathy smiled at Don. "Don't you just love it when a plan comes together?"

Don smiled back. "I sure do...and I'm glad that the Lord has a good sense of humor, too!"

The next time Don was scheduled to address the Committee - by this time now meeting weekly – the scheme was in place. Mr. Johns was fed the erroneous information, two days ahead of the meeting. The Committee asked specifically about the garbage disposal and freezer unit in the kitchen; the questions by the Committee members were framed as if they suspicioned that Don was planning to con his way out of compliance. In Don's pocket was the Inspector's report from yesterday that the disposal and freezer were, in fact, up to standards.

Don explained to the Committee: "I'm sure glad the Mayor is here to witness this...We have discovered that Mr. Derek Johns is an informant, posing as a construction worker for The Factory. His main intent is to dig up dirt about me personally or about The Factory's efforts during this reconstruction and renewal. He, then, reports back to you, either directly or through Pastor Skilling...

"Am I right so far?" No comments but plenty of chair-squirming. Don went on. "Mr. Johns is the informant. But now things get interesting," said Don as he reached into his jacket pocket. "This form that I have in my hand is the Inspector's findings from yesterday that stipulates that the disposal and freezer questions do met his compliance standards."

The meeting room continued with stone cold silence and eyes glued to the floor. Don proceeded with confidence. "You are all privy to this duplicity involving Mr. Johns. Almost from the start, you have wanted to see The Factory go under and for reasons I don't fully understand... even yet! Well, we are not going under I can assure you!"

"Now, see here, Mr. Carlton," interjected the Fire Chief. "We on this Committee are only interested in seeing that your service meets prevailing standards of operation – it's for the wellbeing of our community and..."

"Now, you pay attention to me, all of you!" Don commanded their undivided interest. "Wouldn't you know the local paper and TV news would love to dig into all this further? They would salivate at the chance! We have taken your guff and ill will for long enough. I am sorely tempted to let the cat out of the bag and see what repercussions would come of it..."

More silence. Don resumed. "Part of me would love to see what would happen, but I'm stopped from doing so, because I am a Christian and God would not look favorably on such a step. He wants me to let Him fight my battles, so I can remain in His peace and demonstrate His love to others – even to this Committee."

"So, what do you want, Mr. Crawford?" asked Betty McPherson, with a note of resignation. "Of course, we want to avoid any unnecessary bad publicity, for any and for all of us. How can we avoid that outcome? What are your thoughts, Mr. Crawford?"

"Stop hounding us! Extend some courtesy. Give up your apparent intent to drive us out of business. We are here for the long haul, for as long as the Lord says. We're here to help serve many of the same people you deal with day by day.

"Listen, folks, you have my word, we want The Factory to be in full compliance with all regulations and codes, as much as anybody. It is to our best interest to do so, and it's certainly good for the people we aim to serve.

"So, I guess it all boils down to this: let The Factory follow this compliance do-over in the normally accepted way of doing business, without interferences. That's all we want. That's not too much to ask, is it?"

The three members huddled and conferred in whispered tones. They could not be overheard; neither did Don want to hear. Don turned to the Mayor and smiled as he waited nervously. Finally, after less than a minute, Mrs. McPherson turned to Don with the Committee's reaction.

"Mr. Carlton, you have us over the proverbial barrel. It is certainly in our own best interests to discontinue our close surveillance of The Factory's efforts at meeting the code, so this nasty business with Mr. Derek Johns can be settled and out of the way. That is what we plan to do. No more Committee Meetings. We wish you the best. Good day, Mr. Crawford."

"And a good day to all of you," Don said as he rose from the table to leave. In a parting token of good-will, he turned back to the room and issued an invitation. "We can see the light at the end of the tunnel. When we pass that final inspection, we will host a victory party. All of you are invited." There were feigned smiles from the Committee, but no comments. Faithful friend, Mayor Riley, did say he would be happy to be there.

During the ensuing weeks, the "all-hands-on-deck" attitude continued as The Factory faithful diligently pursued their renovation goals. To an *outsider* it probably appeared to go painfully slow, but not to the Believers. They went about their work assignments with thankful hearts. They knew that God was directing their steps, and because of His direct interventions, many potential problems seemed to simply melt away.

One day, Mark shared in the planning meeting that God told him some things on this topic. He said: "The Lord told me the other morning that Heaven is a remarkably busy place. Our work here was like it was in Heaven. There, no one must work hard or long, because everyone is so efficient and joyful about it. In Heaven you can accomplish twice as much in half the time.

"And then the Lord added this for Don to share with others: '*That's how I want it to be for you*.'"

Day after day Doobie's victory song could be heard up and down the corridors "*Who's gonna take The Factory down? Nobody can, nobody can...*"

CHAPTER NINE –

Destruction was all around except for one place.

T HE FINAL INSPECTION CAME. DON AND HIS crew passed with flying colors! Jenny agreed that she would plan a great victory party for The Factory faithful and the community.

"Praise the Lord!" "Hallelujah!" "Isn't God good!" were heard through all the building. High-fives became the common method of greeting one another. It was a sweet victory to be sweetly enjoyed!

But it wasn't to be so...

The same day as the victory party was scheduled, an unforeseen catastrophe hit little Greensville hard at 3:00 am. It was a category 4 tornado! It came without warning, running from west to east. It zigzagged through the center of town causing a one-half mile of utter devastation in its path. Within twenty minutes it was over.

It caught everyone off guard. To say that it put an immense strain on the emergency resources of the community would be an understatement. This was a disaster like the town had never known before. Destruction was all around the tornado's path, everywhere you looked – except for one place. You guessed it: The Factory!

There were housing needs, food and shelter needs, clothing needs, emergency medical needs. The number of homes destroyed was astounding; nearly a third of the town, as well as numerous small businesses were utterly ruined. Normal day-to-day activities came to a screeching halt! The Governor declared the area to be in a state of emergency, which meant he could call in the State National Guard for assistance with searching for casualties and with general security against looting. Also, emergency supplies, the work of the Red Cross, came pouring in.

In concert with all those emergency efforts, The Factory stood out as a local resource that had the manpower and supplies to play a significant role in the tornado response. And with everyone so concerned about their own personal loss and challenges, and with the local government so disrupted, there was an effort to reschedule The Factory's victory party, but that was quickly scrubbed. In the face of the overwhelming crisis, no one much cared about celebrating whether there were sufficient outlets in the apartment units.

So, The Factory stepped up to the plate and opened its door to whoever had a food, clothing, or shelter need. People arrived by the droves. They walked, they limped, they came in wheelchairs, on scooters, and they came crammed in old pick-ups. But they came. The Red Cross "borrowed" a section of The Factory's parking space to set up their home base, providing food and other supplies. There they also began the important work of triage.

The Red Cross also arranged for hundreds of cots and blankets to be brought in and distributed around town at various venues for the homeless. Many cots went to local churches and schools; some came designated for The Factory's newly set up dormitory.

One Red Cross worker said to Don: "It's a miracle that your place didn't suffer any damage. That tornado must have skipped right over you as it came into town. Pretty lucky, I'd say."

"No, it wasn't luck, it was the hand of God!" Don quickly answered.

"Well, anyway you call it, this old factory was left standing to be able to provide valuable assistance now at this crucial time...and whoever had the idea to set up a dormitory arrangement was a mastermind at planning ahead."

"Yup, you're right about that," Don conceded. "It was the same One that caused that tornado to skip over our factory. We here know Him as Jesus...Well, gotta run inside and help out."

Meanwhile in Greensboro, it was 9:30 am at WMYV-TV. Station Manager, Pat Engels, was sitting with his most popular News Anchor, Samantha Burton and Producer, Gretchen Davis, discussing the Greensville tornado disaster. "Sam, I'm going to send you and Gretchen over to Greensville to cover this devastating tornado. It came as a surprise to the community. With hardly any warning, there was considerable damage - not the least of which was nine known fatalities and another seventy or so wounded, so far. Why don't you take Robbie, with you? It's only about 120 miles west. Maybe you can get something ready for the six o'clock news."

"Pat, I've got something planned for my evening and it doesn't include a tornado in some Podunk of a town nobody has heard of. Why not send Fred; he owes me a favor."

"No, Sam, you're the one to cover this. You did such a great job with the railroad disaster last month. Our viewers really relate to your down-to-earth style and the compassionate sidebars you find to include...Please Sam. Do it as a favor to me?...I think there might be a long vacation in it for you. You like sunny beaches, don't you, Sam?...Please?"

"Okay. Okay already! What do you think, Gretchen? Want to cover another tornado?"

"Yeah. Sure. Don't have a better offer. Remember, Pat, I like sunny beaches just like Sam. Okay?"

"Yeah. Yeah. Yeah. I hear you," Pat replied, playing it like he was the kindest station manager that ever existed. But his bribery seemed to be working. That's all that mattered.

"Well, you two, get going already. An MTV van is downstairs waiting for you...Keep me posted. Call in a run-down every hour on the hour, got it?"

"Bye Pat. Look for me on the six o'clock," answered Sam in her typical cynical and flippant manner, as she rose to leave. Gretchen followed. And soon, Robbie followed her, carrying his camera equipment.

The tragedy of the tornado stretched on for days and days. Don, Kathy and the faithful at The Factory worked tirelessly to address the needs of the community. Amidst the devastation, there were numerous people who lost their homes, who came to The Factory for shelter – some of whom later wanted to remain living there. Between The Factory and the re-purposed Willow Creek Motel, Don and his crew were able to temporarily house nearly a hundred people.

It was also during this time of responding to the desolation that God chose to give Don a special healing anointing. One afternoon, as Don was in the dormitory, visiting with the folks and praying for them, as he often did, the Lord got Don's ear.

He said: "Don, I want you to start laying your hands on the people suffering injury or pain. I will anoint you with a special gift for healing. You'll feel warmth in your hands and that will tell you that the anointing is present to heal. Encourage the people to believe to receive and their bodies will be made whole... Are you ready to begin?"

"Ah...Yes, Lord. I'm ready." Immediately Don could sense the warmth in his hands. He was standing at the side of a Large woman in obvious pain in her back. He said: "Ma'am, you have some serious pain in your back. The Lord wants me to lay my hands on you and pray; your part is to believe and receive. Okay?"

"Yes; yes!" Don did so and laid claim to her healing, commanding the pain to go, in the Name of Jesus! At once the pain left. She smiled brightly and jumped off her cot, to stretch and bend at the waist. She shouted: "I'm healed! I'm healed! Thank You, Jesus!" A relative or close friend was watching nearby and came over to join in the lady's rejoicing.

Soon others beckoned Don to come to their assistance. There must have been twenty or so hands that shot up in the air to get his attention. He felt the same warmth in his hands, so he proceeded to come to their side to pray. Each time the same healing results were evident. A healing revival was taking place in The Factory's make-shift dormitory! And Don couldn't have been happier.

As one might expect, not everyone lying on a cot was keen on the idea. A handful even scoffed. Don didn't care. As soon as one received healing, he was directed to the next by the Holy Spirit. Soon enough news of a *revival* began to cause quite a stir throughout The Factory. Several of the Faithful came into the room to witness it first-hand. One of those was Kathy, who immediately came to Don's side. She felt instructed by the Lord to lay her hands on the people with Don.

Within ten minutes the stirring ended, as the anointing lifted. Don was exhausted but energized to the hilt! He smiled at Kathy standing close by. The only word he could muster through his great big smile was "Wow!" He sat at a close-by empty cot and took several deep breathes. Kathy joined him there.

She said: "Wow, Don. How did this get started?"

"Well, I was just in here visiting with the forks, when the Lord said he was going to give me a special healing anointing. He said I would notice warmth in my hands as a sign of the anointing. So, I just felt led to go around and pray for people, as the Spirit directed me. Many got healed! It was awesome!

"Now the warmth seems to have lifted. I think I'd like to take a break. It was pretty intense."

Before leaving the dorm, he turned to the crowd and said: "Folks, I'm taking a break, but I'll be back, as the Lord directs."

Don and Kathy left the dorm and went to the break room. Kathy opened the conversation. "Don, that was an awesome display of God's healing grace. He always seems to come through for us with a special grace to deal with this challenge or another challenge – and at just the right time."

Doobie poked his head in and announced: "Don and Kathy, I think you will want to see this...Several folks are leaving."

Don and Kathy went to the door and saw about a dozen people walking down the hallway to the front door. Don recognized several of them as ones he had just prayed for and witnessed their healing. One gentleman in the procession came over to where Don was standing.

"Don, Kathy," he said, "My wife and I got healed today, when you laid hands on us, so we figure we may as well leave and give some room to others who need it worse than we do. Thanks folks."

"Oh, you're sure welcome," Don replied.

The gentleman went on with a request of sorts. "You know, my mother-in-law is home in her bed; she may have suffered some broken ribs when she fell over a big tree limb in her front yard...Would you mind if I brought her out here so you could lay hands on her as well?"

"No; that would be quite alright," answered Don. "See ya later..."

Kathy turned to look right at Don. "Well, Mr. Crawford, you certainly started something new today," she declared.

"Well, Kathy, it wasn't me. I wasn't looking for a healing ministry. It was the Lord's doing," he answered.

"You are right, Don. The Lord made it happen...Now will this become a regular part of The Factory's outreach, do you think?"

"I guess so, for as long as God wants it...for as long as He provides the anointing, we'll be available to minister it to others. How does that sound?"

"Great! I couldn't have said it better."

NEW GUESTS IN THE WAKE OF THE TORNADO found their niche at The Factory, wanting to lend a helping hand. Some naturally signed on in the food prep and distribution service. Others helped in childcare and education. Others in security. Others in janitorial services. Wherever a need arose there was always someone who took it on, and most often without being asked. Sometimes people from the community simply walked into The Factory and asked: "How can I help?"

Doobie's garden was essentially cleaned out with the heavy demand. So, local citizens brought in more for the hungry souls. Grocery stores donated generously. Mama Blanchard's food vendors did an outstanding job of keeping The Factory shelves stocked with all kinds of food.

Schools were closed for the rest of the Summer since they suffered a great deal. Many school buildings were structurally compromised and needed extensive repair over the summer months to be ready for fall classes. One by one local small businesses returned to a near normal operation. Many from the community agreed that it would be an awfully long time until normalcy could again be commonplace.

One area in which The Factory stood head and shoulders above other service providers was in attending to the tornado victim's spiritual needs. Many local churches were so concentrated on dealing with their own rebuilding efforts that they lost focus of their people.

Don and Kathy spearheaded ongoing prayer sessions. People could come and go as they pleased, but there was always at least 8 to 10 in prayer, around the clock at first, then less consecrated. And nightly Don provided teaching for The Factory faithful, the guests who joined them, or people from the community at large. Much of the emphasis of the teaching, not surprisingly, was focused on end-times realities. That was the topic that Don seemed most anointed to address — and it was the subject most requested by the people.

The healing ministry continued full force during recovery efforts from the tornado devastation. The man who requested prayer for his mother-in-law for possible broken ribs, did bring her to The Factory the day following his own healing, as he promised.

The lady was brought by wheelchair to the dormitory, where Don was busy laying his hands on those in need, with Kathy at his side. When it was her turn, Kathy laid hands on her rib cage as Don put his hand on her shoulder and prayed. Instantly the anointing came, and the woman was gloriously healed! She jumped out of the wheelchair and did a little jig right there in front of others in the room. It was a grand example of the Lord's healing compassion and a wonderful encouragement to the others awaiting prayer.

One evening about a month after the tornado, as Don was preparing for the evening teaching lesson, he sensed the Lord's bidding for a talk. "Yes, Lord, I'm listening," was Don's usual opening, as he closed his Bible and laid aside his pen and note paper.

"Don, things have been super busy around here," the Lord began. "I appreciate the work you and all the people have done during this crisis.

And more than anything I value your hopeful and thankful attitudes; that means so much to those who have lost so much."

"Thank You, Lord, for those kind words. You have certainly surrounded us with some incredible people...good workers and full of compassion, all of them!"

"Don, do you recall a few months back when I told you that the people who would came to The Factory would begin to highly esteem you and look to you as their Shepherd? Well, it's happening all around you."

"I have noticed, Lord. I have also become aware of Your anointing to deal with that reality. And now Your anointing to heal the sick...that seems to go hand-in-hand with being a Shepherd, don't You think?"

"Yes, I agree...Well, no new instructions to give today. I just wanted to check in."

"Thank You, Lord!"

"You're welcome. By the way, congratulations to you and Kathy..."

"For what, Lord?"

"For the birth of Jenny's baby. It's coming very soon; a bit early but everything's fine. Enjoy the new baby."

"You know the gender, but You're not going to tell me, right Lord?"

"You're right. That's up to Jenny and Jim to share...Well, I'll let you get back to your preparations."

A few days later the baby came! And what a night that was! It was not your textbook delivery. First the baby was about two weeks early. Second, it came so fast! There was not enough time to take the risk of making it to the hospital. So, Dianne was called in on an emergency mid-wife basis. She knew exactly what to do and her calm demeanor put everyone at ease – including a nervous father-to-be and two excited grandparents!

As all the onlookers stood by in Jenny's bedroom – all except for Don, that is – Dianne was coaxing Jenny. "You're almost there, Jenny. Just another push or two! You can do it!"

"Breathe, Jenny. Breathe!" added Kathy as she clutched her hand from the opposite side of the bed. "Breathe! Whooo, Whooo, Whooo."

Jenny let loose with another agonizing groan. "Ohooo...Lord..." Jim was beside himself. He so wanted to help, but he felt helpless, as he stood nearby.

"Honey," began Jim slowly, as he walked closer to Jenny, "Did I ever tell you about my first time to bowl a 250? It was one..."

"Jim, I think now's not the right time for that story," urged Kathy softly.

"But I just wanted to get her mind going in a new direction, away from the pain," Jim insisted. But he yielded to Kathy's advice and took back his position out of the way.

Coach Dianne jumped in again. "Come on Jenny! Almost there! Just one more big push. You can do it! ...I can see the head...here it comes...Oh, Jenny, it's a beautiful baby girl!"

"Good job, mother!" Kathy yelled into the next room for Don to hear. He came running into the bedroom, all smiles. He went to stand next to Jim and put his arm around his shoulder. "That a way, papa. Having babies is easy, don't you think? I don't know why mothers always make a big deal out of it," Don said, smiling, in half a whisper.

Kathy overheard and took issue with Don's remark. "You know why God ordained women to have babies, and not men, don't you? Because you men couldn't take it, that's why! Right, Jenny?"

"I don't know, Mom; ask me later...I'm kind of busy here."

Don piped in. "And a name? You two have a name for this beautiful child?" Jim said, "You answer that, Jenny." She announced: "Her name is Rosalie. Rosalie Anne."

"Oh, honey, that's an awesome and lovely name," said Kathy behind tears of joy.

And who should be waiting out in the hallway but nearly all The Factory Faithful. Doobie took the initiative to force his head into the room and caught sight of Kathy and Don coming out to share the good news.

"Well, Doobie, Ben, Clair, Mark and all the rest of you, there's new life in The Factory tonight!" Kathy announced. "Her name is Rosalie Anne..."

"And she's absolutely beautiful!" Don added, "But consider who her grandma is, and you'll know why, right? You can probably all see her tomorrow; let's give the new parents some space and time the rest of this night. Okay?"

MYTV ANCHOR STAR, SAMANTHA BURTON, was in Greensville through much of the clean-up and recovery from the tornado. She remained in Greensville for nearly ten days straight, and after that she returned on a weekly, then bi-weekly basis, to cover the *"Rebirth of Greensville,"* as she coined it.

Over those many hours together with the citizens of Greensville, she gravitated toward one main player in the tornado drama. You guessed it: The Factory. Throughout her time in town she talked extensively with Don and Kathy – she heard their stories, grew close to their hearts, coveted their joy-filled lifestyle, and applauded their dedication to the ministry.

One day, she returned to Greensville for a follow up on the Rebuilding of Greensville. She stormed into Don's office like a whirlwind and announced: "We've got to tell this story about Jesus coming back. It's something that the world needs to hear and believe in. I've been in on enough of your teaching sessions to know for a certainty that I'm right."

"But how can we do all of that?" Don asked. "You have a full-time job."

"I talked it over with Pat at MYTV – he doesn't get it! He just doesn't get it!" Sam got up and walked around Don's office – she seemed to be fuming as she went. Don noted that she was different – more absorbed, serious, and determined than ever. As she marched around, it sounded like she was talking to herself, some of which could be deciphered. And many of those words that could be understood were, in Don's estimation, mainly expletives – which she was known to express – off camera, of course.

Her ramblings finally ended. She sat quietly again and looked up at Don with a confident smile beginning to form on her face. "You know what, Don. I've been spouting off about how this story needs to be told - pontificating like a crazy woman! But now I'm adding a new wrinkle. Hear me now: This story does need to be told and you're going to tell it! And me? My part? I'm going to help you tell it! Now, Don Crawford, how does that sound to you?

"Wait a minute, wait a minute! Before you answer, I want you to think about it, seriously. Talk it over with your lovely Kathy; sleep on it, dream about it, whatever you've got to do. I'll be back in the morning about nine to hear your answer. See ya later. Bye...Oh, by the way, how is that adorable Rosalie doing?" Without waiting for an answer, she burst out of the office just like she arrived.

No doubt about it, Don considered, *Sam would be back tomorrow at 9:00; and what will be my answer?*

Don sat alone in his office, deep in thought and prayer. "Lord, she's right. This story – Your story – does need to be told for the people to hear and understand. I think You'd agree with that, right? And if there's any way to get this teaching out into the public's home, You'd support that, right?"

"Yes, Don; right so far," He answered. "But...there's a *but* coming from you."

"But...but am I the right person to tell it?"

"Let's not go back to that Moses-complex business again, Don. We dealt with that before. It doesn't look good on you and it certainly doesn't look good on Me. Of course, you're the right person! This is the culmination of all the on-the-job training, study, and leading that you've had over the last many years. This is what it was all for, to alert the world about My return...at least your part of the world.

"I have others across the globe that I've raised up like you for a time and a purpose such as this – to share My return with their constituents.

"Now you know the drill, Don: *'Trust in Me; have confidence in My ways; do your best and I'll make you shine.'*"

"Thank You, Lord. Thank You."

Don headed out to locate Kathy. He had to talk with her about Sam's offer. Or was it more of an ultimatum from Sam? Either way Sam would be here tomorrow morning for an answer.

Don spotted Kathy going into the childcare room. "Kathy! Are you busy? I need to talk," he yelled down the hallway.

"Sure Don. I've got time now. In the break room?" Kathy replied.

"Great. Meet you there."

They met in the break room, which thankfully was empty. Kathy sat at the table and waited for Don to start. Don paced around, then finally sat. He looked Kathy in the eyes, cleared his throat, and began.

"Sam wants us to do a regular series of teaching segments about end-times, that she would produce and promote for public viewing...I later talked with the Lord about it and He gave the green light...So, what do you think?"

"Well...I say, let's get after it! That's what we're here for; that's much of what The Factory is here for, right? That's what all those long hours of study were for.

"Don, this is it! This is so exciting! What do we do first?"

"I'll see Sam again tomorrow. She wants to hear about our reaction. I don't think she would accept anything but 'Yes, let's do this.' She'll give me more particulars then."

"I'm thinking I'll bring that up at this afternoon's prayer session. Okay with that?"

"Yeah, that would be fine. The more prayer the better...Pray for wisdom, for confidence, for all the needed equipment, for the Lord's Blessing. Well, I'd better get started on tonight's lesson."

Kathy stood to leave. She gave Don a big hug. "Honey, we're in this together. All of us at The Factory are in this as well...we both know God will never lead us down the wrong path. I love you, Don. Now, get after that lesson!"

Don went back to his office and spread his Bible and study notes over his desk. *Let's see, tonight we'll talk about the Seals of Revelation...*

yeah, that's it, the Seals. We're probably well into those by this time. Help me, Lord...

As Don finished up his last point for the teaching, he smiled and leaned back in his chair. Quickly he looked over his notes and smiled again; then it came:

"Hallelujah!" Don bellowed.

Both Doobie and Ben Tucker were at Don's door within a minute. Ben knocked and asked Don if he was alright.

Don opened the door to see his two friends leaning against the wall, gasping for oxygen. "Oh, sorry about the yelling. I guess I got carried away. Sometimes the Lord can be so gracious, I don't know how to Thank Him other than yelling. I'll keep the lid on the rest of the day, but I can't promise about tomorrow...Now would you say something, so I'll know you're all right?" No reply from either, just heavy breathing. "Really you two, I'll be alright. Thanks for your concern. See you tonight, fellas."

The meeting room was packed! At least forty were there: Eager hearts ready to learn more about God's plans for the end-times. Sam made sure she was present, with video camera in hand. She positioned herself in the back so she could record the session. As Don stood at the refurbished podium, the crowd grew quiet.

"Folks, it is such a blessing to see so many here tonight. Our topic is the opening of the seven seals, spelled out in Revelation, Chapter 6. As Revelation tells us, God has a scroll with seven seals and the only One found worthy to open the seals is the Lamb of God. As He opens it, one seal at a time, each seal marks the start of something important happening here on earth.

"Let's look closer...but first, let's pray: 'Heavenly Father, we agree as we pray and ask for revelation knowledge to come forth tonight. And we will receive it with joy and reverence. Help me to be clear and truthful. And we all promise to be doers of the Word, and not hearers only. In the Name of Jesus. Amen.'

"We have the emerging of the Antichrist with the first Seal broken. He's depicted as the rider of a white horse, riding as a conqueror. We'll learn more about him later. When he comes on the world scene, he is a good guy, able to broker a peace treaty in the middle east, but later we'll see his true colors emerge. Empowered by Satan, He will become the master of deception and terror, claiming himself to be God.

"With the second Seal, we see a rider on a red horse. He takes peace from the earth and there are wars and rumors of wars. I can hear you thinking: 'But haven't we always had wars of one kind or another?' And, yes, we have, but this is somehow different which I take to mean the wars will be more serious, more treacherous than known before.

"The next Seal, number three, shows a rider on a black horse, and he heralds in a time of severe famine for the earth. Seal four has a rider on a pale horse. His name is Death, and Hades or Hell follows closely. It opens a time of death and destruction from disease and pestilence and plague.

"Do you remember back when the Corona-Virus hit the world with a deadly pandemic. Many thousands died, particularly the elderly or seriously infirmed. I believe that was an expression of Seal four being opened. Now with Seal five we come closer to the worst of it.

"At the breaking of Seal five, things get dicey for Believers, very dicey. This happens when the Antichrist starts his reign of terror. He starts by claiming himself to be God and demanding allegiance from the whole world. He zeroes in on Believers and Jews, from anyone who would profess their loyalty to God Almighty. A time of intense persecution is experienced on the earth. Jesus referred to this time as *The Great Tribulation*.[19] It's a time of grave testing.[20] People riding the fence will be forced to make a choice, to either go all out for God or go with the Antichrist's program that rejects God.

"And where are we on God's timetable for end-times events? Are the Seals still to happen? Have they already happened? I believe Seals one through four have been broken, and we are awaiting the fifth Seal. I

think the Antichrist is in the world now, doing behind the scenes preparations for his sudden unveiling as the Terror Master.

"Jesus called these first four Seals the Beginning of Sorrows [21] – like
early birth pangs. The true, hard to bear sorrow has yet to be birthed,
I believe. It will be as the 5th Seal is broken, marking the start of the
Great Tribulation. During this time of the Antichrist's persecution, martyrdom will become the norm for those who won't yield to his terror
threats. As we'll learn later, for us in this generation who I believe will
have to experience this intense tribulation, there will be two ways to
Heaven – I mean apart from life's typical channel to Heaven through
natural death: the two ways will be either by martyrdom or by rapture."

Don paused. He sensed that the meeting room was silently groaning
with heavy hearts. There were visible frowns on faces, some of whom,
he guessed, would rather be doing anything else at this moment. He
thought: *Lord, You see the faces and know their hearts - should I back off
from this explicit description?*

The Lord spoke by His Spirit. *The people need to know what's ahead;
there's no easy, painless way to present it without it becoming irrelevant, or
trite, or false. But at the same time, let the people know that I will protect
them through the tribulation ahead, as they remain faithful to Me. I want
My people prepared, but not scared.*

Don turned back to the hungry souls before him. "Folks, this is not
easy to digest, I know...But my teaching is taken directly from the Word
of God. This is the inspired Word of God, remember! The Author is
the Holy Spirit Himself. I take this Word at face value. I trust that the
Holy Spirit will help me understand what I'm reading...will help all of
us to understand.

"I know some of you are wondering 'Why wouldn't God arrange for
the Rapture to happen <u>before</u> any tribulation even started'?"

"Yeah, Brother Don, you took that question right out of my mouth,"
said Doobie. "Me, too," chimed in Dianne. Others nodded in agreement.

Mary Kay blurted out her position. "My older brother, who's a
Minister in Kansas, plus my grandmother and both of my aunts, have

told me that the Rapture could happen at any time and it would happen before the hard part comes on the earth from the Antichrist...so, that's what I always believed." More nods of agreement from around the room.

"Well, Mary Kay and all of you with some serious questions on your heart – all I can say is that I am teaching you what I believe the Bible says. The sixth Seal marks the Day of the Lord and the unveiling of some significant cosmic disturbances, with the sun and moon and stars. That happens as Heaven gets ready to receive the living Faithful ones in the rapture <u>and</u> resurrect the Faithful ones that have fallen asleep or died.[22]

"Right after the rapture/resurrection, God's wrath is poured out on the earth. So, there is in my view a Wrath of Satan, followed by a Wrath of God. We escape the second but must face and endure the first wrath.

"And let's not forget what the purpose is for the Rapture: It's so we can escape God's wrath, His trumpet and bowl judgments, which He will inflict upon the disobedient world. That will be utter destruction for those who have turned their backs on God and His mercy, those who have rejected His provision for eternal salvation through Jesus...

"What could be the purpose for why God has us going through some serious testing and persecution during the Wrath of Satan? ...Did you notice I said God would direct us *through* the persecution that's ahead... It's like Psalm 23:4 says: *'Though I walk* **through** *the valley of the shadow of death I will fear no evil'*... With His help, we go through the valley and reach the other side!

"There is a Scripture that tells us Jesus is looking for a Church (actually, His Bride) that is without spot or wrinkle. It's found in Ephesians 5:27. I'm thinking again of those Christians on the fence, about to be forced into a choice for God or against Him. Soon there won't be a fence to ride on; people will jump one way or the other. Either way it goes, Jesus will have a stronger Church in the end. Those leaning His way will become more committed to Him; those leaning the other way will become more enslaved to the Antichrist.

"This reminds me of what the Lord told the Church at Laodicea, through the Apostle John in Revelation, Chapter 3. *'I know your works, that you are neither cold nor hot. I wish that you were cold or hot. So then because you are lukewarm, and neither cold nor hot, I will spue you out of My mouth.'* [23]

"I think we are safe in concluding that Jesus detests lukewarm Christians. Many Bible Scholars believe this Laodicean Church was a picture of the last days church. That's referring to us, Saints! He wants us to be on fire for Him! The passage goes on to say: *'As many as I love, I rebuke and chasten: be zealous therefore and repent'* [24]

"Jesus will end up with His Bride - the Church – being without spot or wrinkle! Amen! And we, Faithful Ones, are His on-fire, committed Church from Greensville!"

Don paused. "Well, saints, this is not exactly how I envisioned tonight's teaching going along... But we're led by the Holy Spirit, Amen? Can I get an Amen out there?"

"Amen!" "Amen!"

"While I believe it is true that we will likely be exposed to difficult times ahead, God has promised in so many places in the Bible that He will take care of us. Those lukewarm Christians, sitting on the fence so to speak, who will be an easy prey for the Antichrist, may easily give their allegiance away to him. But at the same time, they could recognize their vulnerable position and make a new commitment to the Lord! With His help all things are possible, right?!

"I can see that this whole area of staying strong during the Great Tribulation is a topic that needs its own teaching session. As a preview to that, let me say that I believe we can be so focused on Jesus and living safely committed in His *Secret Place* [25] that we can have victory during the Great Tribulation... even in the face of death, we can enjoy victory!

"Some of you might remember this early-on teaching... It wasn't our choice to be born when we were, nor where. That's what God wanted all along, right? So, He must see us as His End-Times Army. Since He wants us to be the generation that will face some super difficult times from the Antichrist, then He will equip us to be able to deal with that challenge. Now, that makes sense, doesn't it? He will anoint us to be His faithful followers.

"And, like the promise says, 'God won't allow any temptation to come before us that is beyond our ability to handle... but will provide us with a way of escape, that we may be able to endure it.' [26]

"God will never leave us, nor forsake us! [27] Never! He is my Everything! I can do all things through Christ, which strengthens me![28] This is the victory that overcomes the world, even my faith![29]

"We could go on and on confessing God's many promises... In fact, let's just do that very thing. Speak them forth and believe them again..."

There followed a volley of praise and speaking God's Word of victory. From across the whole room, every corner, nearly everyone. Even Sam joined in. Don wasn't sure what promise she latched onto, but there was no doubt she was in the spirit of the moment.

After a good five minutes the jubilation finally began to recede. But instead of frowns on their faces, there were smiles of all sizes! Don could see Kathy off to the side holding Rosalie Anne, as excited as anyone. It was a scene to behold. Under his breath Don said: *Thank You, Lord. Thank You! Thank you!*

"Well, saints, I think that's enough for this session. God will see us through whatever lies ahead. We can trust Him; we must trust Him. Let's meet again tomorrow evening. May you richly enjoy God's richest blessings this night and always... And, as we've now grown accustomed to, let me say that Kathy and I will lay hands on anyone in need of healing. We'll stick around for a while."

The people began to trickle out of the meeting room, no one requesting any prayer. Last to leave was Don and Kathy. They ran into Sam at the door. She said: "Great lesson tonight. I'll see you tomorrow, Don, nine o'clock sharp. And good night to you, Kathy."

While some of the faithful met at the break room for a final snack, Don and Kathy traveled on to their apartment. Once inside Kathy opened the conversation: "Well, Don, have you thought about how you're going to answer Sam tomorrow morning?"

"Yes, I've thought about it, and '*Yes*' is what I want to say to her. Sound okay?"

"Yes; still okay by me. I think it could be a great blessing to many people, not just our own but across the country. Who knows where it might lead? Well, God knows, doesn't He...? It sure was fun hanging out with Rosalie Anne tonight. She's such a fine baby; always smiling. I just love her!"

"You Grandmothers always say that! To a Grandmother there are no mediocre babies, especially their own... Say, tonight's session was a bit rocky at times. You could say jaw-dropping... did you notice?"

"I did. Here's what I think: you had some challenging questions thrown at you, but you handled them well. You told the people to trust in God's anointing. You need to do the same. God has anointed you to speak His heart into the people at this crucial time. He'll help you. He wants to. He's invested in The Factory and in this end-times teaching... don't ever forget that Mr. Don.

"By the way, I'll be keeping a close eye on you, so you better watch your step. I don't know if I ever shared this exactly, but the Lord told me to keep you in line and that's an assignment I'm taking very seriously..."

Don smiled. "I wouldn't have it any other way, Miss Kathy!"

CHAPTER TEN –

Yes, let's do it: I believe the Lord is behind this 100%.

T HE FOLLOWING DAY DON WAS IN HIS OFFICE as usual by 9:00 am. Sam walked in five minutes later. She plunked herself down on the chair facing Don. "Again, Don, great lesson last night. I caught it all on video. We could turn that into three 15-minute podcasts to get out on the internet...

"Oops, before I go too far, what is your answer to my proposal – to make those teaching sessions professionally media-ready for distribution far and wide?"

"My answer is *Yes, let's do it*... I believe the Lord is behind this 100%. But what about your job with the station?"

"What Job? The station manager and I had a parting of the ways, you might say. So, you see, I have all the time in the world..."

"Now, wait a minute, Sam! Hold on! You quit your job at the station?"

"Yup. Just up and left. Listen, I'd had it with his narrow-minded, left wing autocratic thinking. He was stifling my creative proclivities, don't you know? So, I quit..."

"You just QUIT?!"

"Don't give it another thought, Don. It's been brewing for some time. Personally, I'm glad it's over."

"So, now what? Are there plans for another anchor job? I'm sure you could take your pick of places to go and work... As you've said to me a time or two: The Sky's the Limit!"

"I know... but..."

"There's that *but*... but what, Sam?"

"But I'd just as soon stay right here – if you don't mind, that is."

"Here?! Oh, that would be great. You could get your bearings here. Help with the videos, check out other TV jobs at a leisurely pace, repurpose your life... Great to have you here. Once you come aboard, why don't you just walk around, get to know people, see what they do, see what draws them to this place.

"Oh, by the way, when were you planning to move in? How about furniture and your other stuff?"

"It's all in the backseat and trunk of my car. I've disposed of all of it. I'm foot loose and fancy free, as the old saying goes... I could move in today, in fact."

"Ah... Well, sure that could work. Let me get a hold of Verla and her cleaning crew and see if one of the vacant units could be ready by this afternoon. Okay?"

"Sounds great, Don. Thanks much for humoring an old TV anchor."

"And now, let me run over to Jerry's. He does a lot of special jobs around here. He'll know where it would be best to store your stuff and who could help today unload your car... Wow, this is going to be something, having you here with us. On behalf of all of us at The Factory, welcome!"

Don rose to leave and hunt down Jerry. Then he thought of another question for Sam and sat again. "Say, Sam, anything you'd like to tell me about what's behind your wanting to be here at The Factory?"

Sam was in unfamiliar territory: at a loss for words. Don patiently let the scene play out.

"Well," she began, "Ever since I met you and Kathy and The Factory Faithful, as you like to call them, I was drawn to your sincere hearts. I knew right off that Jesus was real to you guys. It used to be that way for me, years ago as a teen and young adult, after I went forward at a teen revival and received Jesus into my heart. I just couldn't wait to see what He had in store for my life... Well, wouldn't you know, the world was full of distractions and false promises. I seemed to gravitate to the worst part of what the world had to offer. It wasn't long before I lost sight of God's path for me; my heart grew lukewarm – like those you talked about last night. I was on the fence and then I found a niche that was filled with honors, applause, and acclaim – and Jesus got squeezed out...

"Well, I want that to change. I want to go back to those earlier, innocent years when Jesus was number one. And this is the place for me to do that! I can't thank you enough, Don!"

"You're very welcome... Isn't it just like the Lord, to work this out this way? Hallelujah! Okay, I'm off to find Jerry. Why don't you come with me for a quick tour along the way?"

A FEW DAYS LATER IT WAS TIME for another Planning Committee meeting. The usual were there: Don and Kathy, Doobie and Mark, Ben, and Jim. Don began with prayer and then posed the opening question: "So, does anyone have any *planning* news to share?"

Ben said, "The community work force is really putting out the effort and we continue to be well received, I'm happy to say. Clair is keeping us all highly organized. Sad to say, the sewing machines remain idle; I'm about ready to throw in that towel. The Girl Scouts are starting a new clothing design program and they could use those machines. I think we'll work out a deal with them."

"Good, Ben, keep working on those community relations," replied Don. "And, I think Doobie is busting at the seams to say something, right?"

Doobie cleared his throat and looked around the table. He enjoyed being in the limelight and savored the moment...

"Well, are you going to say something, Doobie, or just sit there basking in the sun?" Don asked.

"Come on, what is it Doobie," Mark added.

"Well, you guys know what day it is next Thursday?"

"Ah, no."

"Your birthday?"

"I have no clue."

"It is the one-year anniversary of when we first went out to look at the empty Factory. Don't you remember? All of us but Jim, and me of course, were part of that day... and obviously Mr. Greyheck was there."

Don spoke for most at the meeting. "I had no idea. One year? To the day?

"Oh, I get it now," added Kathy. "You want to throw another party, is that it, Doobie? And invite everyone and their brother, right?"

"Yup, I sure do, Miss Kathy; everybody I can think of! This is something to celebrate!"

"Well, be sure and include Mama Blanchard. There is always plenty of good food to eat, when you two get together," Kathy said with a smile.

Don exerted his leadership prerogative. "I say, have at it, Doobie. Make it your grandest party ever! I know you will. And I know it will be fun...

"And since I have the floor, let me bring you up to date on Sam. If you didn't already know, she quit her TV anchor job and has moved into The Factory for the time being. She'll be working diligently on taping and producing our teaching sessions..."

"It's not only that," interrupted Jim, "But she's been videoing everything around here: prayer groups, child-care, meal prep, working in the garden, you name it. I sort of made myself an unofficial *Sam Monitor* – just to keep track. She must be amassing a wealth of video... I don't suspect any foul-play or abuse of privilege; I'm just watching... Any objections, Dad?"

"Not a one," Don replied. "I trust you're being discrete about it all... Anything else today for the good of the order? Hearing none I declare this planning meeting over... Until two days from now, that is. Hope you're all coming to tonight's prayer and teaching session."

All arose to leave when Kathy had something else on her mind. "Just one more thing," she announced. All sat back down. When Kathy spoke, people listened.

"Go ahead, Kathy," Don encouraged.

"It's about Cornerstone Church and our affiliation with them. Have you noticed that that there are fewer and fewer Cornerstone people coming out to The Factory? And it's been ages since I've seen Pastor Daniel, except on Sundays. What do you think that means?"

"Now that you mention it, Kathy, I have noticed," answered Don. "I better have a chat with Pastor Daniel. I know we all enjoy the Cornerstone Sunday service... I tell you what: I'll pay him a visit and check things out. Thanks, Kathy... Anything else? Okay, see you later."

THE ONE-YEAR CELEBRATION was a big, gala event in the eyes of The Factory Faithful, with Doobie in charge. There must have been a good fifty people in attendance. Henry and his wife were invited and accepted the invitation, to everyone's delight.

Nearly a dozen children were there: three from Dianne and David, three from Mary Kay, and of course there was the newest, Rosalie Anne – and six children came with guests from outside The Factory: two with the Mayor and his wife, Cecilia; three with Jacob and Helen Ortiz; and one with Pastor Daniel and his wife. All were preschoolers and had a great time together. They loved it when Sam began to play her recorder, while encouraging them to dance. Sam was in her element, all right, entertaining the little ones. Grateful parents were happy to have Sam provide such a fun-filled diversion.

A highlight of the evening was a surprise duet, with none other than Jerry and D.J. Nelson. D.J. played his guitar and the two of them sang great harmony to "It is Well With My Soul." They were encouraged to sing more but they declined. Don made a mental note to ask this twosome to sing again at a later gathering.

David was again on security for the evening. Dianne was proud of her husband's dedication to his job. David had added another to his crew, and it was Jerry Nelson, the one that David had a run-in with about six months before, after the family feud blow-up! Jerry enjoyed his work at The Factory, and David could keep him in stitches with stories about his military career. Twice during the party that night, David poked his head in to give Don a "thumbs-up." Then David would find Dianne and blow her a kiss or two... what a loving couple!

And another couple that was catching much attention were Mark and Mary Kay - as the epitome of a budding romance. People commented on how they seemed to find the silliest of reasons to search one another out and spend time together. Here they were tonight sitting side by side, to no one's surprise.

At one-point Don came by to chat with them. "So, are you two having a good time?" Don asked.

Mark replied, "Sure am. That Doobie knows how to throw a party, doesn't he?"

Don had a specific inquiry for Mary Kay: "Mary Kay, I know that recent lesson about the Seals in the Book of Revelation threw you for a loop. I'm glad to see you haven't thrown in the towel on us."

"No, I wouldn't do that. This place has become my home for Gideon, Levi, and Natalie. But you should know that my brother, the Minister from Kansas, wants me to leave this place. He calls it a cult. He says it is leading me down the wrong path.

"I hate to think I'm causing such a family struggle. I don't know what to believe half the time," she added.

"If you want someone to believe, believe the Holy Spirit. Believe in that still, small voice on the inside... that's the Lord speaking to you through your spirit. He's the one that we can trust to lead us safely. Don't put your trust in me, Mary Kay, or in your brother. Make the Lord your Trust and Confidence...

"In fact, this area of putting our total trust in the Spirit, would be a great topic for a teaching session soon. Thanks for showing me. Bye." Don left to circulate among the other guests. Kathy was content to stay put and hold onto little Rosalie, who was receiving glowing remarks from passers-by.

It was easily recognized that Doobie headed up the festivities, so when he stood at the head of the table for an announcement or to share a silly joke, people turned to listen. No one was prouder of Doobie than Don.

Here's an example of one of his jokes: "Why do cows have hooves instead of feet? Answer: Lactose." Another example: "What do you call a bear with no teeth? Answer: A Gummy Bear."

On a more serious note, Doobie called on Ben to give a capsule description of where The Factory had come over the past year. Ben was happy to do so. As the self-appointed historian of The Factory, he was the most qualified. Besides Ben loved to talk publicly. He spent only twenty minutes bringing everyone up to speed on the growth and challenges of The Factory: through the headaches with making sure the building was up to code, to the trials and tribulations imposed by community leaders, to the stupendous challenge of responding to the tornado devastation.

When Ben was finished, he received a warm round of applause. Then the children took center stage to yell for Sam to play another song. She entertained this time with a spirited rendition of *"Old McDonald Had a Farm."* The children happily added the animal sounds.

No one seemed to want the evening to end. But one by one they finally began to bid farewell and leave. "Another great party, Mama Blanchard, Thanks," yelled Don as he was leaving her and others in charge of clean up. Mark and Mary Kay seemed to volunteer for that job as well. Onlookers smiled and knew one of the reasons behind the couple's sweet gesture was simply to be together.

There was one more item on Don's to-do list. That was to contact Pastor Daniel. He saw the Pastor helping his wife with her jacket and said directly: "Hey, Pastor Daniel, just a quick comment. I'd like to have some time soon to get together and talk. That possible?"

"Sure, Don. Anytime. Tomorrow afternoon?"

"That would be great! Three o'clock? I met you at your office."

"Sounds great. See you then... Nice party and celebration, by the way."

PASTOR DANIEL WAS A BIT STANDOFFISH during his meeting with Don. After some preliminary chit chat, Don asked the obvious question: "Pastor, you seem down in the dumps. Anything I can help you with?"

"Oh, that obvious, huh?" he replied. Don waited for more. The Pastor went on. "I'm having a struggle trying to reconcile these two opposing theories about end-times and when the Rapture is to happen. My training says the Rapture will be the next great event to happen and then we are out of here. But you say that we are slated to be here during the great tribulation. Now it can't be both ways."

Don's heart went out to Pastor Daniel. "I can see the struggle. One has a promise of escape and a one-way ticket to Heaven. The other has only a promise of having to go through some real challenging times. Both views say we will escape God's wrath upon an unbelieving and rebellious world. And we both would agree that when the Antichrist comes into his power, it will be a most devastating time for all inhabitants. The crux of the difference is whether we, the Church, will be here when he comes into his power.

"So, to that question, I say yes – there will be a Wrath of Satan for us to endure. Many, like your Bible College teachers and other Church leaders, say no there won't be any such tribulation to endure."

"I don't have a strong conviction about either way," the Pastor explained. "I think I'd rather have an assurance of one direction or the other, not this in-between stuff!"

"I see the frustration you have – and it's understandable. Can you think of anything I can do to help," Don asked?

"No, not really. I need to work this out in my own prayer time with the Holy Spirit's help..."

"You're right about one thing!" Don interrupted. "That's where the truth lies, with the Holy Spirit. I'll pray for you, Pastor, that you'll find the Truth that you're searching for about these questions. In the meantime, I want to reiterate that we at The Factory are blessed because of your Sunday morning services..."

Don suddenly noticed an ornate plaque, setting in a nearby chair. It looked important. Don inquired. "Pastor, I couldn't help but notice your plaque over there... Congratulations on whatever honor it is com- memorating for you. I'm sure its well-deserved."

"Oh, this?" Pastor Daniel stood to retrieve it. "I'm not all that sure what it's about. Apparently, I've been selected to head up a regional host of Pastors in the Greensville area. Sounds like an excuse to have more meetings, that's what I think. Just what I need!"

"I couldn't help but notice," Don commented, "that it was signed by our Lieutenant Governor, Carroll Leonard... I met that man once at the Mayor's office." Don stood to leave.

"Well, thanks again for seeing me today," said Don. "I hope the good relationship between The Factory and Cornerstone can continue for a long time. Bye for now." Don and the Pastor ended their time with a hearty handshake.

Don left the meeting with an uneasy feeling in his spirit. "Now, what is Pastor Daniel doing with Mr. Leonard, I wonder?"

I was right not to divulge more of my misgivings about the Lieutenant Governor, right Lord? That's how I felt You were leading...

You were right, Don. Pastor Daniel has some issues to work out in his own heart that are beyond your need-to-know. Some of that has to do with Mr. Leonard. I hope I come out on top in the Pastor's struggles, for his own sake. Keep him in your prayers, Don.

That I will do, Lord.

DON LOOKED FORWARD TO THE TEACHING scheduled for that night. He called it: *Two Groups in Heaven.*

Before the teaching started, Don was proud to introduce Jerry and D.J. who agreed to sing another duet. It was again an old, familiar hymn: "*At the cross, at the cross, where I first met the Lord...*" Their effort was much appreciated by the group that had gathered. Announcements were called for. Miss Verla told the group that there is a need for addi- tional volunteers to provide childcare when there were teachings or group meetings.

Miss Verla stated her case. "Barbara and Mama Blanchard need our help. It would be good at least to share in that ministry so they get a chance to hear the teaching. We could all agree on that. Right? There is a sign-up sheet on the childcare door." Several raised their hand to help.

"Anything else?" asked Don.

Ben posed a question. "Where are Mark and Mary Kay tonight? Has anyone seen them? They're usually so good about being with us."

Doobie answered the question. "They're outside somewhere, taking a walk I suppose. They've been doing that a lot lately. Makes you wonder... ya know?"

"Now Doobie before you jump to conclusions, better get your facts straight," Don warned. "Ya know... Sometimes, Doobie, you make me wonder... ya know?"

"What!? What do you mean, Brother Don?"

"Oh, I was just kidding. Couldn't you tell I was pulling your leg?"

"Oooh! Oooh! So that's why my leg hurts so much. Oooh!"

People were beginning to snicker at the antics of Doobie and his chair. Kathy thought it her duty to get the evening back on track.

"Okay, if you two could stop with the Laurel and Hardy routine, I'd like to hear what the Holy Spirit wants to teach us tonight!"

"You are so right, Kathy. Sorry folks, I got carried away," Don conceded.

"Friends, in the Book of Revelation, the Bible describes several groups in Heaven. We'll consider two of them tonight, one by one.

"First is the group depicted in Revelation, Chapter Six, Verses 9-11:

> *'And when He had opened the fifth seal, I saw under the altar the souls of them that were slain for the word of God, and for the testimony which they held:*

> *'And they cried with a loud voice, saying, How long, O Lord, holy and true, do You not judge and avenge our blood on them that dwell on the earth?*

'And white robes were given unto every one of them; and it was said unto them, that they should rest yet for a little season, until their fellow servants also and their brethren, that should be killed as they were, should be fulfilled.'

"So, I take it, this describes those that are slain during the Great Tribulation, or the Wrath of Satan, as I refer to it. We're talking about those that do not yield to the Antichrist's intense pressures to forsake God and give up our allegiance to Him. This is a picture of the fifth seal. More about this later.

"The second group described is in the next Chapter, Revelation, Chapter 7, Verses 9, 13-14:

'After this I beheld, and lo, a great multitude, which no man could number, all of the nations, and kindreds, and people, and tongues, stood before the throne, and before the Lamb, clothed with white robes, and palms in their hands...

'And one of the elders answered, saying unto me, Who are these which are arrayed in white robes? And where did they come from?

'And I said unto him, Sir, you know. And he said unto me, These are they who came out of great tribulation, and have washed their robes, and made them white in the blood of the Lamb.'

"This is a picture of the Rapture, or rather the results of the Rapture: a great multitude who come out (or, are raptured) from the Great Tribulation. This is part of the opening of the sixth seal in Heaven, when cosmic disturbances occur. This announces the Day of the Lord and the start of the Wrath of God, or the trumpet and bowl judgments, from which we escape through the Rapture of the faithful Church.

"Throughout all our discussion about end-times, we need to keep in mind the distinction between the *Wrath of Satan* and the *Wrath of God*. We, God's Saints or His Elect, escape His wrath through the Rapture. However, there is another time of wrath, from the hand of Satan, working through his Antichrist, that happens just before God's wrath. That first time of wrath Jesus referred to as the *Great Tribulation*. And He said it would be so intense and formidable that even the Elect could not endure it. It would eventually overtake even God's strongest saint, if it hadn't been for God cutting this time short! Hallelujah!

"Jesus explained: '... *for then shall be great tribulation, such as was not since the beginning of the world to this time, no, nor ever shall be. And except those days should be shortened, there should no flesh be saved: but for the elect's sake those days shall be shortened.*' [30]

"This description by Jesus reminds me of the passage in 1 Corinthians 10 about temptations. Here Jesus promised two things: first, that He would not allow us to be tempted above what we are able to bear; and second, that with every temptation, He would provide a way of escape so we could bear up under it.[31]

"And in the great tribulation by the Antichrist there will surely be plenty of temptations and pressures to give up, to yield to his terror tactics and turn your back on God. If the pressure is intense, God will see to it that you'll be able to bear it: He'll anoint you with a big dose of His strength to deal with it head-on; or He'll provide you with a way of escape. Our job is to stay faithful, to trust in Him only.

"That's what Peter should have done, instead of relying on his own strength the night Jesus was betrayed. Let's visit Peter again. Remember? Peter said: '*Lord I'll never forsake you... I'll even die for you...*'[32] Poor Peter had no idea how intense the temptation to forsake Jesus would be.

"The days ahead in the Great Tribulation assure us that we too will be sorely tempted, but unlike Peter, we have the advantage of understanding the New Testament teaching on enduring temptations. Also, we have the benefit of having the Holy Spirit in us and upon us, which Peter hadn't yet received.

"Plus, don't forget something we've mentioned before, that the Lord intentionally planned for us to be on the earth during the difficult days ahead. It's not by accident but by His design. I believe we could rightly be called the Lord's *End-Time Army*. So, with God's plan comes God's obligation to equip and empower His Army. No one is called into an army without being outfitted with everything needed for victory...

"Let me pause there. Any questions or comments, Saints? ...Hmmm... Nothing at all? Surely, someone has a comment."

"Well, Don," Dianne began slowly, "I enjoyed tonight's teaching. It tells about some very rough waters ahead but gives us some assurance of God helping us through it all... I think I'll be able to sleep easier tonight."

"Thank you, Dianne."

"I agree." "So do I." "Me, too." "Thanks, Don." Came the replies from others.

More positive comments were made. Don was encouraged at the depth of those remarks. Then a most challenging question followed, from Jenny.

"Dad, how about babies in all this. How is God going to handle that? Do I get to be raptured with Rosalie in my arms? It's a bit unnerving to think about..."

"Yeah, Mr. Crawford, I've been wondering along those same lines," added Nancy Struble, a newcomer from one week before. "I'm thinking of my daughter from Michigan who has two pre-school kids. Will she be going to Heaven with her two hanging on to each hand? Surely the God of Love that we know will make some provision for young families to be and stay together."

Don was stopped cold! He had never considered that scenario. He figured he might as well be forthright and open... "Jenny, Nancy, I've never considered those questions, so I don't know what to say. But I promise you and the other mothers with us tonight that I will go before the Lord for answers. Okay for now?"

"Okay for now, but don't forget," replied Jenny.

"Rest assured Jenny and all you mothers, I won't let him forget," Kathy insisted, as she turned to face the assembly.

Overall, it was a good evening. Before the group broke up, Sam stood aside her camera and caught Don's attention, to give him the "thumbs-up." The session had been safely recorded.

Don waved back at her to signal a "Thank You" for her work that evening.

CHAPTER ELEVEN –

Do you realize what this means, Kathy?

ONE DAY KATHY FOUND AN INTERESTING news article in the local weekly newspaper, tucked away in the corner of page 8. She knew Don would be interested.

"Don, you might enjoy this news story; in fact, I know you will. It's about building the third Temple in Jerusalem. They're almost ready to start."

"What?! Let me see that!" Don nearly tore away the paper from Kathy's hand. He read some highlights out loud... *"This will be Jerusalem's third Temple and plans call for it to be erected in the City of David, not atop the so-called Temple Mount where the Dome of the Rock and Al Aqsa Mosque sit... It's now understood that the former Temple (that Jesus knew and visited) was in the City of David, just to the south of the Temple Mount about 600 feet... What we know as the Temple Mount was more likely the site for a large garrison or fort, housing up to 1000 Roman Soldiers..."* [33]

Don laid the newspaper on the kitchen table, leaned back in his chair, and looked intently at Kathy. "Do you realize what this means, Kathy? We could be weeks, at the most months, away from the completion of this Tribulation Temple."

The news was so overwhelming that Don had to stop and catch his breath and get the right perspective on what this new development really meant. He could only conclude the obvious: "Kathy, this means the time for the Antichrist to show his hand is fast approaching... at least faster than we thought! As soon as that Temple is erected, he'll have his spot to shine... No, no. Bad choice of words! – I mean he'll have his opportunity to show his hand, when he desecrates the Temple's Holy of Holies and demands that the world revere him as God."

Kathy ventured a thought. "Don, this is getting too serious. Before it was feasible for the Antichrist to come into the world and do his thing, but now it is literally about to happen... And you think we only have weeks or a few months before it does happen?"

"I can't think of any reason why the unveiling of the Antichrist would not coincide with the opening of the new Temple. Sounds like something a soon-to-appear global leader would do, just to make his entrance onto the world stage more dramatic. If that be the case, then we're talking about only weeks or so...

"I know it seems awfully fast, but I would think that the Jewish Leaders are, at this time, after all their centuries of waiting, more interested in a speedy build than having an ornate Temple... *'We can add the ornate finishing touches later, let's just get on with implementing the animal sacrificial system,'* they are no doubt thinking.

"We know also that the Antichrist will successfully maneuver a peace accord in the Middle East. How he gets all those warring factions to even sit together, let alone enter a seven-year peace treaty, is beyond me. But the Bible says he will do it... There are passages in the Book of Daniel that talk of this very thing; I'm going to study that this afternoon.

"Say, here's an idea: I wonder if we could identify by name this architect of the peace accord. I've got to *google* the "Middle East Peace Accord" and see what comes up. I gotta believe one of the signatories is the Antichrist himself...Hmmm, the name Gabrinne is ringing a faint bell in my head for some reason...

"Oh, I remember! He was chosen as the first President of the Accord, which is going to have a revolving leadership, much like the European Union. I remember, he was the main architect of the Mediterranean Union, that went into effect a few years back.

"Wow, Kathy! It could well be this Gabrinne guy! This man is already revered by a good part of the middle eastern world. He'll likely be up for the Nobel Peace Prize... And I believe the next go-around for that award is this coming October.

"I wonder if there is anyone else in this crazy world right now who is tracking this thing along the same line as we are..."

Don paused to draw a deep breath. "Whew! Kathy! This is something, isn't it. This must be the focus for tonight's teaching. Let's see if we can get everyone there that's available! Let's both of us spread the word as we go about our day... It's not going to be business around here as usual, not ever again!

"Do we have any doughnuts in the house? I'm suddenly as hungry as a bear... a North Carolina bear at that!"

THE PEOPLE GATHERED WITH HIGH anticipation of hearing something special in that night's lesson. Once there were numerous personal invites extended for the night by Don and Kathy, the faithful began to sense in their spirits that this lesson would be unique. Pastor Daniel was there, with his wife. So was Henry and Louise Greyheck. Doobie and the regulars, of course. Mark and Mary Kay sat together. Even the new lady from a week ago, Nancy Struble, was there again. And faithful Sam was stationed in the back with her camera. People were abuzz as they took their seats. When Don stood to teach, hungry hearts grew focused.

"Folks, I can sense that you're all ready for a notable lesson. First, let me apologize to the mothers out there. Tonight is not about the questions raised recently about children and the Rapture. I'm still working on that one...

"No, tonight is a brand-new topic. It's about the building of the Temple in Jerusalem. And what does that have to do with anything of importance, you ask. Well, it's my hope that at the close of our time tonight, you will have a better understanding of how the new Temple is a significant signpost along God's pathway of end-times events.

"Today, Kathy came across a news article that says that the Jewish people are going to start erecting a new Temple in Jerusalem, the third one in history – but in a much different location than has for centuries been assumed would be the case. Instead of having the new Temple on top of the Temple Mount, where the Muslims have two significant holy sites of their own, the plan calls for the new Temple to be built in what is referred to as the City of David, a 12-acre plot of land that's 600 feet to the south.

"What's special about that? Well, for one thing, this means to me that the Temple can be set up and operational in weeks or months, rather than years. It would have taken years probably to work out an arrange- ment with the Muslims to share that space on the Temple Mount. I can get you more data about the history of that piece of land if you like. Just let me know. Otherwise, let's get on with what all of this means for us today.

"Jesus taught us to be watching for *signs* of His coming. He said we can't know the day or the hour, but we can see some signs and know the season. One of the big signs to my thinking is what the Bible and Jesus referred to as the *Abomination of Desolation* by the Antichrist. This will occur when he goes into the new Temple, into the inner Holy of Holies, mind you, where only the High Priest is allowed, and only once a year! And there the Antichrist proclaims himself to be God! He des- ecrates the Temple first by his being there, and second by his efforts at self-deification.

"Most Bible Scholars, who promote the common view of end-times understanding, say the Rapture is the next important event to happen and there are no signs to be watching for that will signal the coming of the Rapture. It is sign-less; nothing in God's timing is to precede it. It could happen at any moment, they say.

"But I beg to disagree. Jesus tells us to be on the watch for signs, to be sober and vigilant doing so. And to me this rebuilding of the Jerusalem Temple is as important a sign as you could want. When the Antichrist des- ecrates the Temple, that will mark the start of his reign of terror to coerce the world into proclaiming him as God. He'll institute many devilish ways of coercion, done by the will and empowerment of Satan himself. And remember again Jesus referred to this time as the *Great Tribulation*.

"Well, Saints I could go on and on, but let's focus on the practical side of things for a bit. I hope I've made it clear that the importance of this latest development is to show us that the *Wrath of Satan* is about to start sooner than any of us anticipated.

"What can we expect? Overall, we can expect our lives to change drastically. When this might start, or what course it might take is unknown. We'll be on a day-by-day basis to learn more and to listen for the leading of the Holy Spirit along the way.

"We're going to lose many of the freedoms we now take for granted. There will be mounting pressures to do things the Antichrist way; there will be rewards for those who do and punishments for those who refuse.

"One area that is likely to be a concern is that cash as we know it will become obsolete. So, on a practical note, as we plan for these coming days, we need to gather and stock-pile provisions for ourselves. Doobie, how's your garden looking these days? Whatever it takes, get it expanded and growing. Mark, I'm going to count on you in the weeks ahead to help find things we'll need to keep The Factory a viable place to live.

"Questions about travel come to mind. I think travel will become seriously curtailed, then stopped; and our ability to communicate will also. We'll lose smart phone use, computers, too; and cars, planes and trains all run on computers remember.

"I don't want this to be a doom and gloom session. We've said this before, and it bears repeating: *God wants us prepared but not scared*. For sure He wants us to depend on Him for everything we need, and a large part of that is to depend on His Holy Spirit to give us the wisdom we need. Rest assured, folks, we will be taking this challenge very seriously. It should be priority-one for all of us to seek out the Lord, ask for His guidance, His grace, and His ability.

"Let me share on a personal note. Earlier today when Kathy and I first considered the ramifications of the Temple rebuild, I found myself both excited and somber at the same time. Now, another word for somber could be sad, melancholy, or you could say in plain-old English: depressed.

"Then I thought this: *Now wait a minute. Wait just a cotton-pickin' minute! I need to cast the care of that somber mood over to the Lord.* That's what it is, you know, a mood, a feeling, a fickle state of mind, ever changeable, without any real teeth to it. It's just the work of the devil wanting me to stew and fret and begin to question God's faithfulness.

"Well, I tell you this; you all are my witnesses: I'm not going to stew or fret! I'm going to rejoice and be glad! I turn the whole matter over to the Lord. I refuse to worry! I repeat. I REFUSE TO WORRY! I will rejoice in the Lord always! Again, I say I will rejoice! God has got us covered and protected... in both our coming and our going!

"Join with me, folks. Let's keep looking up! That's where our Answer is. Let's not get stuck on looking around at our circumstances; that will only add fear and confusion. No, instead let's look Up! That's where our Help comes from! Amen?"

"Amen!" "Amen!" "Amen, Brother Don!"

Don was proud of his troops that night. They seemed to really catch the importance of the new Temple as a harbinger of the fast-approaching end of days. The session ended on a high note, to be sure. Then Don went by to talk with Henry and Louise, since they were not regular attenders at the evening sessions. "Good to see the two of you here tonight," said Don, as he extended a handshake and pulled over a chair... "Any comments or questions about our topic tonight?"

Henry was reticent, but Louise voiced her view. "It certainly sounds like we're in for some hard times ahead..." Don could sense that she wanted to share more, so he smiled and paused... She continued. "Ah, Don, I don't how to say this exactly..."

"We're not big on proper decorum around here," replied Don to encourage Louise. "Just speak your heart."

"Don, we – that is Henry and I – we are not saved. We don't know Jesus, like you know Him, but we sure want to. Don't we Henry!"

"Yes, Don, Louise is right. Ever since I first got tangled up with your bunch here, I've had a longing in my heart that just keeps growing and growing. Both of us do. Would you help us, Don?"

"Certainly, I will and I'm going to ask my wife, Kathy, to join us. Let me get her attention... There, she saw me and here she comes. Kathy, Louise and Henry are asking to be saved; they want to know Jesus like we know Him. Isn't that just super? We can take care of that business right now. Okay?"

Kathy smiled broadly. "Oh, my, the angels in Heaven are going to be rejoicing tonight," Kathy said gently, as she grabbed Louise's hand. Others began to realize this was a most special moment and they gathered close by to pray softly.

Don continued. "Now, folks, this is not complicated. Let me lead you in a prayer. You repeat after me and mean it with your whole heart... Okay? Here we go...

"Heavenly Father... I know in my heart that I need a Savior... And Jesus, as the spotless Lamb of God, is that Savior... He died for me at Calvary, taking all my sin away... I receive Him now as my Savior... and as the Lord of my life... Come and take over my life, Jesus... I declare that I am now born-again... and filled with the Spirit... a child of God for eternity... and my real home is now in Heaven... where I'll be forever... Amen!"

"Folks, welcome to the Family of God," Don added. Others nearby came over to extend their good wishes to the Greyhecks.

"That's it, Louise and Henry," said Kathy. "Jesus will reveal Himself to you both in the days to come. And you'll know Him like the rest of us around here do... I urge you to get out your Bible and start reading... the Gospel of John is a good place to begin."

"Thanks, Don and Kathy, and all of you," said Louise as she looked around at all the smiling faces.

Henry stood and mustered the biggest smile Don had ever seen on his face. "I believe you'll be seeing more and more of us in the coming days."

"Great to hear. Have a good night. Keep looking up, Henry and Louise!" said Don as they left the room.

"Wow! What an unexpected blessing," Don remarked.

"It sure was," answered Doobie, who extended a high-five to Don, then to Kathy, then to whoever was nearby.

"Thanks, Einstein!"

THE FOLLOWING DAY DON SET THREE goals for himself: to get the Lord's direction about infants and the rapture, to study the Book of Daniel about the Antichrist, and to talk with Mark and Mary Kay. As he set out to go to his office, who should he see in the hallway but Mark and Mary Kay. Mary kay was dropping off her children to Miss Verla and Sam at childcare.

"Hey, Mary Kay and Mark," Don yelled. "Got a minute or two to talk?"

"Sure; we're available," answered Mark. "Where? Your office? Okay."

The three got settled into chairs. "What's up?" asked Mark.

"Well, I was just wondering about the two of you. Rumor has it that you two are... are developing into a couple... like a couple might do who wants more than friendship... Oh, dear, I'm just stumbling along, aren't I."

Mary Kay answered. She looked at Mark and said: "You're right, Don. The rumors are right." She smiled at Mark ever so lovingly...

Mark interrupted: "In this crazy world about to get a lot crazier, Mary Kay and I want something special... It's marriage. What do you think?"

"Marriage? Here? Now? Wow!" Don was taken back. "I don't know what to think..."

"There wouldn't be any reason not to, would there?" Mary Kay asked.

"Well, no, I guess there wouldn't be any reason not to. I can't think of any right off," Don replied. "But just considering the times we live in... I wonder... what ... Hmmm..." Don was momentarily lost for words.

"Listen, what does your family think of all this, Mary Kay?" he asked.

"They're cautious and scared. They still think I should come home to Kansas to get out from under the bad influence of this cult, as they call it. Of course, they've never met Mark in person. We had a video chat with them a couple of days ago. And that went well. But it's not the same I know. One of the things I like about Mark, one of many, is that he helps me understand what the lessons mean. I see you and my minister-brother as having vastly different views on end-times. I'd be lost trying to figure it all out if it weren't for Mark."

Mark smiled at the admiration given by Mary Kay, then he got practical: "Listen, Don, the bottom line here is that Mary Kay and I want to get married. We'd like you to officiate. Mary Kay was going to ask Mr. Tucker to give her away. We want Doobie and Suzy to stand up for us... We've got most of it figured out."

"Sounds like you've given this a lot of thought," Don concluded.

"Another thing, Don," added Mary Kay, "Neither of my parents are living, my grandma in Kansas is disabled. It's my older brother, the Minister, who might object the most to the wedding. I know my previous relationships with men were bad choices with bad outcomes. But now it's different... I just wish my brother could understand."

"Okay, let's say this wedding goes ahead as you want," Don began slowly. Mary Kay and Mark both brightened at the thought and clasped hands. "You need to know that in Heaven, there is no marriage like we've come to know it. On the earth, marriage has a special purpose in God's design, that won't be the case in Heaven.

"I believe every individual in God's Heaven will have their own mansion. So, when we get there I won't be living with Kathy; I'll see her, and we'll hang out together, I imagine... but it won't be like now. And the same goes for you two... Do you get the picture I'm painting here?"

"Yeah, I guess so," said Mark slowly, "but it's still okay with you to get married, right?" Before Don could answer, Mary Kay brought another element to the discussion. "Also, Don, I want Gideon and Levi and Natalie to have the blessing of a real, loving father, even if it's only for a short time on this earth. They like Mark a whole bunch."

"Well, I say then, let's have a wedding!" Don smiled and shook their hands... "Congratulations Mary Kay and congratulations to you, Mark."

The two of them began to rise, when Don added: "Oh, one more thing... Oh, oh, did I hear a groan from you, Mark?"

"No, I'm okay. Whatever it takes to make this a reality. I'm listening, Don," Mark said.

"I need to verify something," he went on more seriously. "Where are the two of you regarding your relationship to Jesus? Would you call yourself a born-again Christian – because, if not, that's the first place we need to go before getting all engrossed in this wedding plan."

"Well, Don, you remember that first night you invited us to give our life to Jesus? That was at the beginning well over a year ago. I raised my hand and received Jesus into my heart. Best decision I ever made," shared Mark.

"Yes, I remember that night, Mark," answered Don, "and it was such a blessing to witness your decision then and see your growth over the months since... How about you, Mary Kay."

"I was born-again several years ago as a young teenager living in Kansas," she said. "It happened through our church youth group. And, yes, Jesus is still number one in my life!"

"I can vouch for that," added Mark.

"Okay, then, that part is over. So, let the wedding begin... Oh, wait, here's another important question," Don went on.

"Now what?" asked Mark, with a hint of surly.

"Take it easy, Mark, this will be my first wedding to officiate," Don responded. "So... let's all just smile for a moment... Take a deep breath.

"Here's the serious question needing an answer. It's simple enough. When? When is this big event to take place? Have you thought about that?"

"We want it to be as soon as possible," they said in unison.

"I think this is where Kathy fits in. I'm going to turn this over to her. We'll call her *The Factory Wedding Planner*. She'll be talking more with the two of you. We want this to be a wedding to remember, don't we?

"Oh, oh. I see two worried faces. Don't worry, you two, Kathy is a fast planner. She'll have your wedding up and going in no time at all... Wow! A wedding here at The Factory. I'm already excited because I get to be the one to break the news to Kathy!

"Thanks for sharing today... Oh! Wait a minute!" Don cuffed his ear, like he was listening to a far-off signal. "Do you hear it?"

"What are you talking about, Don?" inquired Mark seriously.

"I can hear them... wedding bells, chiming over the countryside to say that we will soon be full of processionals, wedding cake, honeymoon... well, you understand. Have a good day, you Lovebirds."

No more did Mark and Mary Kay leave, than Kathy strolled into Don's office from the opposite direction. "Hey, honey, how are you doing?" she asked. Don brightened at the prospects of being able to share the good news about Mary Kay and Mark.

"We're going to have a wedding! Did you hear me, Kathy? We're going to have a wedding. I just finished talking with Mark and Mary Kay about it. It's green lights all the way. And now I'm sitting here across the table talking with *The Factory's Wedding Planner, Extraordinaire*. That be you, Kathy. What do you think?"

"Oh, I love weddings and as you know I've had a little experience at it with two daughters," she replied. "So... When and where?"

"The *where* is here. The *when* is 'as soon as possible.' We have here a case of two love-struck young-ins who want to tie the knot as quickly as they can. I told them you were a fast Wedding Planner, able to accommodate their desires."

"Hmmm, I'd better get going then. I'll get with Doobie, Mama Blanchard, and Jenny, too. We'll get our heads together. Music... let's see. I got an idea along that line; it'll be a surprise. Cake? Reception? Hmmm... Maybe we could skype the ceremony so Mary Kay's family in Kansas could be a part... I suppose you're officiating?"

"Yup. I was their first choice," answered Don grinning from ear to ear.

"I hate to burst your bubble, Mr. Officiator," retorted Kathy. "You were their only choice!"

"Ohhh... do you always have to be so blunt and correct?"

"But that's one thing you like about me, Don. Remember?"

"Yeah, you're right... Just think, Kathy, in an otherwise dismal world, about to fall off the edge of sanity, this wedding will be something to behold! It will be good for everyone's mental outlook, including mine!

"Listen, I'd love to talk more, Kathy, but I've got some studying to do. See you later, Miss Wedding Planner."

"Later. Bye."

Once alone Don got out his Bible and turned his thoughts toward the Lord. There was still that issue about children and the Rapture.

"Lord, I come today asking for wisdom and understanding. As you know it's about young children and the Rapture of the Church... I know children are blessed when the parents are blessed; Your Word clearly states that many times. Surely You would want the little ones, before they're capable of deciding about Jesus, to go with their parents in the Rapture. Wouldn't that be an example of the parents' blessing flowing down and covering their offspring?"

"Yes, Don, you are on the right track," came the reply. "Go back to something you've already studied in Romans 7:9."

Don found the reference and read it again out loud: "*For I was alive without (or, apart from) the law once: but when the commandment (law) came, sin was revived, and I (the spirit man, the real me) died...*"

"Lord, I once heard a preacher explain this verse in this way: *'When I was born and began to grow as an infant, I was innocent; I didn't know sin; I couldn't sin. And if I died at that point I would go straight to heaven (that's what happens to babies who die at birth or are aborted). But when I reached the age of reason and I knew right from wrong, then I needed to have a Redeemer to receive eternal life.'*"

"When the Preacher explained it that way, it made good common sense. That would seem to apply to my granddaughter, Rosalie, still an infant and probably to Natalie, Levi, and maybe to the youngest of Dianne and David's three children. But those children older may have already reached the age of reason. Their parents need to talk seriously with them and invite them to ask Jesus into their hearts... What do You think, Lord?"

"I think you're on target here. This will be good news to the parents who have a young child and a challenge to the parents of older children."

Don continued. "Maybe it would be good for me to meet as a group with the parents involved. I could help them introduce to their children the role of Jesus as Savior if they want. But, as I think about it, maybe it would be better for the parents to do this on their own."

"Yes, doing this alone would be better." The Lord brought forth one additional point. "You might also talk with your childcare workers who know these children. Perhaps those workers could present an emphasis on Salvation and Jesus during their classes. Sam would be a good one to do this."

"Excellent idea! And, yes, Sam would be great at this. The children already love her and enjoy her presence and light-hearted spirit... Thank You, Lord, for helping me get a better handle on all this and for our time together."

"You are welcome Don. Thanks for asking... Now if you ever want some input about officiating at a wedding, just ask. I love weddings!"

CHAPTER TWELVE –

The Factory was buzzing with wedding plans.

OVER THE NEXT THREE WEEKS everyone at The Factory was buzzing with plans for the upcoming wedding. Mama Blanchard oversaw the reception and making the cake. Doobie as the best man seemed more nervous than the groom to be. A wedding dress was personally being made by Clair Tucker. Her husband, Ben, must have told everyone at least twice that he was escorting the bride down the aisle. Mark and Mary Kay had another couple of counseling session with Don. He pronounced them: *Primed and Ready!*

Kathy supervised all the preparations and left no detail unattended. She was ably assisted by her daughter, Jenny. One of Kathy's most delightful and fun accomplishments as *Wedding Planner* was the music for the ceremony. It was a surprise known only by her, Mark, Mary Kay, and Sam. Kathy discovered that Sam used to play the accordion and was good at it. Kathy asked her one day if she would like to have an accordion which she could use providing music for the wedding. And Sam was elated! So, Kathy turned to The Factory's number one procurer of this and that, of the hard-to-find, Mark McKenna.

Mark gave his typical reply: "You want an accordion? No problem. I know some people." Within two days, Sam had her accordion!

It was unfortunate that no one from Mary Kay's family could come to the wedding. Her brother, the Minister, thought he should stay and look after the grandmother. Jenny took on the job of skyping the event so the Kansas family could at least see the ceremony in real time.

Lastly, the construction crew busied themselves renovating the apartment that would soon be occupied by Mark and Mary Kay and the three boys.

One afternoon Don was out back, taking a break and enjoying a nice stretch of sunny weather, when he encountered his dear friend, Doobie, working in the garden.

"Farmer McDoobie, how does your garden grow?" Don asked as he drew near.

"Just fine." Doobie looked up from his crouch amidst the cucumbers.

"You're not making up a new name for me, are you?"

"No. No. As I turned the corner and saw you out here working, it just seemed to fit the occasion... and as I look around, I see some luscious looking tomatoes and many vines of robust green beans. You do have a way with plants, you know."

"I agree. It must be a gift from God. I talk to my plants and I bless them. I remind them that they are fulfilling a most important job: keeping God's children fed and healthy!" Both men found a seat on the little Bench that flanked the garden.

"Doobie, my man, you never cease to amaze me."

"Well... ah... Thank you. I'm just being me."

"Well... whatever you're doing keep it up. Say, wanted to ask: Do you need some more helpers for the garden?"

"No. Not really. Right now, there's not a whole lot of work to do; just watch the plants grow and snare a weed or two. I'll be doing some serious harvesting in a couple of weeks. Then I'll need some assistance. But there's always some people who are willing to come help...

"It's pretty quiet right now... Don, you might not believe this, but there are times when it's real still like this, I can actually hear the plants growing."

"I believe it, Doobie. I believe it because you said it... Doobie, you're a good man. I know the Lord is well pleased with you. Well, gotta run. Working on our next teaching: more about the Antichrist. See you later."

As Don left Doobie and started back to his office, he was hailed down by Clair Tucker, the official-unofficial secretary for The Factory. "Don, I just had an interesting call from a Betty McPherson – does that name ring a bell? – she wants to come out and talk with you about making things right. I told her I would talk with you and call her back. What should I do?"

"Hmmm... Let's see... How about telling her to come out tomorrow about 1:00 o'clock. We can talk then... By the way, have you seen Kathy around?"

"Kathy? I just saw her going into the break room... I'll call Betty back and give her tomorrow at 1:00."

Clair walked briskly back to the office. Don liked that lady; she was always so pleasant and accommodating, and nothing seemed to get her flustered. She could multi-task like no one else. As far as he was concerned, Clair was the *official* secretary of The Factory.

Don was left standing for a moment in front of his office with a choice: to find Kathy and tell her about Betty or to get busy preparing his lesson on the Antichrist. He opted for Kathy and found her alone in the break room.

"Oh, hi, Don," she greeted Don with her typical smile. "Here to take a break with me?"

"No, well sort of. I have something to talk to you about. Do you remember Betty McPherson, Director of Social Services for the County? She was one of the three key players that caused us such anguish when The Factory was trying to get into compliance with those building and city codes?"

"Yes, I remember her. Why?"

"Well, Clair just had a call from her. She wants to talk about making things right between her and The Factory... Clair is calling her back to say I would meet with her tomorrow at 1:00. So, here's a plan. You and I meet with her tomorrow at 1:00 o'clock. Then after about fifteen minutes I'll leave, or Clair can call me and get me out of the office. Then you and she could talk alone. That way you could check her out... her intentions, her sincerity..."

"Don, if the lady is truly seeking to make amends and is asking for your forgiveness, you have to give it to her and right then. If she has any other motive or is not at all sincere... well, that's a different story."

"Okay. I hear you. That makes sense... I don't mean to beg for trouble. I guess I gotta relax, trust in the Lord to guide us and give us understanding. I'll give up any *cloak and dagger* routine I was devising and just talk plain with her. But I still want you with me tomorrow at 1:00. Hey, I know. You could offer to give her a tour. Okay with you?"

"Okay by me. I'll be a second pair of eyes and ears at work."

"Great. Thanks, Kathy... Well, off I go, back to the Antichrist. Now there's an interesting topic, right? There's so much to be known about this man. I won't run out of things to say tonight."

Don turned to leave and looked back and blew Kathy a kiss. Then he reached over and shut the break room door tight, rushed to her side and planted a real kiss. As he left, his final words brought a new smile to Kathy's face: "Hey, that was nice. We ought to do that more often! Love you."

"Me, too, Mr. Don."

Don turned back into the room. *"Me, too,* you say... do you mean *Me too, I love you?* Or, do you mean *Me, too, let's do that more often?"*

"I mean both, you Big Kahuna... Now get yourself studying."

ONCE AGAIN, THE MEETING ROOM was full to the brim. Even some extra chairs were brought in to accommodate the overflow crowd. Don thought it must be the nature of the subject matter tonight that's bringing all the people.

The Lord spoke up in his heart: *It's not just the subject of tonight's lesson, but it's the anointing on your teaching that's bringing the people in.* Don smiled to himself, as he acknowledged the Lord's comment.

"Folks, you're probably tired of hearing me say this, but thanks so much for coming out, for your efforts to better understand these

Coming Perilous Times we live in. That's what Paul called it when he wrote to Timothy long ago.[34] I believe we are living awfully close to those *Perilous Times*. And a large part of what makes these times 'perilous' is the coming Antichrist.

"Just who is this Antichrist? That's our topic tonight. What does the Bible say about him? How is he going to operate and make a difference in our world? Let me read what the Bible tells us... This comes from the Book of Revelation, Chapter 13:

> *"And there was given unto him [the Antichrist] a mouth speaking great things and blasphemies; and power [really, authority] was given unto him to continue forty and two months [three and a half years].*

> *"And he opened his mouth in blasphemy against God, to blaspheme His Name, and His tabernacle, and them that dwell in Heaven.*

> *"And it was given to him to make war with the saints, and to overcome them; and authority was given him over all kindreds, and tongues, and nations.*

> *"And all that dwell upon the earth shall worship him, whose names are not written in the book of life of the Lamb slain from the foundation of the world."*

Don put down his Bible and continued. "The Antichrist is a pawn of Satan that the devil will use to get his agenda accomplished on earth. Long, long ago Satan was named Lucifer. He was the head of Heaven's praise and worship. Then he got to thinking that he wanted to be like God, even to usurp God's power and glory. Recorded in the Book of Isaiah, He said: *I will ascend above the heights of the clouds. I will be like the Most High.*[35]

"Satan was kicked out of Heaven and scholars tell us he took a third of the angels with him. Now he's here on the earth but still intent on being like God. He's about to enter his final bid to dethrone God Almighty, through the Great Tribulation and, at the end, the Battle of Armageddon.

"During the Great Tribulation, the Bible tells us Satan will energize and equip the Antichrist to make war with the saints – that's you and me, saints! We, along with the Jewish nation, will be the focus of his wrath and fury.

"We're more familiar with that side of the Antichrist, the side responsible for terror, death and martyrdom on his way to world domination. And that side of him begins to show its ugly head at the point of the Abomination of Desolation in the coming third Temple. But there is another side to him that accentuates his great skills at statesmanship, diplomacy, and peacemaking, that are in operation before his reign of terror. During this period of peacemaking, he accomplishes what most statesmen and historians would consider impossible: he devises a seven-year peace accord in the Middle East.

"The Book of Daniel says this about him: *And he shall confirm the covenant with many for one week* [seven years]: *and in the midst of the week* [3-1/2 years, or 42 months] *he shall cause the sacrifice and the oblation to cease, and for the overspreading of abominations he shall make it desolate.*[36] This is the Abomination of Desolation that Jesus talked about.

"I believe the world stage is ready for this Antichrist to appear. For some time, the world has been calling out for someone to come and save them after years of frustrating war, conflict, and social unrest. More recently we have pockets of anarchy springing up across the globe, especially in America. It seems that most every country at some point in its formation needs to experiment with Socialism. Anarchy and social upheaval help set the stage. Then, the masses are forced into becoming a hoard of second-class citizens, ever working to satisfy the power-hunger of their leaders. Promises are given. And for each to have a piece of the prosperity pie these promises are alluring to one and all, to be sure. Ultimately, however, the experiment with Socialism collapses. The masses rise in revolt. And society reverts to its former state of disorder... waiting for the next cycle to begin.

"Onto this dark stage the Antichrist emerges. He relates at once to the local powerbrokers seeking celebrity-status in their own land. They run to his deceiving promises for fame and glory, and gladly serve him as minions.

"While, at first, the Antichrist is disguised as a credible and compassionate man of peace with nearly superhuman abilities, no one surmises that he is empowered by Satan to accomplish his amazing feats. Soon enough, however, he shows forth his true colors as he sets out to become savior and dictator of the world."

Don was brimming over with information and Scriptures related to the Antichrist. As the evening wore on, he became aware that he was running out of steam. "Folks, I'm winding down... We'll have to finish this another time. There's so much to learn about this pawn of Satan.

"I believe the Antichrist is on the world scene right now, engaged in some way with the seven-year peace treaty in the Middle East, but his true and personal identity is being shielded by Satan. It won't be long, however, until his anonymity will be over. Then we will find ourselves right in the middle of his provocative terror tactics.

"But... I say, BUT...

"But thank God! Thank God for His Grace! Thank God for the power of the Holy Spirit that lives inside each of us...

"Remember us talking about being *prepared* and not *scared?* Well, I say this: may our getting *prepared* get so big on the inside that it will overpower any *scared* element trying to grab hold from the outside.

"Amen! Amen? Can I hear an Amen tonight?!"

"Amen!" "Amen!" "Amen, Brother Don!"

"Prayer is available if needed. Otherwise have a sweet, peaceful evening with the ones you love."

BETTY McPHERSON WAS RIGHT ON TIME for her appointment with Don. She was somewhat surprised to see a new face at the meeting, that is, Kathy.

Don started. "Ms. McPherson, may I introduce my wife, Kathy. I asked her to be at our meeting and later, if you wish, she could take you on a brief tour of The Factory... So, this is Kathy. And Kathy this is of course Betty McPherson..."

After a brief handshake, everyone had a seat... and waited. Finally, Ms. McPherson spoke up. "Well, Mr. Crawford, Don, as I said yesterday to your secretary, I'm wanting an opportunity to mend the fences between you and me. What I did to you and The Factory during your remodeling phase was reprehensible and inexcusable. I don't know what I was thinking about at the time... Anyway, I'm asking for your forgiveness, and please accept my heartfelt remorse for my critical ways."

Don replied, "Ms. McPherson – may I call you Betty?"

"Yes, please do."

"Betty, I appreciate your candidness on the matter. And as far as I'm concerned, I forgive you wholeheartedly. I would like nothing better than to have this whole affair far behind us. Life is too short, don't you agree; let's get on with enjoying it while we can."

"Well, Thank you, Don, for your forbearance. Thank you. I feel much better."

"Betty, if I might inquire," said Kathy, "You've not seen The Factory since the open house months ago, right? Well, there have been plenty of changes around here since that occasion. We have over forty live-in residents, and several more from the community come here regularly to assist and to receive spiritual help and teaching about the end-times – which is done admirably by Don..."

"We believe that the end of life as we know it is fast approaching," Don added, and our focus is to get prepared for what lies ahead rather than be scared. We can, I believe, live in a scary world without letting fear dominate. Last evening, for example, we looked at the Antichrist and his part in God's end-time drama, which can be quite fear-charged, even for Believers. We do these sessions about three times a week. You're welcome to join us anytime."

Betty picked up the ball. "Thank you, Don. Now here's something you two don't know about me. I know someone who lives here. It's Mary Kay! She's my niece. Or my great niece. I'm a younger sister of her grandmother in Kansas."

Don and Kathy looked at one another with surprise. "Isn't that interesting!" they said almost simultaneously.

"I bring that up mainly to add that she and I talk fairly often by phone or over lunch. And she fills me in on your teachings. I would like to learn more, so maybe I'll take you up on your offer to come out and be a part."

"Another session is scheduled tomorrow night," said Don. "In the meantime, let me get you a booklet that we use around here..." Don searched his bookcase for a copy. "Here it is, called *Coming Perilous Times,* [37] written by someone who I trust knows about the end-times...

"Someone could get up to speed, if they wanted to, studying this booklet. It's been a big help to us. So, here's a copy for you. Got other copies in case you want one to give away."

"Thank you, Don. I'll read it and read it again," stated Betty. "Well, folks, I've taken up enough of your time. Again, I appreciate your giving me the opportunity to receive your forgiveness. And Thank you for your warm welcome and for your invitation to participate out here. I'm about ready to retire. I have some cooking experiences; that might come in handy for you sometime."

Betty rose to leave; Don and Kathy followed. The notion of taking Betty on a tour seemed irrelevant, so it wasn't pursued. Then Kathy thought of something.

"Oh, Betty, I just remembered, and you probably already know, that we're planning on a wedding around here a week from Saturday. Mary Kay and Mark make such a sweet couple. Everyone's so excited. Join us, please."

"I think I'll do just that," answered Betty as she headed toward the door.

"Good-bye Betty," said Kathy. "If you'd like I could see if I could find Mary Kay. You two could visit right now."

"No, I don't have time," she replied. "A staff meeting at the Department to head up in a few minutes. Thanks anyway. Bye for now."

Both watched as Betty headed down the corridor out of sight. Then Don asked: "Kathy, how about a doughnut in the break room. We'll compare notes on Betty."

"Yes, let's go," Kathy replied. The two scampered to the break room and found an empty table.

With doughnut in hand, Don spoke up. "Well, I'll go first... I thought Betty seemed genuine and cordial; a lot different than I remember her from down at the Mayor's office. Then, she was out to eat my lunch for some still unknown reason. I don't know if that mystery will ever be resolved. I don't even want to try... What did you think, Kathy?"

"Like you, I thought Betty seemed pleasant enough and sincere in wanting to apologize," Kathy answered. "So, how about it, Don, problem over? Behind us?"

"As far as I'm concerned, I'd call it over and finished. And I'll feel even more confident about that if she makes the effort to come out here and get involved."

"Oh, hey you two! You're just who I was looking to find," came the bubbly voice of Sam, poking her head into the break room. "Just can't stay away from those doughnuts, right Don?"

"Hi Sam, what's up; have a seat with us," Kathy replied. Sam joined Don and Kathy but passed on doughnuts. She was sure fired up!

"I'm just so excited about life, you know? Ever since moving in here, I haven't really stopped smiling. I get to do what I love doing. I get to hear some incredible teaching. What could be more than that?"

"Maybe a handsome young suitor?"

"No, I don't need that! That's for sure. But I just wanted the two of you to know how well the teaching episodes have been received by the public. We, that is, The Factory, have our own Facebook page and our own YouTube channel. And I have a teaching video of about fifteen minutes that I download to each site, on a Monday through Friday basis. And both of those places refer the viewer back to our Factory Facebook homepage...

"Anyway, it's been so awesome to see the response. It's not that we're *going viral* as they say... not yet, anyway, but we're climbing day by day in the number of *likes* that we get. Thinking about *boosting* the Facebook post, so we would be seen by a bunch of locals who don't yet know much about us... just thinking, mind you."

"Well, I for one am glad that you're doing this and not me," Don shared.

"Me, too, Don," added Kathy. "Jenny first got us up and running with Facebook when she and Jim moved here, but with Rosalie Anne taking so much attention, she hasn't had the time to devote to it like she wants. She told me the two of you got your heads together about The Factory's media presence and she's happy..."

"...she's happy for me to step in and take it over for a while," Sam added.

"Great!" Don concluded, "That's another problem that's been finished today. We're on a roll!"

Kathy changed directions of the discussion when she leaned over to Sam and whispered in her ear: "Did you get the accordion?" Sam shook her head *yes*. "You like it? It's going to work?" Sam shook her head *yes*. All the while Don was looking on curiously, straining to hear a word or two.

Kathy looked on and smiled. "Secrets are fun, aren't they, Don?"

"Depends on what side of the secret you're on, Kathy," he replied. "And I'm out of this one; must involve me in some way... Something about what you got me for my birthday, maybe? But I can't think of anything I really want... Hmmm..."

"Your birthday is six months away, Don!" Kathy clarified. "No, it's something better than that. You'll find out soon enough."

"Well, folks, I'm going to keep moving," announced Sam. "Always something to do around here. See you later."

As Sam left, Kathy began looking aimlessly at the local newspaper, laying on the table. There on the third page was an article about the new Jerusalem Temple.

"Don, look at this; it's about the new Temple going up in Jerusalem," she said.

Don looked intently at the article. It was headed by a photo of several dignitaries standing at the site where the Temple will be located. Foundations had already been laid. You were beginning to get a sense of the actual size by the construction thus far completed.

Don commented: "Looks like it will be much, much smaller than the former Temple... Hmmm, I wonder if one of those dignitaries standing at the site is the Antichrist himself. Wouldn't surprise me in the least. He's probably just chomping at the bit to get his teeth into his upcoming deification program, as he starts his quest for world domination..."

"Okay, honey, I best be going. What's for supper?"

"I call it *chef's surprise*. That should encourage you to come home, right?"

"Anything you make, Kathy, **is** a *surprise*! I'll see you later."

"Wait!" Kathy said. "Was that a compliment? It was hard to tell for sure... See you later."

THE MOTHERS' MEETING WAS WELL attended; six mothers in all, each with concerns and questions about their babies being taken in the Rapture. Don went over his teaching from the Lord centered on Romans 7:9.

"Let me loosely paraphrase this verse: *At the beginning of life I was innocent and knew no sin; later when I came into a time of reasoning, as my conscience developed, sin entered my world. Then it was, that I needed a Savior to gain eternal life.*"

"Is this paraphrase understandable, mothers? *As a little child I wasn't capable of sinning. Growing older my conscience developed and I became accountable for my actions. Then I needed a Savior.*"

"When does this change happen... I mean how old is a child when he or she starts being capable of sin and becomes responsible?" This same general question was raised by all the mothers. Don tried his best to be forthright in replying.

"Well, moms, that's the question of the hour. And there seems to be no clear-cut answer to hang your hat on. It varies from child to child. For some the change might be as early as four-years-old, for others six or seven. I urge each of you to talk with the Lord about it; let Him guide you... He knows your child better than you do.

"Our goal here is to get each child that is spiritually ready to receive Jesus as their Savior – or, to ask Jesus into their heart - to do just that. So, when the Rapture does happen that youngster will be taken out of here, just like his or her believing parents."

"Well, Dad, seeing that Rosalie is only eight months old, I believe I can rightfully conclude she has not known any sin and will go in the Rapture," said Jenny.

"Right you are, Jenny," answered Don. "And, your three-year-old Levi is likely in the same boat, Mary Kay; Gideon might be a different story... and your youngest, Dianne, might also be the same; your two older ones, not sure."

"So, what should we do, Don, if it's not clear?" asked Nancy Struble, with an eye on her grandchildren in Michigan.

"Like I said at the beginning, go before the Lord, ask Him to guide you," Don answered. "Each of you needs to make an opportunity where you can talk with your child about Jesus. You might share your testimony; tell your child about your decision to ask Jesus to be your Savior and live in your heart; talk about why you did that, how it has helped you. If your youngster is anywhere near the age of accountability, your sharing might just open him up to consider taking the same step himself. If they're ready, you'll get a sense of that; listen to your heart. If they're not ready, it's because it's too soon; the Lord will help you see that also.

"I've already talked with Sam about her crew in childcare making Bible lessons take on a *'salvation'* point of view. This will help those children at or near the age of accountability get a jump-start on the Jesus-as-Savior question. Then, when you talk with them, they'll be more primed and ready to participate."

"Sounds like a great idea, Don," several of the mothers said.

"Good. It was the Lord's idea... One final note that perhaps doesn't even need to be said: flood all your efforts along this line with plenty of prayer. Ask the Lord and I believe He'll lead you to the perfect time and place for sharing with your child... In fact, let's start on that prayer right now:

"Lord, thank You for teaching us Your ways. We know that You have a special place in Your heart for children. Help these mothers to share with their youngsters. And, we thank You in advance for their precious hearts to be opened to the truth of Your Salvation.

"It's good to know for sure that it is Your will that none should perish but all should join You in Heaven. So, it's with great boldness that we can pray Your will be done among our precious little ones. In the Name of Jesus. Amen... Anything else?"

Dianne summed it up this way. "Don, I think I speak for all the mothers here, when I say thanks for this meeting and for helping us to set our children's sight on Jesus and on Heaven."

ANOTHER PLANNING COMMITTEE MEETING was on the docket for 9:00 am. "Well, here we are again: The *Intrepid* Planning Committee," Don said after opening in prayer.

"What does in-trep-id mean," asked Doobie?

"It means fearless, daring, or brave," answered Jim.

"Oh, good, that's what I want to be... like *Superman* saving the city from the forces of evil."

"In a way, people," spoke up Don, "to be *intrepid* is like the Holy Spirit making us all Supermen or Superwomen, to stand up against and resist the Antichrist forces of evil! That's been kind of a theme rolling around in my spirit since starting to teach about the Antichrist figure."

"God wants us to be fearless and daring, doesn't He," stated Ben, "as we deal with the devil's tactics of terror?"

"He sure does, Ben," asserted Don. "He wants us to be prepared and fearless.

"Hey – prepared and fearless! I like the sound of that: *Prepared and Fearless*. That could be a new name for us on our *Facebook* page, or for our *YouTube* channel... I'll talk with Sam about that..."

"I like the sound of that as well," offered Mark. Jim agreed. So did Doobie.

"So, what else should we be talking about today?" asked Don.

"Jim, we haven't heard from you in a while," said Ben "Are you and Jenny still glad you moved here all the way from Colorado to be with us?"

"Yes, for sure. This is the place we want to be, especially now after getting an idea of where we fit into God's timetable...

"There is a thing or two I'd like to bring up," said Jim, a bit cautiously.

"Sure, Jim, this is the place," Don said. "What's on your mind?"

"Well, I've taken upon myself the role of *Efficiency Officer* for The Factory..."

"Let's see," remembered Don, "A while back you took on another role. Then you were a *Sam Monitor*. How's that going, by the way?"

"Oh, that's going okay. Not much to report. I don't really think I need to keep that monitoring going... I like Sam. I think her heart is in the right place."

"Glad to hear you say that Jim," commented Kathy, "because I like her too. So, tell us about the *Efficiency Officer* work."

"Well, I just see places where we could be a little more efficient... One example is in the main office, largely held down by Clair. I think she does a fine job, but there are times she could use some assistance, especially when the workers are in there paying for their room and board, mostly on Friday afternoons. I've helped her out a time or two when it gets a little hectic... why don't I set myself to be her assistant when those busy times come. Okay, Dad?"

"Fine by me, son," replied Don, "You know I admire your see-a-problem-and-what-can-I-do-to-fix-it attitude. Keep up the good work... anything else, folks?"

"Yes, I have one more area," Jim interjected. "It has to do with food prep and meals for continuing victims of the tornado. I think our response and presence in the community, to provide food for those in need, could be stronger. I'd like to get that outreach more organized."

Seeing and hearing no objections, Jim went on. "I think we could make it more than a meal or food distribution occasion. Perhaps we could get some volunteers to provide games and fun for the children... Maybe we could get a video teaching episode of you, Don, to show the people. Or, maybe, you could present in person on the back of a flatbed trailer. Maybe some music by Jerry and D.J.? Or, by Sam? Many different possibilities."

"Well, Jim, I am impressed with your heart to serve the people," Don answered. "I tell you what... why don't you corral a few people who might also be interested in this, get your heads together and come up with a definite plan, and we'll talk about it at another Planning Meeting."

"Sounds good," Jim replied. "I will do that."

"Now it seems to me that there's one person in this room who should be as happy as a lark... When we were convening earlier, I looked out and it seemed to me this person was walking about three foot off the floor. Do you know who we're talking about?" asked Don. "No one but the groom-to-be, Mr. Mark!"

Mark looked out at all the faces around the table and grinned from ear to ear. Doobie got in on the act when he said: "Okay, it's my turn, Bro! High Five!" (Swat! Swat! Swat! Swat!)

"That's a good way to finish our business," Don announced. "Have a good day."

On the way out, Don conferred with Ben. "Ben, wait a minute. I had a most peculiar dream the other night. It was like I was listening...

now get this... it will sound strange... It was like listening to accordion music of all things. It was weird... ever happen to you?"

"No, Don, can't say that ever happened to me," replied Ben

Kathy overheard and smiled ever so big.

CHAPTER THIRTEEN –

They all looked so nice in their Sunday Best.

THERE WAS ANOTHER GALA EVENT AT THE FACTORY for all to enjoy, courtesy of Mark and Mary Kay. It seemed that The Factory was developing a modest reputation in the community as a place for a good party. Today was no exception.

Don looked like your itinerant preacher in his black dress pants, loud sports coat, and tie, none of which he had worn for over a year and all of which were out of style and didn't go together. On the other hand, Kathy looked *heavenly*, in Don's opinion. She had on her one and only floor-length, light blue dress that Clair spruced up with a bow here and a tuck there. She was so busy flitting around seeing to last minute details that she missed all the positive comments that came her way from well-wishers. Everyone looked mighty fine in their *Sunday Best*.

The groom-to-be and his best man stood at the front of the meeting room, trying to appear casual, but not fooling anyone. Mark kept asking Doobie, "Is my tie straight? How do my shoes look? Do you have the rings? Can you see the sweat on my forehead?" Even Don's efforts to crack a joke and keep the groom relaxed failed to help the situation.

To no one's surprise, Sam was looking spiffy in her designer outfit, as she sat near the front of the room, waiting for her musical debut with the accordion. She had some soft CD music playing as the people arrived and found a seat. Little did Don or the others know that at the start of the processional, Sam was going to surprise everyone with her musical virtuosity.

Betty McPherson was present, and she took it upon herself to help corral Mary Kay's two boys and little Natalie during the ceremony.

It was arranged that those three youngsters would spend the night with Dianne's three children, in a sleep-over, while the Bride and Groom stayed in downtown Greensville's finest, the *Piedmont Hotel Honeymoon Suite.*

The meeting room was nearly filled and in doing so may have over-reached the fire code limit. The Mayor was there, and he didn't seem to object, and there was no hint of disapproval from Betty. So, the issue was simply overlooked. Other guests included Pastor Daniel and his wife, as well as Henry and Louise Greyheck.

Right at 10:00 am Ben stuck his head in the room to signal that the processional was about to start. Doobie gave Mark a final look with "thumbs up" and went back to join in on the processional. After a few long moments, on cue, Sam stood with her accordion in her hands and began to play an upbeat processional. Don looked over Sam's way with a big smile as he recalled the *secret* between Kathy and Sam that he was not privy to.

As the processional started, Doobie and Suzy led the way. Before long, all eyes were on the Bride. As she walked arm in arm with Ben, she looked so lovely, like she just stepped out of the *Bride and Groom Magazine.* Clair stood in the back beaming from ear to ear, as she looked on her creative work with Mary Kay's dress. Glenda Wilson, a close friend of Mary Kay, was assigned the task of videoing the event, mainly for the benefit of Mary Kay's family in Kansas, so Jenny could stay with Rosalie. She started to video on her tablet and *presto*, thanks to modern technology, the ceremony was streamed directly to Kansas!

Now the eyes turned to Don; remember this was his first wedding to officiate. His hands sweated, his voice crackled, and his tie got tighter and tighter, as he led the participants through the ceremony. Glenda, the videographer, seemed in Don's estimation to be standing much too close to the bride and groom; and in the process probably recorded every bead of sweat that fell from Don's face. But he went on like a trooper!

Finally, after the vows were exchanged and Don gave a brief message on the sanctity of God's plan for marriage, the ceremony ended.

"I now present to you Mark and Mary Kay McKenna, husband and wife," Don announced proudly. Cheers erupted up and down the meeting room aisle, as the Bride and Groom strolled to the back. Then the line formed to greet the new couple individually. No one was happier that the event was finished than Don – unless it was Mark!

Folks spilled out into the halls to allow the reception crew to get to work transforming the meeting room into a banquet hall of sorts, complete with a wedding cake, nuts, mints, and Mama Blanchard's famous sprite-strawberry fizz punch.

It was a day to remember! Finally, after the last piece of cake was eaten and the punch bowl was emptied, guests began to file out. And they did so with many a happy memory to share. Mary Kay's family in Kansas was super appreciative of being able to witness the ceremony first-hand.

THE FACTORY WAS NEVER IN A MORE upbeat frame of mind, than following the wedding, and that lasted for a good two months or so. It was akin to the elation that was felt after having passed the city building code with flying colors.

During this period of relative peace, the New Temple in Jerusalem's City of David was completed and began its long-awaited animal sacrifice rituals. This came much to the delight of local religious leaders. It was officially consecrated on the solemn Jewish Feast of the Day of Atonement, September 30 of that year.

Don, Kathy, and Sam were watching the proceedings from the break room.

"How fitting," Rabbi Levi Radanovich stated at the Opening Ceremony, "that our beloved Temple should begin operations on the Day of Atonement. We have many people to thank for this development, persons that are gathered here today, not the least of which is our newly-appointed Prime Minister of the Middle East Peace Accord, Marschall Gabrinne..."

"There he is, folks," announced Don excitedly looking on. "The Antichrist himself, Marschall Gabrinne... at least that's what I believe. If it's not him, it most assuredly must be one of the other men standing on the dais being recognized... Whoa, time is quickly running out; get ready people!"

ONE DAY SOON AFTER THE THIRD TEMPLE was opened, the hammer came crashing down! The television in the break room that is always on, starting at 7:00 am, had local news interrupted by a *Special News Alert.* Cameras were rolling at the newly constructed Temple in Jerusalem, seven hours ahead, to witness what was being called an *Unprecedented Departure From Temple Rituals.*

"Folks, this is Chief International Correspondent, Janice Martin, in New York, interrupting our programming to bring you this Special Alert. Facts are conflicting, but it seems that Marschall Gabrinne, Past-President of the Mediterranean Union and current Prime Minister of the Middle East Peace Accord, is at the new Jerusalem Temple proclaiming himself... wait folks, let me hear that again," checking her earpiece, *"Yes, that's what I'm hearing alright... Gabrinne is proclaiming himself to be God!*

"I can hardly believe the words I'm saying... Just one moment, oh, good. We now have our man in the Middle East, Curt Block, available for further comment and description. Take it away, Curt."

"Janice, it is now 4:00 pm local Israel time, and 8:00 am eastern U.S. time. Prime Minister Gabrinne arrived at the Temple, I'm being told, about thirty minutes ago. He was not expected here, a Temple spokesman told us, until much later in the day, when a gala Opening Celebration was to be held for the public.

"Although facts here are ever changing and often at odds, as near as I can piece it together, Gabrinne and his entourage arrived without any announcement or initial fanfare and promptly went inside the Temple through the Eastern Gate, brushing aside several Temple Guards in the process.

"His goal apparently was to enter the Holy of Holies section, in the inner sanctum of the Temple, reserved for only the High Priest – and that only once a year, at the Day of Atonement, which is today. And this day marks that unique feast day for Israelis all over the world, so you know all eyes today are on the new Temple in David's City...

"Now is when facts become elusive, but reportedly Gabrinne started ranting about himself being the God of this world. At the same time, Gabrinne's associate and long-time companion, Abrahim Oktbar, placed a bust of Gabrinne atop the sacrificial table in that section, we are being told, but we would do well to get a second confirmation...

"Folks, I sure wish we were able to get our cameras into where Gabrinne is reportedly carrying on, but no news cameras are allowed even close to the Temple at this time... As you can see yourselves, from our camera scanning the vicinity, things here at the new Temple are in a state of chaos and uproar. Temple Guards are here in full force to keep news outlets and the public at a safe distance. We are told that a Spokesman from the Temple will be sharing a news briefing, as soon as feasible.

"Oh, I just heard some news. What? Are you sure?... You're positive?...

*"Now bear with me people, what I'm about to say will sound ludicrous and preposterous to your ears, but I'm learning that the statue brought into the Holy of Holies by Mr. Oktbar is in fact animated in some way... Yes, you heard me right, I said **animated**. The statue itself, is talking; it's affirming and bearing witness to Gabrinne's claims that he himself is to be revered by the world as God..."*

"Curt, this is Janice back on: what in the world is going on over there? You have a statue that's, like alive, talking? Praising Gabrinne? Wow... never in a thousand years... Well, Curt, if you're sure you've got your bearings, take a few deep breaths and take it away again."

"Thanks, Janice. I can see why you would question the sanity of anyone who is reporting on statues coming alive... Now viewers should know I'm standing about thirty yards from the Temple entrance that Gabrinne used. I'm surrounded by a throng of onlookers, clamoring to get a glimpse of Prime Minister Gabrinne. Some, as you can hear, are chanting his name;

some of those are referencing him as God. Others are raising fists in defiance and calling for him to step down as Accord Prime Minister.

"Wait, folks, some movement at the Temple entrance... Can we get a bit closer, Ted, with the camera? No? Okay... To our viewers, what I'm seeing is Oktbar coming out of the Temple enclosure with several armed guards, carrying the statue of Gabrinne. He has found a spot in a small alcove within view of the massive crowd that has gathered here. The statue has been placed on a podium. It looks lifeless... Whoops, I take that back. The statue is beginning to move and talk. I think you should be able to hear it:"

"Follow after prosperity and be forever at peace. Gabrinne will lead us there. He is God! He is our God! Give him your life and he will give you prosperity and peace like you've never known."

The bust continued to hold the onlookers almost spellbound. Then it announced it was time for miracles! "Our Beloved Gabrinne wants all of you well and strong. Come forward and receive your healing miracle!"[38]

Curt continued to report, trying his best to lay aside a swirl of skepticism about what he was witnessing. *"Folks, suddenly I'm seeing people in wheelchairs get up and walk and dance even! Blind eyes are opening. Deaf ears are hearing. Withered arms are being made straight and whole. On and on it goes... Those allegedly being healed are standing and testifying to the crown around them. Wheelchairs, crutches, and walkers are being abandoned and passed through the gathering, out to the surrounding crowded street. As the statue continues to proclaim Gabrinne to be God, I can see that most of the people watching are joining right in and echoing that praise aloud, without reservation.*

"The statue of Prime Minister Gabrinne is unrelenting in declaring that Gabrinne is the world's new Savior. Listen for yourself: 'All hail the God of this world! Praise him; bow down before him. Claim your undying allegiance to our new Savior!'

"I can see at least twenty people in my immediate area who have fallen to their knees, in a prayerful manner that I would take to be an expression of devotion. They have remained in that position for several minutes...

"Let's just scan the camera around my vantage point so you can see what I'm seeing... Many of the people are seemingly suspended in time itself... Believe me, folks, it's hard to describe in ordinary words, what I'm seeing with my eyes. I invite us all to simply watch...

"Well, Janice, it's been almost a half-hour since the wave of miraculous healings first took place. There seems to be now a shift in the proceedings. The statue has stopped its activity, but not any of the crowd has left the scene that we can determine.

"Of course, everyone would like to see and hear Mr. Gabrinne himself, but we're being told that he is going to forego that opportunity until a later time. In fact, he is going right into seclusion, we're being informed, until the fervor here in Jerusalem diminishes. He exited out another door and a tunnel in the rear of the Temple to a waiting limousine, to avoid facing the public.

"Now Mr. Gabrinne's inner circle, his Council of Advisors, as I've heard them called, will be available for all of today's upcoming festivities and, I would guess, will be addressing the practical side of the surge of support from the people. Even now these workers are circulating in the crowd with a petition or form of some sort to have the people sign as a pledge of support for the Prime Minister, I take it ...

"Excuse me, Sir, would you mind showing me that piece of paper you were just given... Thank you much. Hmmm... It seems to be in three languages: English, Hebrew, and Arabic. Hmmm... It does reference a Decree of Commitment *section, calling for a signature and other personal information.*

"Thank you, sir; here's your form back. Are you going to sign this pledge?"

"Oh, yes, indeed! Mr. Gabrinne is my new beloved Savior! I give him my everlasting devotion... my very life! You should do the same!"

"Thank you, sir... Well, Janice, I'm about ready to turn this back to you. But give me a moment to share from my heart... It's more than everyday support from the people I'm witnessing, it's something else, something deeper, something of the soul even, if I might take off my news correspondent hat and editorialize a moment:

"What we have seen today was, in my opinion, an awesome display of the finer side of life. True, there were some unconventional expressions, but overall, it highlighted the best of humanity: the craving for peace, the unifying of the masses, the Hand of Deity bringing physical well-being to those in need... I can only hope that Prime Minister Gabrinne will continue this track of social and spiritual advance in the weeks and months ahead. We all know that this is something the world needs more than ever.

"One final thought comes to mind. There are so many interesting facets to today's story at the new Temple. So many segments of our society have been and will continue to be impacted. And each of these is a three-hour news special of its own. One of those segments affected will be the local religious leaders. They made their position clear right from the beginning; they vociferously stood in opposition to Gabrinne's actions, and understandably so. But it was interesting how their clamor seemed to fade away quickly and without incident.

"Were there threats of retaliation made from Gabrinne's camp, were there immense promises of personal benefit given, will this saga continue at other levels? All questions, I surmise, that will be addressed soon...

"Now, finally, back to you, Janice. We'll be here the rest of this day and the immediate future you can be certain, to bring you all the news that's worth watching... This is Curt Block signing off for now. Janice..."

Don stood from his chair in the break room and considered what he had just watched. It was different than he anticipated. Don expected the worst – for all hell to break loose, suddenly and with a definite punch, right after the Temple incident, but it didn't happen. It was eerie. It was like waiting for the other shoe to drop. Was it the calm before the storm?

It's like the Antichrist came forth into public view, caused quite a stir, and then quickly disappeared. Is part of his strategy, to catch people off guard? Don wondered.

As soon as the TV spotlight was turned away from Jerusalem, Don called for a quick meeting for everyone able to attend. Most everyone, even children, attended. He opened with prayer and then looked over the concerned faces before him. He wished he could take each soul and scoop them into his arms and tell them, *Everything's going to be alright.*

"Folks we have witnessed the Antichrist today, in just a bit of his glory and his mania to be received by the world as God, and more is in store for the days ahead. I don't know what will happen next, or when, but I believe this urging I'm going to share from my spirit is God's wisdom for us:

"First of all, everyone who has cash of any sort – it's probably too late to get your savings out in cash – but whatever you have available let's let Clair collect it and we'll send out Mark and Jim later today to go and buy food and other essentials. Spend it all! In the days ahead it will likely not be of any use to us…And don't forget Doobie's seeds and starter plants for the garden… That reminds me, I've got to make sure Henry and Louise understand this, too.

"Be prepared: travel as we know it will likely become extinct very soon. The internet will be wiped out, which means, no computer access, no cars will work, nor cellphones – no phone service at all! We're going to learn that there are people who want us isolated from the world and from our neighbors.

"Saints, we are entering a time and situation that we've never known before. Many skills and wisdom for coping with these changes we will have to learn as we go. Which means we all must practice patience and God's kind of love, both of which have already been deposited into our hearts by the Holy Spirit. Now our job is to release those blessings from God, so they become an actual expression of our everyday faith and trust in Him.

"Oh, I seem to just be stammering on… Lord, direct my mind and give me the right words to help us be prepared instead of scared…

"Is there anyone who has a comment to share, or a word of encouragement to give?"

No comments were forthcoming. People seemed in a daze, and rightfully so. The usual bright eyes and upbeat spirits Don was accustomed to were vacant that day. He thought under his breath: *Lord, help me to instill in your people a deeper spark of trust and confidence in You.* The Lord whispered back: *That's My plan, Don. That's one thing you need. There's another need: the Holy Spirit and your heavenly prayer language.*

It was like Don snapped to attention! "Hey, the Lord just prompted me. There's something else we need, to cope with what lies ahead, something in addition to our trust and commitment to Him. Anyone guess? It is the baptism in the Holy Spirit, with the evidence of praying and speaking in other tongues. I know some of us have had this experience, but the Lord wants us all to have it.

"Folks, bear with me, please! When we are born again, the Holy Spirit comes into the new believer to reside, bringing with Him the very life of God. But there is a second Holy Spirit experience God wants us to have. And that is to have the Spirit come upon us... So, there are two works of the Holy Spirit. One is to come IN and the other is to come UPON. Here's how Jesus explained it to His Apostles in the Book of Acts: *You shall receive power after the Holy Spirit shall come upon you, and you shall be witnesses unto Me both in Jerusalem... and unto the uttermost part of the earth.*[39]

"In the Gospel of John, Chapter 4, Jesus likened the Holy Spirit experience at the new birth as: *a well of water springing up into everlasting life.*[40] Then in Chapter 7, Jesus declared this: *He that believes on me... out of his belly shall flow rivers of living waters. (But this He spoke of the Spirit... for the Spirit was not yet given).*[41]

"So, Jesus called one encounter with the Holy Spirit as: *a well of water*; the second happening as: *rivers of living water.* The first is the individual's salvation; the second is for the individual to be empowered as a blessing to others.

"I know I'm going on and on, but there is one more Scripture that I want us all to hear about this topic. It's in the eighth Chapter of the Book of Romans. Here Paul tells us: *Likewise, the Spirit also helps our weaknesses: for we know not what we should pray for as we ought: but the Spirit Himself makes intercession for us with groanings that cannot be uttered (that is, in articulate speech).*[42]

"That's speaking and praying in the Spirit. Sometimes there are occasions when we don't know how to pray, because we don't have enough information, or because we just don't know what to say, or we're not sure what the will of God is in a matter. For me, when I can't confidently pray about something or for someone, I start praying in other tongues... and the Holy Spirit will come along side and help me in any number of ways: give me wisdom, intercede with me, get my prayers focused, and comfort and strengthen me.

"Now to get this blessing for yourself, it's simply a matter of asking God and then believing you receive — it's like receiving anything else from Him. Let me see a show of hands: How many know right now they would like to have this Gift?"

Many hands rose. Don was greatly encouraged and went on: "Okay, here's what we'll do... Kathy why don't you come up here with me... I'll lead us in a simple prayer; you repeat my words and mean it with your whole heart. Ready?

"Heavenly Father... I want to receive the infilling of the Spirit... So, I can speak and pray in other tongues... as the Spirit gives utterance... I believe it is Your will for me... I ask for it in the Name of Jesus... and I believe that I receive this as a Gift from You...Amen...

"Now, begin to practice in your new language. Speak forth whatever wells up in your heart and mouth. You're in charge of what comes out of your mouth; it's not the Holy Spirit taking over and forcing you to speak anything. Now, what seems to want to come out might sound strange to your ears, but don't let that stop you, speak it forth anyway... The best way to start is simply to speak it out. Let's practice: Shuma talaba shatolez, keemo no baletass monena, clubatson... "

Kathy, the Tuckers, and others joined in. Don said, "Kathy, let's go around and help the people get started."

Don and Kathy circulated the room, going to individuals to encourage their expression of their new language. Before too long everyone whose hand was raised seeking God's Gift, was praying in other tongues, as the Spirit gave utterance. It was a glorious re-enactment of the Day of Pentecost! Even the two oldest boys jumped right in without the typical adult reservations

After several minutes of people praying joyfully in their new, heavenly language, the room grew quiet. Don then called for anyone wishing to have prayer for physical healing. Two men, relatively new to The Factory, did signal that wish and Don went to each one to pray. Don could feel the warmth in his hands as he laid them upon each man. And there was an instant manifestation of God's deliverance! Almost immediately two others requested prayer: Dianne and Mama Blanchard. They also received easily and with the same results!

Don and Kathy just knew by the Spirit that God was well pleased that day for the Greensville Faithful!

ONE DAY PASSED. TWO DAYS. THERE WAS nothing seemingly out of the ordinary. No further antics or surprises from Mr. Gabrinne. He seemed to be staying out of the limelight. Still, the eyes of everyone were glued to the TV every waking moment, nearly twenty-four hours a day. Don was thankful to still have international television coverage. He knew it was only temporary, however. He reckoned there must be some benefit to the enemy for TV coverage to still be going on, and what that benefit might be was not too hard to understand.

There definitely was a slant to the news being given. Gabrinne was always hailed as a World-wide Benefactor for the oppressed and needy... as the Answer to every human need and longing. So, Don rightfully concluded that the ongoing TV coverage was tainting the minds and expectations of the citizens, getting them ready to acclaim Gabrinne as the world's new savior.

This would be evident in the Middle East and then spring out across the globe. It was like the pebble thrown in the still waters of a pond that causes waves to ripple outward, covering the whole pond.

One country after another was throwing their lot in with Gabrinne. His promises of peace and prosperity seemed so welcomed to the country's sagging economy and civil uprisings, that it was probably a simple choice. And in doing so, that sovereignty also relinquished control of their defense forces to the Antichrist. That man was amassing a great wealth of power and influence.

During this supposed calm-before-the-storm period, some of The Factory Faithful decided to pay a visit outside the Greensville area. For example, Rusty and Barbara from Mama Blanchard's café decided to see their families in neighboring South Carolina. The café had just been shut down by Authorities, so it seemed like the logical time to visit family. Don felt uneasy about their decision. He wondered if they fully understood the risk they were taking. But they were insistent, so they left with his blessing.

A harder travel plan to bless was the decision by Mark and Mary Kay to travel by car all the way to Kansas. It was not a hurried decision, just awfully bad timing, in Don's estimation. They explained that this trip was on the docket ever since their wedding; they had made a commitment to Mary Kay's grandmother to make the trip. After promising to keep The Factory posted twice a day with phone calls, they were given the green light to travel; no, better make that an *amber light*.

Sam tried her hardest to get Don's newest message on the Jerusalem incident onto her usual media platforms, Facebook, and YouTube – but both rejected those efforts. She tried local access TV, but it was showing only propaganda short stories and ads from Jerusalem. Sam was told to submit her message but there was no guarantee it would be shown.

Sam took that to mean: *No and stop bothering me!* But Sam was insistent. Her next approach was to make up some 8-1/2 by 11 flyers that she could distribute to homes in the immediate area. She got her flyers ready and as she left the building she was immediately on the authorities' radar. That was soon apparent when an unmarked van came by and followed her. She looked up and saw drones tailing close behind. Sam had the van in view but moved on as if everything were hunky-dory. When she was spotted putting something into mailboxes, the van driver turned on his siren for an instant and talked over his loudspeaker.

"Lady, it's against the law to put fliers into private mailboxes. I'll have to ask you to stop before you get into serious trouble with the law."

To the young soldier's surprise, Sam came marching over to his van, waving fliers in her hand. She was ready for a showdown! "Young man, I wanted my neighbors to be aware of what's going on in Jerusalem involving Mr. Gabrinne. There's no law against that! Don't you want to know yourself?"

"Let me see a flyer," the officer insisted. He quickly looked it over and shook his head. "These fliers will not be distributed any further. Give them all to me." Sam complied.

"Am I being arrested, young man?" Sam demanded to know. Her righteous indignation was showing, but it was just part of her scheme!

"You are being given a citation," the Officer replied, "for illegal entry onto private property and for distributing anti-government misinformation." He then got out a citation booklet and began writing. "I need to see your driver's license."

"I don't have it with me."

"Where is it?"

"Back where I live at The Factory."

The young officer was getting anxious. Sam noticed beads of sweat on his forehead and thought: *Probably his first citation ever! I could whip this know-nothing with one brain tied behind my back. I've seen them mightier than this one crumble in the face of my grit and Chutzpah."*

As the officer fidgeted, he most likely was wishing he could be doing anything else than facing a challenge from this arrogant lady. Suddenly, the whole proceeding was interrupted by a call over his radio. He rolled up his car window to take the call in private. About ten seconds later, he rolled down the window.

With a forced showing of swagger, the officer announced: "Lady, this must be your lucky day. I've been called to the Armory on important business, so you get off with only a warning. No more fliers! Got it? Next time I'll throw the book at you!"

Sam looked on and smiled. The beads of sweat were still there. "Here, officer, take my Kleenex and wipe that sweat off your brow, before tackling your important business."

The officer drove off in a huff, squealing his tires for a half a block. It was his lucky day really. He had had a run-in with the *Queen of the Bluff* and came out with only minor bruises!

Sam returned to The Factory with a decided look of satisfaction at having out maneuvered that young hooligan. Of course, she didn't get her flyers distributed either. And for that she was sorry. She spotted Don going into his office and yelled at him; he stopped to talk.

"Hi, Sam. What are you up to?" he asked.

"Just had a run-in with a young man dressed up like an Officer. He was keeping track of me. He spotted me out front and seemed intent on following me. I thought he probably wouldn't go along with my stuffing mailboxes with flyers about the latest incident in Jerusalem, but I wanted to try. I think I won in our little skirmish though. It was a hoot to see him squirm and sweat."

"Nothing as exhilarating as winning a good fight, huh, Sam?"

"You got that right... Are you fixing to leave?"

"Yeah, Kathy and I are taking a trip into town to see what's happening there. We'll take the car most of the way, then walk in. Want to join us?"

"No Thanks. I want to get in touch with my former station manager, to see if there is any chance his station could show some of our material. It's a long shot I know, but I need to give it a try. Have fun. Don't let any teen-age Officer boss you around! Bye."

Kathy came to Don's office just after Sam left. "Ready to go, Don?"

"Yup. I'm already... Let's try and make some phone calls on this trip. No telling how much longer these phones will be functioning."

"Good idea. I want to reach Sylvia and try my parents again. But they're seldom available... I wonder how they're doing with what's happening right before their eyes?"

"My main target for a call is my parents," said Don. "I sure wish they had some people they could relate to about all this... someone they would trust, that's a big problem for them, and someone who had a little knowledge about the end-times would make it even better."

Don parked the car on a side street, about two blocks from the square. Kathy did reach Sylvia. She seemed to be handling the changes okay, but Kathy noted a lack of confidence in her daughter's voice as she talked about what was happening in Minnesota. Sylvia promised to stay in touch more frequently. Kathy concluded: "Don, she's not doing well, but wants to let on that she is. I wish I could see her and hold her in my arms. Whew... please help her, Lord."

Kathy's parents must have been in some far-off place with extremely poor phone reception. It was so hard to understand, in both directions. Kathy cut the call short, not even sure if her mother was aware of who she was struggling to talk with.

Don reached his parents, and reception was good. His parents seemed so far removed from any encouraging group or community support, during this difficult time. Don's heart went out to them. He promoted the idea that they could take steps to organize a support group at church, or in their neighborhood – or at least make inquiries with neighbors, cousins, or anyone! But, not surprising to Don, they wanted to struggle along on their own.

"We'll be okay, Don. Don't you worry about us," said Don's mother. "You just watch after that group you have in Greensville. Talk to you soon. Bye son."

Don turned to Kathy as they sat in the car. "Well, they say they're hanging in there. They have a stiff upper lip they project to others. But I know better. They're not inclined to seek for some support from their church or neighbors. But you and I both know this is NOT the time to be a *Lone Ranger*. The Bible warns us about isolation, remember?"

"Yeah, we're not to forsake the assembling of ourselves together, particularly as we see the day approaching – the day of His return." [43]

Kathy felt sorry for Don. "Makes me so glad we have our group of loving Believers, to encourage us every day – and we have each other!" Then Don added the icing on the cake.

"And we have the Lord Himself! Aren't you so happy He's a real part – and the best part – of our lives today!"

"Amen to that!"

"Well, here's where we walk. It's just a few blocks to the town square," said Don. Both got out. Don grabbed hold of Kathy's hand. The closer they got to the square, the more peculiar was the scene before them.

Glad tidings and joyful faces were the norm wherever they looked. The celebratory mood of the Greensville Community seemed so out of place. You would think a major war just came to an end, and the victors were coming home to a grateful Country. Cheerful smiles showed on the faces of most everyone. Don and Kathy quickly made their way to the city park downtown. There they saw more joyful citizens. Enjoying *what?* Don wondered... Gabrinne? His false promises? What?

One came up to Don and Kathy to comment. "Isn't it great! I'm signed up for my $5000 debit card! How about you folks?"

"Nope. We haven't done that," answered Don, walking past the man, to avoid conversation... really, to avoid bringing any attention to themselves. Actually, Don and Kathy had no idea of what the fellow was talking about, but they would learn soon enough.

There was a bandstand in the center of the park, with several officials gathered there, making speeches, Don supposed. Pictures of Mr. Gabrinne were all over the place, on every pole, every streetlight, you name it. Kathy strained to look at the band stand. She saw some familiar faces, like the Fire Chief, Pastor Daniel, and the Mayor was the Emcee of the affair. Looked like some folks were getting ready for the start of a parade. An evening concert was announced, much to the applause of the young people.

Don and Kathy crossed the street for a change of scenery. There they stood at the boarded-up entrance to Mama Blanchard's restaurant. No life or movement was visible peering in through the front window. They turned and looked up and down the street. From that vantage point Don and Kathy caught glimpse of a large billboard with Gabrinne's picture on it, surrounded by a sea of smiling faces and these words: *NEW PEACE ORDER COMING.*

Don shook his head. He turned to Kathy. "Well, honey, I've had enough; how about you?"

"Yeah, I guess so... Here's a question, Don: Those people sitting up there in the band shell, have they already given the nod to Gabrinne, or do they still have time to think about it?"

"I don't rightly know. I would think or at least hope that people have time to carefully consider their position, like the Mayor, or Pastor Daniel. I wonder if all this celebration and hoopla is aimed at taking everyone's minds off the coming changes. I bet underneath all the forced smiles and hardy handshakes, there is plenty of unrest and confusion in the hearts of the people. One thing: I at least appreciate that there is no military show of force, at least not yet."

"Don, let's keep moving. Should we try and see the Greyhecks, since we're so close?"

"My thought exactly. I think they live about six blocks away, on Cornwell Street. We go up here to the corner and turn left."

On the walk to the Greyhecks, it was mostly quiet. The two of them did plenty of thinking but little talking. Finally, they arrived at the Greyhecks front door. They knocked and Louise answered.

She was pleasantly surprised to see Don and Kathy. "Welcome, you two! Come on in and have a seat... Henry is out in the back. I'll call him... Henry! We have visitors!"

"We were in the neighborhood, Louise, and took a chance that you might be home," said Don, as he and Kathy took a seat on the sofa in the living room.

Henry came right in and he too was pleased to see his guests. "Welcome. It's so good to see you two. What brings you our way?" Henry sat on the couch next to Louise and waited.

Don began to explain. "Henry, Louise, we are arriving at a most challenging time. I know you're aware of the scene that happened in Jerusalem at the new Temple a few days back. Well, to my understanding, that starts the Great Tribulation Jesus talked of. Or, said another way, the Temple incident starts the Antichrist on his quest of compelling the world to acclaim him as God."

"But everything seems so quiet and half-way normal in Greensville," Henry rebutted. "I know there are some making a lot of noise at the city park, but that's just par for the course. It will blow over and we'll go on. It will be life as usual again."

"Well, Henry, we at The Factory have done lots of study and searching of the Bible for answers," Don replied. "I believe there is coming – and any day now – a rude awakening. It's going to catch a lot of people off guard and change their lives 180 degrees... I don't want that for you and Louise."

There was a long moment of silence. Henry and Louise looked curiously at one another. Many questions filled their heart, like: *Is all this true? Maybe they're exaggerating? Can it really be that bad?*

Kathy spoke. "Henry, Louise, we don't mean to alarm you. I believe Don is right in this matter. So, we're here to inform you about what's on the horizon for us. At the same time, we wanted to invite you to consider coming out to The Factory, not just to visit, but to live with us there."

"We believe there is strength in numbers, and especially if we are all seeking the Lord for His directions and encouraging one another along the way," Don added. Then he felt the Lord's leading to stop and get ready to leave.

Don stood and offered a final plea. "Folks, I know this sounds like some far-out movie plot, but it's very real. We hope you'll consider our offer, for you to join us."

The Greyhecks were silent. They couldn't fathom the scope of Don and Kathy's alarm and dismal forecast.

Don headed for the door, then turned back to add one last argument. "Henry, I and Kathy believe it's only a matter of time before money as we know it will become obsolete; there's a new system of bartering and commerce on the horizon. Do with that what you want; several of us are liquidating all that we can.

"Plus, and this is my last point: we anticipate that normal travel will very soon be no more. Cars and so many things we take for granted run because of computers in them. We believe the forces of the Antichrist are going to interrupt our computer networks soon, which means travel will no longer be available. It's one of their ways to secure control and force people to comply with their policies."

"Don, I promise that Louise and I will give thoughtful consideration to your words of warning today," announced Henry. "We will stay in touch."

"Good-bye. Hope to see you again soon," added Kathy.

Don and Kathy quickly headed up the block, back toward the city park, to find their way home. "Well, Kathy, we gave it our best shot, didn't we?"

"Yes, we did, Don…But we were asking a lot from them."

"What do you mean?"

"We were asking them to see all this in the same way as we do. And maybe we're just at different levels of understanding… I'm thinking that Henry and Louise need to see some personal value to coming out to The Factory; they don't see that yet. We know that our believing community is about to undergo some most serious challenges, but they don't know that… We need to hold them up in prayer for the Lord's discernment, wisdom and strength."

"Right you are, Kathy… Again, you're right! You are always right! And I'm soooooo glad you are!" Don put on a broad smile and gave Kathy a big hug!

Maybe the Greyhecks are in, maybe not, Don thought, *but one thing for sure, this Kathy is a keeper!*

CHAPTER FOURTEEN –

The NPO strategy: to catch the people off guard.

SOON ENOUGH IT BECAME APPARENT what the NPO strategy was. It was to surprise and catch the people off guard. While seemingly nothing alarming was going on (at least that the people could see), the Antichrist was getting his crafty strategy organized. It was like a cat slowly and methodically getting in position to pounce on the unsuspecting, defenseless mouse.

And what was that strategy? It was presented to the world as the New Peace Order (NPO). This consisted of a series of edicts to make the world totally dependent on the new regime for their livelihood and sustenance.

The first wave of edicts was delivered on a Sunday morning to each door in the community (and, presumably, in the nation) by uniformed officers – really teenagers. The Sunday morning services at the Cornerstone Church with Pastor Daniel had long been discontinued. Officially the Church was undergoing renovations and not open to the public, but Don and others felt there was a different explanation... Something sinister was taking place they couldn't put their finger on.

The Factory's copy of the Edict was found in the mail slot by David on his morning rounds. He brought it immediately to Don and Kathy, sitting in the break room praying and talking, getting braced for another day of confusion, threat, or whatever.

"Thanks, David... Well, here it is, Kathy," said Don soberly. "We've been anticipating further input by the authorities. Here it is... Their plan... their decree!

"Let's call a meeting of everyone; tell the day care staff to bring the kids; call Doobie in from the garden. Tell the work crews to take a break. We've got to all hear this and plan our response."

Everyone who could, gathered in the meeting room. People were trying to be cordial and upbeat. Don appreciated that about his charges.

"Folks, we and probably everyone else in town received our first list of decrees or orders. It was delivered this morning... On a Sunday even! Can we all see how Sunday Morning is only a shell of what it used to be?

"Let me simply read these out loud; we'll get you a copy later if you want. It's entitled **NEW PEACE ORDER (NPO) Agreement**, two pages long. Here we go folks:

> *"All personal cash, savings, and investment capital will be frozen, inaccessible to all local citizens.*
>
> *"Purchasing of food and other personal items will only be allowed with an NPO debit card at NPO-sponsored retail outlets.*
>
> *"All travel by car, train, bus, plane or other conveyance will cease; no longer allowed and no longer feasible.*
>
> *"All existing internet access will be scrambled. No further computer or cellphone use permitted, or possible.*
>
> *"A curfew is in place from 6:00pm to 4:00am. No exceptions. Violators will immediately be arrested.*
>
> *"DISCUSSION: All of the above rulings go into effect immediately, by noon this day; and will be strictly enforced by NPO Officers.*

"We, at NPO Headquarters, realize that these new regulations will provide some burdensome realities for you...

('Oh, brother,' interjected Don, '*burdensome realities...* how sweet of them to be so concerned... oops, sorry for the comment.')

"There is one way, however, to escape those burdensome realities these changes will cause and that is to be willing to give your allegiance to President Gabrinne, for all the good he has done for us and the world. He has given us a new lease on life, with his peace and prosperity initiatives. The world regards and welcomes him as their sovereign, beloved Leader. We all should do the same.

"When you bestow on him your own sure and tireless admiration, you will be asked to sign a Covenant Agreement binding you to uphold all of his new policies. And then you will receive a Mark of Agreement on the forehead or right hand, publicly signifying your devotion to the NPO way of life. Once you complete these steps, you will be issued an NPO Debit Card, gifted with a beginning balance of $5,000, which can be added to through your place of employment and by taking part in various Government-sponsored activities, to be made clear shortly.

"Also, once you have received the Mark of Agreement, you will be entitled to have your right to travel by car returned to you through a minor mechanical adjustment (at NPO expense); your use of the Internet will also be returned; and, you will be free to disregard the curfew rule.

"This document you are reading is a Covenant with the NPO, which the NPO does not take lightly. The NPO

for its part pledges to provide you and your family with
unbounded peace and prosperity. It pledges to provide for
your family's every need being met and every desire being
fulfilled.

('Folks, that's God's doing... providing for our needs and desires. The NPO wants to replace our God and make Him of no importance... Well, I say: **Not on your life!**')

"One final note: You can move up the NPO organizational
ladder as far as you want to go. That will depend solely
on how hard you are willing to work toward advancing
the NPO program.

"Thank you for your attention and your desire to be a part
of something grand, that will establish you as a beacon of
peace and prosperity to the world. To take the next step,
simply complete the enclosed form and return it by mail,
postage paid, to NPO, Greensville, North Carolina."

Don paused and looked around the room. By the stoic look on the faces he concluded that the people were as stunned at the scope of the directive as he was...

"People, it's beginning to dawn on me: you know the forces of darkness have been at work in this community... And why? To cause the current economic downturn... And why do that? To sweeten their offer of a free $5,000 debit card for signing the Covenant, that's why! Gobs of people are going to jump at that chance for a free financial break through."

Several in attendance nodded their heads in agreement. "I was going to call it a *financial blessing*," Don went on, "But it's going to prove to be anything but a *blessing*!"

After a long pause, Don resumed. "Well, people, what can we say: our freedoms are being taken away, one by one. I have marveled that they haven't been more physical from the start, but it looks like that's ending. As of now we can't purchase food and water.

"...You know what? I wish Mark were here, because he'd say, in his undeniably *Rocky Balboa* voice: 'Food and water? Hey, no problem. I know some people!'"

Everyone chuckled at the mental picture of Mark doing his *tough-guy routine.* They all longed for his return with Mary Kay and the boys and Natalie.

"I know the NPO is waiting us out. We are more valuable right now to them being alive. Their number one goal is to sign up as many as possible who will swear a new allegiance to Gabrinne. If they just came in like a bulldozer and forced us to comply or face death, they would be losing a lot of potential new converts.

"So, our immediate goal is to wait them out. And as we do, of course, we will stay faithful to God. Remember always that God wants us prepared not scared... Soon enough they will turn up the heat and more seriously and more thoroughly enforce their new guidelines. Our job is to go on with life as normally as we can and for as long as we can.

"Folks, did you realize we have been living in God's bubble of protection from the very beginning of our time together? I'm talking about His *Secret Place... in the Most High* [44]...where there is no sickness, no accidents. Only peace and well-being!

"They are promoting their *New Peace Order.* But it's only man-made. Well, we have our own Peace Order! It's living in the presence of the Lord... and it's God-made! So, you know it's good and it's going to last... for sure it's going to outlast the NPO version!"

Jim shot up his hand. "Dad, I heard this morning on the early news that for the most part the edicts were easily received in the community without question or conflict," Jim shared.

"They said some arrests were made of persons reacting to the message and tearing up the edicts in full view of officers. These were apparently a few conservative, right-wing holdouts, claiming abuse of their First Amendment rights, and insisting they would rather go to jail than comply with this *Military Coup*, as they called it."

"Thanks, Jim... Any other news to share? Or any questions or comments?" Don asked. "How are we doing on food, Doobie?"

"We have a ton of food laid up for us," he answered. "Well, probably not a ton but a whole bunch, and more is getting ready for harvest. So, we're doing fairly good there."

"What do you think, Doobie, enough to last two weeks? Two months? What?"

"Oh, I'd say, closer to a month," he answered. "The other day when you told us to use our cash to buy food and essentials, I went out and got a bunch of seeds and starter-plants. We need to get another hunk of land ready for planting. That would help...

"Oh, Brother Don, I loaded up on another important item when I went shopping," Doobie added. "It was, you know, paper... t-paper... Toilet Paper! Do I have to spell it out for you folks?"

"Thank you, Doobie," Kathy said. "We'll all be grateful for that, soon enough."

"People, let's have a real teaching session this evening. There's much that the Lord wants us to know. In the meantime, I'm planning on a quick walk downtown, just to see what's up. Kathy?"

"No thanks, Don; I'm going to stick close to home. There's a sweet little grandchild that I haven't seen for about two hours. She'll take my mind off everything else, bless her heart."

Don dismissed the people and got ready for his stroll into town. Kathy was nearby to issue her stern warning to him: "I'm serious, Don! You be careful out there!"

Others nearby boomed out similar alerts: "Take care, Don!" "Be careful."

"Don bellowed back his reply that rang down the corridor: "No, I won't be careful! I cast all my care on the Lord. I refuse to be full of care.

But I will be on the alert, cautious, and tuned into the Holy Spirit! That I will do... See you later!"

Don found the weather nearly perfect for a leisurely walk. As he got closer to the center of Greensville, he again sensed a festive mood among the people. New playground equipment had already been installed in the square; there were pony rides available. Kids were enjoying it all, along with smiling parents. When Don got out of the bright sun, he noticed the outline of some hieroglyphic-like showing of *666* here and there as people walked past. It was the Mark of the Beast, spoken of in the Book of Revelation, Chapter 13. It almost seemed to glow on the foreheads or right hands of the people. The Mark was not on everyone, but on most. The ones with the Mark must have been early signers of the NPO Covenant, Don surmised.

Wow, Lord! It's here. It's for real! The Mark of the Beast. We're past the point of no return, aren't we?

Hold steady, Don! Don't let all the hype and noise throw you off course! And forget about all the smiling faces you see; most of that is phony. The NPO has planted those smiling people. It's all a charade. Stick with Me; I'll see you through.

Thanks, Lord. I'm sticking with You.

Don could hardly move for a second or two. Then who should he run into but Pastor Daniel and Marybeth. "Oh, hi, Don. Isn't it a grand day! Peace and prosperity wherever you look," said a smiling Pastor Daniel.

Don was glad to see no Mark on their foreheads or hands. He commented, "I'm sure glad to see no marks on your foreheads. That's a relief."

The Pastor explained. "No, the Mark hasn't yet come forth, but it will in a day or so; they use some slow-release dye I understand. We have proudly signed our Covenant Agreement. We are now part of the New Peace Order."

"But why Daniel? Why Marybeth? You know this is wrong. This is the ultimate scheme of Satan," Don pleaded but without any effect.

Pastor Daniel interrupted. "Don you have no right to speak that way. You see those gentlemen walking around in the park, with the bright blue jackets? They are NPO officials, looking after things and keeping everything in order. One yell from me would bring six of those fellas over here and you would be arrested so fast it would make your head spin... and that would be the end of The Factory and all your friends out there. So, just be on your best behavior!"

He went on. "If you and your friends had half a brain you would do what Marybeth and I have done. God has promised that our light would shine, that we would be coming into a time of great blessing, showing forth the glory of the Lord.[45] Well, I believe that time is now, and this is how God chose to implement His plan."

"...You mean, through Gabrinne?" Don braced himself for a fight of words and went on boldly. "He is the Antichrist, the embodiment of Satan himself! Surely you don't mean what you're saying!"

Pastor Daniel was nearly at the end of his patience. He turned to look Don in the eye. "Don, I might point out that several of those NPO officers are looking our way right now. They can detect your loud voice. They are suspecting something out of order, just waiting for a signal from me. If I were you, I would quietly turn and walk away...

"Consider my magnanimous gesture as a gift for old time's sake... It won't be long until you're one of us anyway, if you have any sense at all."

The Lord joined in on the admonition. *"He's right, Don. Simply move on. Just smile and move on. Get back to The Factory. That's where you're needed, not here on the streets to challenge the many who have turned their back on Me."*

Don obeyed. Without saying another word to Pastor Daniel and Marybeth, he turned and headed back to The Factory. He didn't greet another person along the way. The reality of what was happening and of losing a friend and co-worker to the NPO was devastating. He sat on some steps of a local house, out of public view, and began to cry, then sob. He cried out to his only sure *Friend*:

"Lord, Lord, You gotta help me keep things straight and keep my feet from buckling under me. Most of all help those You have entrusted to me."

"I will, Don. I will. Just keep looking to Me and listening for My voice... Now, there's another assignment I'm giving you. On your way home, you'll find a young man sitting on a bench near a tall maple tree, about two blocks from here. I want you to stop and befriend him. He's had quite a set back and he's praying to Me for someone to come to his aid."

Don stood, wiped his face, and started to look out for the young man. Just as the Lord said, Don found him sitting alone on a city bench. He did look very dejected, Don noticed. Without hesitation, Don opened the conversation.

"Hello. Mind if I have a seat next to you?"

"No, suit yourself," the young man replied. He was nearly inaudible.

Both scanned the other to check for signs of the Mark of Agreement. "My name is Don Crawford. I live in a big old factory up the road with a group of others."

"My name is Bill Reed, I am... rather, I was, the Pastor of a new church in town, called Glad Tidings. We were just getting off the ground, since about a month ago, meeting at the Civic Center, Room 201, when the Officers came this Sunday morning and told us we could no longer meet there. And why? I have no idea... something about not following NPO Guidelines. Whatever that means!"

"Wow! They just walked in and shut you down like that?"

"But that's not the worst. They threatened the dozen or so parishioners that were there, with dire consequences if they continued with a church that was not officially sanctioned or following the Guidelines of the New Peace Order, whatever that is."

"Dire consequences?!" exclaimed Don.

"That's what they said... so my people got scared and then they scattered. I might as well say, Glad Tidings is finished." The Pastor could barely get the words out.

Don went on, trying to hide the contempt that was churning inside. "So, what are you going to do now?"

"I have no idea," he said. His head couldn't hang much lower. Don's heart went out to him. Then his heart perked up a bit with the young man's next question.

"Sir, Do you believe in prayer...?"

"I sure do. I'm a Believer! I'm an all-out, tongue-talking, going-to-Heaven Believer! So are the rest of the group that I live with. We believe that with God all things are possible."

"Am I ever glad to hear you say that!" came the now-animated young man, looking into Don's face. "That's what I've been praying for... for someone that could help... and here you just happen to come by to sit."

"Oh, it's more than that. God orchestrated the whole thing. He told me about fifteen minutes ago to seek you out and offer you my friendship, as an answer to the prayers you've been sending up to Him!"

"Really? Well, I reckon I shouldn't be too surprised, should I? I'm supposed to be a Believer, after all. I guess right now my faith level is a bit low. But thanks for coming along."

"Say, listen, Pastor Bill, I need to be getting back to The Factory or people will be wondering about me... I have an idea. Why don't you come with me? Stay the night, stay the week, stay longer if you want... at least until you get your bearings back and you hear from the Lord about what to do next.

"What do you think? Is it a go? The people there are super friendly. You'll like them, I know you will. And accommodations are great, simple but nice."

Don stood looking at the young man wrestle with the offer, and the warm smile on his face gave the answer he was hoping for. The Pastor Bill who got up to join Don, seemed to have a new lease on life: "Okay. I will. Thanks for the invitation." A warm handshake followed.

"My car is over here," said Pastor Bill. I've been living out of it for the past month. Let's drive it to your factory. Okay?"

Don gave him the bad news. "Sorry to tell you but cars don't work any longer, as of today, at noon. The internet grid is out of commission, courtesy of the NPO, so cars can't even be started. That could change if I'd agree to sign on to the new Agreement... but there's no way I'm going to do that!"

"I wouldn't either!" echoed the young man, walking to his nearby car. "Let me get my suitcase; its full of my things I want to take with me."

Within minutes the two men were hiking back to The Factory. Don, never one to be shy, started a conversation. "Say, Pastor Bill, I'm curious... where do you stand on God's plan for the end-times?"

On and on went the dialogue and questions, back and forth, all the way to The Factory. Don found out that he and Pastor Bill had more in common about end-times than not. David saw the two of them walking up the lane and came to the door to greet them.

"We were about to send out a search party for you, Brother Don. Looks like this young man with you beat us to the punch... Hello, I'm David.

"I'm in charge of keeping this place safe and running smoothly."

"David, this is Pastor Bill Reed. I literally picked him up from a city bench in town a short time ago. He'll be staying with us for a while. Pastor Reed, this is David. He's a good man. I don't know what we'd do without him and his lovely family."

"Hello, David. Glad to be joining you," the Pastor said with a vigorous handshake.

"David, why don't you help our guest get settled into a room and show him around. I gotta find Kathy – that's my wife, Pastor – and talk with her. Maybe Mama Blanchard could get our guest some grub to eat... We're going to be having a meeting tonight, Pastor. I want you to come and meet everyone."

"Okay. Glad to."

Don found Kathy in Jenny's room – doing what? You guessed it: holding Rosalie! "Kathy, Jenny, Jim... Well, I've got some bad news and some good news!"

The threesome was glued to their seats, waiting for Don's report. "Bad news first," Don went on. "Pastor Daniel and Marybeth have sold out to the NPO. They signed the Agreement, have the Mark, the whole business. I couldn't believe it, but to hear them carry on so profusely about the new changes, you know they're gung ho. They'll probably have a role to play in implementing NPO changes in the Churches in the region. They think this is all part of God's plan to institute a glorious new era in the world through the Church..."

"Wow! This is something," said Kathy. "And for them to think all this is part of God's plan for mankind... How could this have happened?"

Everyone looked on during the longest pause. It was impossible for any of them to fully get their head around this news about Pastor Daniel.

Then, Jim interrupted. "How about the good news, Dad. Let's hear that."

"Yeah... the good news! Guess who I brought home with me today... Guess."

"Don! Stop playing with us. What is the good news!" insisted Kathy.

"Okay. The Lord directed this whole operation. He told me to locate a young Pastor on my walk home, sitting on a bench, who needed a friend. Well, I found this young man and started talking with him. He is a new Pastor in town, as of a month ago, who started a new church, called Glad Tidings.

"He told me the sad story of having his Church infiltrated this morning by the NPO paying a surprise visit. They ordered the Church to close because it wasn't complying with NPO Guidelines. They threatened the handful of parishioners, who all scattered. He was devastated...

"So, I did the neighborly thing and invited him to The Factory. How long he stays is up to him and the Lord. David is getting him settled right now. He said he'd be coming to tonight's meeting."

"Dad, this is something," commented Jenny. "In one day, you lose one Pastor to the NPO fiasco. And on the same day you rescue another Pastor from falling prey to the NPO... the Lord is looking out for us."

"Jenny, I'm not saying he's another Pastor for us," Don argued. "But now that you mentioned it... Hmmm... Could be, I guess; we'll see."

"Now, let's not get the cart before the horse," Kathy cautioned everyone. "Best to let this play out under the Lord's doing without us trying to make anything happen."

"There she goes, folks," Don said, "Being practical and level-headed, and saying for all of us exactly what the Lord would tell us if He was here in person. Thanks, dear... We'll make what you said, Kathy, our *Modis Operandi* regarding new Pastor Bill Reed... We'll *wait and see* how the Lord leads us.."

THE MEETING THAT NIGHT AT THE FACTORY started out on a somber note. "Folks, I do have something to share that's really... well... It's shocking and sad!" Don began slowly. He found it hard to even bring up the business about Pastor Daniel, so he went a different direction.

"But before getting into that, let me introduce a new face to you. Everyone turn around and welcome a newcomer: Pastor Bill Reed, whom I met just today on my walk back from town."

All eyes found Pastor Reed and extended a warm and welcoming greeting.

"He's been in Greensville about a month and started a new church, called Glad Tidings," Don continued. "This morning the NPO Officers paid him a surprise visit in the middle of the church service, to shut them down because they were not operating in NPO guidelines, whatever that means...

"As I heard his story, it reminded me of the time in the life of Jesus, when the authorities came to arrest Him in Gethsemane. The Bible says: *They Smote the Shepherd and the sheep of His flock scattered.*[46] Well, today Pastor Bill's Church was smitten by the NPO and his sheep scattered.

"Anyway, I invited Pastor Bill to come and join us for as long as he wants. I told him this was the friendliest group that ever was, so don't disappoint me. Make him feel right at home. Anything you'd like to say tonight, Pastor?"

"No, just that I'm happy to be here. And I hope to get to know all of you better in the days ahead."

"Wow! A Pastor of few words! Amazing!" said Don... "Well, that was the good news part. Now for the bad news part of tonight's agenda. It has to do with Pastor Daniel and his wife Marybeth... You better brace yourselves.

"I saw them this afternoon, just ahead of meeting Pastor Bill. They are both now Loyalists with the NPO; they have signed their Covenant Letter, swearing their allegiance to the Antichrist."

Gasps of unbelief and muffled groans could be heard all over the room. "I can't believe it." "Are you sure?" "They wouldn't do that, would they?" "Don't they know that's a one-way ticket to Hell?"

"Mama Blanchard, Doobie, and you, Barbara and Rusty... oh, they're not here are they, on their trip west... you guys knew Pastor Daniel well, for many years. Cornerstone was your home church. I'm especially sorry for you hearing this news about the Pastor. I enjoyed going to his Church; I thought of him as a co-laborer in God's Kingdom. No one was more shocked than I was... Anything you want to say at this time?"

No one spoke up for the longest while, then Mama Blanchard made an unexpected announcement. "Don, Kathy, I want to move out here on a full-time and permanent basis. Considering all that's happened and all that lies before us, I want to be as close to my family – and you're all my family – as possible. Okay?"

"Okay! For sure, Mama, we'll make it happen, won't we D.J., Jerry, David, Jim, Kathy, Sam?"

"Sure will," said David, speaking on everyone's behalf.

"Mama, you've been out here for over a week, as our guest, just after all of this challenge unfolded... after they confiscated your restaurant, because you wouldn't take down that poster of Jesus... and wouldn't put up their posters about the NPO and Gabrinne... So, Mama, let's just make it permanent! Do you have enough clothing and personal things with you?"

"Oh, yes. I'm doing just fine. And thank you, I'm already feeling better."

"Great!" Don added. "But that makes me think of others who have been a part of this family, like Glenda, Betty McPherson, newcomer Nancy Struble... anyone else? Oh yes, how about Suzy?"

"How about Henry and Louise Greyheck?" asked Clair.

"Oh, for sure, let's not leave them out," Don replied. "I wonder how they're doing after all this opened up. Maybe I should visit them again."

"But by now," added Ben, "even if these wanted to move here permanently, we don't have any vehicles that we can use to help, because all computers are out and we need computers to make cars and trucks work, right?"

"I wish I knew how the NPO vans are working," said D.J. "They are somehow bypassing the computer system or have a new one installed. There's probably no way I could look under the hood of one of those vans... But if I could...

"Hmmm, What do you think Don? There's one sitting outside right now; David saw it. The driver is still wet behind the ears; he'd be a piece of cake for us."

"Too risky, D.J. I couldn't endorse it. Let's ask the Lord for a better way out of this dilemma... Besides," Don went on with gusto, "What if you could get one of our cars started. What would you do then? Where would you go? You know they'd be on the lookout for any non-NPO vehicle running around the streets... you'd be a rolling target, a disaster just waiting to happen!

"Wait, I just thought of something... and this might work!" Don went on with an air of secrecy. "If you could get one of our cars or a truck started, you could head out to the Armory and run it into the NPO Headquarters! Now that would help our cause a bunch; probably throw the NPO off track for a good two days or so. Of course, we'd lose you for sure in the process... Should I go on?"

"No! No! That's enough!"

As Don began a more serious teaching about: "*How humility is our protection from the enemy's deception*" there was a young Greensville family of five stuck on a deserted county road in northern Georgia. Their car was out of commission, they were hungry as all get out. They had no food, no water, and no plan to give even a sliver of hope for a rescue. They intentionally chose to travel on seldom-used roads on their way back from Kansas to avoid any detection by NPO Loyalists.

As Don was teaching, there came a sudden break in the proceedings... He stopped in his tracks, so did many others. They sat on the edge of their chairs and looked out, gazing, as if trying to detect the faint call of someone in distress. Don listened too, then spoke up.

"Folks, I don't know about you, but I feel a strong impression down in my spirit to pray for Mark and Mary Kay and their children... to pray for their safety..."

"Yeah, I agree, Don," added Doobie and Sam almost simultaneously, "I get the idea they are in some real serious problems... in their car somewhere."

"Let's pray people. We'll start praying in our heavenly language," said Don. All joined in. "Clomata nebo, shirraminas ekanas. Shomato clay-battas klameen..."

Meanwhile, the young family on everyone's mind was coping as best as they knew how with a devastating set of circumstances...

"What are we going to do, Mark?" asked Mary Kay. "Daddy, I'm hungry," cried Levi from the back seat. "Isn't there something to eat?"

"I'm sorry, honey, for leading you guys on this wild goose chase," replied a dejected Mark McKenna. "We should have stayed in Kansas."

"Oh, don't blame yourself, Mark," answered Mary Kay. "We've got to keep praying and believe for God to intervene. He told us He would never leave us, nor forsake us, right?"

She turned to the back seat to address the two young boys. "Gideon, Levi, let's say another prayer for God to help us, Okay? *Lord, our only hope is in You. You have kept us safe so far; Thank You that You love us very much...*"

Suddenly, the car was surrounded by a tremendous bright light. It seemed at first that a couple of Officers may have found the family on that empty road and were coming for an arrest. Within seconds you heard the car door slam, and footsteps came closer to Mark's window.

Mark whispered: "Hold steady, Mary Kay. You too Gideon and Levi. And Natalie. Don't be afraid. God will help us!"

When the person got to Mark's window and looked inside with his flashlight, it was not an NPO Officer. It seemed to be just a young man dressed in everyday clothes, with a soft and pleasant face. Mark rolled down the window. The man spoke up in a gentle and easy fashion. "You folks are in car trouble. I want to help."

"What did you have in mind, sir?" asked Mark.

"I thought I'd give you a ride back home. Where is that?"

"In Greensville, North Carolina, but that's hundreds of miles from here."

"No matter. I'll get you there... Do you have a better option?"

"No sir. I don't."

"I'm not one of the Loyalists wandering around the countryside; you can trust me. I'm part of a group that helps stranded motorists; we've really been busy since the NPO policies were put into effect... Why don't all of you pile into my van behind you with all your suitcases and stuff and we'll get started."

Mark and Mary Kay shared concerned glances as they got their possessions and children together, but followed the young man's leading, nonetheless.

"Do you have anything to eat in your van," asked a hungry Gideon.

"Yeah, do you?" chimed in Levi.

Mark was ready to quiet the children, but he wanted to know the answer to that question himself.

"Yup. We got everything you might want to eat. Why we even have your favorite: Broccoli, okay?"

"Broccoli? Is that all?" bemoaned Levi.

"That would be okay, if that's all you've got, sir," added Gideon, poking Levi in the ribs to admonish him to be thankful for whatever is available. It caused a brief smile on the faces of both parents.

"No, I'm just kidding you. We have potato chips, candy bars, cookies, peanut butter and jelly sandwiches, milk, pop, everything you want! And no broccoli!"

Once everyone got in and settled, the van took off. All hands dug into the food containers and some serious munching ensued. After tummies were filled, the yawning started. The young man said to his passengers, "I know how to get to Greensville. Why don't you all take a little nap. It will help pass the time. There are some pillows and blankets back there for you to use."

The family easily agreed and got themselves nestled in for the long drive. Only it wasn't a long drive. In fact, the drive was over in seconds. All the sudden the van sat at the front door of The Factory! The young driver got out and went to the door and knocked and found David inside. David heard the knock and came closer to investigate. Then he saw them in the van: Mark, Mary Kay, and the children.

David got so excited he didn't know what to do! He ran back and forth, down the hall then back, considering two options: *Should I run and tell Don, or should I stay here and help the McKenna's come inside?*

In an instant the family was standing at the front door, yawning, and stretching, like just awakening from a long nap. Their suitcases sat next to them.

"Where are we?" asked sleepy Gideon.

The parents thought at first this must surely be a dream. "I see the front door of The Factory, I can see David all excited, but this can't be so. We were just in Georgia," said a bewildered Mark. He was holding on to Mary Kay's hand and both at the same instance smiled a smile so big that it covered the night sky!

Mark turned to talk with the young man, but he was nowhere to be found. No sign of the van. No opportunity to say: "*Thank you.*"

Mary Kay summed it up this way: "That must have been an angel. God sent an angel to rescue us!"

"Oh, Thank You! THANK YOU, JESUS!" bellowed Mark. "Your promise is true: You never leave us nor forsake us!"

Then, Don and Kathy appeared at the door, followed closely by a happy group of the faithful. Doobie stepped out the front door to personally welcome the travelers' home.

"Hey, bro, glad you're back. High five!" (Smack) Within seconds the family was surrounded by a crowd of joyful well-wishers.

Doobie took charge and announced: "Let's all go to the meeting room. Mama and I will get some drinks and snacks ready. We've got to celebrate! Mark and his family were lost but now they are found!"

"Don, you'll have to finish your teaching another time," Doobie yelled out as he escorted two excited boys down the hall, one on each hand.

Kathy's excitement was interrupted at that moment. Don noticed her reaching for her phone and nodded that he would go on with the others.

"Hello! Hello! I can barely hear you!" came the faint voice through Kathy's cellphone... "Are you there, Mom? This is Sylvia."

"Oh, Sylvia. Glad to hear your voice. Things are in a state of confusion here; that explains all the noise in the background."

"What's going on? Are you and Dad okay?"

"Yes, honey, we're fine. We just had a family of five brought back to us by an angel. It's a long story, but the family was stuck on a vacant road in northern Georgia, with no working car and little hope of getting out of there. But then an angel arrived in a van and whisked them back to The Factory. I think someone said it was about a ten-second ride."

"Wow! No end to your excitement there. Wow!..."

"Honey, is there something wrong? You sound a little dejected... probably from all the NPO rules coming at us? I can't blame you. Is that it?"

"Oh, I suppose. I wish, I really wish I could be with you there now. With you and dad, and Jenny and Jim, and little Rosalie... All this upheaval and confusion is really getting to me and Mike."

"I wish you could be with us, too..."

"Maybe we could get that Angel to pull some strings, suppose?"

"Well, *all things are possible to those who believe,*[47] the Bible says... Honey, I'm hearing some more crackling over the phone; they are scheduled to quit working some time real soon... Honey, can you hear me? Sylvia? SYLVIA? I'm going to hang up and try to call you back!"

Kathy frantically called Sylvia's number and no response. The phone was dead. Kathy sat in the nearest chair in the hallway and started to cry, then pray. "Oh, Lord, help Sylvia and Mike and the kids. I thank You for surrounding them with the shield of Your good will. May they dwell in Your Secret Place now and forever! ... Shumala nopen... cabolass praysobra... latismani calontes... yay bo nela..."

She continued praying in the Spirit for five minutes and then she was interrupted by Clair, looking for David. "Have you seen David recently? Oh, I'm sorry. I'm intruding."

"That's alright, Clair. I'm fine. I just had a call from my older daughter, and she was going through a hard time because of all this NPO business. And right in the middle, the phone went dead. It just quit on me!" Kathy tried to use her phone again and it was still frozen. "I guess we're done with these phones, Clair. Things are closing in tighter and tighter... I think I'll go and find Don... What did you need David for? Was it important?"

"No, not really. See you later."

A few weeks back there was a big celebration for the marriage of Mark and Mary Kay. Now there was another joyful celebration for their safe return to The Factory by way of Angelic translation!

Over the din of the crowd, Don asked the newest guest a question. "What do you think, Pastor Bill? Didn't I tell you this was the friendliest group ever?"

"Yes, you did," he answered. "I see what you mean."

"Say, Pastor Bill, what sort of work did you do before getting into the pastoring business, if you don't mind my being nosey?" Don asked.

"No. I was a reporter and anchor for a small TV station in my hometown of New Orchard – that's about 120 miles from here."

"You're kidding me! Can't be! No way... this is strange."

"How so?"

"See that lady over near the food table, tall and distinguished looking? That's Sam, Samantha Burton. She used to be a well-known TV Anchor from Greensboro."

"Really? I think I know of her. She covered your tornado tragedy a while back."

"Let me introduce her to you... Sam! If you can break away from the food table, come and meet Pastor Bill... Sam, this is Pastor Bill Reed... Pastor Bill, Samantha Burton. She's been such a blessing around here... Pastor, she knows a thing or two about covering news and making news... Well, folks, see you later; I'm going to find Kathy."

Guess where Kathy was... you're right again, holding Rosalie. "Great party, huh, Kathy? Haven't the two of you bonded by now...?

"Ya know, Kathy, in a way I'm not upset that the teaching got interrupted tonight. This has been a long and challenging day. I'm looking forward to an early bedtime. How about you?"

"I agree. I'm ready anytime. Let's find Mark and Mary Kay and say good night. And then get one last doughnut for the road!"

"No Thanks. My bed sounds more inviting than a doughnut... Oh, maybe I'd better take one for tomorrow morning...just in case!"

THREE DAYS LATER A SECOND LIST of edicts was disseminated. The Factory's copy was pasted to the front door, which David retrieved and brought to Don. Once again, all the faithful were called to gather in the meeting room. Don explained that a new list of rules was just received. As before, he proceeded to read them out loud:

"New NPO Rules: Effective Immediately, for Greensville and sur-rounding area:

"1. *Gatherings in groups of six or more strictly prohibited, unless for NPO-sponsored church services that follow NPO Guidelines; or for other NPO-sponsored events.*

"2. *All churches will immediately adopt NPO policies and procedures, or risk having their doors shut permanently...* ('They got you three days early, Pastor Bill. Likely they had their eye on you for some time... looking for any reason to shut your doors. Why? Who knows! Maybe they didn't like the color of your hair'.)

"3. *All children, ages 4 to 16, will be required to participate in daily NPO-authorized activities at designated locations. All schools, at all levels, will be discontinued, until further notice.*

"4. *Two years of required military service will immediately be insti-tuted for all able-bodied individuals, male and female, 17 to 21, not currently on active or reserved military duty.*

"5. *All varieties of firearms must be turned in to the NPO. There will be guarded receptacles positioned around town to receive the firearms: one next to the shelter at City Park, one at the NPO Headquarters at the Armory, one next to the Post Office, now an Annex of the NPO. All gun stores will be closed indefinitely.*

"Discussion: It is expected that you and your neighbor will do the honorable thing and notify the NPO Headquarters by mail (see enclosed stamped, envelope) of all in your household who will be affected by these new regulations. When you do, we will inform you by return mail of other related details. If we do not hear from you within a week, we will send an NPO Officer to finalize the

sign-up process. Let's all work diligently to make this transition go smoothly."

Don held up the paper to make his next point. "And get this, folks. It's signed by the Greater Greensville Area NPO Steering Committee: Fire Chief, Mac Johnson, Pastor Daniel Tinsley, Betty McPherson, and Lieutenant Governor, Carroll Leonard. And get this: Recording Secretary is listed as our own Verla Martin. Well, she's not our own any longer! Lord, have mercy on her."

Don opened up discussion: "Well that little sign off by the Steering Committee tells us about Betty McPherson and where her loyalties are. That lady is your great aunt or something, right Mary Kay?"

"Yes, something like that. We never did hit it off that well," she answered.

"Really... I wished I had known that when she came out here to make amends for the harsh way she treated us during our refurbishing... I guess we misjudged her, right, Kathy? We gave her a halo when it should have been something else... like a broomstick!"

"Yup. Looks like we were wrong on that call," Kathy replied. "Or maybe not... Maybe Betty really did seek forgiveness then, and only recently decided to side in with the NPO."

"Hmmm... Oh, well, back to our discussion," Don announced. "Let's see which of these policies apply to us? Group gatherings of six or more; yes, guilty. That could be a problem. We're not technically a Church per se, but we do get together for church. So, I don't know about that one...

"We do have children ages four and above, one belonging to David and Dianne and one belonging to Mary Kay and Mark. That could be a problem.

"Let's see, there's no one here age 17 to 21 is there?" Hands go up.

"Yes?" D.J. raised his hands. "Now that could be a problem."

D.J. spoke further. "And Glenda, if she was here, she'd have to raise her hand."

"Hmmm..." Don was thinking about where to lead the discussion...

"But it's not a *problem!* Make it a *challenge*, not a *problem*," Doobie insisted. "That's what you taught us, Brother Don. You taught us that the Bible says we can have what we say... however you define it is how it will be for you, either good or bad.[48] Right? Well, you have to practice what you preach."

"Doobie? Is that you carrying on so in the back of the room?" Don pretended to be scanning the horizon, then pointed at Doobie. "It is you, isn't it! Well, I got one thing to say: Are you ready?"

Doobie sank a little lower in his chair, waiting for the shoe to drop. Don paused for dramatic effect.

"Here it is... Thank you, Doobie. That's what I've got to say. Thanks a whole bunch for holding me accountable and keeping me in line. That's what friends do, don't they? They help one another. I for one appreciate all the help I can get. So, Thanks again, Doobie."

Ben spoke up in a similar theme to that of Doobie's. "Let's make it something we turn over to the Lord to handle. Like the Lord told King Jehoshaphat through that prophet: *The battle is the Lord's and the victory is ours.*[49] Let's do the same thing: give the battle to God and claim the victory."

Mama Blanchard added to the chorus. "Yes, let's give it to the Lord. He'll make it turn out right, and make it turn out for our own good." [50]

"We have a room full of Preachers today, Pastor Bill." Don proclaimed. "And I just love it! Keep it going! Now, let's consider this..."

At that moment, David and Jerry ran in to interrupt the meeting, excited beyond measure. "Don, sorry for barging in like this. You're not going to believe this!" announced David, gasping for air. "Guess who just came in our front door."

"You'll never guess," added Jerry, bouncing up and down like a yo-yo, with excitement.

"Well, let's see," said Don, wanting to prolong the joy of the moment. "It can't be Santa Clause, it's too warm outside... Maybe the Easter Bunny? How about that kids? No, wrong season... Oh, I give up. Who?"

And in walked Henry and Louise Greyheck!

"Henry! Louise! It's you!" Don exclaimed, as he rushed over to greet them with unashamed hugs. "How did you get here? Come up front and tell this story to everyone."

The Greyhecks walked up with Don, both grinning profusely. Henry spoke for the two of them. "How did we get here, you ask. We came in a van, a plain, unmarked van."

Henry looked out and spotted Mark and pointed at him as he spoke: "You see, Mark is not the only person who *knows some people*. I know a few myself. I found one that couldn't turn down my offer to bring us here. And are we ever glad! Thank you for your hospitality, Don, and all of you saints here at The Factory."

As the group applauded, David brought in two folding chairs for the Greyhecks. They sat to listen. Don went on. "Henry, Louise, it's so good to see you here. Welcome to your humble home. We'll get you settled later...

"We were just discussing the ramifications of a new set of policies we received this morning. The NPO is gripping it's strangle-hold on the community tighter and tighter. We now have to deal with the size of our gatherings, no more than six; required NPO elementary school, really *indoctrination* is what it is, for all kids 4-16; compulsory military service for those 17-21; all firearms are to be turned in; and finally, all churches will adopt NPO policies and procedures or be barred shut.

"Now, let's go over these in more detail..."

D.J. interjected. "Brother Don, just what are they going to do if we don't comply? And how do they know how many people are meeting together here? How do they know who has guns? Have they planted video and audio surveillance in here?

"How about if we simply refused to cooperate? Isn't there a rightful place for civil disobedience – when what they're demanding violates our constitutional rights, not to mention our religious freedoms!?"

"Yeah, I agree with D.J." added Sam. "They – and just who is this *they* we keep talking about... They just can't muscle their way in and demand our servitude. How do they get off being the *boss* and we're stuck being the *bossed...*? I tell you, Don, I've about had it with these people!"

Others jumped in on the topic, as Don wondered: *What is the topic, Lord?* People had strong feelings one way, or the other, to be sure. Don was losing the battle of decorum. He looked out at Kathy, as if to ask: *Any suggestions on what I should do?* Kathy shrugged her shoulders in reply. She had no help or wisdom to offer.

"People! People! Let's calm down, please," Don pleaded. After a few more seconds of hubbub, the meeting room did begin to quiet down. "Look! I don't like this anymore than you do. But let's be practical. Our choices are being taken away. As our choices diminish, so do our freedoms...

"And who is the *'they'* you ask. Well, they are the NPO Officers whose job locally is to enforce our compliance with all their policies and to compel us to change our allegiance from God to the kingdom of darkness. The local NPO has as much power as does the organization they represent, which is comprised of a world-wide network of ever-growing, power-hungry villains from the Kingdom of Darkness, headed up by the Antichrist himself, Marschall Gabrinne, who in turn is the pawn, a mere puppet mind you, in the hand of our real archenemy, Satan!

"Here's another angle to this: God mapped out this end-times drama from the very beginning of time. He also planned way back then for Jesus, our Savior, to redeem us from the curse of sin [and Thank God, He did]. But let's not lose sight of the fact that this same God Who set the plan of redemption into motion, is the same God Who set His end-times plan into motion. It's one and the same God!

"As the Originator of Redemption, we might well thank Him as our loving Father. But as the Designer of this end-times scenario that we are presently facing, we might have some trouble referring to Him as our loving Father...

"Yes? No? Am I ringing any bells? Let me hear what you are thinking..."

"Well, Brother Don, since you put it the way you did, I guess I need to get off my *high horse* and face reality," commented D.J. "We're here by God's design... I don't know why He planned it this way, but He did."

"Well, Don, I'm not relenting as easily as D.J.," added Sam. "But I do see that I need to do some soul-searching and prayer, to get all of this into better perspective... at least into some understanding that I know the Lord would be pleased with."

"Thank you, D.J. and Sam. Anyone else with a comment?" Don asked. "Doobie, how about you?"

"Well, I just figure that I need to focus on trusting the Lord and let Him lead the way," Doobie offered. "Course I try to make things as simple as I can, so I don't get lost in the confusion, and you got to admit there are some confusing parts to all this. And one more thing, Don, if I might add," Doobie went on...

"Sure. You've got the floor."

"I remember early on when we got settled into The Factory and you did one of your first teachings, you talked about how it was no accident that we were born into the world when we were. That God planned it all along that we would be walking on the earth at this time, in this town, ready to deal together with the end-times. And since God was responsible for getting us together, He was also responsible for equipping us to deal with whatever comes along."

"Doobie, I remember that teaching. Thanks for reminding me," Don was pleased to answer. "We talked about how we were actually God's End-Times Army, and He wouldn't send us into battle without preparation or without weapons of warfare... Wow, I feel better already! How about you?"

"It does help me, Don, to think that God has made me part of something bigger than just an ordinary life," Mama Blanchard explained. "I say: Bring it on; we'll be ready!"

"Go, Mama!" echoed several in the group. Little Rosalie woke up suddenly at the uproar from members of the group, who by now were offering high-fives to everyone and to no one in particular. (Smack! Smack! Smack!) Pastor Bill joined right in.

"Mama Blanchard! Please keep the hullabaloo back there under better control!" barked Don with a wide smile... "Henry and Louise, are you sure you want to be a part of this motley crew?" The Greyhecks simply smiled at the goings on.

Don turned to a more serious vein. "Well, folks, let me tie a couple of more things together. We're talking about dealing with some harsh realities of these end-times... and, I know we see ourselves as part of God's end-times army. But how do we get prepared and equipped for that role? The Spirit will do His part, but He expects us to do our part. Here, I'm referring to spiritual preparation and spiritual equipping, as you might guess.

"So, Doobie, what is the best way to get oneself spiritually ready for times such as these?"

"Learn how to trust the Lord, and Him alone, with all of your heart?"

"Right you are! What else? Anyone?"

"Praying in the Spirit, in other tongues?" spoke up Dianne, "to uphold our strength."

"Another good answer... Did you know, Dianne, that in the Epistle to Jude, it talks about how we build up our most holy faith by praying in other tongues? [51] We certainly need all the faith we can get, right?...

"Anything else?" Louise Greyheck offered another view. "Thanksgiving! I think we should always have a grateful heart. Without much effort we can look around and always see something to be thankful for."

"Thanks, Louise, having a grateful heart would be excellent help for getting ready for whatever comes," Don said. "And let's not forget a couple more ideas along this same line. One is the Scripture that says: *The joy of the Lord is my strength!* [52] If you find yourself running low on strength, check your joy level!

"And where does joy come from? The Scripture says: *In the presence of the Lord there is fulness of joy.*[53] So, if your joy level is low, check on the amount of time you spend in the Lord's presence!

"The more time you spend in His Presence, the more Joy you have. And the more Joy you have, the more Strength you have... He's got us covered every which way!

"The other spiritual notion that we need to keep tabs on, takes us back to a recent topic along these lines. We talked about the fact that *Humility is our greatest protection against deception.*"

"Don't be deceived, don't believe the devil who tries to tell you that you're so strong or mature, you don't need God's help... That's one of his biggest lies! Don't believe him when he wants you to think that you have arrived unto *Sainthood.* The Scripture says that *Without Jesus we can do nothing.*[54] Nothing of any real value or good, that is... Always remember: What is the best protection against deception? It's humility!

"Stay humble at heart, seek the Lord for everything. He wants to help you through everything. Don't go it alone, thinking you can do this thing without His help. No, seek His help every second of your remaining life...

"Another related Scripture tells us: *Do not forsake the assembling of yourselves together, but exhort one another, especially as you see the day approaching!*[55] Folks, we need one another. We need to encourage one another. I know we do that a lot around here; let's keep it going!

"I hope by now you are practicing your new heavenly prayer language... Pastor Bill, have you received your spiritual prayer language? No? How about you and Henry and Louise having a session later today with me and Kathy, to go over this... Okay? Good!"

Don paused and looked around; then continued. "And remember this: the devil is a liar and the Father of Lies, the Bible says.[56] So, everything (say 'everything'... *everything!*) everything that comes at you from the devil will be a lie. He can't help himself. That's all he knows is lying and deceit! So, if he ever tells you: You're not going to make it – it's a lie! If he tells you: You're too weak – it's a lie! If he tells you: God has given up on you – it's a lie! Don't believe anything he says to you... ever!

"Here's an extreme example. Maybe it sounds too far out, but maybe not: Say Kathy and I are in different cells of a prison, where they're trying to force me to change my allegiance or face beheading, and they come and say to me: 'Kathy has had enough, she changed her position. See here's a picture showing Kathy donning her new *Mark of Allegiance* on her forehead. Since she's now one of us, you might as well join her, so you can live out your remaining days with your lovely wife'...

"I won't believe it. I'll remember this teaching and recall that it's from the devil, so it's all a big lie! With the Lord's help, I'll say back to them: 'I don't believe you! It's a lie! Kathy would never sell out. Somehow you have altered this picture. I'm not moved by what I see nor am I moved by your maneuvers.'"

Don looked out at the faithful with a warm heart. The earlier mayhem and rebellious comments had fallen away. What he saw was an assembly of stalwart believers, arming themselves to fight the NPO with spiritual warfare, and expecting – with God's help – to win each battle... and in the process, to remain faithful to the Lord! He closed with this thought:

"Won't it be great, Saints, to hear the Lord say to us: *'Well done good and faithful servants. You have been faithful... enter thou into the Joy of the Lord!'* [57]

"Folks, I think we're done for now. Thanks for your sharing. I know we didn't really cover the new orders in any detail, but I think we were obedient to the leading of the Holy Spirit, as we took a different direction today. Let's look at the new NPO items later tonight. Have a great day!"

CHAPTER FIFTEEN –

With God's help we will stay faithful!

66 I 9 M NOT ONE TO BE AN ALARMIST, BUT the truth is we live in alarming times! Jesus told His disciples that love (the *agape* love of God planted in the heart of every Believer) will grow cold, for many, during the Great Tribulation. Families will turn against one another. Father against son; mother against daughter. It will be friend against friend. Why would Jesus make such a warning, for His disciples and for us? Because it could happen to us. Yes, to you and me. We need to guard against that possibility with all the might we can find! With God's help we will stay faithful! Amen! No matter what comes our way, we will remain faithful! Don't forget we are part of His great End-Times Army, and He wants us to win! Amen!"

Thus, did Don end up another teaching session for The Factory Faithful. No one moved for the longest time. Then Don recalled another point that he wanted to make. "Friends let's not forget that we will have a visit tomorrow morning by a delegation of the NPO. They want to find out why we haven't complied so far with their new policies: group size, school for the older children, compulsory military service, no firearms, and new Church policies. We have passed their allotted time to agree with the changes; I'm surprised they haven't taken any sterner action."

"Don, do you want us to be involved in any way with their visit? Or should we just go about our day as usual?" asked Doobie.

"Just go about your schedule like normal," answered Don... Kathy and I will be talking with the NPO. And while you're going about your day, be sure and lift us up in prayer... We'll give you a full report when it's over. Have a good evening.

"By the way, Pastor Bill, I'm hoping you'll lead us in another Sunday morning service. Last Sunday was great!"

"Sure. I'd be happy to," he replied. "And I'll get with Sam, D.J. and Jerry for some music... You don't hear an acoustic guitar and accordion together very often for Praise and Worship."

"Thanks for stepping in like this... you're one of us now, Pastor Bill."

"I know. Glad to be here and to be of service!"

EVERYONE WAS GOING ABOUT their day, trying to look inconspicuous, as they waited for the NPO to step up to the front door. At 9:00 am, right on schedule, they arrived. David was the first face they saw. He greeted all five of the visitors and escorted them to the meeting room. David's deadpan look with no chit-chat along the way, signaled to the NPO that The Factory was taking this encounter seriously.

Don and Kathy were seated in two card table chairs, awaiting the guests. After a round of stiff greetings, two of them took a seat in two other card table chairs facing Don and Kathy, while two security officers stood nearby, each flanking one of their leaders. A third guard stood out in the hallway next to the door. The two Officers sitting opposite Don and Kathy introduced themselves as Lieutenant Darrin Williams and as Sergeant Susan Baker. The Lieutenant was the point man.

"As we communicated by letter, Mr. and Mrs. Crawford, our purpose for today's encounter is to find out why you have not responded to the NPO's latest guidelines," began the Lieutenant matter-of-factly.

Don was quick to respond. "Well, Lieutenant, we have no excuse for not responding – other than these two points: First, it is our thinking that we at The Factory should not have to be subject to the NPO policies. We are a non-sectarian group of volunteers, banded together for the common purpose of providing humanitarian aid to the Greensville area.

"Second of all, we are hoping that you and your NPO leaders – in view of our stated purpose to support the advancement of our citizens - would look favorably on us and our situation and put aside any insistence that we comply with and adopt the new NPO guidelines."

The Lieutenant and Sergeant looked curiously at one another... likely thinking: *Do you believe this guy? We're not going to overlook anybody; we don't care how nice you want to be to Greensville citizens...* But their training wouldn't allow them to speak so openly.

"Well, Mr. Crawford," the Lieutenant finally responded. "You put us in an awkward position. We do recognize your contributions to our citizens, but the NPO policies are for everyone to address and agree to, regardless of their profession or station in life... Don't you concur, Sergeant?"

"I certainly do, Lieutenant," she said, scooting to the edge of her chair. "We strive for unity and peace in all that we do. And please believe, Mr. and Mrs. Crawford, that we want only the best for you and all who live at this facility."

"I think it is time to get down to the specifics," Lieutenant Williams proceeded firmly. "This business has gone on much too long, so here's the gist of our position: for every day you stay in non-compliance one of your people here will be placed in custody, at the local County jail to wait out your return to sanity. I mean after all, Mr. Crawford, it would be insane for you to think you're going to override us. You may rebel for a time, but eventually you'll either submit or face a most unpleasant outcome..."

Sergeant Baker looked askance at the Lieutenant and took the lead (kinda like a *bad cop-good cop* routine, Don thought). "Now, Mr. and Mrs. Crawford, I think the Lieutenant may seem a bit harsh, but that's a sign of his utter commitment to our cause. I would guess that he could be talked into a tad more leniency in this matter, if only he could see a token of your willingness to see things our way. After all, you'll have to admit that up to this point we have been accommodating to your group, not pushy, not intimidating, with no show of force..."

"Yes, I have frequently commented that your tolerance and patience have been noted and appreciated," Don answered.

"We value your cooperation," Mr. Crawford. "Let me consult with my colleague for a moment." The Sergeant and Lieutenant brainstormed off to the side, standing at the far corner of the room. Their whispers were evident, but neither Don nor Kathy could decipher any words. The two burly types stood nearly motionless, looking grimly in Don and Kathy's direction. Don just knew that if he suddenly reached in his pocket for a hanky, he'd be on the floor in an instant, underneath one of those onlookers.

Don and Kathy spoke not a word to each other. Finally, the conference was over, and the two Officers returned to the meeting. The Lieutenant spoke first.

"Mr. and Mrs. Crawford, continuing in our effort to be obliging, we want to propose this strategy to bring this impasse to resolution. We will give you an extra day to prepare your people. So, we will expect your group's participation in the school and military service programs to begin on this coming Thursday, rather than tomorrow, Wednesday. And the Sergeant will tell you of our second consideration that I think you'll be pleased with. Sergeant...?"

"Mrs. Crawford, I take it you're a mother yourself?" Sergeant Baker asked.

"Yes, I am. I have two daughters," Kathy answered.

"Well then I think you'll appreciate this point," she went on with a noticeable dose of sweetness. "We would invite the mothers of the four to sixteen-year-olds you have, to attend the proceedings on Thursday, so they can comfort any fears in their children and see for themselves how loving we are with their youngsters. Now, that would be well-received here, don't you think, Mrs. Crawford?"

"Yes, I think it would help a good deal. Thank you," replied Kathy.

"Well, good! This turned out well, don't you think," Lieutenant Williams said as he stood and stretched himself. "Now, our last need is this: We would like the names and birthdates of those that will be coming Thursday. We will be back at 8:30 am on Thursday with two vans: one for the little ones and mothers and one for the young adults."

Don and Kathy also stood. Don said: "Let me take you two to the office where our secretary, Clair, will give you the information you need."

"Lead the way," said the grinning young Lieutenant. The Sergeant followed, then the two bodyguards, who went into the office with their leaders. The third remained in the hall, stationed just outside the office door. David was located by Kathy to come and wait for the two officers, and then to escort them out the front entrance.

After David was instructed, Kathy and Don headed for the break room to defuse from the meeting with the NPO and regain a sense of balance.

"Whoa, Kathy," Don exclaimed. "I'm glad I don't have to do that every day!"

"Me, too!" Kathy replied. "As soon as the two leave we've got to have a pow-wow to tell everyone what's going on."

"Yes, you're right... Let's see, we're talking about two youngsters, age five and up, they are Gideon with Mary Kay and Joshua with Dianne. Also, two young adults, D.J. and... ah, Suzy? No, it's Glenda... Suzy's been gone for quite a while, right? In fact, so has Glenda... Now where are those two?"

Don and Kathy sat without further comment. Then, David arrived and announced: "They just left the building, Boss... boy I wouldn't want to tangle with those three big dudes."

"Me neither, David," answered Don. "Do me one more favor? See if you can locate all of us to have a quick meeting, so we can talk about what just happened. Be sure to be there yourself."

"Sure thing, I'll get them to come to the meeting room ASAP," David assured.

"PEOPLE, KATHY AND I JUST FINISHED OUR meeting with the NPO. How would I describe it? Hmmm... it was interesting, informative... ah... it ended up better than I anticipated. These people, from the NPO, are for real. They are a formidable foe; don't take them lightly. They are committed to their goal, to take over every-thing on the earth and present it to the Antichrist on a silver platter! In saying this, I assume what we can see happening in small-town

Greensville is happening across the globe in one degree or another – and remember all this power-grabbing takeover is being empowered by Satan himself!

"But let's get to the nitty-gritty of our meeting. We have two five-year-olds among us: Joshua Jorgenson and Gideon McKenna. And we have possible three in the 17-21 age group: D.J., Suzy, and Glenda, but the two girls' whereabouts are unknown at this juncture... Does anyone know about the two girls? No?

"Well, anyway, lets proceed in our planning without them... So, this Thursday is our big day! The two boys and their mothers will be picked up at 8:30am for school. The mothers get to tag along all day and check things out. I'm sure that will help alleviate some fears, right? At the same time, a van will be here for the 17-21-year-olds, which right now is only D.J.

"In their mind they extended an extra day to us – that is tomorrow, Wednesday - as a courtesy and a sign of their congeniality... Any comments?"

Stone silence among the Believers. The squirming in chairs told Don that there was plenty on their minds, but no one wanted to open the discussion...

"Don, how about the Mark of the Beast we've talked about or signing the Covenant Agreement. Will we still have to do that?" asked Mama Blanchard.

"Those specific points were not brought up in the meeting," Don replied, "But I know those issues are still on the table. Eventually no one will get by without doing both... I'm sure the NPO is expecting us to comply soon enough."

"So, we having to do these classes is just buying us some time, right Don?" Ben asked.

"Looks that way, Ben"

"So, it seems to boil down to this," Sam summarized. "Either we go along with the program now and sell out to the NPO – or we gain a few more days, maybe a week, by being cooperative, and then sell out or face their dire consequences... It's either now or later – but with the same results!"

"Sam, you have a knack for bringing the whole picture into stark focus. But, yes, you seem to have it accurate – it's now or later," Don conceded.

With Don's statement... blunt as it was, the meeting room grew silent again. Each one faced their own understanding of what reality was presenting them. The likelihood of giving up one's life, as cruel or brutal as that may be, was today being squarely considered... It was no longer off in the distance. It was in the here and now. What personal price were people willing to pay to stay faithful to God? That's the question the Apostles faced, like Peter, and it's the same issue for God's elect now across the world.

Don began praying softly in the Spirit. Soon others joined in, like Kathy, Clair, Jim, Doobie... on and on the participants grew. There followed several minutes of sweet fellowship with the Lord... a moment to be treasured!

As the praying waned, Don broke in. "Folks, this has been a time of precious communion with the Lord."

Ben added, "I believe we would be accurate to call this a foretaste of Heaven itself!" Others nodded or commented in agreement, with looks of gentle peace on their faces.

Ben had more to propose. "Don, everyone, this might sound preposterous or far out in left field, but I'm wondering if we should just say to the NPO: *'We're not going to yield, so just do with us what you want...'*"

Others voiced their agreement. Mama Blanchard said it this way: "Ben is right. Let's just put the whole matter in the Lord's Hands, say our *good-byes* and go on to Heaven..."

"However God's path leads us," David added, "through prison, death, the guillotine, it doesn't really matter – God will be there with us!"

"Yeah, David's right. Let's get on with the inevitable; I'm tired of this waiting!" added Jerry, who then turned to his son, D.J., for a reaction...

"Dad, you're right... I used to dream about starting a gang of rebels that would give the NPO its biggest fit ever, but now I've mellowed...

Now I think we can give the NPO its biggest fit if we just *Let Go and Let God.*"

D.J. then turned to Sam, whom he regarded as a fellow-rebel, for comment. "How about you, Sam, are you with us?"

"What? Me? You're talking to someone who hated to lose, I mean **really** hated it! When I was growing up, I could whip every boy in the neighborhood. I'd just as soon stomp on you as anything! Above all you'd never see me sweat, never!

"But now – now it's all different. Since joining up with this band of Believers, I've grown to see things differently. Now, to lose is to win! To lose to the NPO is one thing, of little consequence really! To go after Life in God's way, is to be the biggest winner ever! And that's what I want! ... Does that answer your question, D.J.?"

D.J. stood on his feet and began to clap and cheer. Others quickly joined in. Soon enough the whole room was cheering at the top of their lungs. And it drew a crowd. The children came in with Miss Clair, and quickly ran to their parents, wondering what's going on? Happy looks on parents' faces gave them assurance that all was well.

Don let the applause fade naturally and then called for everyone's attention. They all took their seat, even Clair and the children. "People, what I have just witnessed from all of you is so very touching and awesome. It is beautiful when people come together in unity. That is a hard slap in the face to the Kingdom of Darkness, who strives to keep us apart and in confusion. Thank you. Thank you! One and all!

"Your comments triggered some points in my spirit that need to be said, so they can get into your spirits, if they're not already there. First, who can say for sure, but Jesus might rapture us out of this quagmire of NPO edicts and threats, before we must face that final threat.

"Second, if we do face that final threat of death by guillotine or whatever, let's not forget what the Book of Hebrews tells us. In chapter two verse nine it says that *Jesus tasted death for every man.* To me that means that I don't have to taste, or experience in the natural, the pains of death. He was my Substitute; He took my place. So, a nano-second before the bullet arrives or the guillotine drops, I, the real me, my spirit man – the part made in God's image - will leave this body and go to be with the Lord. Wow! What a promise that is! Right?"

"Yes, Brother Don!" "What a promise!" "Let's do it!" came the comments.

"We've talked about being God's End-Times Army and how we can expect Him to supply and equip us to walk in victory. He'll never desert us nor forsake us. And He will help us deal with all manner of physical discomfort and persecutions; He'll help us to decipher what is real from what is a lie, or a deception. We need to keep our eyes and ears on Jesus, always.

"That reminds me that the other day I remembered an old chorus we used to sing years ago. I think it's appropriate now. I'm sure you'll remember this one; help me out Sam and D.J., everybody:

Keep your eyes upon Jesus.
Look full in His wonderful face.
And the things of earth will grow strangely dim,
In the light of His Glory and Grace."

The familiar chorus rang through the hallways of The Factory for the next five minutes. (All angels there on assignment for the Believers, joined in, I'm sure.)

"This leaves me with one remaining point to address. How do we inform the NPO of our intentions to not cooperate? I can't call them or text a message or drive my Jeep to see them. I could walk downtown and find the nearest NPO person to help me get the message across to the right source. It would be a fair walk to their Headquarters at the Armory, but I could do that, too.

"I could just wait for two days, until Thursday comes, and tell the Van Drivers in person of our intentions... What else? Any ideas?"

"Whatever you decide, Brother Don, I want to come with you," said Doobie. Then several others chimed in as well, like Jim, D.J., David – all wanting to turn this into a delegation-venture.

Then, Ben stood up and spoke and offered the supreme answer. "Don and everybody, I think this would be best handled by Clair and myself carrying our message to the NPO... Now, I don't want any arguing about this! Clair and I have discussed this very scenario and we agree that we would be the best suited to carry this out. For one thing, I think our grey hair and older age could work to our advantage; it might lead the powers that be to some leniency... I mean, look at Clair's wholesome and engaging face. That alone would trigger the Soldiers better side, don't you think?

"So, let's get into agreement about our plan just like we've been in such agreement all day long. Please, I beg you! This is something we both want to do. Is it okay? Don, okay?"

"Humm... Ben, you got me over a barrel. You and Clair know I love you both, like a father and mother. So, should that love answer *NO* for your safety and well-being? Or should that love answer *YES* to honor your request. Hmmm... Kathy, any ideas back there?"

"No, Don, it's yours to answer..."

"Okay, I say... I say... YES, Ben and Clair. And thank you so much. One caution, Ben: don't try to be a hero...don't be feisty or demanding. Give them our answer and then leave with a pleasant demeanor. Got it?"

"Yes, we got it... and thank you."

"Don, Ben, how about if I tagged along," asked Pastor Bill, "You know, just for the heck of it?"

"No, bad idea," said Don without hesitation. "You're already sort of a *marked man*, you might say, because of your Church closing. They might be on the look-out for you... and have some unpleasant plans in mind. Better to leave it in the hands of Clair and Ben – and God, of course.

"I know there are others here who would volunteer to help out at the drop of a hat if they had the chance. And thank you for that... You know something, there are families by natural birth, but the best family of all is a family of the Spirit. That's who you are to me and Kathy."

Suddenly, a peculiar yet familiar sound could be heard coming from the entrance. It was music with bells, a xylophone, an organ. It sounded like a circus merry-go-round – or, thought Don, like an ice crème food truck from years past!

"Does this sound like an ice crème treat wagon or what? Golly, I'm starting to salivate. I gotta go see for myself! Anyone else coming? Oh, by the way, our meeting is over, till next time! Let's go!"

Don's intuition was right on target! It was a food wagon, but no driver! Curious! Don and the others ran out to it and found all manner of ice crème treats, doughnuts of all varieties, many sodas and lemonade – all that anyone could ask for, who was growing hungry, trying to conserve food from a dwindling supply.

Don was the first to reach into the delightful supply of goodies. When he did, the others quickly followed. They didn't exactly gorge themselves, but it was close. Many gleeful comments were made by the contented patrons.

Don said: "Hey, gang, let's not eat it all right now. Save some for the folks inside! They're also hungry." Then Don noticed something odd: the supply of food never seemed to grow smaller. When one ice-crème bar was taken, another took its place! It was a miracle!

"Oh, God, You are so good to us! Here you give us the food desires of our heart, and it's not depleting! Gotta have another doughnut!"

"Doobie, pass me that chocolate cake doughnut," Don yelled out. Doobie obliged. Ben and Clair were enjoying their ice crème bars. The kids certainly had a great time. This reminded Gideon and Levi of their trip with the angel when they dug into tubs of food.

Don figured it wise to bring the food wagon into The Factory for safe keeping, you know... *Wouldn't want any of this to go to waste*, he thought. So, with only a little coaxing, Don found a crew of four to transport the food inside, to the break room, to be exact. There it stood for the remainder of the Faithful's time at their factory-home.

"Hey, Doobie, I know this snack food is not as nourishing as your garden veggies, but it does hit the spot, doesn't it?"

"It sure does," he answered. "Thank You. Thank You, Lord!"

CHAPTER SIXTEEN –

Ben and Clair were easily spotted by an NPO Patrol

B EN AND CLAIR STOOD QUIETLY AS DON and the others
gathered around them in prayer before sending them out on their
mission with the NPO.

"Lord, we're sending our two faithful ones out into peril, but with
You at their side they won't be in any danger. Thank You that they are
compassed about by the shield of Your good will and favor.[58] We will
maintain our prayer vigil until their safe return. May they draw strength
and vigor from You as they prosper in this important mission. Thank
You, Thank You, for taking such good care of them. In the Name of
Jesus! AMEN.

"Here, both of you take one," Don insisted, handing each a powerful flashlight for their travels. Down the corridor they walked together
toward the entrance, then out into the darkened, cloudy sky.

It wasn't long before Ben and Clair were spotted by an NPO Patrol,
who was traveling the neighborhood on the lookout for curfew violators
or other expressions of civil unrest.

Four soldiers jumped out of their vehicle. The leader barked,
"Halt! Who goes there?" Weapons were drawn, triggers readied, bar-
rels pointed at the Tuckers – hardly a threatening enemy seeking to do
harm or violence. One soldier turned on his flood light, pointing at the
elderly couple.

Ben answered the command: "We do not mean any trouble. We
are unarmed."

The soldiers came around to the front of the van to gain a better
look them.

"It's after curfew hours! You're in violation of the law!" the Officer snarled. "What is your business at this late hour?"

"We wish to speak with the NPO Official in charge at this time..."

"What about?"

"We are representatives from The Factory..."

"Now there are some rebel rousers, if I ever saw one!" sneered one of the young men. Others joined in the snickering. Apparently, The Factory Faithful had established quite a negative reputation with the NPO.

"Like I said, we're from The Factory and we wish to inform the NPO of our decision to not comply with your edicts," brave Ben continued with a notable crack in his voice and shaking in his knees.

Then, Clair herself continued the dialog, with poise: "Perhaps you gentlemen could convey that message to your Headquarters on our behalf, so that we could leave and return to our home... Come on, Ben, let's walk back."

The Officer in charge was taken back at Clair's straight forward approach. After a moment of admiration for her pluck, he again turned adversarial. "Lady, not so fast! Here's what we'll do. You and your friend..."

"That's my husband, if you please," she retorted!

"Whatever! We will take the two of you to Headquarters and you can tell your story to the Sergeant... that's Sergeant Desta; we call him Sergeant Disaster! What happens to you after that is up to him. Got it? Okay, crawl in the back. Jackson will help you."

Within minutes they arrived at the Armory Headquarters. They were led into the main area where several Officers were gathered, busy at work, watching monitors, talking by phone with others out in the field, sitting at computers. Ben and Clair were each given a chair and told to wait.

The Leader from the van patrol went into a nearby office to speak with his superior, the same Sergeant Desta. Soon he came out to greet the Tuckers. He wore a made-up smile that didn't seem to naturally fit his face!

"I understand we have a bit of a problem here," he began politely. "You've decided to not go along with our regulations, is that right? May I know why you at The Factory have come to that decision?" The Sergeant remained standing, rather towering – all six-foot-six of him - over the Tuckers. Arms began to fold, as he shifted from one foot to the other.

"Yes, I can answer that," Ben began. "The overall thrust of the NPO is in direct violation to our Christian beliefs. We understand the world's new-found Leader, Marschall Gabrinne, who is the ultimate Head of the NPO, wants to force every citizen into proclaiming him as Sovereign Lord of the Earth. Our allegiance is reserved for only One, the Almighty God, Maker of Heaven and Earth and His Son, Jesus, our Redeemer..."

"Aarkkk..." The Sergeant and other officers began to cover their ears. "Don't speak that name here, ever! Ever again!"

"You mean the Name of Jesus?" Clair blurted out!

"Yes! Yes!" Sergeant Desta exclaimed. Suddenly, he drew his pistol and cocked the trigger, and aimed it right at Clair, who was sitting six feet away. "Do I make myself absolutely clear?"

"Yes. Yes, you do," conceded Clair in a shaky, muffled voice.

"Clair, dear, settle down; don't do anything rash," Ben insisted, in a loud whisper. "We have others in our company to consider."

"Now there is a wise man," replied the Sergeant. "Listen. Heed his advice." Sergeant Desta put up his gun, grabbed a nearby chair and sat face-to-face with Ben and Clair. He looked at both, tried on another smile, and proceeded calmly.

"Now folks, I believe this is the best solution for all concerned. I'll give you three days – no, make that two days - longer, to reconsider your opposition. I or one of my colleagues will personally come by your Factory this Friday morning by 09:00 to learn of your decision. If the decision is, we will sign the Agreement, great! If it is, we won't sign, you will be taken away to experience the consequences.

"And the consequences, you wonder? We will haul you off to the Recon Center to undergo a range of successfully proven persuasion strategies, to break down any barriers to your acceptance of the NPO program. Strategies that even the strongest-willed opponent could not endure.

"So that's your assignment. Go back to your people and tell them of our little conversation. Make your argument strong and convincing for accepting the NPO as your new way of life. If I don't see some positive results, I'll turn conspicuously angry and vindictive. And you don't want that! Isn't that right, Harry?"

Harry kept his eyes glued to the computer screen: "He's right, folks. Don't make him mad; it won't be pretty!"

The Sergeant continued. "The same Van that brought you here will take you home. Now remember, I'm counting on you to be convincing. Don't test my patience nor my resolve: my patience is short, but my resolve is rock solid!"

Ben and Clair were escorted home, much to the joy of the Believers who were standing guard in prayer at the entrance doorway.

David was the first to spot them. He quickly told Don and Kathy, then Doobie, and the others. The good news spread throughout The Factory like wildfire.

As the Faithful greeted the Tuckers, they all naturally gathered in the meeting room. People waited for Ben or Clair to fill them in on the details. It proved hard to put their experience into words. Ben began the report.

"It was a harrowing time, but the Lord was with us, that's for sure! Folks let me just get down to the nitty-gritty. We have two days to reconsider our position. It's either sign on with the NPO or be hauled off to someplace they called the *Recon Center*, whatever that stands for..."

"Maybe it stands for *Reconsideration*, Don interjected... Sorry, Ben, go on."

"Well, that's about the gist of it all... the choice is before us to make, with two unappealing options... what else can I say?"

The group was silent. Each was wrestling with the choice facing them as a family and individually.

"Give into the pressure to do things the NPO way, or face a new level of their persuasive ways," Don presented the alternatives.

"Don, we already made it clear to them that we opposed the NPO plan. I suppose they thought that some might reconsider if they knew they had only two more days to weigh the alternatives," said Ben.

"Probably so," answered Don. Then he asked the burning question on everyone's mind... "What would the Lord want us to do?"

"Well, I don't like either possibility, of course," Sam offered, "but considering the question of what the Lord would want me to do, that would be to not give in. So, that's what I'm going to do! Anyone else?"

D.J. said this: "Dad and I have thought a lot about this, from every angle. One possibility that's looking more and more viable is to head out on our own in the dark of night and pray for the Lord's protection as we go. We know this city like the back of our hand. There are lots of places to hide. Who knows, we might be able to outwit them or outlast them. It's worth a shot... to us."

"Whoa! Pretty drastic, D.J. But I might be thinking about the same if I was your age. And Jerry, you're okay with D.J.'s plan," asked Don?

"Yeah, I guess so. I trust that God and D.J. will help to keep me safe. And if we die, well that's no major deal. Like you've taught us, Don, *to be absent from the body is to be present with the Lord.*"[59]

"How about the rest of you? Where do you stand on the question of staying, or going out on your own?" Don asked. "Doobie?" "Mama Blanchard?" "Jim?"

"I'm staying put," Doobie asserted!

"So am I," echoed Mama.

"Jenny and I are staying here, Don," said Jim convincingly... "And I'm planning to be raptured with Rosalie in my arms," added Jenny.

"Let's see... who haven't we heard from? The Greyhecks, David and Dianne, Mark and Mary Kay... Suzy's been gone for several days without saying goodbye; only the Lord knows where she's at... Oh, I almost forgot our newest member, Pastor Bill..."

Don looked out at his family, and the compassion of God welled up in his heart. He began to sniffle, then cry softly... "I love all you guys, you know that, right?

"I take it some are still working on their choice, so I'm not going to push the matter... Here's something I will say, however... since we only have two days left, I say let's be thankful for those two days, right Louise? Thankful! Let's make them as special as we can. For one thing, just think of all the ice-crème and doughnut treats that we have at our disposal..."

Henry Greyheck stood to make his position known. "Louise and I will be staying here at The Factory with many of you... but I just wanted the brave ones heading out on their own to know that in my bedroom closet at home there are three rifles and all the ammo you'd ever need... there's a kitchen window at the back of the house that's not locked. That'd be your way in... In a way I wish I could join you."

Louise tugged at his arm and he sat again. Then she said: "Henry you're not 22 again in the Army Rangers! For us to stay put is God's best plan for us." Henry shook his head in agreement.

Another round of silence ensued. Then, Kathy stood to make an announcement. "Here's something I propose, that won't mean anything to the rest of you, only to Don... I propose for our last two days that The Factory have a new name... (Don was not aware of what was coming)... and that name would be *CRAWFORD CITY*."

Kathy promptly sat down, but Don got it! He smiled from ear to ear, then he cried. At the same moment he began to dance, doing a little jig right where he stood. Others looked on and laughed at the sight before them. They didn't understand the significance of *Crawford City*, but they appreciated Don's exuberant response.

Don wanted to explain so the people could better enjoy the moment. "Let me tell you what Kathy's announcement meant to me. Years ago, on a day or two after our elopement, I was bragging to my mother that someday I was going to make it big in Real Estate and have a city named after me. Kathy offered the name of Crawford City, and that was going to be it. Except I never made it big in Real Estate."

"Yes, you did make it big!" Kathy yelled forth, standing again. "You sorta own a factory, don't you, at least part of one, and not everyone can say that!"

Don ran back to Kathy and gave her the biggest hug you ever saw. Onlookers began to applaud. After the hug was over Don found a nearby chair and collapsed in it. He began sobbing; others gathered around and comforted him. It felt good to Don to release a wealth of pent-up emotions.

Softly at first, those coming around Don began singing: *Keep your eyes upon Jesus, Look full in His wonderful face...* More and more joined in until the meeting room was filled with the beautiful chorus, one of Don's favorites!

Don looked over at Kathy and said to her: "Honey, why don't you close the meeting; I can't."

Kathy walked to the front of the meeting room and looked out at the precious faces she had come to know and love. "Folks, this meeting is closing – I was about to say, it was coming to an end, but I think this meeting room will get a lot of attention over the next two days. Let's just think of it as an ongoing meeting that never ends but may pause from time to time... Stay close to the Lord; He is our strength and wisdom, now and forever. Bye for now."

As the meeting ended, everyone mulled around the room and the break room next door. It looked like people were in a state of shock, not quite sure what to do first. Certainly, there were no experiences to call on about how to deal with what they were facing – no one had ever been in this situation before: namely, having two days before being carted off to someplace called a Recon Center!

Don, Kathy, and several others gravitated to the break room. But even the bright colored doughnuts with *sparkles* on top didn't look appealing to Don, nor anyone else. Sam stopped by for a quick visit. "Hey, Don and Kathy, I enjoyed that story about Crawford City. I think I and the kids will stay busy tomorrow making some *Crawford City* signs to go up here and there. We're also going to do some *Thank You, Lord, For Our Time Here* posters – the more colorful the better."

"Sam, Sam, Thank you so much for all you do around here," said Don. "You add color and grace to our lives every day..."

"Yes, you bring out a certain sparkle in us all. We don't thank you enough," added Kathy.

"Now you guys aren't going to get mushy on me, are you?" she asked with a smile, as she got up from her chair.

"No. No. Don't worry about that," Don confided, as he returned her smile.

"Kathy, Honey, I'm beat. Let's go to bed."

"I'll be there as soon as I visit with Jenny, to make sure she's doing okay."

DID THE NEXT TWO DAYS GO BY in a flash or drag on and on? Hard to say for sure; there were times of both. The general atmosphere seemed subdued; not necessarily sad, just quiet... pensive maybe. Activity level was low. Not much to do; no ongoing projects to attend to. I mean, why scrub a floor you'll never see again. Sam and Mama Blanchard did keep the children occupied and involved in artwork and games. It was good every now and then to witness their gleeful cries during a hide-n-seek game, or to overhear the singing of their favorite song: *"Old McDonald had a Farm."*

Without presenting the question out loud, several people wondered what the upcoming experience would be like for the little ones. There likely would be times of separation from parents. Parents wondered how much they should talk about things like that, versus making the remaining time as pleasant as possible. But really, how could you prepare them for what might be ahead – how could you prepare yourself, for that matter!

Several people enjoyed taking a leisurely stroll around the area. Days were bright with sunshine; wind was light. Great walking conditions – or, better said: walking and praying. Praying was probably the single most common activity for the Faithful. And part of those prayers was dedicated to asking for safety for those who had left The Factory, to strike out on their own. These included Jerry and D.J., along with Pastor Bill. It was assumed that they stayed together in their venture, and the hope was that we all would be reunited in Heaven.

Don had a couple of ideas he wanted to share with the group, who convened at his request in the meeting room, children included. Don sat in a chair rather than take his usual spot behind the podium.

"Folks... I asked for this time together to share a couple of ideas with you, for our remaining day and night together. First, and Kathy hasn't heard this yet, I plan to drag my mattress out of my room and put it into this room tonight. Let's make it a sleep-over to top all sleepovers! What do you think kids?"

"Yeaaa. Yeaaa!" They approved.

"And what do you think of the idea, folks?"

Everyone looked around at each other to get a read on how the idea was being received. Most everyone nodded in agreement. Doobie said: "Sounds like fun, Don. Count me in!" Others concurred. Just to make sure, Don asked about Mama Blanchard and the Greyhecks. The Greyhecks said "Yes."

Mama was not sure. "Don, I'm a bit uneasy about sleeping on the floor. Getting down might be okay; it's the getting up part that concerns me... but if there was a way, I'd love to be here."

"We'll make a way, won't we David. You could have two mattresses or the whole bed in here. Somehow it will work. Great... *I love it when a plan comes together!*

"Now, folks, listen; this is serious! What famous TV action star made those words famous? I've been searching my brain for that answer for a long, long time."

Henry had the name, but he wanted to tease Don first. "I know who you're referring to. Here's a clue first: He usually lit up a big cigar before saying that phrase... ring a bell?"

"Hmmm... cigar? Wait! Wait! It's coming to me... no... Need another clue."

"The actor's real name has the initials of G. P... ring a bell now?"

"GEORGE PEPPARD! I got it – finally! Thanks Henry... Thanks! I can rest easier tonight... Well enough of my shenanigans...

"Here's my second point. This is strictly optional about joining me, but I'm planning to put on the best clothes I have for tomorrow's trip. I know we'll likely discard our civilian clothes right off, but I still want to dress up a bit. And on my face, I want there to be a big smile and a calm, confident look. They'll be expecting us to be resistant, sad, afraid, fighting all the way... I say, let's surprise them... Let's impress them with our calm and cool manner... Gentle as a lamb. Okay? Comments?"

"I love it!" Sam yelled from the back. "Just where do you come up with these ideas, anyway?"

"I don't have any fancy clothes," said Doobie, "But I'll wear the best I have."

"Great, Doobie... I'm sure you'll look handsome."

"Well, Don, I figure we're not taking any clothes with us," reasoned Dianne, "So, I might as well wear the best I have... And David can wear his one and only tie, okay, Honey?"

"Great!" David answered. "I'll be as stylish as can be!"

"I don't know about my own best clothes," shared Jenny, "but I have a cute little dress in mind for Rosalie... and Jim, you'll go along with this, right?"

"Sure will," he replied.

"Count us in on this dress-up plan," said Louise.

"We're in, too," Mary Kay added.

"Well, that's about it... we'll be the best-looking gang they ever saw. Thanks, people, for going along with these ideas."

SOON ENOUGH, AS EVENING CAME, the meeting room turned into nearly wall-to-wall beds on the floor. Don and Doobie came in with their gear at about the same time. Don said to his young friend, "Doobie, why don't you put your mattress next to mine... right here close to my blue pillow."

Surprised, Doobie was eager to comply. "Sure Don, that would be great."

The room grew full of people. Some were chattering away with their neighbors. Others were quiet, as they looked around at their friends for the past two years. Last to settle in was Mama Blanchard. David arranged for her to have a two-mattress arrangement. She said she felt like a Queen, overlooking her subjects. Of course, to be expected, the six kids were wound up. For the time being it was all a big party to them.

Don leaned over to ask Kathy: "Maybe this wasn't such a hot idea, including the kids."

Kathy replied, "Sure it was. They're just running off a little steam; you remember how kids are when the rules have changed..."

"...You mean like acting a little squirrely?"

"That's right... It's the same way you do now as an adult."

"What? You take that back, or..."

"Or what Don? Remember where you are. In a room full of people... many of whom are looking at you right now."

"So, noted... I think I'll turn over and talk to Doobie for a while."

"Good. I'll talk with Rosalie."

"Hey, Doobie, how are you doing?" asked Don.

"Ah... well, okay I guess..." he answered tentatively. "How should I be doing?"

"Just the way you're doing," Don replied. "No one knows how to act in a situation like this...Say, Doobie, can I ask you something – something personal?"

"Sure, go ahead."

"Where did your name *Doobie* come from? I've always wondered. Is it a given name? A nickname? Or what? Do you mind telling me?"

"No, I don't mind. It came from my younger brother, Mark. There used to be a kid's cartoon on TV that had a big dog in it named Scooby Doo. When Mark and I watched it together, he would point and try to say Scooby, but it came out Doobie. Then I'd pretend to be a dog and he would giggle and call out Doobie! Doobie! So, it just stuck. And that became my name for everybody to use."

"Thanks. Course then I came along and wanted to change it to Einstein... You know, Doobie, when we get to Heaven, we won't have this old body to lug around. At first, we'll just be our spirit man and soul; later we'll get a redeemed body to have for eternity. My point is your brain is part of your physical body. Your brain may have come into this world with a few circuits off kilter, but once in Heaven it will be your spirit that matters. You'll be as sharp as a tack, you'll probably have the whole Bible memorized, and you'll sit down with Einstein himself and discuss your latest mathematical theories – if you want to, that is...

"Oh, Doobie, my man, you're going to love Heaven! Just love it! I know. Oh, by the way, to finish your story, what was your real first name, the one on your birth certificate?"

"Now, don't laugh, Don... Okay? Promise? It was Harold!"

"Harold?! Harold?!" Don broke out in raucous laughter. "Shhhh..." Don tried to quiet himself to a whisper. "Harold... you don't seem like a *Harold*. I like Doobie a lot better."

Kathy turned back to Don, smiling. "Hey, you two quiet down!"

"Ooops. Sorry, Miss Kathy," Doobie said softly.

"Me, too, Miss Kathy," added Don, trying to stifle a snicker or two.

The evening wore on. One by one the children fell off to sleep, cuddled next to parents. The mood of the room grew somber, solemn... meaning that thoughts were drifting toward the morning, when the NPO vans would come. Don took the occasion to suggest that people, as they felt inclined, share any prayer or thought about tomorrow. Most did.

David started. "Lord, help me and my family to be brave tomorrow. The people might act scary, but we don't have to be moved by that. Help us, like the song says, to *Keep our eyes on Jesus*."

Sam joined in: "Lord, help me to keep a smile on my face and to keep my thoughts in line with Your will."

Mark was next: "Lord, thank You for bringing me a family to love, besides my big brother, Doobie. Help me to make You proud tomorrow."

Clair spoke for she and Ben "Lord God, it has been the highlight of our life so far to be part of this mighty end-times army from Greensville. Thank you for watching over us all... I can't wait to get to Heaven!"

After a long pause, six-year-old Gideon spoke up. "Jesus, You live in my heart and You'll never leave me... I believe in miracles. You did a miracle to bring us home from Kansas. I believe You'll do more for us in the days to come. Thank You. Amen." (*I think that boy will be a Preacher someday, and maybe soon,* thought Don.)

Joshua was listening and wanted his turn. "Jesus, help my family tomorrow wherever we are going. And, like Gideon said, I believe in miracles, too." *(Sounds like an assistant for Gideon,* Don thought. *May miracles happen, Lord, just like they believe.)*

Jim had the floor. "Lord God, I don't know how you'll do this but make a way for Rosalie to be raptured to Heaven in Jenny's arms. Thank You. Thank You." Jenny looked on with a confident, peaceful countenance.

Don got up to turn out the overhead light and returned to his bed. "No patrol tonight, David, enjoy the presence of your family... Good night everyone."

Like the TV family of old, *The Waltons,* there followed an avalanche of "Good Nights" from all over the room...

Don turned and had one last word for Doobie. He whispered: "Doobie, you know that I love you. Right? But this you didn't know... if I had a son, I'd hope he'd be just like you."

"Really, Brother Don, Thank you. That's mighty nice of you."

"And guess what I'd name him... guess... It would be *Harold,* just like yours!"

CHAPTER SEVENTEEN –

For sure our biggest challenge ever!

DON THOUGHT HE WAS THE FIRST TO get up that morning. But he was wrong; it was Ben. It was 6:30 am. "Ben you must have gotten up before the chickens this morning," commented Don, as he ran into him in the kitchen.

"Well... this is going to be a day like no other," he replied. "I didn't want to waste one moment of it..." Suddenly Ben had to steady himself on the counter. He looked for the first chair to sit down. Don was concerned about his friend.

"Ben, what's wrong? What's going on?" Don insisted on knowing.

"Oh, it's nothing. A little light-headedness that's all. It will pass."

"Let me pray for you." Don put his hand on his friend's shoulder, as he prayed: "Lord, You are our Healer. This light-headedness was defeated over 2,000 years ago at Calvary. I join my faith with Ben, and we stand in agreement: Light-headedness, you must go! We delight in sending you out of Ben's body and out of this building, in the mighty Name of Jesus! Now, GO! Amen!"

"Thanks, Don, for helping me remember that we have been given authority over sickness and disease. I'll have to keep that in the forefront for the days ahead... I think part of it is the uncertainty of what we are about to face."

"I hear ya, Ben. I know what you mean. It will without doubt be a great challenge for all of us – for sure our biggest challenge ever. The goal is to *Keep Your Eyes on Jesus* like the song says, and not on our circumstances; not on the actions, words, or threats of the NPO... But I know you know this and I'm preaching to the choir... Ben, you and Clair have been the pillars of faith for this community. You, me, Clair, Kathy, we all have to keep strong and focused on Jesus for the sake of the others."

"I know that, Don. Right now, I'm not doing my best, although the light-headedness is gone. Thank God! I'm believing to walk in God's strength this morning, this day and for the rest of my time on this earth."

"Amen to that! Just think, Ben, Heaven is our home and soon enough we'll be there... with Jesus... our permanent, for-all-eternity, home! Hallelujah! Now that's something to shout about! So, another HALLELUJAH!"

Soon enough the other Factory Saints rousted themselves and one-by-one made their way to the kitchen - meeting room area. And were they ever spiffy looking! Don and Ben greeted each hearty soul, with a smile, kind word, and acknowledgement of how marvelous they looked. Each had on their best church-going clothes.

Don addressed everyone, either singly or by family, to say: "Folks, I'd say breakfast is on your own today... I might have one more doughnut before our guests arrive... Did you notice I called the NPO our *Guests?*

"Doobie, what does the Bible teach us about what we call things?"

Doobie was quick to answer. "Whatever we call a thing is what it is to us."[60]

"Great! You got it!" Don replied exuberantly, to help create and model a positive atmosphere among the Believers, but Doobie wasn't finished.

"...If we call it bad, it will be bad to us. If we call it good, it will be good. If we call it a challenge, that's what it is, if we call it a big problem, then we're defeated already."

Sam got her two cents worth in. "Just between you, me, and the fence post, today is going to be one heck-of-a *challenge*... I can't even imagine. Lord, Lord, help me, help all of us, to be calm under pressure, to be ever quick to call on You for help, and to always... ALWAYS! see You as our Strength and our Protector..."

Don led the people in a giant shout: "And everyone said, AMEN!"

By this time, Kathy was up and dressed, looking gorgeous, in Don's estimation. He went to her to grab her hand, kiss her on the cheek, and posed this important question: "Honey... how's my tie... straight?"

"Yes, dear, you are *styling* today," she answered, as she tweaked the tie just a bit. Jenny joined in the exchange to give a *thumbs up* to her father from across the room.

Jenny was of course holding sweet Rosalie. Looking on at the two of them, Don couldn't help but reflect: *Lord, I don't know how You're going to make it happen, but I believe with Jenny and Jim that she'll be raptured to Heaven with Rosalie in her arms. I think I was speaking Your heart when I gave her that assurance.*

The Lord answered: *Don, yes, you were speaking My Heart... that dream will be fulfilled. Just see it done in your heart and believe. Oh, by the way you have a visitor coming. I sent him.*

As if on cue, Don slipped away from the crowd and headed down the hallway to the front door. There stood a tall, handsome young man with dark, curly hair, wearing a pleasant smile. Don opened the door and greeted him without apprehension. "Hello and welcome to The Factory. We're all gathered in the kitchen."

Don seemed to know the very nature of the visitor's coming. They walked down the hall without saying a word. When they arrived at the kitchen, everyone's attention was suddenly riveted on the stranger. And he spoke to all in a relaxed and confident tone:

"I come from the very Throne of God with a message for you. God is well pleased with your work here and with your undying devotion to Him. He wants you to know deep down in your hearts that He will provide all the strength you'll need to endure whatever lies ahead... In the Name of Jesus, may His BLESSING rest upon each of you, now and forever. Amen."

With that said he promptly turned and walked back down the hallway. Don remained behind with his friends. A sacred hush fell over the Saints, which could have remained for a long time, except Don broke in to announce: "Folks, it's now 8:00; we're one hour away from the

NPO arrival. I think we should move into a special time of individual and family prayer however the Lord might lead." Everyone obliged easily. Don and Kathy went to their bedroom for time alone.

At ten of nine, the Believers slowly came together and began to gather at the entrance to The Factory. Kathy looked over at the wall nearby and saw one of Sam's creations: a one by four-foot poster that read *Crawford City* in big bold, red letters. She had an itch but stopped herself from going over to retrieve it. *Best to just let it be,* she thought, *and have the next occupants wonder what it meant.*

Right on time four NPO Vans arrived at the front entrance. Everyone took a long breath, wiped sweaty palms on pants and dresses, adopted their best smile, and waited for the *Guests* to arrive. David was ready to open the door. Several soldiers and what looked like two Officers piled out of the vans. Sergeant Desta was not on this assignment.

Again, guns were drawn and at the ready, in anticipation of a confrontation with The Factory Faithful. Cautiously they came to the door, peered in; then David opened the door and held it open as the NPO walked in. Two soldiers remained outside. David handed the keys to the one that seemed of highest rank. He was not expecting that gesture! Then David returned to join Dianne and the children.

No one spoke for the longest moment. Finally, the head Officer snapped an order, brandishing his pistol conspicuously. "Okay, everyone, line up against the wall, and no trouble from any of you!"

Don stepped forward and spoke for all: "There will be no trouble, Officer. We are ready to go." Another unexpected gesture for the puzzled Officer. The NPO was anticipating a clash with a roaring Lion; instead, they came upon a peaceful Lamb.

The Officer's subordinate took over to outline practical matters. "Mothers with nursing children step forward and go with Corporal Lynch." Jenny did so and was escorted outdoors, to the waiting van.

"Next, let's have mothers with children under ten years of age. Line up over here with your children." Dianne and Mary Kay did as they were told. They were taken outdoors by a second female soldier, to another van.

"Now," the junior Officer continued, "we separate the women and the men. Women, go on with this soldier to van number three." Kathy, Sam, Mama Blanchard, Louise, and Clair followed the soldier.

"Men, go with the remaining soldier to the last van." Don, Doobie, Ben, Jim, Henry, Mark, and David went to the van.

"Is there anyone else here in the Factory?" The question was posed to no one in particular, but Don replied halfway through the front door. "There's no one else here; you have us all."

Understandably, the children were the most shaken by the whole incident. Mary Kay and Dianne did their best to quiet their fears.

In caravan style the four vans made their way out of town, over a lengthy trip taking at least an hour. The vans traveled on winding roads away from other traffic. There were no windows in the back to look through for signs of where they were headed; and the front windows were blocked from view. Passengers had to sit on hard, bench-like seats. A time or two Don tried to softly offer a word of encouragement. Each occasion, however, he was chastised by a nearby soldier also sitting on the bench and told "There will be no talking." Don wondered how that restriction was going over with Sam in the women's van.

The caravan finally arrived at their destination. In a slow and arduous manner, the vans were emptied one by one. The last to do so was the men's van. As they got out and stretched their legs and looked around, they could see they were in the country at what looked like a former prison. There was no sign of the rest of the Factory Saints. Don and the other men filed in the entrance. When they did there was still no trace of those who went in before; no recognizable voices were detected. It was like they had simply vanished!

Once inside the NPO squad that transported the Faithful got ready to leave and turned the men over to prison guards. First on the docket was a sign-in at a make-shift registration table. Verla, the Librarian, assisted, with the help of Suzy. Doing so they both intentionally avoided any eye contact with the Factory men. No talking was still the rule. The men were led to a room off to the side for a change of clothing. Gone would be their *Sunday Best*. Instead, they donned drab, prison garb. No one's outfit fit exactly, but they were stuck with it for now.

Next was a long walk to what would become their communal prison cell. It was in a large cell-block area where other cells were located, each with a group of from five to eight men. There were enough cots in each cell to sleep eight.

Austere comes to mind in describing the setting. No frills, no privacy, no view, not much cleanliness either. Little food; sparse water. The cell block housed about ten group-cells and was guarded by a dozen or so NPO guards. All around the walls, even in each cell, were huge pictures of Gabrinne, the NPO logo, and colorfully designed messages to encourage the cooperation of its prisoners. And worse than that were the incessant messages or commercials heard over the PA System, that would carry on for ten minutes or so, every hour on the hour of the day and night.

This ten-cell cellblock had a command center of sorts, clearly visible to all. It housed several soldiers, watching monitors, wearing headphones. Don and the others correctly surmised that the main activity of the command center was to spy on the prisoners. Likely each cell had a video camera or two and a microphone at work. Try as they might Don and his crew were unable to locate any video or audio devices in the cell.

Don's cell had another cell of men on each side. But with the overriding rule of no talking and learning of the horrific consequences if caught, no one wanted to speak to neighbors. Right from day one, Don was itching to talk. He wanted some information and he was tired of biting his tongue. So, he devised a scheme: he would call out to one of the guards and see what happens. If nothing else, he reasoned, he could rightfully claim ignorance, and surely, they would extend some grace to a *Newbie*... Did Don ask the Lord about his plan. No!

"Guard! Hey, Guard! Please come here! It's important," Don yelled forth. Within seconds two guards arrived. They were perhaps thinking that Don had reconsidered his views and wanted to embrace the NPO.

"What's the trouble?" asked one of the soldiers.

"Is the rule about no talking in force all the time? Or is there ever an opportunity to speak with others?" Don asked.

"It's the rule all the time! Now SHUT UP!" the guard barked loudly, as he clanged the butt of his rifle on Don's cell.

The other guard added this tidbit: "If you're caught, it's two days in the box ... right, Chauncey." A man by that name answered from the adjoining cell.

"He's right. Two days in hell, I call it. You don't want to go there."

"Okay. Thanks, Chauncey," Don whispered as he turned away and sat on a cot. The two guards returned to their positions.

Just settle in, Don, came the familiar, soothing voice of Jesus. *Remember I'm looking out for you and your friends. Count on Me to help you, all of you, over this initial adjustment challenge... And, by the way, you wanted to talk? Well, what are we doing right now? Talking! I'm always available. Don't go at it alone! I will be encouraging the others as well. And I'll keep you posted on their lives.*

Thank you, Lord. Thank You, Don answered, as he laid down on the cot. Then he wondered about when a meal would happen but decided against raising that question. He and his friends must have missed the meal for the day – there's only one – so hungry stomachs prevailed that first night. And with no windows in the cellblock, it was hard to decipher the time of day it might be. All prisoners gave up wrist watches at intake. So, prisoners slept whenever it felt right.

Soon enough, the cellblock settled into a routine of sorts, and one day blended into another. Over time the men found an easy, workable solution to how to pray without words. They entered into agreement to gather and pray silently, whenever anyone requested it. Whoever took the initiative to start a prayer session was signaling to the rest that they wanted some prayer. Prayer sessions on the average happened three or four times a day. With arms on one another's shoulders, or hands clasped together, the group bowed their heads and prayed in silence. A clenched fist became a signal to each other that an "AMEN" (So be it!) was being pronounced, and the session did not end until all seven men could register an *Amen*. Soon they got skilled at sensing in their spirits what the prayer-initiator was struggling with and their silent prayers became quite focused.

Often the vehicle for prayer expression was simply praying in the spirit under one's breath. And on nearly every occasion prayer ended with humming softly the now familiar chorus of *Keep Your Eyes Upon Jesus*. Guards looked in on the humming as a questionable activity; it was perhaps close to talking but no words were spoken. No repercussions came from the humming practice.

Not surprising other cells looked on curiously when the Factory Saints were assembled for prayer. *If only the other men in the cellblock could talk freely*, wished Don, *What specific prayer needs would they identify?* Soon enough Don's friends began to expand their prayer horizons to include praying for the ladies, mothers, and children, and even for other men looking on.

ONE DAY ABOUT HALFWAY THROUGH THE second week, Pastor Bill was arrested and brought to Don's cell. He had a wild story of his arrest at a vacant farmhouse, which he couldn't convey except in broad gestures and facial expressions. He looked well, except for scratches and bruises from his flight in the country to escape from the NPO. D.J. and Jerry were still on the run. It wasn't long before Pastor Bill caught on to the rhythm of the cell, silent prayer in the spirit, and the humming of *Keep Your Eyes Upon Jesus*.

No one around the cell blocks was sporting a **666** sign on their forehead or right hand, so Don figured they were Believers who hadn't succumbed and sold out to the NPO. Perhaps among the prisoners there was a smattering of rebel-rousers, the disenfranchised, or Constitutional

Freedom-Fighters, as they were known, who also hadn't joined up with the NPO, but that was only a guess.

As if near starvation and minimal drinking water, and the ever-glaring NPO propaganda wasn't enough of an incentive to give up on your allegiance to God, there was another, more gruesome practice in the cell block. Every day one prisoner was picked out for *Special Duty*, as the guards called it in jest. This meant a session of focused torture.

As the prisoner was brought back to the cell, he hardly was able to walk and he was in obvious pain, holding both hands limp and off to the side with great care. Their hands had been brutalized, likely many bones broken or crushed. But at least their coming back to the cell meant they hadn't sold out – and that was cause for jubilation. The prisoners from the man's cell welcomed the poor soul back. They wanted to clap and hoot but dared not be so frivolous. Unfortunately, they had no way to help the man with his injuries. The bucket for drinking water was the only resource available, to provide some relief from the pain.

Not everyone who was taken to *Special Duty* returned with signs of torture. Instead, they came back sporting a visible 666 mark. As part of the NPO routine, the returning prisoner would be paraded all around the cellblock, accompanied by P.A. taunts and reminders that all the torture could be avoided by a simple change of mind. It proved to be a powerful message for all the onlookers, and undoubtedly paved the way for others to reconsider their position. If those looking on wanted to implement that change all they had to do was call out to the guards. The guards would come immediately and rescue the defector out from their cell. So, as time passed, the overall number of prisoners began to dwindle. More were leaving the prison as an NPO Loyalist than were arriving from the outside.

One day, Mark was chosen as the target prisoner for *Special Duty*. Just like the others, Mark was carted off by two guards to God knows where. The Prayer Group had a nearly day-long session for him. Finally, Mark came back to the cell in the same condition as others who didn't give in. He was barely able to walk and both hands were in a crumbled mass of bones and bruises, hardly recognizable as hands.

Chauncey had been watching. He picked up his metal cup and threw it against the wall as hard as he could. He was furious. He grunted and snorted like an old bull in the pasture. He paced up and down and others in his cell gave him place.

The P.A. voice yelled out a warning: "You better cool down, Chauncey, or you're headed for more trouble than you can imagine!" Chauncey gave out with a long, anguished groan, and then grew silent.

Immediately the prayer warriors in Don's cell convened again. Mark put his limp hands in the middle of the circle; others, ever so gently, laid their hands on or below his and prayed silently in the spirit. After a few minutes, a crackling sound could be heard. It was coming from Mark's hands as bones were being repaired and put in their proper place. It was an amazing healing miracle that astonished the onlookers from neighboring cells. As they could risk it, they joined Don and his friends in the celebration of God's miracle... with mixed, muted expressions and movements. By this time, they had caught on to the sign for AMEN being the clenched fist – and looking out Don could see many clenched fists in the air, in praise to God for His Victory! And there was none bigger than Chauncey's!

The undeniable miracle was a big boost to the cellblock, a source of inspiration to all prisoners and a painful reminder of defeat to the NPO. It helped many to better tolerate the horrible living conditions, the food and water deprivation, the ongoing P.A. barrage of pro-NPO messages, and the no-talking rule! Many other cells took up the practice of silent prayer groups for themselves.

IN A DIFFERENT PART OF THE OLD PRISON, the ladies and children from The Factory were faring a bit better. They were out of view and earshot from the men. All but two of the women were in one cell, which included Jenny and Rosalie. Mary Kay and Dianne, along with their six children were in an adjoining cell. During the daylight hours the six children were taken to another section for classes and indoctrination into NPO values. Much prayer went up for the Lord to shield these little ones from falling prey to their tactics.

Now came the time for a drastic change. Four of the older children would be sleeping at another site, and the two youngest would return to the mothers after classes.

Slowly the NPO principle to win over the children was being implemented. The theory was that children won over to NPO values would prove to be staunch Loyalists in the end, so the NPO was willing to invest time and patience into this strategy. During a time of transition, Mary Kay and Dianne could see their children in person from 4:00 to 5:00 each afternoon in the children's new sleeping quarters.

You might say that the NPO presence for the women and children was much more lenient than for the men. Talking was tolerated, even encouraged; food and water supply was ample; and bathing and personal hygiene were promoted. Unlike the men's situation, there was little emphasis on coercing anyone to consider changing allegiance to the NPO. The thought was that once the man of the family switched his loyalty and took the Mark, he could then be incentivized to work on his wife's commitment and that of the children.

While the NPO theory made sense to most, it wasn't about to work for the Greensville group. Why? Because it didn't consider that the two oldest children, Joshua and Gideon, were born-again believers... that these two believed in miracles and had undaunted faith that God would see them and their families through to victory. It wasn't uncommon to see these two young *End-Times Soldiers* grasp hands and pray, right out in the open, whenever they sensed the prompting.

The lessons they heard from NPO staff during the day were sprinkled with fun and games, and various snacks – aimed at making the lessons more appealing. But, like Daniel and the three Hebrew children from the Old Testament, who refused the King's *dainties* - Joshua and Gideon set their hearts to not fall prey to such schemes from the enemy.[61] So, every day the two of them alone or with their mothers prayed for God's discernment to know what was true and what was not.

Part of the strategy of working with youngsters was to begin challenging the authority and wisdom of parents, even their love, while beginning to present the Antichrist as the One with final authority and all wisdom, and the only One who truly loved them. The two boys saw through these obvious falsehoods. At a *thumbs-up* signal from one or the other, they began to softly pray in the spirit.

After a time, all the children joined Joshua and Gideon in living apart from mothers, except the 4:00 to 5:00 time slot was still reserved for family visits. NPO staff Officers continued to be surprised at the calm demeanor shown by the children and their mothers. They just knew there was something different about this group. And the unruffled manner on display made the NPO consider the Greensville group an even greater trophy to win over.

After a few weeks, a plan for their long-term protection was devised and implemented by the Lord, Who in turn shared it with the children and mothers. Here was how the plan unfolded:

One evening when the six children were asleep, a visitor arrived unawares – not unlike the angel who came to help Peter escape from prison.[62] It was a lady, an Angel named Hannah. She took the children out of their locked quarters and walked right past guards as if invisible to them. Then they went on to outside of the prison walls. A short walk away there was a waiting cottage, that was not visible to the natural eye, but very real indeed. Here there were six beds and a goodly supply of food, drinks, and clothing. There they would all wait for God the Father to signal it was time for the Rapture of His Saints. And during that grand event they would be reunited with their parents.

The next morning the prison was in an uproar over the disappearance of the children. Search parties were formed and sent out in all directions. They searched high and low, but with no success. Out the windows of the cottage the children and Hannah could witness the frantic search and note by the faces of the workers what frustration they were going through. There was not even one clue found about how the escape happened or where the children went. Video cameras that were situated everywhere in the cell blocks caught no record of the escape. It was like they simply disappeared!

One Officer said to his cohorts: "We coddled that group from Greensville too much, and I won't make that mistake again. When we find them, they'll regret they were even born! And you're telling me that the mothers had no clue about the escape? That's preposterous! Well, it's no more *Mr. Nice Guy* for them. That group will rue the day of the escape, mark my words!"

Over time the intensity of the search waned. No clues were discovered. It seemed pointless to go on. Soon the search was discontinued, and the topic was dropped. But at the same time, those overseeing the women prisoners adopted a different, more austere and unfriendly strategy.

All the time of the search, Don and his group would get a hint or two in their spirit about what happened. They knew in their hearts that the children were securely away from the prison. Where exactly was not known; everyone believed and thanked the Lord, however, that the youngsters were being kept safe.

One day Don talked with the Lord, along these lines: *Thank You for keeping the children safe, wherever You have led them…*

I know where this is going, the Lord interrupted. *You want to know about Jenny and Rosalie, right?*

Well, yes, Lord, that has been on my mind…

Well, you'll be happy to learn that Jenny and Rosalie are dwelling safe and sound in My Secret Place. She has said of Me: Lord, You are my Refuge and my Strength, I shall not fear [63] *and I have honored her faith… What does that mean in everyday living? It means if any NPO Officer should have a negative thought about Jenny or Rosalie My Grace will flood her with favor and blessing, and the hurtful thought will go up in a wisp of smoke. The NPO Officer will end up blessing her when they initially meant to cause distress. They'll come away scratching their head, saying* "Why am I so nice to that person; I don't want to be, but I just can't help myself."

Oh, Thank You, Thank You, Lord. I love You... You never cease to amaze me!

ONE DAY THERE WAS A PECULIAR MESSAGE overheard on the P.A. system, during a time of commotion, at a shift-change for the guards. Two Officers were talking, not aware that they left the mic hot for all in the cellblock to hear.

One said: "So Captain, what are we going to do?"

The Captain answered: "We need to get a bigger quota of Loyalists, so start to rachet up the persuasive methods... I don't care how you do it: physically, psychologically, whatever it takes. In one month, our Recon Center is expected to turn 70% of the prisoners into Loyalists. Currently we're making the grade only 45% of the time...

"You're smiling, Sergeant... Why is that?"

"Sir, I'm smiling because I know just what cell of men to focus on; that creepy group from Greensville... This will be a pleasure, Captain!"

"Well, I don't care who you start with or what you do – just get the numbers up, so the big brass will be proud of us!"

The Sergeant highlighted the start of this phase of the program called *Loyalty for All*, by bringing in a guillotine to the men's cellblock. It sat there for two days in plain sight with no further explanation. Everyone was free to imagine whatever they wanted to about it.

On the third day, the NPO brought in a huge watermelon, placed it under the blade of the guillotine, and after calling for the men's attention, promptly released the blade. The severing of the melon, accompanied by a clear squishing sound and a splashing of the melon innards, made for quite a dramatic demo. If anyone tried to say they were not impressed to their core, all the others knew they were lying! And everyone in the cellblock knew, without having to be told, that they were all slated for the guillotine if they continued to renounce the NPO program.

In a strange turn from policy the rule of no-talking was lifted for the men's cellblock. The premise was that more fear could be generated in each cell if the men were free to talk to one another out loud about what they were feeling... and the more fear, the more a man would be willing to give in. Following the watermelon incident, several men did in fact ask to sign the Loyalty Covenant. The cellblock went from 52 to 37 in a matter of hours.

All of Don's cell held steady, except for Ben and Henry. They were feeling at the end of their rope, both physically and emotionally. In fact, Ben asked if he could be the first to go to the guillotine from his cell. He presented it as a personal request.

"Don and all of you, I'm asking that I be the first from our group to go to the guillotine. I'm at my absolute end. I know I wouldn't have gotten this far without the Lord's help and strength every day. But now I sense His go-ahead... So, would that be okay with you?"

The others gave their quick approval. All the men knew the Bible says: *To be absent from the body is to be present with the Lord.*[64] So, they recognized Ben's request as meaning he would be the first to be with Jesus and experience Heaven. And that awareness was a cause for celebration among the Saints.

Next to speak up, and with basically the same kind of appeal, was Henry. The men had noticed that Henry seemed to be declining of late in his zest and resolve. So, his demand to be the second was also received easily by the men.

"Ben and Henry," Don began. "You two have been a great source of encouragement to me and all of us. So, we want to honor you by saying *Yes* to your wishes... It will only be a short time before we'll all be together again anyway. And against the backdrop of eternity, a few days or weeks is only a drop in the bucket... I sense in my spirit that the Sergeant wants to focus on our cell, so when he gives the opportunity, we'll announce Ben as the first choice."

That opportunity came quickly, that very evening, in fact. The guillotine technician arrived and prepared his apparatus. Ben was escorted to the scene. He sat on a small bench, had his eyes covered with a blindfold, and was asked if he had any final words. Ben looked heavenward and at the top of his lungs mustered a hearty "HERE I COME, JESUS!"

He then leaned over and was strapped in position under the blade. The technician counted to three – *one, two, three* – and the blade dropped. *BAMM*. It was over. Most looked away from the carnage. Man, no matter how depraved, was not created with any appetite for such a slaughter.

Waiting in the wings was a clean-up crew. They rushed on the scene to retrieve the body and put it a bag, and then begin mopping up the blood. The executioner himself left the scene immediately after the blade dropped. Don suspected that he sought refuge to emotionally disengage from the death he caused, and to prepare for the next demand by the NPO.

Don's heart went out to all the men in the cellblock who just witnessed this carnage, who were not Christian, but were fighting against the NPO under their own power and resolve. They had no heavenly connection or hope. Don spoke to the Lord about it.

"Lord, can I speak forth to a group of the men about receiving You as their Savior and Hope of eternity? Would that be wise?"

"Don, your heart's desire is commendable, but your method is not wise. Instead of blaring out a message for all, that the NPO would soon stop, pick out just one man on each side of you to speak to. I will prepare their hearts before you. When they receive, then they can take the same message to their cellmates, and then share it with their neighbors in the next cell. It will become like a river of living water in this place... Oh, and Don?"

"...Yes, Lord..."

"Thanks for asking this time."

"...Yes, Lord."

Don turned to his cellmates with excitement. "Men, I've been talking with the Lord about sharing Jesus with our neighbors. The Lord says to do it one-on-one. I know who I want to talk to – its Chauncey..."

"I'd like to do the same with the other cell," said Mark. "Doobie, why don't you join me; I'd feel better if you did."

"Me Mark? ... You want me? Yeah, that would be great! Thanks, Mark."

"The rest of us will be praying for you all," added Pastor Bill.

As Mark and Doobie went one direction, Don went the other. He spotted Chauncey and signaled that he wanted to talk. Don opened the conversation. "Nice that they're letting us talk out loud, huh, Chauncey?"

"Yeah, it is... Say, I don't get it. One of your men just got guillotined and you're acting like it's no big deal...Didn't your heart go out to the old guy?"

"Yes, my heart went out to him but more than that, my heart rejoiced for him."

"Rejoiced? That don't make any sense. Why would you be happy?"

"I rejoiced because I knew he was going on a straight course to Heaven, to be with his Savior, Jesus. That man had that blessed hope in his heart, just like all of us in here have... Is that something that's in your heart?"

"No. No, can't say it is."

"You mean you've stood against the NPO all this time, relying on your own strength? Wow! That's something. I don't think I could have lasted this long on my own effort; I need lots of help. And that's what Jesus has given me and all the men in our cell... He has given us His strength for the day-to-day challenges, and He has shown us deep down, that to leave this earth is a one-way ticket to Heaven."

Don stopped there to give Chauncey a chance to digest all he heard. Hearing no comment Don closed with this: "Well, Chauncey, if you ever want to talk more about this stuff, just let me know."

Don turned away and took three steps, and Chauncey signaled he wanted more: "Wait, Don!"

"What's up, Chauncey?"

Chauncey spoke is hushed tones. "Well, to tell the truth, I'm getting mighty weary of all this. In fact, I don't know how much longer I can take it. I'm about ready to flip out! Or do something crazy!

"I want what you and your men seem to have: a calm, a peace, even a confidence that I know I don't have inside. Can you help me get there?"

"Sure, I can. It's a case of receiving Jesus into your heart. He wants you to acknowledge that you need Him - and you do; all of us do. He wants you to call upon Him and make Him the Lord of your life... We could do that now."

"But I'm not real big on religion and all that praying business."

"I'm not big on religion either; we're talking about a relationship with Jesus, not religion. The Bible says: '*Whosoever shall call upon the Name of the Lord shall be saved*.'[65] That means saved from hell and eternal punishment and saved for Heaven and eternal happiness... and to have the strength to deal with the daily challenges in this place. So, Chauncey, are you ready to make a personal commitment to Jesus?"

"Ah... Yes. Yes, I am. What do I do?"

"Just follow me in a brief prayer and repeat it after me as I go along. Ready? Here we go: 'Jesus... I need saving... I call upon Your Name... and Your Name means *Savior*... You died for me on a cross... And it was more agonizing than any guillotine... But you did it because You loved me... I receive You now as the Lord of my life... In the Name of Jesus, I pray... AMEN...

"That's all there is to do, Chauncey. Jesus now lives in your heart and He wants you to trust Him every moment."

"Wow. WOW!" A smile as big as the Grand Canyon grew on Chauncey's face. His cellmates came to him after Don's exchange, wondering what had transpired. Chauncey shared with them... then Chauncey shared with the men in the next cell over. On and on it went, one cell to the next. Like wildfire the Good News about Jesus spread through the whole cellblock over the rest of that evening and all the next day. True enough, not all were positive about hearing the Good News, but most of the men were.

In the days that followed the number of men throwing in the towel to the NPO dwindled to a mere trickle, much to the disgust of NPO officials. Their strategy of compelling more to become a Loyalist by display and use of the guillotine seemed to backfire.

The plan presented was for the guillotine to be in use twice every day, mid-morning for the men and late afternoon for the women. Contrary to the hopes of the NPO, both stations had similar results: fewer than expected conversions to the NPO. And that disappointment for the Officers was a hard pill to swallow.

"It's these so-called *Christians* from Greensville that have caused the whole strategy to boomerang on us!" said the Sergeant to his Captain. "I hate all their talk about Jesus and Heaven and such things as that... there's got to be some way to break through their Christian shell and grab them where it really hurts..."

"Well, you better find it fast, Sergeant. The Top Brass are planning a visit here at the close of this week and they'll be looking for results, not excuses!"

"If only we could find the children they came in with, that have disappeared. That would give us some leverage to turn minds around.

"I heard of one Recon Center at Benson Harbor who had wives beheaded while the husbands watched, standing ten feet away. But the guys ended up so traumatized that afterwards they were of little use to themselves or the NPO."

"Keep searching, Sergeant. I'm counting on you to make this look good!"

No new ideas with any chance of success came into the minds of the NPO; so, if nothing else, it was business as usual... guillotine executions.

One evening Don gathered his men for a meeting of the minds and spirits. He looked around at his faithful charges: Doobie, Jim, Mark, David, and Pastor Bill. The two missing – Ben and Henry were already in Heaven.

"Men, I sense in my spirit that use of the guillotine will be continuing for us and for the women. Thank goodness all of this is being shielded from the children, now living in safekeeping somewhere close-by I believe.

"Lest we get complacent or lazy in our spirits, I thought it good to gather and proclaim again our dependence on the Lord for even our next breath, let alone His strength to ward off fear and confusion – two of the enemy's main tools to keep us off-guard... What do you think?"

The men were more than willing to comply. Don added this: "And I took the liberty to invite Chauncey and his cellmate, Billy, to join us. Let's go closer to their cell... Welcome Chauncey and Billy."

One by one the men offered their wisdom and shared their heart... David started.

"Don, you are so right about the enemy's tactics; he wants to keep us in fear and confusion... But the more we stay zeroed in on the Lord, the more He keeps us insulated from the enemy's ways..."

"We need to stay focused in our spirits, we need to be alert and sober for the devil's tricks and be quick to cast all our care on the Lord... and NEVER doubt God's love..."

"One of the enemy's tricks is to try and keep me focused on my surroundings; he wants me to question God's compassion and have me doubt His desire for me to walk in victory, but I'm not going to cooperate with that. I'm going to resist every contrary thought that comes in..."

"I've learned that staying centered on God's love is a full-time job, that takes a lot of commitment and effort. And the enemy is quick to throw a wrench into the whole thing. But let me tell you, the enemy is not going to win! I'm going to win!..."

"The enemy casts doubt in my mind about whether I'm good enough to earn God's love; I know I could never be good enough to earn His love. I just thank God for Jesus, Who gave me His Righteousness and made me a child of the Father..."

"Thanks, guys, for those heavenly thoughts; there's a mountain of truth in every one of them... Anything you'd like to add Chauncey? Billy?"

"Nope, not really" said Chauncey. "I'm just so glad that I learned about Jesus... that He died for even a big loser like me!"

"But you're not a loser anymore, Chauncey," insisted Doobie. "Now you're a child of God, and before not too long we're going to see each other in Heaven!"

"Well men, I believe we're coming to the close of this chapter. This prison thing is about to end. I don't think the Cavalry is going to ride in here and save us from the NPO. No, I think there's another way it's going to close, by way of that life-shattering devise we can see before us... there must have been a devil who inspired the invention of such a wicked thing as a guillotine.

"So, I figure that we will each have our turn – our turn to give glory to God in death. I believe we've given Him glory in our lives, and now it's time to do the same in our departures...

"Lord, we're counting on You to see us through to the last breath we'll have on this earth... We so love You, Almighty God, and Savior... Jesus our Lord, Forever. AMEN!"

The last to depart from the woman's side was Kathy. Given opportunity to say any final words, she elected to yell forth: ***"See you in Heaven, Don!"***

The last to depart on the men's side was Don. The executioner asked Don if he had any final words. He said: "Yes I do... ***To God be all the glory!"***

The onlooking Sergeant reacted strongly over the PA system: "Aargh! Don't you ever quit?! Charley, make this one as slow and as agonizing as you can. I want to see this guy suffer - really bad!" His words echoed throughout the complex.

Did that cause any alarm for Don? Not in the least. His perpetual smile didn't even flinch. Don knew the Scripture that said: *"Jesus tasted death for us."* Don was emboldened by knowing that Jesus experienced the pains of death in his place. As well as he knew his own name, Don knew he would be in Heaven a nano-second before the guillotine blade made contact – so he would miss out on all the agony the Sergeant had in store.

That's what Don's protracted smile conveyed. Before being blindfolded Don and the Sergeant caught sight of one another, as Don looked up at the Command Center. In a profound way, both understood that they were from two different worlds, serving two different Gods, and their paths would never cross again... ever.

The Lord's final act of mercy for the Greensville End-Times Army was to do for Jenny and Rosalie what He did for the six children. One evening well after dark, Hannah came into Jenny's cell and led her and Rosalie out to safety.

Within seconds Jenny and her baby arrived at the same cottage where the six children had been living. There they all enjoyed God's bountiful blessings until being Raptured to join awaiting loved ones.

CHAPTER EIGHTEEN –

Look at you! All dressed out in White!

ONCE IN HEAVEN DON JOINED a sea of other martyrs. All were given a white Robe of Righteousness and told to wait a while longer.[66] Among the myriad of Saints, Don finally spotted a friend from The Factory.

"Hey, Doobie!" yelled Don. "Look at you! All dressed out in white! You look great! What a place this is! Right? More magnificent than I could have ever imagined! Wow!"

"Hi, Don. Great to see you!" yelled back Doobie.

"Have you seen any of the others?"

"I thought I saw Ben and David a while back, but that's about it."

Don approached Doobie. He couldn't say he was walking and he couldn't say he was gliding, but he was moving in some fashion and with little effort. He got close enough, so he didn't have to yell.

"Hey, Doobie, let's hang out together. I figure over time we'll begin to see the rest of the gang."

"Sounds great to me," Doobie answered.

"Have you looked around much, Doobie, at all the sheer beauty!?"

"Mostly what I see is people, tons of them, all dressed in white robes," he replied.

"These are the ones who gave up their life during the Great Tribulation, many I figure, by way of the guillotine, like us. What we are seeing are the results of the fifth Seal being broken by the Lamb of God.[67]

More familiar faces showed up. Don greeted them all. "Oh, look who's coming by! It's Sam and Dianne! Hi you two... Wait. There's another. It's Mama Blanchard! Hi, Mama!"

"Hi, Don and Doobie. Good to see you," they answered. Then Dianne posed a question for Don. "Don, help me understand: my three children are still on the earth, waiting in that cottage by the prison with the Angel... when and how will they arrive in Heaven?"

"Dianne, your three and Mary Kay's three children will come here during the time of the Rapture, along with any other Saints who survive the Great Tribulation. And don't forget those who will have died a natural death in God's Grace in times past will be raptured also... actually, resurrected. Their spirits are currently in Heaven, but when the Rapture is called for, these Saints - and us included - will go to receive a new immortal bodies.

"Imagine some of the current residents of Heaven that will go with us... It's like a Bible *Who's Who*: How about Peter and John and Paul. There's Abraham and King David and Mary. And how about all the ordinary people, like someone's great, great grandma Tillie, and maybe Albert Einstein, right Doobie? I sure hope you get to meet him someday! The list goes on and on...

"So, don't give it another thought, Dianne! In due time you'll be squeezing all three of those boys...they'll probably look different, but there will be no denying they are your three sons."

"Thanks, Don, I was thinking and hoping it would be something like that," Dianne said... "And Jenny and little Rosalie will come here then, too? Correct?"

"That's right... Wow! Just look around, people! Is this awesome or what!" exclaimed Don.

TIME IN HEAVEN WAS UNLIKE ANYTHING the new arrivals experienced before. What is an *hour* anyway? Sixty minutes? What's that? The time it takes to watch a glorious sunset or have a family dinner? Heaven exists beyond the dimension of time. And travel is its own mystery for newcomers. It seems that you can take as long or as short as you want to travel from here to there. It's automatic; just think of your destination, and you're there. And no vehicles needed!

Also, so many earthly expressions of natural life are irrelevant in Heaven. There's no day or night! No decay, no dust! No shadows! No one hurries! Everyone is busy and works. But no one labors! No one sweats. No one is weary! All activity is purposeful and anointed. Everything is done with ease and great, great joy!

Forget about *hours* or *days* or *light-years*. People in Heaven can learn to get their minds around much heftier concepts such as **forever** and **eternal.**

Before too long Don and the others encountered most of The Factory Faithful. They were gathered in a garden-like spot, amid a lush green meadow. Flowers of every kind were all around, sporting vibrant colors beyond the limits of the color spectrum. And the fragrance!

"Oh, the fragrance!" noted Sam. "It's out of this world! Whoops! I guess we are out of the world. How could I forget!" Others looked on with knowing smiles. They were thinking the same thing as Sam.

Most noticed a commotion brewing off to the side, a few hundred yards away. As they strained to see what was happening, an Angel came by announcing: "Jesus is coming! Jesus is coming! Get ready! Jesus is coming by!"

Soon people came nearby to gather at what was becoming a pathway for Jesus. It was excitement like the newbies had never experienced!

The commotion proved to be a crowd of people coming alongside of Jesus as He made His way through the meadow, greeting and blessing the people. Closer and closer the entourage came. Finally, Don and the others could see the Master! First just His head, then His full body. But His Face; what a beautiful face He showed forth, and the glow was undeniable!

Don and his friends found that earthly words could not describe what they saw. Jesus looked at each one individually; for a moment it was like each in their turn had His undivided and loving attention. Most of the onlookers were speechless. For sure all were touched deeply at the awesome sight. And the fragrance that accompanied Him was magnificent! Don was reminded that this Jesus has been anointed as King of kings. In the Gospel, shortly before the Last Supper, Mary anointed Jesus with expensive perfume and the sweet fragrance filled the house.[68] Now in Heaven He has been anointed as our King and Lord, and the fragrance will continue forever.

As quickly as He arrived, Jesus moved on His course to greet others. All around people strained to catch one last glimpse. The Angel assured the onlookers that there would be an eternity to enjoy the Presence of Jesus.

The crowd began to disperse. Don looked around and asked of no one in particular: "Where's Doobie?"

"I'm over here, Don," he answered. Don went to him and then suddenly he couldn't contain himself. He started dancing! And it was with Doobie, hand in hand, round and around. It was an unrehearsed, beginner-style square dance with plenty of whooping and hollering, like you might hear at an old foot-stompin' barn dance. You just know Sam was itching to get her hands on her accordion. She and Dianne joined into the dancing. Passers-by saw the dancing and jumped right into the middle of the festivity without reservation. All the newbies would learn that in Heaven spontaneous celebrations of praise spring up all the time.

Others from the Factory came to Don and his group, including Kathy. Don beamed in delight and rushed her way to give a giant hug.

"Kathy, you look... great!" Don gushed forth, thinking there must be a better word to use for the occasion. Kathy returned the hug. Both knew it was different than they had enjoyed on the earth, but it was welcomed just the same.

Ben and Clair stood nearby, as did Jim, Henry, and Pastor Bill. They all knew that others would be coming soon. Then Don had a premonition that something undeniably wonderful was about to happen. Instinctively he grabbed Kathy's hand and motioned for the other Factory friends to stand back, alongside them and make space for special visitors. There in the clearance stood two new faces. One was a handsome young man looking about age thirty; the other was a younger girl. They were beautiful to behold and most pleasing. They both looked intently at Kathy and Don, without uttering a word. Don took the initiative to speak.

"Hello, there. You look familiar in some way. We're Don and Kathy Crawford. Who are you?"

The young man stepped forth and answered for both. "Hello and welcome to Heaven. My name is Greg. This is Elizabeth. I was your son for a short while and then I died at age three. I've been waiting here for you ever since."

Kathy gasped in delight. She was overwhelmed with excitement. She said softly, "Hello, Greg... It's really you; I'm so glad to meet you... I'm at a loss for words..."

"Me too, Greg," added Don. "And this pretty young lady, Elizabeth...?"

She spoke up. "Yes, my name is Elizabeth. That name was given to me when I arrived in Heaven after about three months of life in your womb, Kathy. I didn't make it to full-term. Do you remember, Kathy? And Don?"

"Yes, I remember that well," Kathy answered. "That happened in between the birth of your two sisters, Sylvia and Jenny... Oh, what a joyful, unexpected blessing to see the two of you!" Kathy went over to the twosome and shared a gentle hug with each. Don stayed put; he had his own way to rejoice.

"Kathy, you took the words right out of my mouth." Then he turned to Elizabeth and Greg to explain, "When I get this way, I just gotta yell – I gotta yell for pure joy!" Don replied.

"PRAISE THE LORD! HALLELUJAH!" he bellowed out. Others in the immediate area heard and did the same... "Praise the Lord!" "Hallelujah!" "Thank You, Jesus!" Soon enough a volley of praises went forth. No one in Heaven need search for a reason to Praise the Lord; those reasons are all around. Without much planning praises echo forth continually.

Greg and Elizabeth moved to stand beside Kathy. Next, two sweet little girls, about age eight it appeared, arrived out of nowhere and stood in the midst. They asked for Sam and Mama Blanchard. Both ladies came forth to visit with the girls.

"Hi. My name is Willamena," the first one began. I want you to know that you two have been chosen for a special job in Heaven - if you're willing. That job is to help provide childcare. Here's Jessica?"

The second took over. "Hi. I'm Jessica. You will learn that there are a lot of children here in Heaven, who don't have a natural parent or grandparent to encourage them, as they grow. That's how it was for me and for Willamena. So, God has made a way for such children to receive special childcare, with the help of particular ones like you He has called out and anointed. We need your help to bring up the children in the nurture of the Lord. Are you two willing to help?"

"Yes! Yes!" they answered simultaneously

Willamena exclaimed: "Oh, Thank you... very much!" Then she added, "Another reason we are here is to escort you to your Mansions. Once you get settled in, we will come and find you. Okay, Sam? Okay, Mama Blanchard?" Both nodded with delight!

Jessica smiled in sharing one final piece of news. "One more thing. Waiting for you, Sam, in your Mansion is a special surprise: it's brand new, made in Heaven, and it makes beautiful music. Can you guess?"

Sam could hardly contain herself with excitement. She rushed over to Jessica and Willamena and gave each a big hug. Soon enough Mama Blanchard joined the group. The rest of the onlookers were beaming with joy from ear to ear.

Mama Blanchard turned to the bystanders and announced. "I want to use my given name in Heaven. Please, from now on just call me *Maria*," she said. The foursome turned to leave the scene. Within seconds they were off on their adventure. One second visible, the next second gone!

Don and Kathy were next. Doug and Elizabeth were to be escorts to their two new mansions. "Kathy and Don, are you ready to see your new homes?" Greg asked. Don looked at Kathy with unbounded excitement; both shook their head "Yes!" Without further ado, that foursome darted from the scene. Heavenly travel was awesome to experience!

Other new faces arrived at that area as escorts. Most often it was a family member and current resident of Heaven who had that privilege. For Doobie and Mark, it was their parents whom they hadn't seen for years! For Ben it was an older brother, Harold, who died many years back in a car accident. For Clair it was a stepmother, Lois, who brought up Clair in a godly household until her untimely death when Clair was a teenager.

For David and Dianne, their escorts were older cousins, Sean and Gloria. Before leaving the scene with them, Dianne had a question. "Gloria, I want to make sure I'm available and in the right place to greet my three sons here when the Rapture happens. There won't be a problem will there?"

"No. No, Dianne. You will assuredly be the first to welcome your three children to heaven... along with David of course. God would make sure of that happening!" Dianne smiled joyfully. "Okay, then, I guess I'm ready for whatever's next."

For Pastor Bill, his escort was his mother, Katrina, who died in his childbirth. What a sweet reunion that was! Mary Kay was escorted to her mansion by her grandfather. He had a double blessing for Mary Kay when he arrived; he was accompanied by Mary Kay's grandmother and brother, who also remained faithful during the great tribulation.

Last to have escorts from the Factory Faithful were Henry and Louise. And their escorts were Louise's parents, Abigail and Charles. Understandably Louise was elated at seeing her parents. Henry was happy for her but wished that his own parents had come. *Maybe they didn't make the same commitment to Jesus that I and Louise had made,* he thought. He then looked around at the utter beauty and glory of Heaven and any hint of sadness quickly vanished. Then he heard these happy words from Charles...

"I know you're wondering about your own parents, Henry," he said. "I saw them not long ago. They're here and looking forward to welcoming you and Louise." Henry's heart rejoiced!

A few from The Factory were still unaccounted for. First there were D.J. and Jerry, who left the others to fend for themselves on the run from the NPO. They could have died and are now somewhere in Heaven unknown to the others, or they are still on the earth in the throes of the *Great Tribulation*. Only time will tell.

Also, unaccounted for were Barbara and Rusty, who left the group at The Factory early on to venture out on a car trip to South Carolina to see family. Don hoped they would be among the happy throng to witness Heaven.

SOMETIMES WOMEN ARE RAPTURED TO HEAVEN in a special, unique condition. Knowingly or not they are pregnant when the trumpet calls. One prime example of that was Jenny herself. She suspicioned that she may have been pregnant but was not certain. If Jenny had been part of those from The Factory who gave up their life before the Rapture, like Don and the others, she and the new baby would have immediately come to Heaven – likely in the same wave of glory! Rosalie, as promised, would have accompanied her mother, traveling in her arms.

But Jenny's situation was different. She and Rosalie were on earth awaiting the Rapture of the Church for their entrance to Heaven. At the time of the Rapture, she would receive her new glorified body. And the baby inside would have come forth and have the same happen to him or her. Jenny could be arriving with Rosalie in one arm and the new baby in the other! What a sight that would be for her parents, as they watched for her coming! Three supernatural, glorified bodies arriving at once!

THE LONG-AWAITED DAY of the Rapture finally arrived. The Factory Faithful instinctively reconvened for the special day, as their spirits led them back to the same meadow where they first encountered Heaven. One by one they came to wait for further instructions.

Don, one of the first to arrive, went over to two Angels standing by and asked: "Is this the day of the Rapture... is that what I sense in my spirit?"

"Yes, you are right. This is the day of the Rapture. We got word not too long ago. The Lamb of God is about to open the Sixth Seal, and you know what will happen then?"

Don finished the thought. "Then... get ready earth! You are about to see the most glorious cosmic show ever... *the sun will be darkened, the moon will not give any light; the stars will fall from the sky; and the heavenly bodies will be shaken.*" [69]

"Right you are, Don," said the first Angel. "It's the Day of the Lord! This is the day we all have been waiting for. His Saints who died in Christ, like you and your Factory friends, will be *resurrected* and rise first with a glorified body to meet the Lord in the air." [70]

"Then His surviving saints on the earth, like Jenny and the children," added the second Angel, "will be given their new bodies and will be *raptured* to join with the others and meet the Lord." [71]

"Oh, I can hardly wait for the Trumpet Call, when the Angels will gather the elect from the four winds," Don said. "Wow!... What a day!... Oh, hi, Kathy. Are you ready?"

"Yes, I am. I know you're ready, right?"

"You betcha," Don said. "I'm ready to get my new redeemed, immortal body...I can see that the Saints are beginning to depart and follow Jesus. It's like they are simply stepping off the edge of Heaven, going to the earth. Our line is starting to move us along. Oh, Glory!

"I can see that the multitude is breaking up and travelling in different directions. I wonder...could each Saint be headed for a different part of the earth maybe? If so, perhaps their destination is to reach the locale and time zone in which they lived...They might have family in that same area watching the Glory of Jesus unfolding before them... Hey, what do you think, Kathy?"

"What Don?!" she replied. "Look...I'm kinda busy in the middle of this Rapture thing. I want to make sure I'm doing everything I'm supposed to... You can tell me later what you're seeing. Okay?"

"Alright; no problem," Don answered, but he continued anyway with his one-way description of what was happening before his eyes.

"Oh, I get it now! Kathy...Jesus is going to take His time with the Rapture. You know how some people think the part in 1 Corinthians 15 where it says *in the twinkling of an eye*[72] means that's how fast Jesus will conduct the Rapture business – but it really refers to how quickly we put on our new incorruptible bodies. *In the twinkling of an eye* it happens! So, I'm thinking this Rapture is really a 24-hour matter; Jesus will move around the earth through every time zone, for the whole world to witness His splendor! And there will be opportunity as He encircles the globe, for people who haven't sold out to the Antichrist to make a personal decision for Jesus...Wow! How vast is God's mercy!

"Kathy, now I can see that there are numerous people coming up from the earth. They have heard the Trumpet Call and the shout of the Archangel. They are sporting their new physical bodies – and they are all beaming from sheer excitement! People to my right and left are recognizing these travelling upwards. Wow! It's like family-reunion-time all around me!"

"Where's Jenny and Rosalie, Don? We should be seeing them, shouldn't we?"

"Here they come. I can see them! And it's Jim...he's leading them along. Get ready, Kathy! ...Hi, Jenny and Jim! And there's baby Rosalie..."

Jenny was itching to announce to her father: "Dad it was just like you said, I was able to be raptured with Rosalie in my arms." And she spoke with an exuberance that could not be denied!

"Hi, honey," said Kathy. "And there's little Rosalie. It is so great...Wait a minute!...What's going on? Don, do you see this?"

"I see another baby...in Jenny's other arm...I'm flabbergasted!" replied Don softly. "Jenny, the other baby...What?...How?"

"Mom, Dad, I didn't know but I was pregnant when we were all taken out to the Recon Center. So just now when I got my new body, so did the baby inside me. It all happened *in the twinkling of an eye*... she suddenly came forth and laid in my arm. Isn't she beautiful? She looks about the age of Rosalie already, don't you think? A name will come later."

"Thanks, Jim, for finding these precious ones – all of them!" said Kathy. "You didn't see Sylvia along the way?"

"No, Kathy, we didn't," Jim replied. "They should be along any time...Well, see you later, Mom and Dad." Off the four of them darted heavenward.

"Kathy, I reckon it's about our turn to receive our incorruptible bodies. I don't have any idea what we're supposed to..."

ZAP! ZAP!

"Kathy, it just happened. We have our new bodies! ...Oh, my, look at you: you're a Freshman Co-ed again...You look great! Beautiful! No grey hair, I might add."

"And you do too, Don. Handsome. Rugged. Thirty-years-old! Wow!"

That's the way it was for both those going from Heaven to the earth to receive their resurrected body - and for those raptured from the earth going up to heaven sporting their new, glorified bodies.

It was a joy-filled occasion for everyone: not only their being clothed with an eternal body, but their meeting up with loved ones in the process. In Heaven there are no elderly, no weakness or affliction, no frailty - only 100% supernatural, flesh and bone bodies just like Jesus, now equipped for all Eternity! Glory fills their veins instead of blood!

Ben and Clair were a good example. They came alongside for an instance. Clair was showing off a head of beautiful auburn hair and a definite twinkle in her eye. Ben was also appearing about 30, in the prime of his former life, with the body of an Olympic athlete. He had a head of handsome, curly brown hair, as well.

On and on it went. One glorified body after another rising off the earth. At first travel seemed slow, but then gained momentum, the closer they approached the Light, which was the bright, shining presence of the Lord stationed above.

Don and Kathy's travel was now headed up, to Jesus. They never did return to the earth. No, their transformation experience took place in mid-air. For many of those coming from the earth, their transformation seemed to occur a step or two into the air.

Don looked around and saw a familiar subject off in the distance. Then, as if responding to orders from above, the twosome turned and came to him. It was his parents! Glory! And shortly behind them was Sylvia, Mike, and their family. Oh, my, what a reunion! His parents looked like a much younger version of themselves; handsome and robust, and with faces that lit up the atmosphere. Sylvia and the kids looked about the same as Don remembered them. But it was their faces and their smiles that gave them away as now being citizens of Heaven. In seconds Kathy joined in the wonderful reunion, right there midway between earth and Heaven.

Don's thoughts turned to D.J. and Jerry. In a moment of time, Don saw them on the earth in a wooded area not far from Greensville that had become their home on the run. Then Don had the privilege of seeing God's Rapture firsthand. Two beams of intense light shone around D.J. and Jerry; the beams seemed to pulsate, growing brighter and more intense. The trumpet sounded and the angel summoned.

They knew what was going on; they stood motionless except for shaking knees, and wanting to yell and scream for joy, but daring not to. Suddenly the beams of light lifted them off the ground and in the twinkling of an eye, they were **ZAPPED**. And up they flew. Within seconds they were met by a woman that they recognized as Jerry's wife, Darla. Excitedly the threesome arrived where Don was, but sped right past, with hardly a wave. Don knew what their destination was: it was above with that Majestic Source of Light Himself!

Another traveler came close enough to smile and wave. It was a young-looking Chauncey from the Recon Center! He was travelling with a young woman and two young men – his family Don presumed. They were chattering away. Chauncey looked Don's way and gave the biggest wave ever. His broad smile was infectious!

Who should come by next, but two happy families with a slug of kids. Mary Kay and Dianne were reunited with their children; Mark and David tagged along behind. The kids seemed like young teenagers in appearance. They all spoke and greeted Don and Kathy...and again it was those faces that stood out so. Don and Kathy waved back and watched the excited families head upward.

Things then seemed to come to a standstill. There appeared to be some reason that Don and Kathy had tarried so long before returning to Heaven.

Don asked: "I don't know why we're still here and not back in Heaven, but I just want to stay here for now." Kathy agreed, "Me, too... But not sure why."

It was fun to watch the activity that day, the family reunions, the new, redeem bodies, the beaming faces...

Don spoke to his Friend. "Lord, is there something You want us to do? Is that why we're lingering here?" The Lord answered both Don and Kathy:

> *"Yes, I have a reason for you to stay. It's to talk to Doobie. You see, since he got his glorified body, he is looking quite different than before. This new body is the one I originally meant for him to have, which he never got. But now he's not sure how others will take to the new look. He needs a bit of encouragement from you two. I knew you'd be agreeable. Bye for now."*

"Kathy, here comes Doobie...Wow! Does he ever look different!"

"Hi, Doobie," Kathy began. "You look so handsome in your new, redeemed body..."

"...and so tall, Doobie. I bet you're as tall as Mark. Maybe taller. Wow!"

"I can see you're not so happy about the change," Kathy observed, "but this is just like the original body God designed you to have...He told us that just a minute ago."

"I think the new look will give you a commanding presence around other people. They'll naturally look up to you, Doobie...literally *look up*."

"So, you guys think this is not too drastic a change and people won't mind, right?" asked Doobie sincerely.

"Not at all!" insisted Kathy.

"You're still the Doobie they have grown to know and love," Don added.

"Well, if you think so...Ya know what? Since I look so different, maybe I'll just make the change even bigger," Doobie stated.

"What do you mean," asked Kathy and Don together.

"I think I'll just go all out and use my original name – Harold!" he smiled.

"Sounds great Doobie – oh, I mean, Harold."

Kathy noticed a traveler coming by. It was Mark. "Hi, Mark," she said.

"We haven't seen Doobie for the longest time," Mark stated. "Oh, sorry to interrupt. Who's this with you?"

"Mark, meet a former *Doobie*; but now a *Harold*," Don set the record straight.

"What?" Mark leaned in to talk softly to Don. "Are you telling me this tall, handsome guy you call Harold, used to be my older brother, Doobie?" Mark was puzzled. He shot some questions:

"What was the name of our first dog?" *"Jackie."*

"What street did we grow up on?" *"Western Avenue."*

"What was your mother's maiden name?" *"Johnson."*

"Wow! You are Doobie!"

"Now, I'm Harold."

"Sorry, Harold...high-five big brother." WAP!

"I'm ready, Don. Let's move up to Heaven," said Kathy. "We've got some catching up to do with family and friends...And I'm sure your parents are waiting to see more of you, Harold."

"Yes, I'm ready!" Don answered..."Me, too," Harold and Mark added.

"Lead the way, Kathy!"

THE WRATH OF GOD FALLS ON THOSE WHO have rejected Jesus. When Seal Six was broken in Heaven the **Day of the Lord** [73] occurred, with three purposes: to resurrect the dead in Christ, to rapture all living, faithful Believers, and thirdly, to pave the way for the out-pouring of God's wrath.

The first two purposes were fulfilled; Don and his people were wit-nesses and participants of that. The remaining objective was about to be unleashed, through the Trumpet and Bowl judgments. This occurred at the opening of the Seventh Seal.

The Bible records: *"And when He had opened the seventh seal there was silence in Heaven about the space of half an hour."* [74] So awesome, so terrifying was the coming Wrath of God going to be...

At NPO Headquarters in Greensville, North Carolina, the scene was utter chaos! Those with the Mark of the Beast were sorely mourning this grand event because they knew deep down in their spirits that it was too late for them. Their fate had been sealed! The only thing that lay before them now was the wrath of God!

Across the globe, those who had rejected God now cried out: *"Mountains fall on us and hide us from the face of Him that sits on the throne, and from the wrath of the Lamb. For the great day of His wrath is come; and who shall be able to stand."* [75]

While all this fury was being poured out on the earth, those in Heaven lived in a different existence. All they knew was peace! Don and his friends were enjoying life to its fullest, and more of God's good-ness was being revealed to them day by day. They knew they would have all eternity to discover the depths of God's love.

Before long Heaven entered the Millennial Reign of Jesus. [76] That was a thousand years of Heaven's Glory without Satan and his devils. By then the False Prophet and Antichrist had been thrown into the lake of fire for all of eternity! The Devil, Satan, was locked up in the bottomless pit for a thousand years.

During this Millennial bliss, the Marriage of the Lamb with his Bride, the Church, was celebrated with gusto! According to Mama, I mean *Marie*, the Marriage Supper was, in all aspects, simply awesome!

Jesus took the occasion to bring honor to Don and his faithful com-pany. The Lord issued this proclamation throughout Heaven. Amidst a volume of cheers at the Marriage Supper, the proclamation declared the following:

**Be it known to all of Heaven that
The End-Times Army of Greensville
is hereby decommissioned.
It served The Kingdom of God
with great distinction.
Thank you, Faithful Servants.**

BIO – PHIL T. PORTER

Phil is a retired psychologist, who has lived and worked most of his life in the Midwest. Since becoming a Christian, forty years ago, he has been interested in the Biblical study of End-times. At first it was more a fascination with end-times realities, like the Great Tribulation, the Antichrist, and the Rapture. Now the interest is in sharing with others what the Bible teaches about these approaching realities. Phil's heart is to help the Church become faithful and committed during these perilous last days. Hopefully, this novel accomplishes that purpose.

ENDNOTES

1   Genesis 12:1

2   Matthew 9:36

3   Hebrews 13:5

4   Philippians 4:6

5   Proverbs 3:5

6   2 Corinthians 8.9

7   Acts of the Apostles 3:7

8   John 20:24-27

9   Exodus 4:10-12

10 Matthew 24:21, Mark 13:20

11 Revelation 13:16,17

12 1 Thessalonians 4:15-17, 1 Corinthians 15:52-54

13 Matthew 24:21

14 Matthew 24:9-12

15 Matthew 26:31-35

16 James 1:2

17 Romans 4:17, 14:14

18 Isaiah 43:19

19 Matthew 24:21-22

20 Revelation 3:10

21 Matthew 24:7-11

22 1 Thessalonians 4:13-17

23 Revelation 3:15-16

24 Revelation 3:19

25 Psalm 91:1

26 1 Corinthians 10:13

27 Hebrews 13:5

28 Philippians 4:13

29 1 John 5:4

30 Matthew 24:21

31 1 Corinthians 10:13

32 Matthew 26:35

33 "New Findings Suggest Israel Can Build Third Temple, Now" from Israel Today daily newsletter, *www.IsraelToday.co.il.*, 2-18-20, by Bert Boersma. Lays out evidence that the previous Temple was located in the City of David, not on the Temple Mount, as commonly understood.

34 2 Timothy 3:1-5

35 Isaiah 14:14

36 Daniel 9:27

37 Coming Perilous Times"- Self-published Booklet, by Phil T Porter, 2012, update 2015, 87 pages. (Available on Amazon.com)

38 Revelation 13:14-15

39 Acts 1:8

40 John 4:14

41 John 7:37-39

42 Romans 8:26-27

43 Hebrews 10:24-25

44 Psalm 91:1

45 Isaiah 60:1-3

46 Matthew 26:31

47 Mark 9:23

48 Mark 11:23-24; Job 22:28

49 II Chronicles 20:15

50 Romans 8:28

51 Jude 1:20

52 Nehemiah 8:10

53 Psalm 16:11

54 John 15:4-5

55 Hebrews 10:24-25

56 John 8:44

57 Matthew 25:21

58 Psalm 5:12

59 II Corinthians 5:8

60 Mark 11:23-24; Job 22:28
61 Daniel 1:8-20
62 Acts 12:3-10
63 Psalm 91:1-2
64 II Corinthians 5:8; Philippians 1:23
65 Romans 10:13
66 Revelation 6:9-11
67 Revelation 6:9
68 John 12:1-3
69 Mark 13:24,25
70 I Thessalonians 4:16
71 I Thessalonians 4:17
72 I Corinthians 15:52
73 Joel 2:10,11,31
74 Revelation 8:1
75 Revelation 6:15-17
76 Revelation 19:7-9

CPSIA information can be obtained
at www.ICGtesting.com
Printed in the USA
LVHW052110150321
681607LV00018B/654